ILLUSION OF A BOAR

LAND MYSTERIES

CELIA LAKE

ILLUSION OF A BOAR

In March of 1944, four magical specialists are brought together at a secret camp for an even more mysterious mission.

Hypatia and Cammie adopted each other as sisters twenty years ago, during their school years, after Cammie's mother married Hypatia's older brother. Cammie has been neck deep in signals work since the start of the Second World War, while Hypatia has used her gift for sympathetic magic and materia to support the war effort. All while keeping up the proper standards for ATS girls, of course.

Pulled from similar work in Scotland, Claudio knows the most about what's needed and about what resources might actually be available. That's a big problem, but he's far more worried about his chosen brother, Orion.

Orion's war had been comparatively simple until six months ago. After an injury invalided him out of active service using his magic to support the front lines in the

Mediterranean, he came home to find betrayal. Now he's figuring out where to begin rebuilding any sense of himself and his place in the world.

None of them have enough information or access to resources for what they're being asked to do. And they're doing it in a camp that has no idea what to make of them and that has its own deep secrets. When the challenges keep coming, they have to figure out whether and how they can trust each other and whether their objective is even possible.

Illusion of a Boar takes on the run-up to D-Day inside the magical community of Albion, figuring out what magic could help turn the tides in their favour. It's about trust, choosing new paths, and just maybe taking a chance on love and romance. The fifth book in the Land Mysteries series, it can be read in any order.

Learn more about the world of Albion and future books at my website, celialake.com. Additional information linking characters, places, and timelines is available at bit.ly/celia-lake-wiki

CHAPTER I

C ammie frowned as the truck finally let her out in front of a couple of small huts. One of the men hopped down to drop her trunk near enough to the doorstep. She made herself offer a smile and a wave as they drove off. Now, of course, she'd be trying to figure out for the rest of the day if they'd been nervous to be out on this edge of the property. Or maybe that was just her imagination. Something smelled wrong, but she had no idea yet what it was.

She straightened up, considering her welcome so far. Or lack of welcome, as it were. Getting here hadn't been too hard. She'd taken the portal to London and the train out of Waterloo station, then followed the instructions she'd been given to get a lift to the camp from a despatch car who'd be waiting at the train station.

What she'd found when she arrived was a well-guarded gate, fenced round with wire and wood. Cammie was precisely on time, only to find that no one was there to meet her. The despatch driver had pulled away as soon as she'd got papers signed over.

1

Cammie had been left standing there with her trunk and typewriter case, while no one did anything quickly. The man at the front gate had summoned an officer, who'd peered at her papers as if she'd forged them. Then he'd gone to talk to someone else. After an hour, they'd finally sent someone round with a truck to drop her in the right place. Cammie would have thought she'd interrupted someone's very important tea break, but this was England. Tea breaks were endless.

Her looks were against her, when it came to people taking her seriously, even if she was in uniform herself now. It was the downside of being among non-magical folk. Her father came from perfectly excellent Great Families stock. They were First Families on Grandmama's side, Second on Grandpapa's, as Albion reckoned such things. She just had to mention the name Octavian Gates, or refer to Grandmama and Grandpapa. Their names still had the proper sort of resonance, and people assigned her the sort of status that meant they didn't argue too much.

And of course these days, Mum and her step-father Ibis were also just as well known and respected, if for entirely different reasons. Mum had taken over the book-shop in Schola village when Cammie was still in school there, a year after Ibis had started teaching. Between them, they knew nearly everyone worth knowing, and quite a few people who still had to earn that particular marginal note on their permanent records.

Here and now, though, she was visibly mixed race, with an accent most non-magical folk couldn't slot into a tidy box of assumptions. Educated, yes. Precise, yes. As fluent in both French and German as in English, yes. And in Arabic, not that anyone asked about that one. But it wasn't Oxbridge, it wasn't posh; it wasn't any of the usual markers of being worth knowing or more importantly worth listening to that they used.

So she'd had to rely on other things. Besides her orders, which apparently weren't quite enough. This time, the trick of having a sweetheart in the RAF had done its usual magic. At least, it had once she'd actually been able to get a word into the conversation that wasn't her name or assignment. She blessed the fact she'd had a few days with Duncan in October, as well as a day last month. She'd kept tight hold of a couple of sharable stories.

Not that she'd seen him since then. Or even got much in the way of letters. He couldn't have his journal, too much chance someone would spot it in his barracks or wherever he was sleeping and wonder. They were confined to the ordinary sorts of letters that had been passed through the ordinary sort of censors, which meant half of them were blacked out, and she suspected she was only getting two letters in three at best.

He'd started up on the second round of combat missions just before she'd seen him, and now it was waiting and worrying and hoping he'd make it through. Odds were he wouldn't and that was the hell of the thing, because she loved him and wanted to be able to think about a future with him. And she couldn't yet.

At least this would be a distraction. She'd now been assigned to a quite secret project, in a camp that was apparently full of them. When they'd yanked her out of her previous work, last week, they'd told her that much. Assigned with three other people, names not given. Not that she hadn't figured out one of them that night.

She let out a long breath. Time to face the huts, and how dismal they likely were.

There were three, all Ministry of Supply standard huts, but oddly arranged. Two of the huts faced away from the camp, toward a wooden fence topped with barbed wire. A stone wall curved along about five feet inside the fencing and maybe fifteen from the doors of the two huts. It wasn't tall enough to keep anything out, but it might make a place to sit outside without other people in the camp seeing. Cammie suspected the wall was original to the property, providing a nominal division between the estate and Richmond Park on the other side of the road.

She made the two sleeping huts about eighteen feet by twenty-six; she knew the things were modular. One module wide, some number of modules long, and they were placed side by side, with a few inches gap between them. The third ran along the back of them, what looked like the whole length. Cammie hoped the location meant the two sleeping huts would be reasonably private. With her luck, it'd be the spot people went running or marching or whatever six times a day instead. The working hut faced back toward the rest of the camp and the main house of the estate it was on, but there was nothing else near them at all. There were a good hundred feet, maybe closer to two hundred, between them and the next building.

The men in the truck had dropped her trunk in front of the right-hand hut, fair enough. She nudged the door open, bringing her typewriter case with her, to find something that wasn't at all what she expected. The last time she'd been housed in one of these, there had been small cubicles down in a row. There had been just enough for a bed and a trunk and her personals. A tiny stove and whatever else had been down at the far end, with the loo and showers in a separate building a hundred feet away.

Instead, she was confronted with a small sitting space, and the rest of the hut divided up by wooden walls. Sound probably carried all through, though they could fix that right up with charms. The front room had a wood stove in the corner, flat, so they could heat things on it, but with no sign of pot or kettle or any sort of actual cooking equipment. Nor was there any cut wood or coal in evidence. At least it was spring, and they wouldn't be relying on it for heat overnight much. And again, charms could do a lot there. There were two easy chairs of indeterminate age, a window with a blackout curtain pulled over it, and a slight smell of mildew. There was a single desk in the corner, with an unpleasantly angular chair.

Maybe there was room to rig up a gas burner, if they gave up the desk or found another table somewhere. And there were at least hooks by the door for the outerwear and hats and all that. She pulled the service cap off her hair, tugging a curl back into place and anchoring it with another charm.

The rest of it was also odd. The place had its own bathing room, loo and sink and bath in a longer narrow room off the short hallway. That was unusual, to have their own instead of a hut for ablutions, as the term went, somewhere central. There also wasn't any visible water tank, and she didn't think this was the magical sort of design where it'd be hidden.

The bedroom was - oh, that would have been a problem, except she knew who she'd be rooming with. She'd shared rooms plenty of times the last years, but she hated it. And normally it was not at all recommended for anyone doing complex magical work. Two beds, enough space between them for two battered dressers, and room along the opposite wall - the one with the door in it - for trunks. No wardrobes or anything like that, but more hooks on the wall.

Tight quarters, the door to the bath and loo opened into the hall. That was going to be a regular pain in the neck, likely also the hips and knees and elbows. Barely enough room to move around in the bedroom or sitting room. Cammie had done this kind of sharing before. On the other hand, she only had to deal with one other person here, not half a dozen women. And well, she knew exactly what she was getting, and that was actually a joy.

She'd expected some of this - shabby quarters, tucked away from whatever else was at this camp. Certainly, she'd expected to have to make do. On the other hand, this was peculiar in ways she hadn't expected. That bathroom, for one thing, and the shared sleeping room, but only for two of them. It made her wonder what the hut had been used for previously.

At least she had some options for the cleaning. She considered and then charmed her trunk lighter once she was sure no one was looking. She dragged it in, and claimed the bed near the window, because she knew she'd win that argument. Cleaning first, then unpacking. It was the least she could do. But before she got into that, she wanted a look at the hut next door, and their working hut, whatever that meant.

The hut next door was just the same, down to the last detail, just mirrored to keep the two bathing rooms next to each other. Also in need of cleaning, but she wasn't going to do that for them, at least not before anyone got there. Lend a hand, maybe. If they weren't awful. But it set up things badly with strangers to do the cleaning first off.

They'd expect it, and Cammie was having none of that. She'd do her fair share, absolutely, but more than that was the sort of thing she did as a gift, not an expectation. Mum would say a good thing too. Cammie was competent at cleaning. Mum wouldn't have allowed anything else. But it wasn't where she excelled, and everyone Cammie knew was clear about that.

In this case, she suspected someone was going to have

to have a conversation with the plumbing, and see if they could knock together something to get reliably warm water. Poking her head into the bath, she saw a water tank on this side, with a large pipe running out the wall, across the gap into the other bath. That'd make it easier to coax, then. And there was electricity. They'd make do. Anyone serving these days was very good at making do. And she hoped the other two with this particular assignment were just as competent as she and her own partner in creative solutions, as her previous assignment's bunkroom had put it.

The beds here were just as spartan, and the hut had an immediate identifiable mustiness. She was sure there were mice somewhere in the walls, and perhaps she might do something about that later too. Tonight, if all went well. Just another particular way of being of help. One that made use of her actual gifts.

That done, she circled around to the last hut, nudging the door open. This had only a few tables, a handful of chairs. Five, in fact, one more than there were beds. They were the sort of worn things that had gone through a number of lives before ending up here, with scuffed leather and mended patches. The tables were wood, and broad; that was at least better than some places she'd been. No other equipment though, at all. There was a note waiting, saying simply, "09:00 sharp. Tuesday." That was tomorrow morning, then. Nice of anyone to have told her on the way in.

No sign of anywhere to get food, though she gathered there was some sort of canteen set up on the grounds. Maybe there'd be a way to bring food back, at least some of the time, or have one of the four of them go fetch it. Socially, food was a trick, especially when working on something that absolutely couldn't get talked about. In this case, couldn't get talked about for twice as many reasons as most people doing secret work.

Right. Time to get down to work. She made her way back to what was now her hut, for better or worse, at least for the duration. There were cleaning supplies on a shelf in the bath, and she ignored those, instead going to her trunk and rummaging out a smock. Then she hung up her hat, took off her uniform jacket, rolled up her sleeves and put on the smock, and got to it. Magic was decidedly a help, and within an hour she was the sort of tired she hadn't felt in a while, magically, but the bath was in much better state.

Cammie was just contemplating what she could rig up for a cup of tea when she heard the door rattle. "Hello? Cammie?"

CHAPTER 2
HYPATIA, A FEW MINUTES LATER

Hypatia knew her sister was here. The signs were unmistakable, honestly. It wasn't anything visible, or even really audible - though that tune was one of Cammie's favourite things to hum while she was focusing on something else. It was, instead, a feel in the air, or in her magic. Hypatia let down her case - her trunk was supposed to follow tomorrow or the next day - and waited, one foot back behind her, bracing.

As always, she didn't have to wait long. Less than ten seconds, and Cammie was barrelling into her, picking her up and twirling her around, for all Hypatia was actually taller. "You!" Cammie set her on her feet again. "It's been ages."

"It's been a year." Hypatia rubbed her face. "A year? Yeah. Ibis and Pross got that cottage, he had research to do, and we both managed to wrangle leave. You've been horrible about writing, did you know that, even with this?" Cammie had written as soon as she'd got her assignment, even though no one had actually mentioned Hypatia's name. On the other hand, there weren't that many people who likely fit the description.

"You have also been horrible about writing. And honestly, you should be better at it." Cammie took a step back, hands on her hips, the smock flaring out beneath them. "I get most of your news through Mum and Susanna."

Hypatia grinned. "Missed you too. Guessing you have the bed by the window?" She gestured at the case. "I've got a trunk coming sometime. They said tomorrow, if we're lucky it'll be Friday."

"And if you're not, it'll be Monday. I'm assuming you've got all the urgent things with you."

"I have been doing this a while, you." Hypatia reached out and tapped Cammie's nose. Very different from her own, far more snub than aquiline and also a different shade of brown to the skin. They were not sisters by blood, but simply because they were. When her brother Ibis had taken up with Pross, Hypatia had been willing to be helpful to Pross's daughter. It was the right thing to do, to help her get settled at Schola, be friendly.

Only then two things had happened. First, and probably most important, Cammie had also been sorted into Owl House. She'd started as a first year in 1926, when Ibis had begun teaching and Hypatia was in her fifth year. Not prefect, thankfully, that would have taken entirely too much time away from her research and projects. That was a common problem in getting prefects for their House, though Cammie had gone on to be one and had done quite well at it. On the other hand, Cammie liked both patterns and talking to people, and being a prefect was full of both.

But second, the two of them had turned out to get on really rather well. It wasn't just the ordinary things, though those too. They were comfortable together, reading, chatting about what they were reading, then going back to being quiet. They didn't step on each other's mental feet. If Cammie needed the window open a bit, or someone to lend a hand from time to time, well, that was easy enough. And Hypatia knew Cammie would always find time to help with research, even the odder things.

Besides. All Hypatia's other family were in Egypt, except for Ibis. Mama and her two older sisters had stayed in Cairo when she and Ibis had come back to Albion after Papa's death. Hypatia had visited, several times now, but her home was in Albion. Even if, at the moment, it felt like a more tenuous fortress of a country than it might ordinarily.

At any rate, somewhere in the middle, so smoothly neither of them could actually put a date to it, she and Cammie declared themselves sisters. Sometime right around their first solstice properly together was when they counted from. Pross had been staying out at Schola, and the staff had been exploring older traditions, a couple of which had decidedly unexpected consequences.

Ibis swore she and Cammie didn't look alike, but they sounded and felt alike, the way they wielded their magic, how the resonances of it worked. And he was an expert in sympathetic magic, as well as the Materia that he taught now. Hypatia could feel the differences, but she'd gone into a different line of the sympathetic magic work, and also of course she was feeling all of it from inside herself. It was like hearing her own voice on a recording, and how differently it sounded when it was coming from outside her own head.

Even after Ibis and Pross had Susanna, a new baby niece, that didn't change anything. Cammie and Hypatia had both helped Pross out, they'd delighted in time with

Susanna when they could manage it among their own lives. Hypatia had been wisting after another holiday like the last one before the War, all of them at the seaside for a delightful week.

Now, though, she shook her head, and followed Cammie back to the bedroom, noting on the way that someone - almost certainly Cammie - had done a fine job with the bathroom. Priorities. "Pross said she'd see about sending along some blankets and such for cheerful, if we think we're going to be here more than a week or two."

"I've seen no hide nor hair of anyone other than the men at the gate. Or information, other than a note of a meeting tomorrow at nine sharp." Cammie said, levering the case onto the end of the bed, with a plain Army blanket. That was another thing. Both of them liked vibrant colours. Living in the beige dun brownness of the ATS's idea of sensible blankets would drive them both up a wall within a month unless they did something to improve it. And they probably couldn't pull out the colour changing charms here, like Hypatia had at her last posting. They'd need a visible excuse of a shipment, and sheets and such that didn't have Army markings.

"You took on the bathroom? I'll do here and the front room, if you like." It was probably a fair trade, maybe still leaving Hypatia owing a bit. "What's the water like?"

"Tank in the other hut, we should be able to do something useful with it, communally. Metal tank, of course. If it doesn't take charms well I'll eat my service cap. Oh, and there are mice around. I'll do something about that tonight if I get a minute." Cammie looked pleased at the prospect.

Hypatia let a delicate shiver show. "Appreciate that. I don't mind them if they stay out of my way, but they never do, somehow."

Cammie grinned toothily for just a moment. "Glad to.

And it's been a while since I got a good hunt in. Cover for me, and we'll be grand."

"Besides, if you're out, you're not snoring." That was, well, older sisters had some obligations, and Hypatia wasn't going to neglect her duties here.

Cammie laughed. "You sleep through it, you always do. I have tested." She sat with a thump - and a small puff of dust - before getting up and doing a series of rapid charms to clear that. The second time she sat down, just as energetically, there was much less of a cloud.

Hypatia shook her head and turned away to unpack what she had with her. Spare uniform, all her clean blouses and underthings, her daily kit, and the rest of the case full of books. That was right and proper. At least half the trunk was books too. "You bring your typewriter?"

"I did, it's under the bed right now." Cammie gestured with a foot. "There's a hut for work on the back of this. That's where the meeting note was. I didn't like to leave the case in there overnight, not until we've got a better sense of the place."

"Rather off by ourselves, and that's good and bad, isn't it?" Hypatia turned around once, getting another look at the space. "Wonder who they had in here before us. Just pair and pair."

"There are rumours about this place. Secrets," Cammie said. "More than a few stories. I'm not at all sure how many of them to believe. And it's a curious setup, the rooms and the bathing facilities. Like they didn't want whoever was here mingling with the rest of the camp and using the same ablutions hut."

"What did Ibis and Pross say about them?" Hypatia managed to hang up the spare service dress uniform jacket and skirt. She left the slacks in the case. She likely wouldn't need them yet, but she set the boots out under the bed.

There were hooks on the wall for some things, and - well, the rest of it would have to live in the trunk when she got it here. There would be room for two trunks on the wall with the door pushed toward the corner so they had room to move around just a little. Awkward, but manageable. And a lot better than the last posting, where it had been six of them in the hut, and someone was always coming or going, no matter the hour.

Then she took out the small box tucked safely into the suitcase. She'd have to see if she could get a growing plant, but in the meantime, she'd have to make do. Hypatia set the malachite crocodile on her dresser, tucked into the tin she'd set up as a portable shrine. Closed, it looked like a trinket box. Open, the crocodile sat on a bed of blue resin, decorated with the proper materia: flecks of solar gold, an edge of shoreline done in crocodile eggshell, and a little stand of reeds in the corner made of papyrus stems. It had accompanied her everywhere since she'd made the tin up a decade ago. Here, the shrine could stay out in the open, Cammie was sensible and properly respectful, even if she wasn't, herself, devout.

"You know how they pay attention." Both Ibis and Pross - and Cammie's father, Octavian, as well - had done Intelligence work in the Great War. They all had well-informed opinions about how things were going in the current one. "Mum said she didn't have enough informa-tion to make a proper judgement, which suggested some degree of competence somewhere. You know how she gets."

Hypatia grinned broadly and turned back to her case, taking the books out. "Anything we can use for a bookshelf?"

"Not that I've seen yet. But there's so little furniture in the other hut. They must intend for us to ask for what we need, or at least look the other way if we go sort it out ourselves."

Hypatia shook her head. "Make do, want not." It had the singsong tone of the childhood sort of lecture, and Cammie burst out laughing. Once she started, it had Hypatia tumbling into giggles herself, for no good reason other than the fact she desperately needed a release. And whatever had brought them both here - which they still didn't know much about - at least they were together.

She was trying to get her breath back when there was a shout from the hallway. "What in the bloody hells..." It was a bellow, the sort of man who thought volume was power. On the other hand, there was a decent chance that was some sort of superior officer. Or someone who had a superior officer's ear. Both she and Cammie managed to swallow their giggles, stand up and face the music. Hypatia cleared her throat. "I was unpacking." She almost said 'sir', and then decided against it in some twitch of intuition.

A bare second later, a man in Army uniform appeared in the door, almost looming. It took Hypatia a moment to place him. He was wearing service dress, not the battle dress uniform of most of the men she'd seen so far today, no regimental affiliation obvious. He had the brown leather gloves on his hands that went with the service dress. Service cap, rather than one of the other options, firmly in place over brown hair, and he hadn't removed it. Then she got a better look at his face - the light was shading it to start. Pale skin, medium brown hair.

"Sisley." She waited a beat. "What title, please?" Technically, among people from Albion, it should be Lord Sisley, until he indicated otherwise. Hypatia wasn't a barbarian, she read perfectly good Greek along with her other languages, and she paid attention to that sort of detail. On the other hand, for all the Sisley name had a lot of weight in Albion, it wasn't a title that carried over to Britain, not anymore.

"Captain." It came out curt and gruff. "Mistress Ward, Mistress Gates." Then his eyes focused on their own uniforms. "Subalterns."

Cammie nodded once. "Just so. Begin as we're going on?" Then she tilted her head, as irrepressible as Cammie often was. "Though if we're working closely together..." She let her voice trail off.

He jerked slightly. "Do you know who else?"

"There's two beds on the other side. I was told four of us total, so one more person. And there's five chairs in the other hut, meant to be a workroom." Hypatia let Cammie talk. She was the more extroverted of them. More usefully at the moment, she was also somewhat less intimidated by someone of Lord Orion Sisley's background than Hypatia could be. That was thanks to her family, but mostly that Cammie generally carried off being just a tad brash in a way people thought was charming rather than irritating.

Orion Sisley had been a year ahead of Hypatia at Schola, not that their paths had ever particularly crossed then. There had been a mess with his great-uncle that Ibis and Pross had ended up tangled in, though that was ages ago. And she didn't think this Sisley particularly held a grudge, but how would she know if he did?

He'd been in Fox House, showy and sure he was going to go on and rule the world. And he'd done a fair bit of that. Before the war, he'd made a name for himself as a duellist and specialist in the sort of arcane magics that impressed a lot of people. Not Hypatia, because she went at those sorts of things from a different direction, but she could respect skill when she saw it. More to the point, she knew that Isembard Fortier thought well of Sisley, and she'd need more than casual encounters to go against that bit of information.

And it wasn't like she had much to go on. They'd been at the same place at the same time, oh, a handful of times before the war. Mostly when he was visiting Isembard at Schola, and Hypatia was there to see her brother and Pross and Susanna. And Cammie, when Cammie could get free, of course. But it wasn't as if they'd ever particularly talked.

He nodded once. "Do you know anything about food and cleaning and all that?"

Cammie shrugged once. "I did the bathroom here. Hypatia was going to do the front room and the bedroom." Very much not volunteering either of them for the other side. "The usual charms brought up the dirt easily enough. Whoever was here didn't leave it in an awful state. I'd guess it's been empty a month or two."

Sisley took a step back, and his eyes narrowed. "And?"

CHAPTER 3
ORION, LATER THAT AFTERNOON

Orion took a breath, clenching both hands down at his sides, then regretting it. The scar tissue on the left still burned and pulled where his missing fingers weren't. So did the stretch along the wrist and fore-arm. He'd have to dig out the salve as soon as he got a minute alone. That would help a bit.

He hadn't known what to expect from his orders, but it wasn't anything like this. Right now, it felt like another insult, piled on top of all the other insults and injuries of the past six months. First he'd had to figure out how to get to the camp, which had involved a bumpy ride from a pickup point in London that had rattled his teeth, with the others in the truck wondering why he wasn't assigned somewhere else. Why he wasn't back in the fighting that he understood, and was bloody brilliant at. He hadn't said anything. Orion had learned that lesson well enough. He couldn't be suave like a Fox should be, nor charming. He could at least shut up, and give the illusion of control.

It hadn't helped. He'd heard a whisper or two, he was sure that was about him. There'd been the glances. They'd been dropped off at various points, and as the truck pulled away from the last, with just Orion and one other on it, plus the driver, the other man had pointedly turned away.

Now he was here, he certainly hadn't expected to be confronted with two women, both confident and sure of themselves. They weren't giving him any space to learn what he needed to, not before something else ambushed him. It seemed like they'd already settled in, claimed one of the huts for their own.

They even looked more put together than he felt. Both were dressed tidily, hair in place, even Gates, who had black curls he remembered as a confusion of chaos when she was younger. They were standing their ground.

One part of him respected that. The rest of him wanted to scream and hit something. Or since he couldn't do that - bad for the scars, again, as he kept being reminded - to work out his frustrations some other way. No duelling salle here. A punching bag was out of the question, too. He'd take up running again, likely. His feet worked fine, and it didn't need his hands. And they were on the edge of Richmond Park. That would give him a nice long route to run to exhaustion if he could get the time.

Which was the other trick. He had no idea why he was here, if this was punishment or someone's idea of a reward. Orion weighed asking about it in his head, using the checks and balances Isembard and Thesan had taught him over the years, far more useful guidance than his parents had ever offered. He had another flash, now, of them breaking it down for him, all the things other people did without walking through the steps.

The maths worked out well enough. "May I ask about your orders here?" He tried to keep his voice well over on the polite side of the scale. He largely failed, but it at least came out more neutral than aggressive. "Mine weren't specific at all."

Ward tilted her head, looking at him like, well, like she was an Owl. She was allowed to peer at people, thematically speaking. Though most Owls of that sort liked to deploy a pair of glasses to help the effect. "Excellent question." It made him feel like she considered him a rather dim dog, who'd done something marginally clever, and he did not like that at all. Also, it did not give any further information.

He waited, folding his arms over his chest, and just let the silence drag out uncomfortably. His mother had taught him that one, and it was as effective for him as it was for her. More, maybe, he did have broad shoulders. The overall mien was a bit like a wall.

Ward shrugged. "I've a guess or two, but that's only from knowing since, what, Saturday, that Cammie was also being posted here." She nodded at the other woman. "She's got signals experience. I've got," she frowned, considering something, then cast a brief charm to check there was no eavesdropping, then another to ensure more privacy. Orion felt them cast, deftly, and the slight pop like ears did, diving down in a pool. "I've got sympathetic magic experience. I've been working on other projects, the whole war. You?"

That was tricky, wasn't it, about three ways round. Orion cleared his throat. "Overseas, parts unspecified. I've been back in Albion, on an extended leave, since October." He'd been in the heat of fighting in the Dodecanese islands, and before that part of mobile raiding forces in Europe. He'd been brilliant at the fighting, that was the hell of it. He knew where he was when he was fighting.

Then everything had smashed into bits. At this point he couldn't measure out how much of what he felt now was healing and what rehabilitation they could offer, what was fury at his now ex-wife, and what was the process of disentangling their magic, contracts, and agreements.

He'd been able to prove the adultery three times over, magically. His memory under oath, truth compulsion on her telling, and of course the tidy bit of blood magic that made it clear Decima's unborn babe absolutely wasn't his. Given that, the decree nisi had gone through in Albion quite quickly, just a fortnight or so, in legal terms. But the actual ritual work had turned out to be a patch of brambles. And of course the decree absolute took six months, and wouldn't be done until the end of April. They'd only finished all the ritual aspects in mid-February, and then he'd been warming a bench in various hallways, waiting to see if he was fit for anything useful.

Well. Warming a bench and helping Isembard out when he could. It made a change from dealing with Mother. He'd made sure to spend time with his children, but neither Melchior nor Sybil knew him all that well. He'd been serving abroad, only a leave here or there, from the beginning of the war, when Melchior was barely two. Sybil had been born after one of his early leaves, and he'd never lived with her, day in and day out. Mother and his aunts were better set to raise both the little ones. And after what Decima had done - or rather, the way she had done it - the courts had given him full custody. Pointedly, with comments about war heroes with supportive female relatives being much better able to raise the children.

It wasn't the done thing at all for Decima to be bedding her lover in her husband's bed, when he might walk in at any moment. More to the point, when it broke every single of their marriage agreements. The negotiation of that had taken half a dozen solicitors representing the various interests when they'd got married in the first place, and most of six months. And Decima had thrown it all away, for no good reason.

He could still see the agreements in his mind, the way he mentally added lines and arrows and rubrication. The one about discretion, the one about privacy, and most certainly the one about using multiple methods of contraception. Orion forced his mind away from the memory, because it would make him furious again, and that wasn't going to help anything. It hadn't yet, anyway.

He coughed to bridge that, and the growing silence. "My background is in duelling and patterns and various of the martial magics." He'd found himself a place there, though it made his fellows in Fox House eye him a bit oddly. Foxes didn't get their hands dirty in the heat of battle. Foxes sent Boars and sometimes Bears to the heat of battle. "A bit of geomancy. I was doing artillery work, mostly, or the support for it." Complete with explosions entirely too close to his person. It would have been better, honestly, if the one in the Dodecanese Islands had killed him dead.

Only it would have hurt Claudio and Isembard. Possibly just the two of them - and Thesan - would have actually missed him. His younger brother and mother would have been sad, but they'd have gone on the way they had after Father's death. His son was far too young to inherit the land magic. There would have been a regent, but there were traditions for that and Mother was absolutely capable of it. He turned away now, for just an instant, to cough again. "Pardon, the dust in here."

"We need to do a bit more cleaning. I don't know anything about food, or whatever. I assume there's a canteen here somewhere, there's enough people around for one, but I don't know where." She hesitated. "They might respond better to you asking than to one of us."

Orion's chin came up, and he considered that. "Anyone given you difficulty?" Difficulty he could do something with productively, maybe. He knew where he was with that sort of problem. He wasn't sure about these women, or why they'd been assigned here - it was a very mixed set of skills so far. Plus the fact the two of them had been assigned together. Surely anyone who knew them in specific knew they were near enough sisters, or at least that was how they went at the world. Like he and Claudio did, and he respected that, even if they weren't his sort in every other way than sharing magic.

"I haven't given anyone the chance to." That was Gates, meeting his gaze directly. She liked a bit of a fight, he suspected, and that was something he hadn't guessed about her when they were at school. Not that he'd paid much attention to her. He'd only seen her when he was visiting Isembard and Thesan, and she happened to be around to see her mother or stepfather.

"Any idea when we're getting our fourth?" Orion weighed the options. "I could go do reconnaissance about the catering options, and come back and let you know."

Both women visibly considered this, and then Gates offered, her tone suddenly precise. "Seems like a reasonable trade. I don't want to clean another bathroom today, but I could tackle your front room if you see about food?"

Orion nodded once. "Fair. You said the usual charms were fine?"

"I used Fomalhaut's Advantage, Hessing's Third, and the variant on Coller's Practical I learned at school. Nothing fancy."

She clearly did her own cleaning a lot more often than Orion had done magically in a very long time, but he still remembered that. Or at least, mostly. He'd have to see how Hessing's worked for him now. It required both hands, and

23

he still hadn't worked out how to rebalance that sort of casting reliably. "I'll give it a try, then." He could be agreeable. Somewhere, long-forgotten, he had learned manners, and whatever else these women were, they weren't actually Decima. It helped they looked nothing like her, either of them. Decima had her pale, much-praised looks aided by various potions to make her hair sleeker and more golden, and cosmetics to bring out eyes and lips and who knew what else.

He was about to fall into that particular mental pit again, he could tell, when he heard steps from the front door of the hut. "Rather Portal Square around here, isn't it?" Then he turned, and his eyes focused, and all the air went out of his lungs.

Claudio. The last person he'd ever expected to see here and now. The person he most wanted to be near. Claudio was his chosen brother, his friend, and one of the only people who wouldn't blame him for things. Claudio understood, and if he didn't, he'd listen as long as it took for him to get a grasp. Orion leaned against the wall with one shoulder now. "You're supposed to be up north."

"Reassigned here." Claudio looked every bit the proper nobleman, in ways Orion never quite felt himself. He was dark-haired, with the sort of sharp handsome features that did well on hortatory posters encouraging young men to do their bit for the country, and young women too. The uniform suited him as well as it had last time they'd been in the same place. Orion thought Claudio had dropped near a stone in weight since his service dress had been properly tailored. Claudio's mother would not approve, and that made his mouth twitch up.

Then Claudio caught a glimpse of the two women who'd come up behind Orion. "Gates. Ward." He nodded, politely, leaving off the titles. "I have a bit more information on what we're about, but can I have a few minutes to put things away?"

"We were going to do a bit more cleaning." Gates spoke first, then there was a tiny pause before she added, "Captain Warren. And I'd just traded Captain Sisley here the cleaning of your front room in exchange for him figuring out what the canteen's like or where we can get food. We might manage a bit of cooking on the stove, but there's no pots or kettle or fuel."

"Cooking, not either of our strengths." Ward put that in, firmly. Orion got the sense neither of them wanted to be stuck with it, which was fair enough. Too many men dumped everything like that on the ATS, as if the women were assigned to do everything a mother might, as well as their own work. And if these two had significant signals and magical experience, there were plenty of other things they were skilled at that were needed far more.

Claudio nodded. "Fair enough. How about thirty minutes or so? I assume there's no option for tea yet. We'll have to see about that, too."

Gates nodded. "I'll see if I can get the stove going. I've something that will do to boil water in my kit."

"Grand. Do we all have something for a mug? I've got some actual tea with me. Reconvene in thirty, then." Claudio had a gift for making the statement neither an order nor a suggestion, but something that rode the line between the two. He pivoted neatly, and Orion followed him without a pause, matching stride as if it hadn't been months - years - since the last time they'd been able to do so.

CHAPTER 4
CLAUDIO, MOMENTS LATER

Claudio knew Orion was right behind him as he walked out of the one hut and made two sharp right turns into the other. Once they were in their bedroom, he flung out the magic that would ensure their privacy, no matter how thin the walls were. "How are you really? Both hand and heart." They hadn't been able to talk about anything terribly personal in the journals. There was too much chance someone might catch sight of it. And it had been hard to get letters out, too. Claudio hadn't had leave of any kind for months. Not since, what was it, last March, except for a day for research in Schola's library a fortnight ago.

Orion must have known it was coming. He had followed Claudio in, standing by his trunk but not yet bent over to unpack it. He didn't look up. "You know you're the first person to ask that. Outside Isembard and Thesan." The last bit was a bit grudging. "About either part of it."

"Well, other people are like that. We've known so for a long time. You haven't answered my question."

Orion pivoted to sit on the bed like his legs wouldn't

hold anymore, with a creak of springs and dust in the air. Claudio mentally filed that away, that no one had particularly prepared for their arrival. "How am I supposed to be? My hand's mangled, the divorce went through promptly, my ex-wife's about to have another man's child. She couldn't even be competent about that bit." It was bitter, angry, and entirely justified, really.

"And?" Claudio could tell that wasn't quite all. Quite a lot of anger still, given that it had been months. Something in Orion was furious, a boar pawing the ground and about to charge.

"And your mother made it very clear last week I should put any idea of challenging again for the Council out of my head." Orion's voice was sharp, low, absolutely death on wings.

Claudio felt his heart skip. "She didn't." Oh, she was so high-handed, she never stopped being high-handed. "Just her? Not Cyrus."

"She's quite enough, thank you. I don't need to hear it from him, too. You know how they are about injuries. Lasting visible ones."

"Edgarton uses a cane." Claudio knew that wasn't a sufficient retort, but it was the one he could start with. Orion had made the attempt at a challenge for a Council seat in 1939 and not succeeded. His family had been quietly furious, and Claudio's mother had been fuming. And then the challenges since, both Claudio and Orion had posts that meant they couldn't get back for it.

"He uses a cane, but he's got all his bits, he's more than mobile enough when he needs to be. And he's got at least two-thirds of them terrified that he'll pull out some bit of mind-reading their deepest secrets if they push too hard on that point."

Claudio let out a snort. "Well, they're not wrong."

Then he shook his head. "Mother is, though. No reason you couldn't make the attempt again, and you'd find out what the Land thought. Which is actually what matters."

"Not that it's a particularly urgent question unless someone gets themselves killed. But there is a war on." Orion shrugged, and Claudio exhaled. So his friend, his brother, had had all the devastation of the injury, and learning that his wife was unfaithful in the worst way possible. Decima had rubbed his nose in it, and hadn't cared about hurting him. And then he'd had the thing he'd been supposed to be aiming at near all his life tossed aside. It'd make anyone stroppy. And, well, Orion was given to stroppiness by nature.

"All right. But now we're here, and together, and I'm glad of that." Claudio was, but he'd put it that way for a reason. "Achilles?" Claudio hadn't heard much about Orion's younger brother for a bit.

"Still posted in North Africa. We only hear anything erratically. The last time was..." Orion frowned. "Two months ago? Mother worries, but there's nothing we can do about that." Of course she would. Orion's mother was his father's second wife. Hector, Orion's older half-brother, had died in combat in 1917. Like a lot of families, they'd gone into this war knowing what it meant to wait in the silences between letters. It was all about quietly hoping it wouldn't be the short telegram with announcement of a death next.

Claudio nodded. "And who knows how much mail's getting through, between the censors and ships going down and whatever else." He half turned away, considering the space, not sure what to say next. There was a lot he ought to say, and he didn't want to put any of it into words.

Orion called him on it immediately. "What's happened to you, then, that you're not telling anyone about?"

"I never can hide things from you." Claudio leaned against the wall now. "And I don't want to. Don't you start about that." He shrugged. "I'm exhausted. What we're going to be doing is more of that. I'm worried about a lot of people."

Orion's eyes widened. Then he nodded, working through the implications quickly enough. "Isembard. You've seen him - when?"

"Starting there. A fortnight ago, gather I just missed you." Claudio agreed. "It did him good to be able to help you, but there've been three more deaths. You know how he blames himself. Or how it hits him. Thesan, too. And you getting near blown up almost did him in, not that he'd have said so to you, I expect."

Orion snorted. "We are all very good at not saying things, after all this time. All three of us. Though in this case, I did get that look from Thesan, you know the one. And then biscuits and cider, and they were the best thing I'd tasted in, I don't know, two years. My last leave."

"Ah." Claudio let out a sigh. "Yes. Maybe we can talk her into a care package here? If she can figure out something that works with the rationing." He flicked his fingers. "I don't want to get into the details until we talk with the women, but we're here for a bit, assuming we're any good at the assignment."

"Define a bit? Also, you haven't answered my question. Fair play."

"You need to be read in first, and make the oaths on it. But months, not weeks or days." Claudio waited for that to hit. Something long enough that they'd get some time together. And, so he devoutly hoped - and Claudio was on average not actually devout - without anyone directly trying to kill them for a bit. "And yes, I'm not answering your question. Give me a min to think about how to put it."

"Gives me a sense of the scope, then." Orion pushed himself upright. "Do you want the bed by the window?"

Claudio considered. "Would you rather have your back to the wall, or be nearer the door? I don't know which way you're more comfortable these days."

Orion grunted. "I'd like to be up a flight of stairs with a couple of windows and at least three exits from the room. But there's lots of things I can't have anymore, and that's just another on the list."

"Thought so." Claudio considered the options. "And the wall behind us is the other hut. We could maybe magic a door if we wanted to. But not tonight." He grimaced. "Definitely not tonight."

Orion raised an eyebrow. Claudio expected him to press again at the unanswered question, but instead he glanced around. "They know we're magical, then."

"Mmhmm." Claudio turned away, moving to open his trunk and hang things up.

"And we're in together. Not separate quarters." Most magical folk did very badly sharing sleeping space, especially if they were doing any kind of intense magical work. "And we're all officers." Claudio and Orion outranked the women, but that was normal, given the relative command structure of the ATS.

"Just so. It's the two sets of us because - when this was pointed out by higher ranked people than either of us - they thought we'd get along well enough it wouldn't be so much of a problem. That, and the skill sets mesh."

"How do you know so much about this? Are you in charge of the thing?" Orion came over to start working on his own trunk. "You take the bed by the wall. We can swap around if it turns out not to work, right?"

"Right." Claudio shoved his trunk over to make room for Orion to rearrange his. "And I'm not in charge. Some related experience. Patience, you. Even if it's not your best virtue."

"Don't feel like I have any bloody virtues at the moment." Orion grunted again. Claudio was on one hand almost glad to hear it. He'd rather Orion be honest, at least when they were in private, like this. But at the same time, it wasn't the thing anyone wanted to hear from a friend— or brother. The two of them had been in Isembard's particular care while they were students at Schola. Isembard had been a combination of bodyguard, duelling master, and a professor for their classes in the ordinary way of things. Most important, though, he had been one of the only adults in either of their lives who'd really listened to them and cared what they wanted.

Oh, Claudio's mother wanted all the best for him, at least by her own standards of what was best. And Claudio had more or less met his father's expectations until his father had died a decade ago. Twelve years, in May, if the world made it to May. That seemed a very long way from now, for all it was March now. Claudio could tell he was tired, bone deep, and that wasn't going to get better any time soon. To make it all smartly right by their standards, he should be on the Council like Mother, and like Father before her. And he wasn't, but there was still time for that. So Mother kept saying.

Electra, Claudio's own wife, was not inclined to the utter shambles Decima had created. But she was certainly not a source of solace. She'd taken over one of the family's country houses up in Norfolk entirely once she'd had Minerva, the second of their contractually agreed children. Even four years later, she was still rather annoyed that Mother hadn't ceded the Trellech townhouse to her. She alternated between visits to Trellech and whatever amusements she made for herself.

Electra nominally supervised the children's nanny and governess, but Mother honestly did a lot more of that, despite being terribly busy with Council duties. It was what was called a cordial marriage, but it was a lot more cordial when Claudio wasn't remotely present. Even thinking about making a proper show of it was exhausting, and it was one reason Claudio hadn't tried to get leave. It would be show and pomp and circumstance if he did, and it was far easier to put his head down and keep working.

Now Claudio let out a breath. "Doing the kind of thing Isembard's talked about. The things that leave marks on you, inside. Not as bad as he had it. I've not been in direct fighting? But that's a thing that weighs on me, too." There wasn't anyone else he'd say that to, even Isembard himself. Maybe especially Isembard himself, who'd blamed himself for a number of things he'd done in the last war, down to the death of his best friend. Rubbing those raw edges again wouldn't do anyone any good.

"And it's exhausted you." Orion frowned at him, before coming closer, then lifting both hands to cup Claudio's face and look him in the eye. Claudio felt the smooth leather of Orion's gloves on his skin, a beat before he noticed consciously that three of the fingers in the left glove felt different. Something solid, fitted in the gloves, charmed to move with the index finger, he suspected. Not something Claudio would ask about, straight out, not yet. He waited for Orion to read whatever he was looking for, then finally his brother by choice pressed forehead to forehead for a breath before backing up. "I missed you. More than I knew."

"Me too. I keep," Claudio's voice caught. "I'd say no one told us it would be like this. Being grown up. Being responsible. But Isembard did. Mother did, too, and Father. Though much less usefully."

"All the flashy bits, parties and fun. Power, but in a civilised form, at least in public. Not so much of the sharp edges." Orion nodded. "I keep thinking of Isembard sitting us down and explaining things. Wishing it was still like that, rather than having to figure it out ourselves. Always a step behind where we should be. And it's not as if we actually have power, it turns out."

It made Claudio laugh, but the laugh came out hollow. "Like that. Right. We need to talk to the women a bit. I desperately need a spot of tea, if Gates has come up with something." He snagged the tin out of his trunk. "And then cleaning and the canteen, or whatever it is. My advance information was short on the practical."

Orion had backed up, but now he didn't move, folding his arms. "How dangerous is this thing we're doing? No, I don't mean that." He reached to rub his face once, then tucked his hand back, folded under his arm. "What kind of dangerous is it?"

"The kind of thing where there might be nightmares, later. The ones with horrors and gaps and wondering what you've done. The uneasy ones." Claudio had those one night out of three, on average, at the moment, and he suspected this was going to make it worse. "The sort of thing where we won't be able to talk about it after, with anyone who's not read in. Which is part of why I'm glad you're here." That was one thing he'd learned well from Isembard and from other veterans of the last war. Having someone - even just one or two people - you could talk to, who understood, could make a world of difference. "And that's before we get to the potentially dangerous magic."

"Ah, that one. At least we've got some experience and training with it." Ah, there was Orion's bravado. It had been entirely missing, so far, and hearing it, just a titch of it, made Claudio feel a bit better.

"We do. And we're in it together." Claudio titled his head, then tossed the tin of tea in his hand, a little shallow bump. "Tea?"

"Tea." Orion nodded. "And I'll do the bathroom. Might need a h— a little help with it, not sure how the magic's flowing."

"Good thing to try it on, and of course I'll help." Then Claudio nodded once more, and they went back over to the other hut in companionable silence.

CHAPTER 5
CAMMIE, THAT EVENING

I t was more than thirty minutes before the men came back, closer to forty-five. But in that time, Hypatia had made excellent inroads on cleaning the other two rooms of the hut. Cammie had spent the time excavating her mess tins from the bottom of her trunk and then going and finding some wood for the wood stove. There was a stack by the side of the hut, which - well. They were back to mice in the vicinity. Possibly also some rats, voles, or moles, and it was possible there was a snake or two lurking. She avoided sticking her hands or any other extremities into any crevasses and gaps, though she took note of them for later reference.

By the time the men knocked, quite politely, she had water at a boil. Her own enamel mug and Hypatia's were waiting, and she'd snagged two chairs from the workroom for the moment. Warren was rather more polite. He had knocked, waited on the doorstep, such as it was, and then waved them to the more comfortable chairs. Sisley had lingered behind, and Cammie wondered what they'd been talking about. Sisley looked better, something in his colour, the indefinable shades that pale-skinned people showed more easily that she'd learned to read.

"Oh, you did get the hot water going. Orion, mind wrangling the cups? I remembered the tea, but. Mine's at the top right of my trunk." Claudio glanced over his shoulder.

Cammie would have expected that to put Sisley's hackles up, the casualness of the comment. Sisley just nodded. "Sure." He disappeared, coming back before anyone in the room had worked around to saying anything else, with two matching enamelware mugs. She caught a glimpse of the dots of paint on the bottom, a common way for people to mark their own. Her own mug had a little squiggle, and Hypatia's had a triangle, a gesture at a pyramid.

Once they had all four mugs, Warren pulled out a small tin, and added some crumbled tea from a tea brick to each mug. "We'll work out something better - a proper kettle and teapot, I'm hoping - soonish." He spoke easily, as if this were a stroll in the nearby Richmond Park. It was intended to make them relax, but it put the hair up on the back of Cammie's neck. She crossed her ankles properly under her, quite aware Hypatia would have comments if she didn't do the done thing.

"You said you had some information about why we're here? All I got was the information to report today, and that Hypatia was also assigned." If Cammie couldn't be pushy about his tone, she could ask a different question. There were certainly plenty of different questions on offer.

"First things first. Formalities in public, when other people are around, certainly. But when it's the four of us, working - and I suspect it will be just the four of us a lot of the time - do you wish to stand on ceremony?"

Oh, that was unfair. If the women said they wanted

formality, it would turn into something stiff and edged. If they suggested they were all right with something more casual, it was a quick downward slope toward the men assuming that a lot of other casual things were on offer. Cleaning, managing laundry, fetching the food, for starters. And quite likely, angling toward sharing a bed, or at least favours. Cammie wasn't up for that, and she was certain her sister wasn't either.

Fortunately, Hypatia was there before her on those points. "Names are one thing. The implications of the names are quite another." She lifted her chin.

"And how much time do you spend talking with Alexander Landry, then?" Warren was grinning now. "Not when we've been there, but I'm guessing some."

It made Hypatia's mouth quirk up. "Before the war, there was a regular Sunday wrangle over supper whenever the bohort matches didn't run too long. You must know that."

"He was Isembard's mentor, the way Isembard has been ours." Warren's gesture took in Sisley, too. "And Alexander does have quite a spiel about names and their implications. Sensibly so." He spread his hands out, more genially. "I'd just prefer not to be saying 'Subaltern Ward, Subaltern Gates' every other minute. And I suspect you'd like it the same way round."

"To be fair, it's not like we save that many syllables." Cammie said, letting a certain drawl into her voice. Her mates at the last posting would have known to worry. So did Duncan. When she got like this, she was on the prowl for something, and her target was decidedly not safe. Hypatia did not kick her ankle, so she kept going. Then she flicked her fingers. "If it's first names all round, then Cammie and Hypatia." She refused to be Camilla.

"Claudio and Orion." Warren - Claudio - counted off

on his fingers. "For savings of, let's see. Four plus four plus four plus four is sixteen. That's rather geometrically balanced. Versus two plus three plus three and three. Eleven. That's thirty per cent more efficient, give or take some decimals."

It was not the answer Cammie had entirely expected. He wasn't standing on rank or position, though he could do both. They were both captains, a rank above Cammie and Hypatia. "And you're all right with this?" She hesitated just a fraction and pointedly added, "Orion?"

This time Hypatia did tap her ankle, and Cammie ignored it. She was watching Sisley's face.

"Orion." He shrugged one shoulder. "Claudio's ideas are generally pretty sound. Though I would also like to hear more of what you know. Now. Claudio." That last word wasn't a growl, not the way Cammie was sure he could do without much provocation. But it was being direct.

Claudio spread his hands, not seeming to mind. Most people would mind that sort of growl, especially from a close friend. Claudio just went on, as if it were entirely ordinary. "Two other things. Anything we should all know about what to avoid? The usual around not startling each other? Knocking before entering the other hut, bar utter emergency, which includes fire, attack, bombing, magical disaster, etc."

The list made Cammie snort. She glanced at Hypatia. "We've all been doing this enough to have the things we startle at, sure. I need a fair bit of time on my own outside, if I can get it. I'll let one of you - Hypatia, usually - know when I'll be back. Obviously, not when we're needed for something."

"Running, or something of the kind?" Claudio asked.

It was a casual question, but she suspected he had multiple reasons for it.

"Trust me, she means the 'on her own' bit, or she's misery to live with. And seeing as that's me, she'll get the time." Hypatia cut in smoothly, perfectly.

Claudio lifted his hands. "I do a fair bit of running when I can. So does Orion. We'll make sure to go a different route if you're out, that's all." Cammie tilted her head, trying to read his expression, and utterly failing. Orion's face was set in a pleasant enough mask, but at least with him she was sure he was covering several sets of thoughts. Both of them were obviously of Fox House, but Claudio was vastly better at it. "All right. Usual sorts of privacy charms. Do we need to beat on the plumbing with a magical sort of mallet?"

"I like that you're practical." Hypatia said. "We've both tested the loo now, but the hot water on this side isn't great, if you'd have a look? The heater's on yours. Cammie's certain there are mice around. She's got a gift for making them be elsewhere. I'm sure she'll see to that promptly."

Orion grimaced. "Mice. Why is it mice?"

"It could be snakes. Or spiders. Though if we had snakes, we'd likely have fewer mice." Hypatia pointed out, with a vicious amiability. "Anyway. The building's been here for a couple of years, I'm guessing there's a few inches space between the two, from the size of things. Mice."

"I was - well. On the march, mostly, until." Orion shrugged once then didn't finish that sentence. "Right. Privacy charms, we'll see about the hot water. See to our own spaces and split the cleaning for the shared, and all that. And we'll figure out food when we know what the options are." He hesitated for just a beat. "I'm not used to having the ATS around. I was in combat settings, fairly far afield. I'd not mind a bit more about what you've been doing."

Claudio picked up the implied question before either of the women needed to come up with anything like an answer. "Which brings us tidily to our next point. I can't tell you three - any of you, don't ask, Orion." That was easy and relaxed, as if he was anticipating that growl and getting in ahead of it. "You'll get read in tomorrow. And besides I don't know a lot about the specifics. But I was working on a similar enough project up north for the past six months or so. There's only the four of us working on it here, they needed people who could work closely, share living quarters, all that. And while I don't know a lot about either of you women, I'm quite sure you're competent." He gestured. "Research on my end, applied research, a lot of work around incantation, a good dash of alchemy and materia and sympathetic work. A little of a lot of things."

Orion picked up without missing a beat. "Combat, as I said. No longer suited for what I was doing, came back here to recuperate, and here I am." Which didn't make it clear what had needed recuperation. Shock, possibly, battle strain. He didn't look at first glance like he'd had a bad injury, though she noticed his gloves were still on. "Duelling, some ritual magic, a lot of artillery work most recently, a number of martial applications of things."

Hypatia nodded. "Sympathetic magic work, here. Resonances between things, some of the precautions on magical kit, all that sort of thing."

"Signals work. Decoding, nothing I can talk about. I'm fluent in French and German, and good at a couple of others." Cammie considered, then added. "Walking out with an RAF man, when we've had the chance, which we haven't for a year. But I know a fair bit about how that works, now, or can ask, things he can share."

"Does he have a journal on him, or no?" Claudio asked, leaning forward.

"No, he's in barracks with a lot of non-magical folk. Too much risk. But he gets his mail fairly promptly when the censors don't hold it up too much. And we've got our own private codes." That wasn't revealing too much, she thought, particularly since she was in signals.

Claudio clearly added it to a stack of other information in his head - he was letting her see that, she was sure. "Right. Appreciate that. What I know about this camp is that we're on our own in a lot of ways. We'll be reporting to someone specific, who's not based here. We'll be given our line of work, and we can ask for materia and supplies. Thinking creatively is encouraged, so long as it works. This camp, though, there's a lot of secret work going on, and I suspect they won't want us to mingle much. We'll find out about the canteen."

"So we're stuck with each other's company. I'm guessing that means not much in the way of, oh, entertainment shows. Just a lot of work." Hypatia frowned. "Books?"

"Books we can get in. Likely something like a gramophone or radio. I suspect not a lot of leave time. They were squirrelly about it at my last place. Too worried about someone talking. Whoever gives our orders will be magical, but the people they report up to aren't, and they don't understand that oaths actually hold for us."

"If they're properly made." Orion leaned back, crossing one ankle over his other knee and cupping his hands around the mug. "Can we send for some comforts, do you think?"

"I'd wait a few days, but oh, we can rise to a teapot, something to listen to, whatever reference books are needed for the work. There's a portal near the old palace at Sheen, a hair over a mile's walk, but again, leave will be hard to come by. We should get mail promptly enough." Claudio flicked his fingers. "With the appropriate cautions around who you consult. People under oath, the Official Secrets Act or equivalent."

Cammie shrugged. "Fairly sure that includes both my parents, to be clear. And I think half the staff at Schola, at least."

"Isembard, for certain." Claudio agreed. "So we should be able to get copies of things, several ways around. Good to know, thank you."

Cammie inclined her head. He had a way about him, Claudio did, of making a 'thank you' into something that had a soft weight to it, that mattered. Like patting a dog who would then wag his tail. She found it fascinating, because it irritated her, but he was also quite competent at it. Not overusing it, not abusing it, but measuring out its effectiveness. Then she heard someone's stomach growl.

Orion grimaced. "That's me. Shall we go hunt up food? Bring you something back, for tonight, and we can finish making things tidy, get a good night's sleep before tomorrow? Ta for the tea and the water to make it." He was far less suave about it, but he made a point of saying it, and Cammie hadn't expected that.

"Good plan." Hypatia stood up. "I've got dust to get out of two beds."

"I'll have a go at your front room while you're gone, then." Cammie said, standing up. "And get out of your way after that."

"There's a fine plan all round. Appreciate that, Cammie." Claudio stood, and Orion immediately followed him, almost entirely in sync. They took their mugs with them, and the rest of the block of tea, but with any luck tonight's meal would come with some more.

CHAPTER 6
HYPATIA, THE NEXT MORNING

The night before had gone smoothly enough. They'd had a middling supper. At least it was warm, though it was mostly beige and unseasoned. One of the men had thought about a warming charm while bringing the mess trays over, and at least the mess tins took to magic well enough. Cammie and Hypatia had finished cleaning up their hut until it was presentable, if not actually terribly comfortable.

While they'd cleaned, they'd talked out their working theories about the two men. Both of them had noticed how Orion and Claudio walked together, entirely in rhythm and apparently without trying. How they treated each other was another bit of mystery, particularly the ways something in Claudio had evened out Orion's stroppiness. Neither Hypatia nor Cammie knew quite what to make of it, or what it'd mean for their work.

It wasn't their closeness that was a mystery. Hypatia had seen them at Schola, with Thesan and Isembard, out of term time, in their younger and more relaxed days.

How they fit together, though, she didn't understand. Orion was older, but deferred to Claudio in ways that might even work out here and now. Claudio didn't presume on that, but he did make things flow, once he knew which direction he wanted to go. It was all curious and not the way things were usually done, and that would gnaw at Hypatia a good bit until she and Cammie got rather a lot more data to work with.

Once it was properly dark and the noises of the camp had quieted down, Cammie had waved and ducked out. She'd been gone for perhaps two hours, with a certain amount of squeaking, scrabbling, and muted chaos coming from the space between the two huts. When she'd come back in, she'd been a smug little thing. But Cammie had more than earned it, and Hypatia had just handed her a mug of tea. Herbal this time, mind, it was easier to come by. They'd made sure their shoes were polished, their uniforms ready, and Hypatia had fallen asleep listening to Cammie's even breathing. Not even much snoring, some things did actually change.

The four of them left their huts at precisely the same moment, ten to nine, all turned out neatly in the appropriate service uniform. Hypatia knew there'd been quite a lot of fuss about the design for the women, they were supposed to look smart in it. Cammie looked well, and Hypatia had made sure all their hair was up and staying put. Claudio held the door for them, and they took seats on rather decrepit chairs.

Precisely at nine, the door opened. Orion started, and so, worryingly, did Cammie. Both of them flung themselves into standing, and into a salute to - a woman. Claudio and Hypatia were standing an instant later, doing the same. The woman was an ATS Junior Commander, to be specific. Not anyone Hypatia knew, and that was also more than a little curious. She was significantly younger than either Cammie or Hypatia, first half of her twenties, at best. She had dark hair up in a Victory roll, her uniform was impeccable, and she had the sort of self-possession that Hypatia was used to seeing on the women from Fox House. She looked like one of the women who'd been born and bred to that sort of control for generations.

"At ease, have a seat." Her voice was just as crisp as the rest of her. Hypatia read that immediately. She'd been in the same position often enough, having to hold someone's attention by sheer force of personality, and what that was going to cost in the long-term. The chairs creaked as all five sat, with the Junior Commander crossing her ankles neatly under her chair as if she never sat sloppily, ever.

None of them spoke, they all knew better than that. To be a Junior Commander at that age - the equivalent to a Captain, Claudio and Orion's rank - suggested significant competence. And besides, she knew things they didn't yet, and only a fool would toss the chance to learn more away. Hypatia folded her hands and waited. They hadn't been told they could take notes, and that was a sign in and of itself.

"Good morning." The younger woman nodded. "You may refer to me as Junior Commander Roberts. I will be asking you for a number of oaths this morning. The first of them is that you will not, by any means mentioned or otherwise, attempt to determine my actual identity. If such information should be presented to you, you will speak to no one about it, even each other. You're all competent to make the oath, yes?"

That had the dual meaning, of course, that they had magic sufficient for it, and that they knew how to form an oath on the spot. Each of them did, more or less in the expected format, covering the various exigencies, including chance information falling in their laps. Once that was handled, Junior Commander Roberts nodded again. "You all attended Schola. I did not, but I did make the Pact at twelve. I am here as your liaison with a particular unit, handling highly secret material. Before we go on, your oath to keep what you hear today, and during any part of your work with this unit entirely secret. In this case, you may of course discuss with each other, but you may not consult outside experts unless we have cleared them first."

Again, they made a round of oaths, making Hypatia suspect there was at least one more coming. She felt the magic twining around her, not exactly strangling but certainly pressing a bit. Like wearing a frock that was perfectly tailored for her, but didn't exactly allow free movement. Or her uniform, case in current point. She sat up a little straighter. Ummi would approve.

The younger woman nodded, "One more. You swear that you will work to the best of your ability. You will be forthright and honest with me or another designated contact about what is important, what is feasible, and what you cannot achieve with the limitations at hand. Those limitations will likely include time, resources including materia, labour, skills, and a number of others."

There was slightly more hesitation at this, but that sort of shortage was to be expected, and all the more so when it was a highly secret project. Claudio led in this one, his voice steady. When he finished, he cleared his throat. "You know my background, of course."

"Yes. And I do hope you'll share whatever you've learned that might be helpful in this situation, about how to approach the problem, though not, of course, operational specifics." Junior Commander Roberts settled back in her chair. "First order of business. We will have some ordinary sorts of supplies arriving before lunchtime.

Tables, desks, a teakettle and something to heat it on. Arrange it so that no one who is not keyed to the wards will be able to enter this space. Violent repulsion version, please. I trust you can all handle the results of that if it snares someone."

Hypatia snorted. "If you know our backgrounds, you'll know that Cammie and I help pick students out of Schola's warding when we're visiting. And I'm quite clear that the gentlemen have similar skills." She was being courteous, but she caught how Claudio's head came up for a moment at that, focusing on her. She'd chosen her words precisely, thank you. Both in naming what they were, and what she hoped they'd be. Though she was beginning to have strong suspicions that what they were being asked to do had nothing to do with gentlemanly codes of conduct.

"Just so. We'll set the wards before I go. You can advise jointly on whether you think anything else is necessary." Then Junior Commander Roberts went on. "Bluntly put, your assignment is to mislead, magically. We have the non-magical side covered, or at least that is the plan. As Captain Warren knows, we are implying the presence of the Fourth Army, focusing on fictitious divisions based in southern England."

Orion cleared his throat. "The Fourth Army used the badge of a white boar's head in the Great War, King Richard III's badge or near enough. Was that intentional, or a chance?" He added to Claudio, not nearly as quietly as he perhaps should have, "The Somme, 1917, and then reformed later on, for the Hundred Days offensive beginning in Amiens. Almost all under General Sir Henry Rawlinson. He had a long military career, starting in the Sudan, died in, erm. About when we finished school, if I remember right, so at least he's not around to object."

Junior Commander Roberts coughed. "Military history

later, please. The boar is by chance, but if you find it of use, do inform me. More to the point, it is key to several initiatives that the Germans and Axis powers be deceived about where and when a major attack will come. Not in the general sense, of course, they must expect that France is the likely country. But which part of the coast, exactly when it will happen..."

Cammie opened her mouth, then closed it before Hypatia could kick her ankle. Instead, Orion cleared his throat. "And we are in this particular location - rather than, say, Trellech - why?"

"Because the rest of the camp is dealing with deeply secret material, some of the people consulting with you will be coming here. It is easier to arrange a transfer of information here than in Trellech. Or, for that matter, in London or Dover, where a number of them are working."

Claudio said, with a posh drawl that was at least two-thirds effect, "Didn't go to the right school, old chum."

It made Junior Commander Roberts snort. "Just so. They're public school boys, Eton and Oxford, mostly. A few exceptions. But they do want to know where you went to school, and who your people are. And none of you fit what they expect."

Cammie shrugged. "That's nothing new. Ma'am." She was polite, of course. "So what are we to do, then?"

"Once we've got the warding set properly, I'll walk through the range of the assignment with you. Captain Warren was working on a similar project based up north. I am sure he will have ideas and be able to explain to you some of the practical parameters. The goals are, however, two-fold. First, to support the deceptions being created in various forms, both practical and, shall we say, intellectual? Passing of inaccurate information through known agents, and so on."

Hypatia nodded slowly. "I heard a story about a ritual in Ashford Forest, the first year of the war. That sort of thing, letting observers get information?"

"That's one form of it, yes." Junior Commander Roberts agreed. "You have better sources than I'd expected."

To her surprise, Orion spoke up. "Possibly the same one, ma'am. I had the story of that ritual from Alexander Landry. We happened to have an evening in the same hedge at one point."

Junior Commander Roberts blinked several times. "Well. I suppose you were all selected for good reason." She seemed a tad over her head, and Claudio stepped in, Hypatia suspected, to smooth things out.

"The other part of it, ma'am, is the larger question of needing the deception to hold up magically. Knowing what we do about the Nazi approaches to magic and ritual, certainly the Italians have their own, and all that. That's some of what we were working on up north, how to lay the proper signatures magically that would imply efforts on that part. It's not just about tricking the eye, but about tricking all the senses, including the magical."

"Quite. We still do not believe that enemy agents have access to anything that would allow them to confirm those signatures in Albion proper. But once the invasion begins, we will need to make the proper show of it. Magical fireworks, as it were. Only far less directly visible."

Cammie was chewing on her lip now, thinking. "And you've got the four of us because we've got a range of skills. I have an idea how the signals work has been going, for example, what kinds of information get conveyed and what gets mangled. Hypatia has the materia and sympathetic magic work. We're going to want a significant sand-table map, aren't we? With the appropriate bits of earth to anchor the sympathetic vibrations."

"Don't ask for much, do you?" Junior Commander Roberts looked amused. "We should be able to provide, however, at least for the coastline." She nodded then. "Just so, on principle." She looked up at the men.

Claudio spoke more carefully now, choosing his words. "Me, because I was working on the same thing up north. I have a good idea of both what's needed, and what they're doing. Not that we need to do the same things, precisely, but it would look odd if they didn't play off each other. And Orion..."

"I have actual experience on the battlefield. No. Right. I see what you're aiming at. And a small number, people who can get on in tight quarters, who don't mind being away from others for a long stint." There was something guarded there, like a shaky wood walkway over a deep chasm.

"Exactly. Now, you can draw on materia available - I'll have a list for you with the other things arriving. We can arrange a proper sand-table, but you'll have to set it yourselves. You can eat in the canteen, but honestly, everyone here would rather you didn't, or at least not very often. We can arrange to have meals ready to be picked up, or possibly brought round and left somewhere nearby. Supplemental rations, sufficient for the magical work, though not very interesting food. Laundry of ordinary uniforms and sheets and such will be picked up on a schedule from the road nearest the front of the hut. Captain Sisley, we'll make arrangements for leave for the land rites, as you confirm the necessary dates and times."

Hypatia saw a tiny twitch of his mouth, as if he had been ambushed by it, out of expectation. Curious, that. The rest of it was all reasonable enough, and honestly,

Hypatia was glad they wouldn't have to do either set of that. Along with all the other reasons, they were going to be working hard and stretching their magic enough as it was.

Junior Commander Roberts went on. "You are not expected to keep to military code in your own private housing, but don't let anything show that shouldn't. You may exercise in Richmond Park, but do not go nearer the centre of town or interact with people there without advance leave. If you meet someone out walking or running, you may talk about the current weather, the weather in the recent past, and the forecast for the next few days. Polite and meaningless comments about attendant dogs and small children are also permitted." She raised an eyebrow when none of them commented. "It wouldn't do to be rude. And besides, that sort of rudeness draws attention."

It made Cammie snort, irrepressible. "True. I do like a good walk, when I can. And the work itself?"

"The work itself, let us see to the wards, by which I mean you talking through what you want and me approving it and making sure it's done." Which put her own skills in a particular light. "And then we'll talk through the outline, and what equipment and materials you need to start. I do have a journal, though I am only able to check it once a day. Generally later evening, due to other demands of my work."

"Can't risk anyone seeing it," Cammie said. "My boyfriend's in the RAF, same problem. Too many people, right at hand." That at least got the four of them up and moving. It was time to take a good look at the hut they were in, the construction of it. Then they had a twenty-minute discussion sorting out the warding they were going to use.

Which was what Hypatia had suggested at the beginning, with a clever modification Orion suggested. As a place to start, it was somewhat promising. Neither man had got on his high horse about knowing best. There had been a good give and take. And the work got sorted without endless rounds of discussion.

CHAPTER 7
ORION, THAT EVENING IN THE CAMP

B y the time they finished up for the day, Orion had a headache gnawing at the base of his skull. He kept a civil tongue in his head with Junior Commander Roberts, whatever her actual name was. Her features had that faint hint of familiarity, but he'd been drilled in all the magical families of note for decades. At this point, they rather swam together unless he was paying close attention and, ideally, consulting some notes. And of course, he didn't have those with him, they were all packed away at Fairlight.

And who had the time right now? His mother would give him that look. The one that made it clear he was failing at several things at once, and she was sure there were others to add to her list. His father - well, his father had died. Which was part of why Orion was in particular parts of his current mess. If he hadn't inherited out of season, he wouldn't have had to marry when he did.

Orion had been told to avoid scandal, ever since Great-Uncle Phineas had got himself in heaps of trouble over a mix of the Research Society and some very uncouth ritual choices. Isembard had finally explained some of it several years later, when he realised that Orion was still fuming over it. Father had been on the Council by then, for years. But Great-Uncle Phineas had held the title, the land magic, and all the power and influence in the family. And outside it, too. The Council worked differently, and Father had not been one of its more prominent members.

At any rate, Orion had had more than enough of behaving himself once they had cleaned out the working hut. They'd set up a number of tables and desks, space for a sand-table, and several sets of cupboards suitable for storing materia. All at once, he'd just been done. He'd grunted, "Need a walk" and gone without looking back. Even at Claudio.

Not that he'd needed to look back. It wasn't like Orion didn't know what he'd see. Claudio would be looking after him, worried - quietly worried - before he turned back to do what needed doing, as resolutely as a gentil parfait knight in any bit of mediaeval lore. Orion knew how fake that felt for Claudio, too, but Claudio was far better at the show of it. He always had been. Also, better at the truth of it, and that was a thing Claudio wrestled with most nights. Orion knew that.

Now, he went off to make a circuit around the more remote areas of the camp. He wanted to get his bearings, and he didn't much want to go out into Richmond Park yet. It was getting on for sunset, maybe quarter to six, and he didn't want to get caught out on unfamiliar land when the shadows started looming. Not until he had a better idea where he was and what was around them.

There had been those odd noises last night, for one thing, something in the walls. Something hunting, he'd thought, before dismissing the idea as implausible. There'd been scrabbling squeaks that broke through the sound charms a few times, and that sense of something stalking. Not hunting Orion, that was a different feeling, and one he knew entirely too well.

Claudio had watched him, then kept the conversation on other topics. Somewhat safer ones, catching up on people they knew. Not quite as many deaths as Orion had feared, but more than anyone wanted. That was the way of it. These conversations, whenever they happened, were like that. Always, it seemed. There was no escaping that part of the war, any more than he could escape anything else.

He picked a small rock up in his right hand, tossing it up and down a couple of times. After he'd tossed it higher in the air, he heard a shout behind him. "You. Halt. Hands in the air."

Orion let the rock fall to the ground near his foot, both hands in the air. No point in being difficult here. It wouldn't do anything. It might make him feel momentarily better, but he could get that with a drink and less damage to his reputation or his remaining fingers. "Yes?" He tried to keep his voice relaxed and at ease, but he could hear his pulse pounding in his ear. Bloody combat reflexes, why couldn't they go away, some small benefit to go with all the awfulness?

"Who are you?" The voice drew closer, coming from Orion's back left. Part of him was calculating exactly what charms he could get off, quick and quiet enough they'd pass in dim light for something that didn't break the Pact.

"Captain Sisley. Just assigned here and arrived last night." Orion kept his voice calm. Two-thirds of making this work was sounding right. Right accent, right mode, right body language. Isembard had taught him that. How not to get into fights unless he meant to, and how to end them properly if he did. Nothing his parents had taught him had been half as useful.

"What project?" The other man came closer, and he was wearing an enlisted uniform, battle dress.

"Can't tell you. Secrets Act and all that. I've got papers, if you need to see them." The Junior Commander had made sure those were all properly stamped and managed. She was very efficient, even if she'd been rather in over her head in a couple of ways.

"Take them out slowly, with one hand." The man kept him in close visual contact. No visible weapon, but that didn't mean much. He must have a service piece on him somewhere if he was on guard.

They were in his right breast pocket. "It might take me a minute. Have an injury to my left hand. I fumble with it sometimes." He waited for the other man's nod, before he worked his finger and thumb into the interior of his jacket, the false fingers along for the ride. He'd got quite good at most of the ordinary movements of his day. He'd have to add this one to the list of things to practise when he was alone. The papers came out without too much trouble, and he held them out.

The solider peered through them, flicking back and forth, then he nodded. "This part of camp's off-limits. You should know that."

"Pardon. Only been here a day, still getting my bearings. I've been to the canteen twice now, that's it. Can you point me that way?"

Before either of them could say anything else, he heard a voice off to his side. "There you are, Sisley. Good evening, Corporal. We should get a move on, get our supper so we can get back to what needs doing." Claudio, of course it was Claudio smoothing things over. Always stepping in with impeccable timing.

If it were anyone else, he'd sulk. No one should be that deft with this sort of thing, so implacable. And yet, he couldn't and wouldn't resent Claudio for it. Claudio was who he had been born to be, raised and made to be. Blaming him for being good at it would be just as unfair. And besides, Orion had some idea of what it cost his brother. Now he let his hands settle by his thighs. "I had just asked for a pointer back to the canteen. I appreciate your quick action, corporal." He couldn't see the insignia from here, but he absolutely trusted Claudio had it right.

"Sir. Sirs." The man cleared his throat. "Back this way, if you please, and it would be better if you checked with your superior officer for a map. If you're looking for a walk, best out toward the Park. The front gate has some guides, if you need them."

"Appreciate that. We'll get out of your way now, then. Besides, I want my supper." Claudio turned on one heel, and Orion moved to settle into place beside him. This time, he made an effort not to sync up, as they did naturally. They were so used to adjusting for each other's pace and posture after so many years duelling each other and with each other against the world. Metaphorically and quite literally.

Once they were well away, Claudio cleared his throat. "Talk a little. When we can find somewhere we're sure no one's overhearing?"

"Sure." They found a clear bit of ground, no one visible within twenty feet at least. Orion called up the charm that would muffle the sound around them and light up anyone who was lurking under charm or magical artefact. He'd rehearsed it painstakingly, in his life Before, and now it was still useful. There were a few flickers of people at the edge of the reach, forty feet away or so, but no one closer. "I don't know how long we have."

"Me either, but I didn't want to risk doing this closer in. Not until I can have a good look at all three huts for listening charms and the like. I think it's more likely they're only reading for certain emotions, but I want to check to be certain."

"You think they'd go so far?" Orion tilted his chin, then he read it in Claudio's face. "You know they would. Because they've done it before."

"Mmmhmm." Claudio let out a long breath. "Being at the front, in the face of the enemy, that's one kind of brutality. And one I don't know." His family hadn't exactly pulled strings to keep him out of the fighting. But they'd certainly rearranged some of Fate's threads to get him assigned somewhere his skills would be highly useful. "But this is high stakes work. Pulling all the stops out."

Orion grunted. "And what does that mean for us?"

"Making sure we're getting on. That we're not cracking up under the pressure." Claudio hesitated. "Or rather, not cracking up in ways that mean we can't work. So long as we can work, they don't care much how we feel."

Orion turned, looking Claudio up and down. There were lines there, on his face, that hadn't been there before. "You were doing the same thing up north?"

"Same sort of thing, different objectives. And I was on my own with it a lot. They asked me what would work better, and I said people who were used to working together. That you were likely to be available. I didn't expect the women."

"What do you think of them, then?" Orion glanced back toward their little trio of huts. "I don't know what to make of them."

"Competent. I've seen bits of their records, and of course I know their reputations. Sharp wits, memories like steel traps. Cammie's supposed to be very deft with signals work. Not just the translation, lots of people can translate, but figuring out the implications of wording. We might need some of that. And Hypatia's near the top ranks for people doing her kind of sympathetic magic work, with ritual skills Alexander approves of. And she's practical enough to make her one of Thesan's go-tos when they have to plan a big student event, to make sure there's no gaps they've missed."

"High praise, all three." Orion considered that. "And they're a united front against the world, aren't they?"

"Like us." Claudio looked down at the tramped down grass under their feet. "Do you mind that I dragged you into this?"

"Not thrilled about the deception involved, honestly. Everything I've done so far has made it clear that people get killed that way. Not knowing what's truth and lie and distraction." Orion swallowed. "But I'd rather be with you than somewhere else."

"It offends your sense of right and wrong, doesn't it?" Claudio's voice was very quiet now.

"Yeah." It came out as a little bark of a cough. "Give me a nice honest battle charge any time. I know what to do with that." He hesitated, then went on. "I was a complete pain when we were at Schola, a lot of it. Until Isembard started taking time to explain things, not just what I was supposed to do, but why. Why those things? Why that way? Why I was making life harder for myself over and over? And then I wanted to fight things. As if fighting would make things better."

"You ever talk to him about what House might have suited you better?" The sentence came out so casually that it took a moment for it to register in Orion's head. Not something he and Claudio had ever talked about before. It was admitting that the entire pinnacle of their world was built wrong, that it had irresolvable flaws.

"Yeah. You?" Orion kept his voice as relaxed as he could, which didn't feel like much.

"You should have been in Boar, I think. Bet he thought so too. It'd have taught you how to put all that wanting to fight somewhere useful. Somewhere..." Claudio lifted a finger. "Somewhere it would feel useful. Not like you were duelling shadows. Ghosts."

"That." Naming it made him feel like his stomach had dropped out from him, that it was that obvious he was faking things, often badly. Orion let out a long breath. "You?"

"Always thought I'd have made a good Owl." Claudio glanced over. "Seeing the two of them today, the way they went about thinking through what we'd need? People. Fox House people, I mean, always put down Owls as all thought, no action. You know all the jokes, same as I do. But they were, they were efficient, they were sharp as anything. Fast at it. I don't know, there was something there I didn't understand until today."

"Fairly sure Isembard also made it clear to you why sensible men don't bed people they work with, unless they're entirely sure where it's going," Orion pointed out.

"Hey, one in two chance of it ending really well, based on his experience." Claudio pointed out. "I mean, there was the thing with Mistress Loft in the library, his first year. But then there's Thesan, and you can't deny that's worked out. Far better than either of our marriages."

"Mmm." Orion did his best non-committal noise before asking, "That bad for you, too?" '

"Electra's done her duty. She has her own life. I have no idea if she has a lover, but so long as she keeps the agreements, I won't fuss. I haven't seen anyone I liked enough to consider figuring out how to trust. And it's not really fair to someone to have to hide it, is it?"

"That's a statement that needs a lot more drink." Orion didn't really want to think about the many implications there, not for Claudio, not for himself. "Think we could go collect food and then come up with a list of what someone could ship us? Starting with some brandy or whiskey or I don't know what. Enough for a nightly glass? I suspect we're going to need it to look forward to."

"Food, then lists, yes. Something better for blankets, too. Mine itched all night."

At that, Orion pulled the charms back into him, feeling the slight burn of the magic as it merged into his own again, and they set off for the canteen.

CHAPTER 8
CLAUDIO, MARCH 12TH

Claudio rubbed his face. It was Sunday, in that infinite time between mid-morning and luncheon. Orion had gone out for a run maybe half an hour ago once they'd brought some order to their hut. Claudio's mother had sent along a crate of supplies, blankets and slippers and a few practical lamps. He appreciated the decent soap she'd included, and the charmed cedar to keep moths and other insects away. But she'd also sent a box of things that had no place in such a hut. He'd have to arrange to send back three entirely inappropriate rugs, a fine porcelain tea set, and the stained glass lampshade. He might, in fact, keep his formal dinner wear, though he didn't expect to need it anytime soon and, in any case, his uniform would likely be more suitable.

She had also sent along a letter, inquiring in quite pointed terms about how Orion was doing. He'd have to work up a suitable answer to go back. He'd have to figure out how to word it, the sort of thing he wouldn't trust to a journal. Just a seal that would only open under her hand. And he'd have to find something distracting to ask about.

That would get her onto a different topic. Possibly what Gabriel Edgarton was up to right now. That could keep her occupied for hours or pages, whichever was relevant in the moment. It was not at all subtle of Claudio, but in this particular case, he was fairly sure Mother wouldn't notice.

Finally, though, he'd run out of things he could rearrange in the hut. There was only so much of it to work with. He hadn't seen a sign of a mouse since the first night, nor of anything else untoward, and he was grateful for that. He snagged his uniform jacket from the hook, slipped it on, straightened it without thinking about it, and went out the door.

The weather wasn't bad. It had actually been dry since they'd arrived. For a moment, he thought no one was about, but then he spotted one of the women sitting on the wall, facing off toward the park. Though, given the fencing, all he could see were the uppermost bits of trees, and the sky above.

By the time he'd got about ten feet away, he'd identified the figure as Hypatia. Her hair was up in a smooth Victory roll under her cap, compared to Cammie's more chaotic styling. He came up to one side, clearing his throat audibly, so as not to startle her. She half-turned, without the sort of start that suggested she'd been anywhere near combat herself, then nodded once. "Claudio."

"Orion went out for a run a bit ago." It was not the best conversational opener he had in his arsenal, but he'd done worse. And he had been looking for a chance for a casual conversation, one on one, for days.

"He was just setting off when I came out. Cammie was a few minutes ahead of him. I wanted to let the place air out a bit. We did a fair bit of cleaning up first thing, including some bleach and such." Likely several potions to improve things, then.

"I just finished some of that up. Orion helped, of course. My mother sent a crate of things along, since we're likely to be here a bit. Some of it is more useful than others, but I expected that. Are you all right for comforts? Now they got the desks and your sand-table sorted for the work?"

"Ah. Pross and my brother sent things along, too. A veritable run on crates." Hypatia tilted her head. "What sort of things did you get?" Then she gestured. "Feel free to have a bit of wall. Not that it's mine to offer, I suppose."

"Thanks." Claudio came around to hop up onto it. It was comfortable to sit on, a nice bit of sturdy stone, flat across the top. It was at a height that just let his toes dangle without being uncomfortably awkward to get up on the thing. "My mother has odd ideas about what would be helpful. Three fine woven rugs, and I don't dare let them near the floors. Stained glass lampshade. Beautiful, but no."

"My. No. Pross was a lot more sensible, I think. Cleaning potions, some fresh blankets - we wanted colour, not the Army browns, if we could get it. A couple of rag rugs for the bedside, but those were rags when they started, and if they're unsalvageable when we're done here, they've had a long noble textile lifespan."

"Rags you knew well, then?" Claudio kept his voice light, but something in how it came out - that he was teasing, perhaps - made her stiffen.

There was the sort of awkward silence that Claudio had wanted to avoid before Hypatia spoke again. "Pardon."

"I was thinking I should apologise to you. Look, I want us to get on - all four of us. But I obviously pushed a bit too far." That was all entirely true, but also he was clear that honesty - so far as he could be honest - was the strategic choice here.

Her shoulder twitched. "It's not you, really. But I'm not good at that sort of, I don't know, back and forth. Not my skill set." She let out a huff of a breath. "What does it mean to you, getting on?"

"Being comfortable around each other. Though I admit, Orion and comfort don't always run together smoothly." And right now, here and now, he needed things to keep working. For Orion's sake, for his own sake, for the war's sake.

That, in contrast to what he'd said just a little previously, made Hypatia laugh. An honest laugh, he thought. She shook her head, fondly amused. "Cammie's not always exactly comfortable. I love her, mind, top to bottom, with all her joys and flaws. But easy, not the reliable thing."

Claudio felt himself laughing, a deep laugh, the kind he hadn't had in far too long. "Oh, Merlin Ambrosius, you too? That makes me feel better, honestly."

Hypatia glanced at him, then smiled a little. "He was getting on my last nerve yesterday, when we were wrapping up. No, I lie. Pretty much all afternoon."

"You hid it very well, I only noticed the last five minutes or so. Also, I forget that other people are on average a lot less tolerant of ten minutes of monologue on little-known historical battles." That bit had, admittedly, been earlier in the day. Orion was still on relatively good behaviour.

The rest of the afternoon, though, had been harder to pin down. She'd given as good as she'd got, honestly, but the afternoon had been a crescendo of her being more and more pointed about her skills and knowledge. Claudio braced one of his hands so he could lean on it. "Glad to help with that kind of thing, if you want to figure out a way to tell me he's getting to you."

"You'd do that?" Then she caught herself. "You'd know how?"

Claudio shrugged. "I've been doing it for years. What is it, twenty-one years now, how'd that happen? Since Isembard started at Schola."

"Not before that?" Hypatia frowned. "I mean, I know a bit more than the average person like me about the Council, because Alexander does turn up when he can. And Pross was helping Thesan with some research when I was still around a fair bit."

That was an interesting question. "We knew each other, certainly. But when Isembard started, or the summer before, I mean, they'd started getting more worried about, well, the sort of thing that needs a bodyguard. There was a lot of talk, no one really explained it to either of us. We got told he'd be teaching, that he'd be keeping an eye on us in particular, and teaching us duelling. And whatever they were talking about, you know the sort of voice, everyone agreed he was an amazing duellist. Which he is, now I know a lot more about it."

Hypatia nodded once. "Had a hard time after the War, I know. He's said, more than once, that Schola was the saving of him. But he'll round on anyone who says it was Thesan being, I don't know, an angelic civilising force."

"Oh, he's told me stories. And a couple of times I've been there. You could sell tickets and make a mint. He's excruciatingly polite about it, too, but it's all those skills at trimming back a student who's gone too far, the precision of it." Claudio considered. "He got lost in a bottle, he says. And then Orion and I got thrown in together. Anyway. By the next year, Orion and I were spending a lot of time together and Orion wanted to fight a lot." Claudio considered. "Well, he still does, but he doesn't actually fight as often anymore."

"People?" Hypatia's voice was cautiously curious now. Good, he'd wanted to get her talking more comfortably, and this was information she really should have. Both of them should have. Besides, if he managed a bit better, he should be able to clarify some things he wanted to be more sure of.

"Some brawling with people who were unpleasant. A lot of just being angry at the world. Isembard taught him a lot of what to do with that."

Hypatia hesitated. "Any particular reason why? I'd have thought he didn't have a lot to be angry about, from the outside."

It was the 'from the outside' that made Claudio even consider being honest. He took a breath. He could say a lot of different things here, and most of them were public knowledge. "Orion has a lot to live up to. Both of us do. He had an older brother, Hector. Half-brother, technically, but Orion didn't care about that. Golden boy of the family, charming, skilled. He was killed at Vimy Ridge in 1917. Orion looked up to him no end."

"Of course that's a blow." Hypatia let out a slow breath. "I don't know that one, but I know about having much older siblings. What it's like to look at them and want to match up to what they've done."

Claudio hadn't entirely put that together. There were ways in which he was mystified by siblings still. He nodded slowly. "And then, instead of Orion being aimed for - well, the Sisleys often go in for military service. And he'd have done well enough there, in the ordinary sort of peacetime skirmishes. Only then all the expectations came and landed on his shoulders. His father's first, but Orion knew what it'd mean in time, even if no one expected his father to die comparatively young."

"The late Lord Sisley was…" Hypatia paused, doing maths in her head.

Claudio saved her the bother. "Sixty-five. When everyone expected it'd be at least another five or ten years before he retired from the Council, and some years more before he died."

"I'm sorry for that." The thing of it was, Hypatia actually sounded sorry, not just making the platitude. She went on, more quietly after a moment. "My father died when I was thirteen. Cammie was nine when her father died. We've talked a good bit about it over the years, the way it changes everything else around it."

Not something Claudio was going to get into in any more depth. Certainly not without talking with Orion about it first. Both of them had their own complex feelings about fathers and death, and they weren't for sharing. He cleared his throat instead. "Anyway. Somewhere in there, Orion started listening to me more about where to aim it. How to make it useful."

"Even though you're younger." She seemed to be chewing on something.

"These days, the year between us barely matters. We're grown men, with wi—" He caught himself. "Children."

"Right." Hypatia sounded more cautious again. "There were things in the papers, I'm sure you know."

"Know, got sent the clippings, heard all the gossip through the journals about six times over. I've been worried about him. There are a number of reasons I wanted him on this project, but most of all, I was worried about what would happen to him out on his own. His mother and aunt have his little ones, but they barely remembered him when he got sent home."

"His ex-wife?" That was even more cautious, but Claudio was delighted she was asking, that she felt she could. It gave him some hope they might manage to work together, the four of them, without tripping each other up into mines and unexploded ordnance.

"One of our sort - you know, Fox House, right sort of family. Strong enough magic, though she never apprenticed. More or less arranged, though when they started out, they liked each other well enough. I don't know exactly what went wrong, or even if it was just that he was off at war and she got bored." Claudio wrinkled her nose. "I'd believe that she just got bored, actually."

"And he - there's no good way for me to finish this sentence, is there?" There wasn't, and Claudio appreciated that she had the sense to know it.

"He got injured, invalided out, and once he was recovered enough he turned up at his family home, the landed estate. Fairlight's just south of East Grinstead." Claudio shook his head. "Beautiful name for the estate. The town's a bit less so. Both date back to the Domesday book, mind."

"Isn't that where the hospital is, burn victims, and such?" There was a queer note in her voice now.

"Yes." Claudio hesitated. "A particular reason you know that?"

"Cammie's sweetheart's in the RAF. Doing well, but - I suppose you do know the statistics. Half of them die, a quarter more end up in a prisoner of war camp if they're lucky. He's on his second round of missions now, and..." Hypatia shrugged. "You can hope and pray and whatever else all you like, and it doesn't change the raw numbers much. Even with magic. Anyway. Two of the men he'd trained with ended up there. Some help, people were very kind, but."

That held a lot of weight, those three letters. "It must be hard." Claudio paused. "Anyone you're particularly worrying about like that? Orion and I do have access to some news that's not through official channels, if that's ever a help."

She shook her head quite quickly. "Gods, no. Not for years now. Well, technically. February of '42. I've been so busy since then, it hasn't mattered." Claudio knew that tone of voice quite well from the inside, the one that was insisting loudly everything was just fine, no problems here, when there were definitely scars of the non-physical kind. They might have healed over a bit, but that didn't stop them from aching.

"I'm not going to ask. Just one thing, hear the question out, would you?" Claudio wasn't sure how to put this, all of a sudden. But he knew he had to press a little, because he needed these people to be all right with him. It was a slow-growing fire, a neediness he didn't have words for, couldn't explain to Orion most likely.

Her chin jerked once in a nod.

"Is that why my teasing, earlier, hit you oddly?" Claudio kept his voice even. "I mostly want to know to have a better idea what not to do. Like I said, I want us to get on. This will be a whole lot easier, all round, if we don't tread on the sore spots. All four of us."

She went silent and still for a long moment, like all her attention was going to thinking. She'd done that a couple of times so far, fallen so deep into her work nothing else mattered. "A bit. That's on me, though, not on you." It came out like she was saying what was expected of her. He wasn't satisfied with that, but he wasn't going to push, not here and now. Maybe he'd get the chance in a bit. Isembard had taught him that bit of pacing, far better than his mother ever had.

"Let me know if I do it again, please? I mean it when I say I don't want to make you uncomfortable. Or if Orion's too much." He hesitated. "He had an injury. That's what got him invalided out, it's the kind of thing that changes what he thinks about himself. Not mine to talk about the details, to someone else, but so you know. I'd put some of his moods up to pain, but he's always had them, at least a bit, and it's been years since we were in the same place any length of time. The journals are a wonder, but they're not the same."

Hypatia snorted. "No, not at all." She let out her breath, slowly. "Anything you want to know about me, then? Or Cammie, what I can share."

"You were both Owl House, I know that. But she's four years younger, a first year in our fifth. After her mother and your brother Ibis got together." He'd never had Ibis as a teacher, which was a help here.

"Mmhmm. Ibis thinks you have some skills. For the record. I did check. That's part of what provoked the supplies. We have a fair bit of herbal tea now, and a good kettle, and a decent small stove, enough to heat up tinned stuff and all. Assuming we've got enough magic at the end of the day for it." Which might not always be true.

"That will be good, then. Sometimes, I just can't with going to the canteen, or what they're serving up. And it's only been days." Claudio thought through things. "And you've been doing sympathetic magic work, straight through. Were you in with all magical folks?"

"Yes. Cammie wasn't, though. Straight signals work for her. And you must have been somewhere at least mixed? If it was like this?"

"A larger hut, a dozen of us, but also working on some other projects. They didn't really know how to use us, I think. I'm a bit more hopeful here. Not least because of the company. I think all three of you are a good bit more creatively minded."

"That is not something I've been called often. Cammie,

maybe. She knows what she wants and she goes for it. The trick is getting her to care in the first place. But she does about this— she knows, I mean. Duncan."

"Her sweetheart?" Claudio didn't really make it into a question, and Hypatia nodded. "Anything that could help, any of them, that's a good place to care." Then he looked up. "She's coming back, it looks like, or at least I assume so. Not many women around here, had you noticed?"

"I had." There was something very dry in her response. Before Claudio could ask about it, Cammie was nearly up to their bit of wall. She was cheerfully talking about a bird she'd seen on the walk, and there was a nest of dusk-spines in an untouched corner she'd found. Hypatia was laughing and saying she'd have to tell Ibis. There was obviously some sort of familial joke about hedgehogs and their magical kin. Claudio let it roll over him, not listening to the words so much as what the two of them sounded like when they were reasonably happy and relaxed.

It had been an informative conversation, in several directions, and he was a bit more hopeful this might actually work out.

CHAPTER 9
CAMMIE, MARCH 15TH

By the next Wednesday, they had settled into a routine. Up at half-seven, a cold breakfast of food brought from the canteen the night before, plus some tea. Both huts had kettles now, run by a touch of magic. That was good. No one had to get the stove going. And they didn't have to be civil to each other before they were properly awake.

More to the point, Cammie and Hypatia didn't have to be fully done up in uniform until they went out the door. Neither of them much cared for it. There were worse uniforms out there, but the fabric was chosen for sturdiness rather than comfort, and they weren't tailored the way magical clothes usually were. Hypatia was having a harder time with it. Since her last posting had been all magical, she'd been able to get away with wearing a blouse and skirt of her own a lot of the time unless there was some sort of official meeting.

At this point in the war, Cammie was used to her uniform, but she didn't really want to be. Still, it was nice to have more privacy, and better by far to have some hours where she didn't have to be fully presentable all the time. And nice to share the morning with Hypatia, who was not inclined to chatter until there had been tea, unlike some people she'd shared housing with the past few years.

They were working hard, too. Right now it was mostly research, which meant that they spent hours in the workroom, and then hours more in their huts, reading through various articles and books. By now Ibis had sent along a number of things. Cammie had her own references, and she was sure the men did as well.

She made a point of keeping up with her physical fitness. If she got dumped back into the general ATS work in a few months, she'd regret it if she didn't. But also it just felt good. She liked being out on her own, seeing what she spotted. She had to go find her own fun that way. Right now, she was still scouting out where might be an option to indulge in some of her other physical habits.

They'd got through the morning's work reasonably enough, and paused for lunch. That was sandwiches from the canteen, a pot of soup they heated up on the stove, and tea. Always tea, though at least they got reasonable rations of it, especially when supplemented with decent herbals from Pross and Ibis and Schola in general.

It was after lunch the problem started. Cammie had been working on some initial analysis of the signals options. She hadn't been talking much about it, because it was fiddly and because she wasn't sure of the parameters yet. She'd figured out enough that while Orion had a bit of practical signals knowledge - not surprising, given his artillery experience - he didn't have any of the more nuanced theory. Hypatia did, but there was also a point where she gave up and made encouraging noises and Cammie had to solve her own problems. Sometimes talking it out at someone was, in fact, helpful.

Hypatia had been working steadily on setting up the sand-table for the sympathetic magic she had in mind. It covered quite a lot of territory, and it stretched out over fifteen feet long and about eight wide. It was far enough across Hypatia was having to do a lot of the detailing with a series of shafts of wood with different tools on the end, mostly the one like a pencil or a pointing finger. It reached from London south, then a foreshortened view of the Channel, since they couldn't do much with the water proper. Then there was the northern half of France, across toward Spain and the Netherlands.

Whatever it was they were doing, it was France that mattered, Junior Commander Roberts had made that clear. It at least simplified the maths. Or the geography, or whatever the term was here. Cammie tended to think about what they were doing as maths, as much as anything else, but that was training and habit speaking.

The men had been talking quietly, on and off, working at another large table with several maps spread out, considering different points. Cammie had caught snippets of it, about the local geography, where there were rivers or mountains or particular limits, like there being only one bridge. They'd gone back and forth for a bit, each of them sending question and answer, like a game of tennis.

Cammie had started paying a little more attention when Hypatia's voice got that strained note in it. Cammie had heard that before the war, the days her sister had turned up at her flat, needing a drink and a shoulder, usually because someone had ignored her very real skills. Once because he'd tried to pass off her work as his own, which was an insult to scholarship as well as to Hypatia.

Hypatia was the calm one of the two of them, easygoing unless someone hit in exactly the wrong place. She was the one who talked Cammie down when needed. And sometimes when the problem would be more usefully resolved with teeth, but people didn't do that. But Orion got under her skin. He hadn't been rude to them, not up to this point, but he kept wanting to know why they were doing things a certain way. It never quite devolved to telling them their work, but he'd been weaving along that line more than enough to become tedious.

It was too much to hope that Orion would notice and do something different, of course. He forged on, heedless, his voice louder and a bit deeper. Hypatia had said something sharp and fast enough that Cammie couldn't catch the actual words. Everything went the wrong kind of quiet, the sort that brought Cammie's head up instantly.

It was far too much like the silence after a bomb exploded, just with a great deal less dust and obvious destruction. There was a moment of hesitation, and then everyone was loud, talking over one another, all in a clutter.

Cammie put her hands over her ears and waited it out, as patiently as she could. She would like to bite someone, actually, but as she wasn't sure who needed biting first, that wasn't an option. Well, it wasn't an option for more reasons than that. She pushed back from her desk, though, and got the wall behind her. The other three had settled into a sort of line. Hypatia was shouting, her hands on her hips, and Orion was shouting right back. Claudio had a hand on his shoulder, but from a little behind, as if he also didn't want to get into the middle of it.

Cammie couldn't actually blame him for that. But someone was going to have to do something, and that someone was her. She let out a piercing whistle and then followed it with a silencing charm. She chose the one Mum had taught her, for when hordes of students kept her up at night when she wanted to sleep. She was very good at it now. She'd had years and years of practice.

The room went silent, comically so. She could see Orion's mouth moving, then the confusion on his face. He leaned forward, but Hypatia stepped back smartly. She didn't turn her back, but she put more space between them. Only when they'd ended up a good ten feet apart, and not near so visibly angry, did Cammie let the charm drop.

"Is there some reason for that?" She tried to keep her voice civil, but she wasn't doing very well at it. It was all sharp teeth and nipping bites, even in a few short words. "Come on. Behave better." Her chin went up, and she waited.

Hypatia folded first. She had the most sense. Her hands came down to her sides properly and she took another couple of steps back, until she was standing next to Cammie. Cammie, for her part, immediately shifted to let her fingers brush Hypatia's back, feeling the trembling there.

Claudio backed up a bit more too. Cammie just kept watching, letting her face take on that expression she knew made others so terribly uncomfortable. Women weren't supposed to be that fierce. Ask her if she cared. Finally - she'd counted out about ninety seconds - Orion backed down, stepping beside Claudio.

"Thank you for pretending to be civilised." Her voice was sharp enough to cut glass, but she didn't care right now about being nice or pleasant.

No one said anything for another count of five. Then Claudio's voice broke the silence. "You have some skills you didn't mention." He sounded cautious, most of all, with a little hint of what seemed like appreciation. She hadn't expected that, she'd expected him to be affronted.

"Not just a pretty face." Cammie agreed. Both men took a half step back, and Cammie gloried in it. This was a particular kind of chase and hunt, and oh, she hadn't had a chance at this in quite a long time. She'd been very well-behaved at her previous posting. "Why were you arguing?"

Both men closed their mouths. Beside her, Hypatia said, her voice precise in the way that meant something had hurt her, and badly, "Orion didn't care for how I was setting out the sand-table." She paused for just a fraction of a beat. "I'm using Thorinson's approach from the appendix, not the better known take from Grimalfi."

"Of course you are. And obviously not Twaft. No one sensible uses Twaft." Cammie said, as if it were entirely normal to have conversations about areas of magic that were not her own speciality, at a near enough expert level. Though of course it was, for them. She couldn't do what Hypatia did, but she could talk it through and be helpful that way. Then she tilted her head. "And?"

"Why would you do it like that, though?" Orion burst out with the question before Claudio clapped a hand over his mouth. Orion didn't fight it, at least, though he pressed forward for a few breaths before subsiding again.

This time, it was Claudio who spoke into the silence. He coughed. "Orion also wasn't sure what you were doing, Cammie. Hypatia refused to interrupt you."

"Well, I'll have to start working the sequence over from the beginning. There's an hour's work wasted," Cammie agreed. She focused now on Orion. "Don't think I'm much use, then?" Why not make it an outright challenge, get this nonsense out of the way. Beside her, she heard Hypatia suppress a snort of amusement. Good, her sister was doing better.

"I apologise for my assumptions, Mistress Gates. Mistress Ward." It was a somewhat grudging apology, even with the formality. Or perhaps because of the formality. Claudio thought so too, because a moment later he was elbowing Orion, who grunted. "I was an idiot. We shouldn't have interrupted either of you."

"No." She let out a breath, then she switched languages into fluent Arabic, turning slightly to Hypatia. "Good grief, men are rather a lot, sometimes. These men, in particular."

Hypatia snorted, half-smiling now, switching languages just as smoothly. "You're just enjoying toying with them, aren't you? Both of them."

"Oh, yes. I mean, here I am, I could be saying entirely innocent things like the book is on the table, the table is full of sand. Or I could, I suppose, swear at them properly." Arabic was a glorious language for it after all, and she indulged herself in a good few sentences of invective involving camels, ancestors, habits, and secrets. She stopped only when she was sure Hypatia was going to lose it laughing. "They really don't like that we know things they don't, do they?"

"Not at all." Hypatia shrugged. "I'd say make them do our cleaning for the night, but I'm not actually sure I trust them to do it to our standards."

"Rather not, no." Cammie considered. "They could clean up in here. And finish setting up the bookshelves properly." Which were currently a pile of shelving and several crates of books.

"Oh, that's fair. Maybe they'll pick up something by osmosis, handling books. Though to be fair to them, it was mostly Orion being awful."

"Doesn't matter." Cammie let her lips quirk up in a smile. "You all right now, or should we keep annoying them?"

Hypatia didn't answer in words, just the single shift of

her shoulder, the one that was all about getting on with it, despite the obstacles in the way. Right then, they could talk about it more that night, when they were private. Or talk about something entirely different, whichever Hypatia preferred.

Cammie judged she'd pressed the men as far as she needed and swapped back to English. "If you want to make it up to us, finish setting up the book shelves tonight, would you? After you fetch supper."

Orion opened his mouth and closed it like a fish, then he glanced at Claudio, who nodded once. "That's fair." Orion was grudging, but he was at least responding. "Um. May I ask what your signals work involves?"

"I did a fair bit of training with Major Giles Lefton, my apprenticeship, though also a lot of maths. It's come in very handy for signals work. That stack is a set of things that might or might not have some magical information in it, I was trying to work out if it did. But it's in at least two languages, it's got some odd abbreviations, and I'm starting to think whoever wrote it was throwing in some Magyar. There's a dictionary in one of the boxes I'll need for that. Mum sent it along."

That got both men blinking. "Um. Pardon. How many languages do you have?" Claudio asked, after a moment.

"Was that not in whatever of my files you got to see, Claudio?" That one hit home, she could see his face sharpen, then he let out a huff of breath, shaking his head no. "English, French, Latin of course, German, Arabic, as you've just heard, a few bits of ancient Egyptian, and enough Magyar to make a bit of sense of it. Dad's speciality. Not Ibis, my father. And I had a project just before the war that had me looking at some Portuguese."

Her father Octavian had died when she was six and a bit, old enough she remembered him, but not nearly well enough. She'd spent a summer going into her last year at Schola wading through all of his papers and writing, and Mum had explained as much as she could. He'd had darker skin. Grandfather was one of the Second Families closer to their African roots than many.

But Dad had given her that curly hair. And her eyes had been Mum's blue, when she was young, before settling into his brown, though there were other reasons for that. Most of all, he'd given her a sharp curiosity, the kind that went hunting and chasing without pausing for breath. That was what she made offerings for, entirely in private, for whatever advice might come from her father beyond death about how to use that sharpness in the proper way and for the right cause.

"And you're trying to figure it out because..." Claudio held up his hands immediately.

"Because if we're going to do things to magically mislead the Germans and whoever else might be looking, we need to have an idea what they expect to see." She kept the 'isn't that bloody obvious?' out of her voice. Mostly.

Claudio swallowed once. "There's someone I could possibly ask about that. I know he's sworn in on this." He looked at Orion. "Mother's going to hate it."

Something in that made Orion laugh, suddenly, a barking laugh that changed his entire face. "She will. I think you should do it."

Neither of them explained, and Cammie decided it was better not to ask. They were on calmer footing now. "You decide about that. We'll wrap up, and I'll take my notes to the hut for the evening and see how far I can get through it. After a bit of a walk. A run if no one's around to disapprove of women being active." Because some people had very odd ideas about women exerting themselves. Still.

"We'll have supper back here in what, an hour? That give you enough time? And Hypatia, can we help you with anything?"

The practicalities took another minute or two to arrange, but Cammie went off humming to change into her PT gear.

CHAPTER 10
HYPATIA, MARCH 17TH

Hypatia ran her hand through her hair, and then sighed as two of the hairpins came out. She pulled the rest out with quick motions, stepping back from the sand-table to drop them on her desk. She got to work coiling her hair back into a low bun at the nape of her neck. It would let her put her uniform cap on when she left the hut.

It gave her a moment to sort out what everyone else was up to. The two men had taken a tea break half an hour ago. They hadn't interrupted, but Cammie had set a cup down on her desk. And, bless her names, put a keep-warm charm on it. It was still pleasantly hot to the touch. That did it.

Hypatia ducked around the desk to take a seat and put her feet up for a few minutes on the small crate she'd tucked inside the bottom of the desk for the purpose. What senior officers didn't see wouldn't hurt anyone. At least in this case. Besides, to be technically correct, the crate itself, turned on its side, held several small boxes of supplies that could live there as well as anywhere else.

The real problem of the day was that she was nearly done setting up the sand-table, and she had no idea what to do with it. In the pragmatic sense of the assignment at hand, that was, rather than the skill sense. The principles were all well developed. First, taking a bit of something - sand was easy to come by, easy to shape, easy to mend. Then she had to connect it magically with tiny vials with samples of earth from the places the model mapped to.

With the table set as it was, she should be able to mark certain kinds of magic in play - major protective or destructive magics, for example. And, with a good bit more effort, she should be able to imply certain kinds of magic there, from her place here. The whole thing had a number of hypothetical statements built into its very existence. But it should work for what they needed. Probably.

Of course, it wasn't as if they were working in a proper workroom, without outside influences. Depending on what needed to be done, she could arrange for one somewhere. Schola, almost certainly. Ibis would help. He understood the score.

She thought back to the last time they'd talked about that, directly. He didn't talk about his own experience doing Intelligence work in the Great War much. He'd been based in Cairo, and his gifts for languages - Cammie had built on that - had been useful there. And the way he'd known Cairo as a native son of the sand and heat and the twisted alley ways did. He'd carefully kept his other skills hidden, the fact he could shift shapes.

And that was tricky. Both of them were used to navigating the way people made assumptions about them, because they were half-Egyptian. Not unknown, in Albion, but Papa's lineage had been respectable rather than impressive enough to erase that effect.

Shapeshifting, though, was a problem for anyone who did it. There were still far too many ridiculous comments about shifters being less than human in some essential way. No one with their sort of skin or parentage could afford to press on that point more than they already did just by existing in the world. And then there was the shape itself. She'd known for a long time he found the fact he turned into a hedgehog something that made him blush.

But he'd explained, that day, sitting out on one of the stone walls overlooking the ocean, the other part of it. That if people knew you could shift, they'd send you on the dangerous missions, the ones that were entirely impossible. That they, the amorphous 'they' with power, would treat you as disposable. And as he'd pointed out, a hedgehog might have sharp points, but they were not actually built for combat. They'd left a lot of things unsaid in that conversation, even though they'd both been quite sure no one was at all nearby.

They both had those habits, now. There had been a day, still in 1939, in the first months of the current war, where Hypatia had woken, muttering protection charms in the dark. She closed her eyes, head hitting the too-flat and too-lumpy pillow, and she'd known. There was no going back from living through the war. Either she did her best, or she'd have a hard time looking in the mirror the rest of her life.

But doing her best meant sleepless nights, things she couldn't talk about, things other people wouldn't understand. It would change whatever relationships she had. There, at least, she was luckier than a lot of people. Cammie was here, and whatever else they'd both done in the last four and a half years - and seventeen days, her precision insisted - they could share this. It made it a bit better. Ibis understood, and she was fairly sure he was doing some ongoing consulting, all secret, this war as well. Pross understood, even if she was in slightly less over her head.

Cammie was luckier in love, though. Her Duncan - Hypatia had only met him twice, fairly briefly - was just as fierce about facing the world as Cammie was herself. They made a fine pair, sharp and brave, with a visible confidence that caught the eye.

Hypatia, well, her sharp edges came out when she was upset, or focused on something else, or had had a poor night's sleep. Her last two relationships had wrecked themselves on that rocky shore, as surely as ships without a lighthouse. And the few fleeting ones before that had barely got started before the men found something else to do with their time, or before Hypatia did.

That had been why she'd been out with Ibis, really. She'd wanted someone to be with who loved her. Who'd always loved her. Who thought she was worth loving. A brother's love wasn't the same thing at all as anything romantic or erotic, but it had given her comfort when she'd desperately needed it. Desperately needed it and hadn't been able to admit it.

That was a thing big brothers were for. The best sorts of them, anyway. She wanted to pay it back to Susanna, as she could. Being a shoulder that wasn't a parent, for all Ibis had stood in for their father from the time Hypatia had been about to start at Schola. Papa's death had changed everything, in some ways, but Ibis had been there, steady as one of the great stone statues. Or the great English oaks and yews, because Papa had been English, through and through, as much as Ummi was Egyptian.

She'd been entirely lost in thought, enough to go

through two-thirds of her tea. When she looked up, Cammie was standing there, the pot in her hand. "More?"

"Imhotep's favourite tools, yes." As it usually did, that particular turn of phrase made Cammie grin. She poured more tea, poured another cup for herself, and then perched on the corner of Hypatia's desk.

"Cammie. What if someone comes in?"

"Someone won't. And we've checked the charms on the window, to prevent people looking through what, a dozen times now?" Cammie didn't move. Hypatia didn't have the energy for that futile argument. And besides, it wasn't as if she actually cared that Cammie pushed the boundaries of furniture on a regular basis. "What did you get stuck on, then?"

Hypatia saw the two men - over in the other corner along the short wall - look up cautiously. She waved a hand at them. "No need to pretend you're not eavesdropping. That's ridiculous."

They'd both been rather cautious since Wednesday's argument. Not as if Hypatia - or Cammie - were fragile, but as if they were trying to make sense out of something they hadn't expected. It had kept them civil. Orion's questions had been more measured and better spaced out. Mostly, they'd let Hypatia alone to do her work.

Though Orion had apparently been taking his commentary out on Claudio. Hypatia had overheard bits of four different monologues on different historical battles, all without any direct relevance to their work. Claudio had taken it in good humour, though, interjecting an occasional question or murmur while he got on with his own tasks. Hypatia wasn't sure if he'd put himself in the middle on purpose, or whether that was just how things usually went for them.

Claudio laughed and stood. "We could use another tea

break. And I can run to biscuits. Let me step around and grab a few from the tin. Be right back." From that, she diagnosed that they'd got stuck on something too, though she had no idea what. They'd just taken a break, but well, tea was a good excuse. And for a wonder, their senior officers weren't hovering over their shoulders. Hadn't been seen at all, since the first day, actually.

It left Orion to move a couple of chairs closer, and to pour two more mugs of the tea. Cammie peered into the lid, and then went to refill the kettle and set it up ready to boil water for the next round. Two minutes later, Claudio was back with biscuits, small round ones, enough for two each. "Thesan sent these along. The hives at Schola are still doing amazingly well, and they got a few oranges from the orangery at Arundel."

Hypatia blinked, but then the smell hit her. The citrus was a fresh breeze, clearing out the fog in her head. "I'll have to thank her. I hadn't realised, I mean."

"That it's delightful to have something that has a bit of scent, and that - well, I suppose it's technically beige, but an entirely different sort?" Claudio's lips quirked in a smile. "I'm sure she'd tell us to share, not that I've told them you two are here. I mean."

"That's the knot of operational secrecy, isn't it? And I don't know what her oaths are about this. Though it'd be right handy, actually, we could use someone with better locational magic skills."

"What line of them are you interested in?" Cammie reached to grab one of the biscuits, took a bit, and her face lit up with the pleasure of it. Strange, how small a thing could do that these days, and yet, well. It had been some time since either of them had had this kind of sensory pleasure. Make the most of it, while they could, definitely.

Also, it gave Hypatia a chance to gather her thoughts.

"I've almost got the table fully set up." She wanted to admit she didn't know what to do next, but she knew perfectly well how that would go. The men's tasks had to do with planning, at least that was how they'd divided things, but they hadn't wanted to talk about it. Forcing the point now would harden the civility they'd got from Claudio and Orion so far. They'd been more polite for the last two days, but that had limits. It always had before.

They'd look for reasons to chip away at her work or dismiss her ideas. Orion had challenged near every one of her choices in how to lay the thing out on Wednesday, asking for chapter and verse and citation to the page. She'd gone to sleep with the argument replaying in her head, how none of it satisfied him.

She knew the patterns. It had happened several times before, and she was, among all the other things she did, a student of history. Or at least, trying not to make the same mistake more than twice. And that one in particular, she'd done the same thing half a dozen times with the same bad end.

Now, she cleared her throat. "Could you talk a bit more about what we're looking at, strategically speaking?" Having the table would do very little good if they had no idea what to do with it.

Claudio took a moment to savour a last crumb. Hypatia wondered suddenly if he was taking the time to think, if he needed it, but if that was the reason, no sign of it showed in his expression. "That's the trick, isn't it?" He let out a huff of breath. "I might be able to talk to someone who could advise us, but I'll have to go through getting permissions. And it's one of those things where the right hand doesn't know what the left hand is doing."

"Left foot, more like." Orion made the comment with a sharp grin. Claudio snorted and otherwise ignored him.

"Someone you both know, then?" Hypatia asked. She was trying to think who it might be, who'd be an effort to get permission to talk to.

"Socially, yes. One of the horde who shows up at the solstice rites." Which did in fact cover a few hundred people by obligation, and several hundred more hoping some of that would brush off on them. Not much use in narrowing anything down, then. Particularly not for Foxes, who were already overlapping that set.

"And until then?" Hypatia gestured. "It's not like we can sit around not doing anything."

"You heard the briefing. Some attack by sea, some air cover. Do we know anything much about either of those before we get into the land options? Leaving aside the German magic question, we need to do more research on that. Right now, stick to hiding our own passage, protections, that sort of thing."

"Last time I saw Duncan," Cammie's chin came up, a bit aggressively. "We got to a bit of talking about what the risks are. Magically, I mean. For one thing, the machines are finicky. A whole lot of the bomber command are superstitious as all get out - not that they don't have some reason to be. But it'd be hard to get them all to have a thing with them, or even paint something on the plane. I don't think you could arrange it, all the necessary planes. And they shift in and out of service a lot, or the one you were thinking of crashes or what have you."

"It would be a challenge," Claudio agreed. "But surely something that might foil whatever detection systems would be a help?"

"Yes and no. If it clouds too much, they look like German planes to the anti-aircraft batteries." Cammie shivered. "He knew several people whose planes went down because of that. Not good ends."

"Not sure any of us get a chance at good ends right now." Orion grimaced, then pushed back, to go circle around behind them. Hypatia watched Cammie, who was suddenly watching him intently, the way she measured any potential threat in her own particular idiom. Claudio didn't seem particularly bothered, or not more than the conversation warranted.

He steepled his fingers. "So we probably want to consider some options - no idea what they'll ask us for. But we won't focus on that. I agree, the ways it could go wrong for our boys are rather high. Things to bring up protections of any kind?"

Hypatia flicked a finger. "Fogs are easy enough to do if you can manage the coordinate flying. We might manage hints of, I don't know, things that look like tanks in one place. My last post, someone had a story, third hand, of someone building wooden shapes to do the same thing. We could do a bit better than that, probably."

"That's definitely worth doing. What about ships on the Channel, fogging them out or obscuring where they are? Not the same issues as the planes."

Cammie leaned forward a little. She was still paying attention to Orion, who was still pacing, a bit like a bored lion at a zoo. Not roaring, but there remained the sense he might any minute, or that he just had a moment ago. "Worth some investigation, sure." There was a little twitch of her head. "What about the land magic? I don't know much about how it works there."

"Neither do we." Orion said, before pivoting and pacing. "Differently. Isembard might know. I can probably write that up in the journal and let him tell us if there's more that would be worth a visit?"

"Please." Claudio said. "What we need right now is the overview, anyway. You could make a request for whatever summaries are in the Schola library. That would cover it nicely to be getting on with, and not be that unusual a question. Especially from you."

"Glad the title's bloody good for something, then," Orion said. "I'd write Alexander, but he's off doing something again, last I heard."

"Deep in it, I gather." Claudio agreed. Though at least Hypatia could follow that one. Alexander's father had been French, his mother Egyptian. She'd mostly heard bits of the latter side, both from him directly, and from Cammie, who'd done some language practice with him while he was still teaching at Schola. "No, we'll start with Isembard. He'll be honest if he can't help, and he might have ideas on who else to ask." Then he straightened up. "Does that give you somewhere to start thinking about what to do?"

"Enough for the moment. Let me do a bit more research on my end, and we should talk through things again, in more detail, when we've all done that? It's Friday now, so I don't know. Next Wednesday, for cleverness?"

That brought Orion up short in his pacing. "Do you really hold to that nonsense about planetary days as at all relevant to timing? I mean, haven't you read Horatio Wilson on the topic? You must have."

That, well, was the sort of argument she wasn't going to ignore. "I have, but you obviously haven't read Circe Hemmingshaft. Or Alicia Waters-Bryant. Never mind your classics." Within a minute they were well into what some might reasonably call an argument, and that Hypatia would call a vigorous academic debate. Well, a vigorous academic debate at high volume, but Orion was at least matching her in including citations. And he was being more measured about making his arguments than last time. Five minutes in, she noticed Cammie slip out, followed a minute or two later by Claudio. She put her back into the ongoing argument now no one was going to tell her to calm down.

An hour later, neither of them had won, and that was annoying. Orion was also annoying. When he'd run out of arguments, he'd just abruptly bowed and left, quite swiftly, leaving her alone at her desk in abrupt silence.

CHAPTER 11
ORION, EARLY EVENING

Orion ducked out of the working hut. He knew Claudio had wanted to finish up a letter to his mother. He was sure his brother would catch him up by the canteen in a few. It gave Orion a few minutes to clear his head, and enjoy the reasonably pleasant spring evening. Or at least, it wasn't being actively unpleasant. No rain, they hadn't had much this month, and a comfortable temperature with his uniform jacket on.

A little quiet on his own wouldn't hurt, anyway. He was pleased with how today had gone, honestly. After Wednesday's row, he'd listened to Claudio. He always listened to Claudio whenever he could get his wits to run faster than his tongue. He'd been careful the last two days. But it had felt fragile, in all the ways that had always seemed treacherous to him. The things no one ever explained, he was just supposed to make sense of them.

Hector had. His elder brother had the family gift for politics and interpersonal relationships that had entirely passed Orion by. Father had been quieter about it than many, but any man who'd navigated the Council for thirty years had all those skills and more. But then Hector had been killed in the Great War, and all the expectations had fallen on Orion's shoulders.

Orion would have done much better in a different era. Four hundred and fifty years ago, he'd have flourished in the Wars of the Roses, at least as long as he lived. He understood those battles. Given another decade, he'd have ended up under the banner with the white boar, Richard III's own badge. The wars then were bloody, awful in ways beyond counting, but they'd been human and direct in a way this one wasn't. It was even worse now Orion couldn't actually fight, and he was stuck in this land of social necessities and working at a distance.

Oh, he was doing better with it now than when he was younger. Isembard and Thesan had explained a lot to him, both while he was at school and regularly during his apprenticeship and entry into adult life. Claudio had done even more of it, explaining in a low voice who this person was, why that particular topic was sensitive. These days, Orion could manage people he knew about quite well, really. Mostly because Thesan's tricks about keeping track of who was who worked brilliantly. And more importantly, he knew or could look up what they cared about and what they wanted to avoid.

For all this war wasn't like the mediaeval ones, it had simplified everything, actually. Not in kind ways or comfortable ones, except for that one thing. When he'd been in the midst of the fighting, his role was quite direct. He took the orders he was given and he made them work out, lobbing shells and whatever else at the enemy, aided by a bit of magic. It wasn't his job to sort out the political consequences. And as a captain, he'd been able to get to know each of his men.

Which was a different sort of problem when they'd

died, but he'd been warned about that in advance. Before he'd been posted overseas, Isembard had made sure he'd had a chance to talk to veterans of the previous war who'd been captains. That had helped no end, even though this war was far different than the endless slog of the trenches. It was one more gift he treasured, in a chest full of them.

Orion had been quite good at that sort of fighting. Surprisingly good at it. He'd been trained to it, some ways, all his interests in martial magics coming together with the modern explosives and artillery. Until, all of a sudden, he couldn't do it anymore, and he couldn't do much of anything else. That was a hopeless line of thought. He'd promised himself - and Claudio and Isembard and Thesan - that he wouldn't let himself get bogged down that way if he could help it.

Anyway. This afternoon had been a reassuringly academic argument. He still wasn't sure of at least half of what Hypatia was on about, why she was taking the line on it she was. But it had been a much better wrangle than Wednesday. He was pretty sure, at least three-quarters sure, that she'd enjoyed it. Or at least hadn't been offended by it. She hadn't started shouting. Which had, in hindsight, been something he should have spotted at least three steps earlier. Isembard would give him such a look for that.

It wasn't good to annoy his allies into shouting, for all sorts of reasons. Especially when the four of them were working together so closely for the duration. And she really was clever. He had figured that out in the first day or two. Both of them were. He'd caught himself listening to the way they batted ideas back and forth, a rapid-fire series of references and allusions and abbreviations, built up of long familiarity with each other's work. Like he and Claudio did, but in an entirely different area of magic.

He'd made a loop up the main road, and was coming back to circle before heading for the canteen, when he heard. "Hey." His chin came up, and he moved a little so the light was a bit more of a help. "Yes?" He couldn't quite see their ranks, but chances were decent he ranked them. Three of them.

"You're with the lot over at the edge of the camp, aren't you? That group of huts. Two ATS girls?"

Women, not girls. Orion's chin jerked up. "Four of us, yes."

"You don't eat in the canteen." The three came a little closer. Lieutenants, all three. He ranked them, then. That might be a help.

Orion shrugged. "We were told better not. And it's not like we can talk about what we're doing."

"Lot of that going around the place." One of the men stepped forward. Years younger than Orion, he thought, though it was hard to tell, the way people aged so fast now. "But you all have it easy. Not many ATS around our parts. A few, but mostly they talk to the senior officers." He shrugged. "Got to be nice to have someone type up your notes and make the tea."

That, now, put Orion's hackles up. Or whatever it was you called them in people. "Oh, they're quite skilled, the both of them. Signals experience, for one thing."

"Not a lot with you lot, though. I mean, there's only the two of you doing actual work, surely. Only so much to pass along. We'd know if you got regular despatches, and you don't."

Orion was not at all sure what Cammie was up to. He was quite clear that the maths for some of it was well over his head, and it wasn't as if the non-mathematical parts were simple, either. But he was quite sure it was a lot more than relaying messages. Or would be, soon enough. "To be honest—" No, he couldn't finish that sentence, that he felt they were making more headway than he and Claudio were. For all sorts of reasons. "I said, can't talk about our work. Made an oath on it, and I keep those." He would have anyway, without the magic, but he could feel the press of the Silence on him, the way it was twined into him.

"But you're not saying what they're good at." The man in the middle was getting more aggressive. Orion had done it often enough himself. He could read that just fine in the set of the shoulders, the way he had one foot in front of another. The other man had done some boxing, maybe, which was not something Orion had specialised in, but enough of duelling carried over, except for actually hitting people. Orion had some practice at that, too, in the usual sort of mild brawl that happened sometimes. All right, moderately often, every quarter or so, for him.

He shifted his weight slightly to match, slowly enough they probably wouldn't notice. Orion tucked his bad hand behind his back, setting his shoulders to allow free movement with the other. "No. Because that would be telling."

These men weren't magical, they hadn't made the Pact. He couldn't explain to them that Hypatia was working at a magical level that maybe fifty or a hundred other people in the country could touch, as far as he could tell. Like the best of the alchemists or the ritualists or the materia specialists. Or if she wasn't in the top hundred yet, she was going to be bloody soon. He hadn't followed the details today, but that didn't mean he hadn't understood she knew them.

"And you're off by yourselves with them. Usually they tuck ATS girls up in barracks, all together, with some old dame to keep an eye out. No fraternisation outside of dances and all that. How'd you get so lucky, to get company on the regular? Even if they're not up to the standard of beauty I'd choose. You got some skill means they want to keep you happy?"

There was a nasty note there now, or rather he was certain that it had to be in there. It was the sort of thing that was only said nastily. "Say that again, would you?" He didn't want to throw the first punch, but Isembard had taught him how to be ready, if it was needed. Provoked. And what counted as actual provocation, not just Orion justifying his moods. Which went double or triple right now, because they were supposed to be on the same side.

"Oh, everyone's guessed there's some reason you've got them. Maybe nothing too overt. But something to keep you sweet."

Orion was a hair's breadth from throwing that punch, feeling the way his weight would shift, his hip would twist, and someone's jaw would be feeling it. Then he sucked in a breath. "No one, in all my life, has ever accused me of being sweet."

Before the others could say anything, there was a sound. "Hold, there." Sharp command voice, someone who was utterly sure of his rank and position and how to use it like a weapon. Claudio. Orion immediately folded his right hand behind his back as soon as he placed the voice and took a step away from the group. Claudio would read that, how close it had come. Orion could feel the muscle in his jaw twitch now. That was going to ache in a bit. Then, a beat later, still pitched to carry but not a command, exactly. "Sisley. I was just on the way to fetch our supper. Something a problem?"

This was where it was tricky. He could tell Claudio now, and they'd know Orion had told. He would, of course, tell Claudio later, but if he passed it off as nothing major now, it would ease things in the moment. And likely make things trickier for the women later. "These lieu-tenants had some questions about what we're up to, and what the ATS women are doing as part of it. Of course, I made it clear we can't talk about our work."

"Quite right." Claudio somehow made it sound simul-taneously cheerful and easy-going and also brisk and no-nonsense. "We've more work to be doing tonight, fellows. We should go along and grab our supper, get back to it."

Ten seconds later, there were a handful of rather slap-dash salutes, and then the two of them were heading off to the canteen. Orion had to make sure he didn't match Claudio too closely when they might be seen, though of course that would actually be much easier. They collected the food, including tomorrow's breakfast, and Claudio sweet-talked one of the cooks into a couple of extra apples. He didn't say anything about the conversation, too many ears to overhear.

On their way back across the camp, Claudio paused. "What do I need to know before we get back? You were going to hit him, weren't you?"

"Need your advice on it." Orion swallowed. Then he could taste a bit of bile in his mouth. "Ugh."

"Flask?" Claudio shifted the food he was carrying onto one hip, rummaging inside his jacket for a small flask and handing it over. "Give me your food for a minute."

A swallow of it - the sort of whiskey that was for drinking when someone needed a bit of bracing, not for flavour - was a help, in fact. Orion let the burn of the alcohol work through him. "They were implying - more than just implying - that the women were doing favours of a particular kind. To keep us happy. Because normally they'd be in barracks, always going around in a group."

"That's the rub of it, isn't it? Different mores." The women of Albion - all right. It wasn't that men didn't take advantage at times. But a woman who had strong and well-trained magic, anyone who'd gone to Schola, she had defences of her own. Slow ones, even if she didn't have faster ones. And she'd have family or teachers or people who'd notice, and all the social pressure that could come to bear. It didn't avoid every problem, but on the whole, women had a lot more equality. Albion had quietly been sending women along to combat for centuries, too, unlike the United Kingdom. "Is it going to be a problem for them?"

"You're asking me?" Orion blinked, startled. This was not a problem he should try and solve. He could feel the edge of frantic desire to be doing anything else rising rapidly. "I don't know. I don't even know whether to tell them to avoid leaving our area - but Cammie's going to want to get out, at least, into Richmond Park."

"Give them the information, then. After supper. No sense getting into the muck of it on an empty stomach." Claudio had mastered that particular practical aspect long since. "Break out a bit more of the whiskey as needed. That's what it's there for."

"Yeah." Orion closed his eyes. It was easier to admit it when he couldn't see Claudio's face. "I was about to hit him. And I mean, on the one hand, I think I was justified. On the other hand, it would have made a mess."

"A lot of a mess. I'm not sure you understand enough of how much it would be. So I'm glad you didn't. That I came along." Claudio let out a hiss between his teeth. "We're on tenuous ground here, a dozen ways."

"The kind of thing I don't see until I'm up to my knees in bog. Right." Orion let out a huff of breath. He didn't entirely understand this one either, but he would add it to the long list of things where he took Claudio on trust. That trust had always been justified before. It made his head hurt, though, not just his jaw.

"Like that. Right. Bring the food, let them eat, I'll figure out how we go about telling them what they need to know."

CHAPTER 12

CLAUDIO, SATURDAY EVENING WITH THE OFFICERS

"Here we are, then. Have you been in the house before? So much more civilised. Pity we can't manage an officer's mess in here too, the huts are so loud. But we can have a drink in here. Used to be the butler's room, I gather, quite separate from the rest of the house, but Ecks here is on duty, needs to be handy. There you go. That's no one's particular chair."

It was the oldest and most battered of the upholstered chairs, but it was in fact the sort of chair one expected in a smoking room in this sort of place. Latchmere House was a large but not particularly notable Victorian house, turned over to the War Office in the last war. Claudio had not previously been inside, but, well, he had been invited in tonight. He'd been told it was mostly offices and working space in this part. No details, they'd been careful to avoid any information about what that work actually was.

It had happened when he'd gone by himself to bring the trays and tins back after their luncheon. One of the other officers had called out, "Captain, a word?" and Claudio had obliged. It had been the sort of conversation

Orion would have found terribly frustrating, since it was full of things no one was explaining and that didn't fit the models of how things were supposed to go.

Would he - just him - like to come round for a drink tonight? Supper in the officer's mess, if he wished, beforehand, a break from his usual company? Now Captain Warren had been here for a bit, it might be nice to talk officer to officer. Claudio could do those maths quite easily. They wanted to learn more about the four of them, perhaps about the project. Most likely, wanting to know how likely it was Orion wanted to punch one of them in the nose. Also how amenable the women might be to a bit of time in private.

There was nothing to it but agree, with an amiable, "If you'd check it's all right for me to join you for supper, certainly. And a drink or two after." He'd left it with them, to make it all right with the more senior officers. But Claudio knew how this game was played, all the many forms of it, just as well as the senior officers did. Better, likely. He'd grown up watching this particular kind of dance of favour and intrigue from before he could talk. Certainly before he consciously remembered. Father had lived and breathed the use of protocol to wield power. Mother wasn't far behind him, though her style of it was noticeably different.

He was the most presentable of the four of them, by far. They thought they could have a sensible conversation with him. Sort things out like gentlemen who played by the same rules. Claudio didn't, of course. He worked by rules they didn't understand, and that he couldn't speak of. But he was just as used to that dance, by now. He'd done it up in Edinburgh, and he'd expected it here. Right about now, really. And he'd already learned several things of interest.

Last night, they'd talked the problem through with the

women, neither of whom were at all surprised by the assumptions. Tired of them, honestly. Cammie had commented that she'd at least been spared turning up at dances and looking agreeable, and Hypatia had snorted. There were stories there, apparently, and at least not entirely unpleasant in the retelling. Neither woman much wanted to change their habits on account of those three lieutenants or whatever others might have similar thoughts. Claudio had suggested it might be a good idea to let someone know if any of them - he and Orion very much included - were going to be away from the huts any length of time.

Hypatia had agreed, as had Cammie, but a few minutes further on in the conversation, Hypatia had tilted her head. "Would you carry a stone in your pocket? Something that could signal a problem? I'll have to find something suitable or send for something from Ibis. They need to be the same material, then linked."

Claudio had said, immediately, he'd be glad to pay whatever costs, if beads or some such would be easier, and they'd got into an amiable discussion of the different methods of doing that. He'd very much like to know if Orion needed a hand, even more than with the women. To be honest, Orion was more likely to get himself into trouble of the trickier type.

The discussion had been excellent, too. Orion and Hypatia had not actually spatted with each other about methods. Cammie had mentioned several different categories of information that might be useful to convey, and how to achieve that with a minimally complicated item. By the time they'd dispersed to go back to their various research for their actual assignment, Claudio had felt rather better about the whole thing.

Which made the contrast to how he felt now all the

more stark. The bevy of officers had been cordial enough over supper. Though that conversation had foundered once he'd shaken his head at the queries about where he'd gone to school or university. "Privately educated, chaps." He'd not had much practice making it disarming and firm before the war began, but these days he'd said it so often it flowed off his tongue.

None of them knew of Schola, he was quite sure. He knew enough now to read the touch of the oath on the Silence, that everyone magical - everyone in Albion, rather - made at the age of twelve. Besides, they were all around his age or a bit younger. If they'd gone to Schola, Isembard would have known them, and Claudio likely would have met them at some point. If they'd gone to Dunwich or Alethorpe, it was a bit less likely. But he'd still know the family name and the shapes of their faces, or enough to look for other cues and hints. There was none of that. It made things easier, on the whole, but it would make this evening harder.

It wasn't as if they could talk about their various work over supper, so it had devolved into the usual sort of safe topics. Fond memories of sport, both the more organised sort like cricket and rugby, neither of which Claudio knew much about. At least there was also chatter about the more individual country amusements of hunting and riding and fishing, which he did. Various hijinks at university came up, though that was often marred at this point by one or the other mentioning a name, and then the fact the chap had died, and when and where, before moving relentlessly on in the sentence. Now they were more in private, or at least as the non-magical counted it, Claudio expected a bit more prying. He'd had the sense to do a charm as they came in and counted three listening devices.

"There you go. Brandy is what we've got at the

moment. Hope that's fine. Here's to a good time, chaps. And to the king's health." Claudio was handed a glass. He echoed the toast, not very loudly and without putting much weight into it, and then took a sip. Not horrific brandy, but not particularly good, either. But they were all making do, in every dimension. He settled back in his chair, knowing the body language would be something they read. He was the perfect illusion of someone entirely at ease, trusting that the others around were just like him.

"So, Warren." It was a last-names-only sort of crowd, at least in Claudio's case, though he'd heard a few of the more usual sort of nickname. Beetle, Robs, Ginger of course, there always had to be a Ginger. Someone puzzlingly named Ecks, which seemed to have nothing to do with any other name he used. And a Bunny, who admittedly was well nick-named, he looked remarkably like a permanently startled rabbit. "You've been here, what, a fortnight?"

"Ten days." he replied, lifting his glass slightly. "Thrown in the deep end, a bit, though I'd been working on something related up north." From this point in England, up north covered quite a lot of territory.

"And your people?"

"Isn't the term 'of local respectability'?" Local certainly wasn't true, Father's name had been known - and often feared - not only throughout the magical community of England and Wales and Scotland, but also throughout the British Empire. He'd been head of the Council for thirty-five years and on it for fifty, before his death in '32. Mother had joined him on the Council fifteen years ago, and the whole thing had shaped - and warped - every part of Claudio's own life.

He considered how to put it. "Father died twelve years ago, Mother's rather younger." Father's third wife, in a desperate attempt to produce an heir to succeed him in all things. That was Claudio, and thus far, he knew he was a disappointment. A redeemable one, perhaps, especially compared to Orion, but a disappointment. Not that his mother ever said that outright. She didn't need to. Claudio knew how to interpret all the things she didn't say. "Family home in Surrey, near Guildford."

"Chance you might get leave and see your people?" That was Ginger. "A day away from here's worth a lot."

"We were told leave would be hard to come by. I don't mind, much. Mother's terribly busy doing her bit, too." Which ran to decidedly more active sorts of work than the average bandage-rolling, fête-throwing, tea-hosting sort of volunteer work of the average society woman. If she wasn't out on Council business, she was in the household alchemy lab, making up needed potions. Her last note had suggested they were building up a backlog of stamina and endurance variations for something, not that she'd said so directly. But she'd been complaining about the quality of the ginseng available, and exploring the combination of rosemary, mint, and sage, properly run through alchemical distillation processes.

"Just you, then?" That was a too-casual question.

"Oh, I'm married. The sort of expected thing. We get on well, but I'm certain she doesn't miss my being around. My son is off at prep school, my daughter's not quite four." Which left it nicely ambiguous. If he'd said 'tutoring school' the way he would in Albion, they'd have pegged Tiberius's age to within a year or so. He shrugged. "I knew what it'd be like when I took the posting. And we do have a long history as a family of doing our part. Not career Army or Civil Service, usually, but whatever skills apply."

He could tell, from the little ripple of reaction, that none of them had children, or at least none they knew anything about. Sweethearts, likely, several of them. "Then you're not likely to want to come along next time there's a dance? Not here." Ecks spoke quickly at the end, to make it clear. "No outsiders here. But there's a base, Americans, a couple of miles away, and we go round there for the entertainment from time to time. Whoever's not on duty."

"Not really my thing, no. And as I said, we're expected to stay put."

"The other man with you. Captain Sisley, yes?" That was Bunny, and Claudio suddenly was sure the man wasn't as daft as he looked.

"We've been friends since our younger days. And our families are the sort that support each other's projects, by and large." Claudio let a hint of warning creep into his voice. Just enough to make it absolutely clear he wasn't going to stand for insults, now or later. "He does actually know how to behave, but he's had a bad year. He was posted out in the Greek islands, got invalided out. Glad to have him on our project. I know I can rely on him." It was all utterly true, those sentences.

Beetle, who seemed to be the one the others looked to, considered that. "Loyalty's a virtue. So long as it doesn't get you in trouble, too. Though I'm wondering if there's a reason neither of you've had a promotion, above Captain?"

"Oh, that's the kind of work we've been doing." From a couple of things Junior Commander Roberts had said, he was fairly sure that there were several majors on the committee or group that was overseeing them. He'd been overdue for a promotion before his last posting, and so had Orion, but the kind of work they were doing didn't encourage it beyond a certain point. On the other hand, Isembard had finished the Great War as a Captain, and had no shame at it. Claudio would rather model himself on that, considering everything. "You know how it is."

"And nothing you can say, then. Robs was saying it must be grand to have the women to do the typing and the tea and all that. But your - your friend." That, now, had a cautious note to it. "Took offence."

"Oh, they've got their own skills. Signals work, research expertise. A bit of this, a bit of that, working on projects with some relevance. From before the war, both of them, not just what the ATS taught them."

"And neither of them's married?" That was Ginger, leaning forward. "I mean." The others glanced at him, and there was that uncomfortable moment. "They're not from the colonies and whatever, are they, either of them?"

"Both come from families with long ties in England." That was, in fact, quite true, even if it wasn't entirely as these men would assume. "Ward was born in Egypt, but her father was English. She's been living here since she was something like ten." He let himself show a slight shrug. "Gates is seeing an RAF flyer. Bomber command, his second round of active duty."

That got a little rock out of Ginger. "Ah." He was someone who knew the death rates and had them at the tip of his mind. "Right."

"Also. I'd not want to be on her wrong side. I'm not sure what she'd do, but she's not one to suffer idiots. Ask Orion, if he's inclined to be sociable."

That got a suitable roar of laughter, and then there was an offer of a lighter for a cigarette, and the talk shifted a bit. None of them shared much about their actual work, but Claudio managed to pick up a few things. There were quite a few separate spaces around the camp, little huts isolated from each other, not sharing ablutions or eating spaces. Each of them had soldiers supervising, but these men were doing other tasks, something related to analysis. None of them were dense, but most of them seemed quite set in their ways. Unlikely to see outside the narrow box of their upbringing, schooling, and the paths their lives had driven them down, like sheep.

Claudio had often thought he'd rather be a goose or a goat, setting off on his own. It was likely Orion's influence. Without Orion, Claudio knew he'd be a lot more like these men, so sure he was right, he couldn't see any other option, walking in his father's footsteps without any idea of the consequence or costs. By the time they showed him back out of the main house, he'd had a fair bit of brandy, and he had plenty to think about for the coming days.

CHAPTER 13
CAMMIE, MARCH 30TH

The fortnight had gone smoothly enough. They were making some progress on their work, moving from figuring out the broader parameters of what might be possible into the refinements that led to actually doing things. Cammie was considering her options for the evening, after a long day's work.

Whatever Claudio had said to the various officers over drinks, it had been effective enough. The officers nodded politely at Cammie and Hypatia when they were visible. The enlisted men saluted when appropriate. There were other ATS women, but Cammie thought they were all secretaries. Whatever the reason, the other ATS women didn't approach or invite their company. If she hadn't had Hypatia handy, it would have been rather tedious. But she did, so there wasn't a problem.

Orion had also been more or less manageable, by which Cammie meant a number of extended lectures about historical battles, brought into check by Claudio's cough or elbow. Orion had taken it with good humour, in that case. He'd disappeared for a day on the equinox and had come back crankier than usual. That would have been the land rites. If a few historical monologues helped with the cranky, they could cope. Probably.

Hypatia had claimed the workroom for a purification ritual after hours the same night, after taking over the bathroom for a good hour before she started, which had been a tad annoying. The pipes clanked loudly enough to be distracting, for one thing, and she'd run more hot water four times.

The longer they'd been here, though, the more questions Cammie had about the place. She was sitting on her bed, peering out the window, when Hypatia came in from the front room. "I know that look." Her sister frowned. "You couldn't have done this last week, at the new moon?"

"Nope." Cammie shook her head. "It'd have been too obvious. But they're working on things in their hut, you're here. And I..." She jerked her chin toward the window.

"How long?"

"You know I don't have a good sense of time like that, and it's not as if I'll be wearing a watch." Cammie shrugged again. "I want to know what all the other little huts are. What's up with that big long block that no one goes near unless they're on duty? What we're surrounded by. Well, not surrounded, we're off on the edge. Metaphorically fenced in by, as well as the wood fences and the wire. It's making me itchy."

"And we can't have you getting itchy. All right. Don't take too long, though? It makes me nervous." Hypatia tilted her head. "What do I tell them if the men come by looking for you?"

"Headache, I've gone to bed. Or I've got my nose deep in something. That one's true enough." Cammie grinned sharply, then stood and started stripping off her uniform. She put on an older worn skirt and a visibly darned shirt.

Likely she wouldn't need the cover coming back, but if she got stuck somewhere, she didn't want to wreck her good uniform pieces. Hypatia didn't bother looking away. They'd seen each other dress and undress hundreds of times by now. As Cammie did up the last buttons, Hypatia went to push the window open a couple of inches.

Cammie laughed, just once, then she flung herself at the bed, changing in mid-flight into her other self. Four feet, a nose that could follow all sorts of new threads, and fur. She shook herself out, then waited a moment, twisting her head up to peer at where Hypatia was. It always took her a moment to let her eyes adjust and remember what it was like to have four feet and a great deal of spring in her steps.

Hypatia snorted and put her hand down for Cammie to climb up. She could scale the wall, likely, there was enough texture to grip, though nothing as good as a tree trunk. But why go to the effort when Hypatia could give her a lift?

"You're still in your winter coat, though the summer one's coming in. So you know." Hypatia lifted her up to the window ledge. Cammie arched her back, swivelled her nose around. Still a pretty pretty ermine, then. Or more or less one. Rather than the beige stoat, beige like the ATS uniforms. Not that she expected any trouble from people out hunting for fur here. The white would glow more, though, so yes, she'd be careful.

Cammie nosed at Hypatia's hand one more time, then slipped out of the window, down the outside wall, and bounded off in the lea of the hut. She wanted to stay out of the open pathways - too much chance of owl, and certainly too much chance of a car or truck. She lifted onto her hind legs to sniff and orient herself. The question was where to go first. There were various huts scattered over the property, but she'd got the impression that many of them were housing.

She was curious about the main house, but even more so about that sort of annex that stretched along one side away from it. She'd start there. Cammie made her way from hut to path to tree, along, keeping a wary eye, ear, and nose out for any signs of movement. That was the annoying thing about owls. In this form, she wouldn't hear them. Foxes, yes. Automobiles, yes. Owls, no. She considered it a hilarious irony, given her House affiliation at school.

Ibis had found the fact she turned into a stoat unexpectedly startling. She'd demanded he teach her to shift, her last year in school, in trade for her helping tutor several students in other things. He'd given in, because - well. Because Cammie was fierce and determined.

It hadn't surprised her to turn into a stoat, not really. Or rather she'd expected some moderately sized mammal with teeth and claws and a will to use them. England and Wales offered a reasonable variety, foxes and badgers and various sorts of weasel, as well as cats and dogs. She arched her back, revelling in how good it felt. No weasel, her. She ran with her back arched in bounding leaps, not slinking along the ground.

A few minutes got her over toward the main house. The annex stuck out awkwardly, a much more recent addition than the original building. She couldn't get inside. There was entirely too much risk of getting trapped in there. She could shift back, but that would cause other problems. But smells carried a lot of information, and there was always the chance she'd overhear something interesting.

Only she didn't. She circled the outside spaces, keeping on the far side, away from the camp. She could pick up some smells. That there were, hmm. More than twenty people, probably. Too many to differentiate. But none of them were making much noise. There was no music on, or radio. She didn't hear snatches of conversation she couldn't make out through the muffling of the walls. There weren't the sounds she'd expect of a guard in Army-issue boots making the rounds, even though she was pretty sure she observed for at least half an hour.

Toward the end of that, she scampered up the side of the building, using a drain or pipe of some kind. She got an angle through a slit of a window, bars over it. There was more of a scent here. Stale, very unwashed human, not at all pleasant. It had fear in it, and the sort of fear that had gone on for a long time. It wasn't just the sudden sharp burst of being right under bombs dropping during an air raid. There was a distinctive difference with this nose. With her human nose, too, honestly, but even more so now.

Cammie couldn't figure out how to get a good enough angle to peer inside the window, but the couple of tries she made suggested small rooms, even cells. She'd got a snatch of a metal door and a metal-framed narrow bed. Worse than the ones in their hut, by a long shot. Also worse than the usual ATS bedding issue, the 'biscuits' of three thin square mattresses that more or less made up a bed. If they could be convinced to stay put. Cammie had managed fine, having both sticking and cushioning charms in her personal arsenal. But the other women had to make do with tightly folded and tacked together sheets if they had spares.

She recognised this as un-stoatlike. Her human mind was skittering away from the implications. If this were a prison, there were really two options. Either it held enemy aliens, or it held domestic threats. Probably not both at the same time. They were, from the snippets of gossip she'd heard, treated differently. After a bit of consideration, and waiting to see if she saw or heard or sensed any other movement, she circled around the building, until it came out at the wall at the front of the house. She could almost certainly get herself through a gap in the fence somewhere, but there would be men on duty, and that was the sort of risk Hypatia frowned about.

Instead, she reversed direction, going back the way she'd come. Carefully she made her way up toward where she thought most of the staff housing was, not that she'd been anywhere near that on two feet. Cammie thought it was rather a long way, given the size of the camp. They seemed to want everything near those cells to be quiet, none of the ordinary noise the inmates might expect. And it backed onto the park, so there wouldn't be other noises from houses nearby or whatever else.

The staff huts were a bit more what she expected. She circled between them, eavesdropping on the ordinary sorts of off-duty grumbles and distractions. Complaints about the cold, and only having a bucket of coal to work with. The blandness of the food, which made Cammie glad again that Ibis had sent along a solid set of herbs and spices for flavouring, and plenty of salt. Two card games, both with people playing terribly badly. Cammie thought it suggested something about their other skills, this far into the war. Someone who wasn't a cutthroat card player by this point should not be trusted with complicated lines of work.

She did find several huts of ATS girls. Women. She hated that particular bit of terminology with a burning passion, though she'd known just as many who loved the thrill of it. Mostly, she thought, in her more cynical moments, women who'd never had the experience of sharing dormitories as schoolgirls. She'd done it for the two necessary years before getting her own room. She had hated being piled in with others, in a hut of six or eight or more beds.

It wasn't just her magic, or the fact shifting had been next to impossible. She just liked space. And quiet. That made her consider, and she found the far fence line again, and went on the prowl. She always felt better after a proper bit of hunting, and she could do that before she went back to reassure Hypatia she was fine. Well, physically fine.

Two mice and a rat later, she clambered up the side of the hut again, slipping through the window. She launched herself off the sill into a twisting somersault that had her landing on her bed, more or less seated, back into a shape with two legs and two arms and opposable thumbs.

Hypatia was lying on her stomach, propped on her elbows, book in front of her. "Show-off." She sounded relieved. "What'd you find out?"

Cammie swallowed. "Is there tea?" She would, in fact, like to wash the taste of rat out of her mouth. That one had been in something particularly nasty, even by her other form's sense of taste.

"Wash up. There should be hot in the boiler. They did their washing a bit ago. I'll get the kettle started." She went off to the front room to do that. Cammie checked the time - eleven, not as late as it could be - and decided she would run the hot and hope the pipes wouldn't be too annoying.

Fifteen minutes later, she'd scrubbed herself down, done the charm to clean her hair and wrapped it up for the night so it wouldn't go everywhere. She was back on her bed, feet pulled up under her. Hypatia had got under the covers. "So."

"It's a prison. I'm not sure who for, but there's a whole

block of cells, that building off the main house. Entirely too quiet, rather brightly lit."

"So, not the sort of place where they tuck people who need to be kept out of public, but who are probably harmless." Hypatia let out a fast set of something, one of the prayers she liked. "That's not good."

"If it is spies, it'd explain why they stuck us here. Rather than - I mean, we could have been working in far more comfortable conditions, with more access to, you know, a library," Cammie said.

"But if they're getting information here, or, yes." Hypatia blew air out in a huff. "Do you think the men know?"

"Maybe not." Cammie considered. "Do we tell them? They're going to want to know how I know." That was the rub of it, if she admitted that.

"You were chatting up that guard at the gate, two days ago," Hypatia said, cautiously. "Any chance he'd have let something slip, that sort of thing?"

"I could maybe have gone for a walk when they were bringing someone in?" Cammie frowned. "It is lying to them."

"It is not telling them something you keep secret for very sensible reasons. And yes, I did check the charms, and I know you did too." Hypatia pushed herself upright again.

Cammie sighed, and then decided her feet were in fact cold, and wriggled into bed. "You don't trust them, do you?"

"They have been better than they might be. Even Orion. But that's a low bar, and we both know it. So do they, actually." Hypatia sniffed. "Did you hear him today? Pushing about Claudio's thoughts about the ritual signatures?"

"At least he does it to Claudio, too? I was wondering if he'd feel left out," Cammie said.

"I was assuming he mostly did it to us, honestly. Though I suppose Claudio's not been leading on the theory discussions as much as we have." Hypatia fell back on the bed with a thump. "I'm still stuck, for the record." She'd been beating her head against a wall of whether a line of echoing sympathetic effects would be useful for two days now. Cammie knew, from long and sometimes bitter experience, that they had at least another two days of it, most likely. With a decent chance of interrupted sleep, if there weren't an air raid before then. "Sleep now?"

"Sleep now. Or rather, reading, then sleep. You can have this when I'm done, likely tomorrow." Hypatia waved the novel she was reading in the air, and she wasn't far from the end at all.

"Grand. Mum said she'd send along some more soon as she can." Cammie turned on her side and reached for her own book, waving the light on her side a bit dimmer.

CHAPTER 14

HYPATIA, APRIL 11TH IN THE WORKROOM

"Look, I know you think Keller's the best on sensory impressions, the colour associations. But that won't work if there's too much rain. Or it gets dropped in the water." Orion leaned back, hands on the desk behind him.

Hypatia bit back the first three things she thought of saying before settling on something that was probably forgivable. "Had you bothered to ask what the actual goal is here?"

Orion came up short, his eyes flashing. She could see his shoulders clench, the way his hands shifted, then he pulled them in front of him, cupping left hand in the right. "Beg pardon." He cut himself off. "I'll be outside for a few. I need a smoke."

No one moved until a count of twenty after the door had near banged shut behind him. Claudio had been working at his desk, but hadn't moved, not even when Orion left. Hypatia looked over, now feeling sharp herself. "Not going after him? Or to apologise for him?"

"Not right now." Claudio sighed, and there was something tired there, all of a sudden. "He should make his own apologies, and I hope he'll work round to that soonish. He's being awful right now."

Cammie swung herself to sit on Hypatia's desk, on the half that didn't currently have papers on it. "I don't suppose he's got a good excuse for why."

"What makes a good excuse? There's a war, we're head down in a task that seems impossible. Past the initial settling in, where everything's expected to be chaos. Honestly, he was a lot happier with regular explosions on offer. Not bombs, that's different. Aiming them at other people, or military targets, whatever you want to call it. He's always wanted to fight. But no, he's been more and more on edge the last week."

They'd told the men about the camp on Monday, after Cammie had had a useful encounter with one of the guards here. It wouldn't have given her enough to work with without her scouting mission, but it had provided her with a couple of entirely accurate sentences to quote back. Orion had been furious then, in a way that had disturbed Hypatia. She couldn't make it make sense in her head. No logic she applied made sense. He wasn't - so far as she could tell - upset about there being prisoners, directly. Or about the fact they hadn't been told. It was about something else, that ran deep and broad enough it made him inarticulate.

If she hadn't known better - she'd seen enough of his records to be sure of it - she'd have thought he'd been in a prisoner of war camp himself, at one point. But that wasn't it. Claudio hadn't either, so it wasn't a, what was the word, displaced anger.

"He is not supposed to be fighting us." Hypatia tried to keep the tightness from her voice and utterly failed, though at least she was not breaking into tears. She should probably excuse herself before she did. "We are not the enemy."

Claudio's jaw clenched, just once, and then it came up, that position of a man of power refusing to admit to a weakness. "Depends how you count." Then he lifted his hand. "I don't mean that like it came out. You're doing your job. Both of you. But there are sharp edges, all over. For him. For me, too, I'm just less—" He stopped there, like whatever might have come next would be entirely too revealing. "You're both very competent, is the long and short of it. And he doesn't like the position he's in, six ways round. Only half of one is about you."

"And you're apparently both unsure of what to do with competent women." Hypatia snorted, then half turned away. "I'm going to get bloody all done for a bit. Cammie, are you up for a walk to clear our heads? Think you can make nice with whoever's on gate duty about not fussing over it?" They did tend to go out at hours that didn't match the usual sort of shifts, and that caused questions. Some of which got funnelled back to Junior Commander Roberts, who then had to say something about attracting the wrong sort of attention. It was a pointless rigmarole that they'd all rather avoid.

"Sure. Can I change my shoes?" Cammie pushed herself off the desk. "Back here in an hour or so?"

Claudio considered the clock. "How about we aim at supper on the early side, at five, and pick up again after? I'll knock on your door when I've got yours. Ninety minutes."

"Hope it's better than last night." Hypatia shook her head. "Honestly, you'd think the cooks had never met anything remotely like a flavour."

Cammie didn't say anything until they were changing to the more worn pairs of shoes from their current uniform sets. It was spring, there was mud even if there hadn't been a ton of rain recently, and they both knew about keeping a presentable set for show. Cammie glanced at her watch. "Ninety minutes is enough for a good round in the park."

They walked along the path toward the gate. Their hut was tucked into a curve of the fencing, nearest the Park. There was a series of huts between them and the main house, used for storage so far as they'd been able to tell. Cammie led the way, half a step in front of Hypatia, neither of them talking much. There was a sense of somewhat oppressive quiet on this half of the camp at the best of times. It was both helped and complicated by the soundproofing charms on their own huts.

Hypatia let Cammie do the chatting once they got to the gate. "Odd time for you girls, isn't it?" The man on duty was obviously someone Cammie had talked to before.

"Fells. Afternoon. Yes, they shooed us off for a break while they set up the next thing. We're making the most of it. Going to be at it until late this evening, I'm sure. All right if we take our walk in the park? Back in oh, under an hour and a half?"

There was a little murmured conversation with the other guard on duty, then a nod. "We'd want you girls back by five. There's some traffic coming in sometime this evening. Best be out of the way."

"Of course. Wouldn't want to interfere. Say, did you hear back from your Alice, since, when was it, Tuesday?" Cammie chattered along in that vein for a minute or two. In the process, she got the other guard's sweetheart's name out of him - Gladys. Also worries about mines in the Channel, shipping, some of the usual grumbles about rationing and how hard it was to get coffee. She finished it up with a cheerful "Well, best get on."

Hypatia waited until they were well into the park, no one near them visible. "I don't know how you do that. They look at you like they don't know what to make of you. Five minutes later you know the names of their girls, their pets, their cricket or football team or whatever, and I don't know what else. I can't do that."

"It's all in asking questions, and not caring too much about the answers. It's not hard." Cammie shrugged, blithely cheerful, then amended, "For me." Annoyingly cheerful, honestly, but she'd had a rough day too. If she bounced back faster, it wasn't her fault. "I mean, I keep track. It's handy later. You saw with Fells. If he's talking about footie, he's not wondering so much why we're out for a walk mid-afternoon."

"Point." Hypatia let out a long breath. "Do I need to apologise to Orion?"

"Do you think you've done anything to apologise for? Gods' sakes, Hypatia, and I do mean the plural there, there are times you're entirely too civilised for your own good."

It at least made Hypatia snort, which was almost certainly Cammie's first intention. "Someone should be. You do very well with it, but it's mostly because you're rather competitive about being sociable." She shook her head. "He was reminding me a bit too much of Virgil." Her more recent and not at all missed boyfriend, or whatever one called him. Sweetheart was the wrong word. He'd turned out to not be the first and not have the second, so far as she could tell, except in a purely anatomical sense.

That was her ongoing problem. She hadn't figured out - and maybe she was done trying - how to tell when someone was sincere, in the first flush of meeting. People put on pleasant faces and their best manners, to start out. Only then, she kept being surprised when that was covering for something far more selfish and petulant.

Sometimes worse. Not that she couldn't be self-absorbed and tedious, she absolutely could be. But she mostly did it about her work, about projects that actually mattered, not just about her personal pleasures. For as annoying as Orion was, she thought he was more like her on that front. When he was actually upset, not just congenitally stroppy, it was about something bigger than him.

Cammie's steps paused for a second, when Hypatia didn't go on out loud. "What in particular?"

"You know Virgil had that thing about assuming he always knew better than I did." Though now that she said it out loud, that wasn't quite right. Not about Orion. A false note, and she knew enough to listen for that.

"And about one time in twenty, he almost had a point." Cammie cocked her head. "All right, I admit that you do like to lean on Keller's takes on the colours through other senses. But in this case, I think there's good reason for it. You want all the sharpness and the tang of it in whatever we're putting together for that, the things that cut through to the hindbrain and the centres of fear." Then she caught herself. "Better leave that for later."

"Rather." Hypatia sucked in a breath, then let it out slowly. "So, should I apologise to Orion?"

"Only if he does first. It's good for him to not be on top, I'm sure. And it wasn't like Claudio was jumping to defend him. For once." Cammie shook her head. "Not sure what to make of that. But see what he says when we get back and if he's at all decent about it."

"And if he's not?" Hypatia wanted to jam her hands in her pockets, and knew she shouldn't, they were out in public.

"If he doesn't, you are entirely capable of competently professional communication and nothing more." They walked along for a bit. "Virgil, really?"

Hypatia shrugged. "I didn't tell you all of it." A lot of it had honestly embarrassed her, both at the moment and ever since. She'd thought he was a decent sort to start out with. Charming, certainly, and from a long line of mildly distinguished specialists in sympathetic magic. She'd enjoyed swapping sources and research with him. Until.

First, he'd snagged several of her ideas without checking with her. Second, when they'd gone wrong - because he hadn't actually checked on the assumptions she'd been working from - he'd blamed her for that. He'd never - quite - got violent, but she'd worried about it a few times. She'd have worried more, except they were both living in shared quarters, and he was always well-behaved around other people. Besides, as he'd said, violence was for the lower classes. Cutting comments, coldness, and outright plagiarism were the way the posh set did things, apparently.

Orion might remind her uncomfortably of Virgil, but she had to admit, Orion at least was far less of a hypocrite about the violence part. He'd served at the front, doing dangerous work, and magically complex work, at that. She respected that commitment, and the risks it involved. Even when they'd been arguing, it had only been shouting. He'd never attempted to press her into a corner physically, or put her at risk of getting hurt. Orion also hadn't used the words that would hurt most, now she thought about it. He'd been aggressive, absolutely. But it was the sort of aggressive Cammie often was, and she was fine with that. From Cammie.

Maybe just because it was Cammie. There were a lot of things Cammie did that other people couldn't get away with.

After a few minutes, they picked up a quiet conversation about the novel Cammie had been reading, the history

Hypatia had passed along. Then a letter from Ibis and Pross to both of them with the latest school chaos, mostly the reasonable unhappiness of the local merfolk based at Schola. And of course the trials and tribulations of keeping all the chickens, pigs, sheep, and cows healthy, the school's ongoing obsession to help manage with rationing.

They'd made most of the loop, coming into the southeast corner of the park, where they saw a group of men in American uniform. They seemed to be talking as the women came down the path closer to them. Most of the group walked back toward the gate to the street, while one waited for their approach. "Afternoon. You're ATS girls, aren't you?"

Hypatia rather thought any sensible person should be able to recognise the uniforms by now, but she supposed it was always possible whoever this was had newly arrived in Britain. She took in the details, this was a Major, so someone well enough up the ranks she'd certainly not comment on it. "Sir, yes."

"We've not seen you at the dances over at Camp Griffiss, have we? I think I'd remember seeing someone like you." Hypatia could not, for the life of her, figure out how to take that. The man himself sounded like he was from New England. Certainly not south, but she'd heard Alexander mimic accents just enough when telling some of the tales of his travels to be fairly sure of it. He had tanned skin, a sort of active outdoors mien, shoulders that filled out his uniform well, and dark brown hair under his cap, just long enough to have a bit of a wave to it.

"Camp Griffiss?" Cammie took the brunt of it. "We're kept quite busy at our work, Major."

"Of course you are. But - are you posted near here. You must be?" Then he glanced over to where their camp was and raised an eyebrow. "If you're there, we've got a number of other ATS girls coming for a dance on Saturday. You should come along. I'll make a note. Your names? And you're both British?"

This was, if not an order, uncomfortably close to one. There wasn't much wriggling out of it. If he actually asked at the camp, they were readily identifiable. "Gates and Ward." Cammie said after a moment. "Camilla Gates, Hypatia Ward. My family goes quite a long way back here, both sides."

Hypatia could answer the other. "And my father was British, my mother's Egyptian." She was fairly sure why he wanted to know. Being anything other than white could be tricky with American troops. On the other hand, there were likely some posted - if it was a large camp - who weren't. That would be a whole complicated tangle to navigate too.

"Fantastic. We've got an excellent band playing. Bring your dancing feet. We're sending a truck over at six-thirty, meet everyone by the gate, and we'll run you all home at eleven." He hesitated. "If there are soldiers working with you, they're welcome too. Just let, who is it, right. Let Captain Graves know. Everyone calls him Ecks, I believe."

"We'll pass that along, sir." She and Cammie were both quite clear there wasn't an option, other than perhaps sufficient illness to be in the infirmary they'd never seen and didn't much want to see. If it came to actual illness of any complexity, they'd be sent off to Trellech, but that was harder to explain all round.

"Good. Well, must get back to it. Saturday." He offered a nod, then turned and walked off without another comment.

They watched him go in silence. Cammie sighed. "Suppose I can't get out of it by saying I have to wash my hair, can I?"

"Did that ever actually work for you?" Hypatia asked. "At least we needn't worry about what to wear. Service dress for these things."

"Have you ever actually been to one? They're rather awful by our standards. All the worst parts of a formal social event in Albion. Decidedly less in the way of potions to dull the worst bits, and having to make plenty of small talk with people you'll never see again. The dancing's often better, but that's a help for me, not so much for you."

"On the other hand, you can say the same thing over and over?" Hypatia offered. "Ugh. Well. I suppose we'd better let the men know. And you'll want time to darn your stockings properly between now and then."

"Can I trade you for it?" Cammie asked hopefully. "Bathroom and taking your turn cleaning the working hut?"

"'You really hate darning, don't you?" Hypatia slipped her arm through Cammie's.

"Darning stockings. Everything else is fine. Stockings are a horror." Cammie grumbled amiably about that until they were almost all the way back.

CHAPTER 15
ORION, APRIL 14TH AT SCHOLA

"**A**gain?" Isembard brought his hands up, signalling a momentary pause.

"Don't you need to be somewhere?" Orion took a moment to pull a handkerchief out of an inside pocket and mop his forehead. They'd been going hard at the duelling for near an hour. It was Friday afternoon. Orion had finished with the research in the Schola library that was the excuse for this visit. He'd expected an hour or so of Isembard's time, but not more than that.

"Stay for supper, will you?" Isembard pulled the flask of water on the strap over his shoulder up to take a long drink. He didn't turn away. He was watching Orion closely now. In anyone else, the proper word would have been scrutiny. "Not with the seething young hordes. Thesan said she'd cook."

"You're cheating." Orion found his hands on his hips, all the stubbornness coming out. Of course they'd have figured it out, how tangled and knotted and broken up he was inside. Of course they'd also actually bring it up.

Orion was fairly sure a lot of people noticed it, but no one else, bar Claudio, would have said anything.

Not that Claudio had said anything on Wednesday, when Orion had arranged this trip. He'd done it grimly, feeling like he needed to be away from the camp or go screaming off into the wilderness. Or as much wilderness as one could locate in a well-tended park, anyway. He hadn't expected waiting for the divorce to be final to wear on him, but it was far worse than waiting to go into battle. His anger and frustration at the necessary delays felt ridiculous, along with everything else he felt about it. Or rather, tried not to feel.

Isembard spread his hands. "Using all our advantages. Anyway, she's already got the two of us free from the staff meeting. There wasn't anything there we couldn't skip for once. So if you don't stay, we'll be doomed to amusing each other."

That made Orion laugh, suddenly, the sort of barking laugh that was half hysteria and half honest humour. "Like you couldn't come up with something. Sir." Emphasis entirely on the up. He'd paid attention to the many ways they loved and showed it, since he was a schoolboy and they'd first fallen in love.

Quite a flavour of envy, sometimes, of wanting something like that, and being increasingly sure he was never going to get it. Or get to give it to someone else, either. More so now. It would hurt to be in the midst of it, and then go away. But maybe, just maybe, he could borrow a bit of it to keep him going a while longer. Until something changed, something killed him, the war ended, or the world ended. That was a cursed depressing line of thought, for all it was true.

When he met Isembard's eyes again, he nodded, once.

"I could use some advice, actually. Something I don't understand. Not the specifics of our work."

"Thesan's made the proper oaths, Official Secrets and all. If it helps." That came with a worried look, which meant it was something new in the last month or two, and also something magically complicated. "Anyway. One more bout, you can use the second bath to wash up. She's scrounged up enough things to make a good supper." Without further conversation, they set to it again.

By the time they were done, Orion was dripping with sweat. Isembard had pushed him hard. And he'd pushed back just as much. His mentor was breathing hard and wiping his face. Knowing he'd been able to manage that made Orion feel abruptly better. He was glad, though, that he'd borrowed a set of duelling togs. They desperately needed the laundry, and he couldn't send them out with his uniform and linens.

Fifteen minutes later, they'd closed up the salle properly and climbed the stairs to Isembard and Thesan's rooms halfway up the building. She'd greeted her husband with a kiss on the lips, Orion with a kiss on the cheek, and then shooed them off to bathe. He'd changed into cloth gloves for the duelling. Now he pulled them off for the bath and let his hands fall under the water, where the aches slowly faded enough. Soaking in a proper magical bathtub was sheer joy. She'd set out bath oils he liked, the ones he found soothing. The soap was soft on his skin rather than pragmatic cleansing. Part of him wanted to stay there forever.

Except there were the smells. And those were amazing. Orion got back into his uniform, though he left the jacket off, then added the silk glove liners and the leather gloves. By the time he made it back out to their sitting area, Isembard was setting out plates. "Leo?" he asked. Their daughter would be eating in the Great Hall at the Fox House table. She was a third year now. She'd been a bit gangly last time he'd seen her, growing into the height she'd got from Isembard. Leo would normally be up here after supper.

"Down with Helena for the evening. He's currently making himself helpful gathering up eggs. We'll need to wrap up by eight. I got us out of the meeting, but not out of my marking and prep for the evening class, besides Leo's bedtime. And I do want to see him today more than in passing. When do you need to leave by?" Thesan swept by, dropping a plate of rolls on the table. "Jam, but no butter. Hope you can make do. We've got extra jam at the moment somehow."

"It's a mile or two back from the portal on the other end, so I'll need to make nice at the gate no matter what time? Maybe go downstairs to meet him on the way out?" Orion felt especially unsure with children, but he'd known Leo since before Leo was born. More to the point, both Thesan and Isembard had outright told him what Leo liked and didn't, as it changed, and that helped. A few minutes later, there was a pie plate, with a browned crust, a smell of herbs, and somehow, miraculously, cream. Behind it, there was something sweeter, apples and spices, that suggested heaven was coming with the pudding course.

"How did you put this together?" He'd been eating canteen food again for long enough he'd almost forgot what other food tasted like. And, well, it let him duck the more complicated question some more. A little while longer.

"The cows are coming into milk. There's cream and just a little butter in that and cheese. We've been lucky with eggs. Mum figured out a new sifting charm for flour, so the chickens get the bran and we get the fine white. And the pie's herbs and veg, besides the dairy. Apple crumble, for later." That explained the spices.

"You shouldn't have." He half-stood when she shrugged off the apron and settled down in her usual chair, as Isembard poured out cider for all three of them.

Thesan tilted her head, observing him as intently as she observed stars, which was to say, exceedingly. "I absolutely should. And you've, hmm. Three things you don't want to talk about. Before we get into that, how's Claudio?"

She always managed to do that, get the number right. Isembard chuckled, then listened as Orion talked about the easier parts. He had a letter from Claudio for them both, and ones from Cammie and Hypatia to pass on to Ibis and Pross. The kind of thing that could avoid censors and journals and being read by anyone it wasn't meant for. Though of course all of them had kept their oaths about their current project.

That took them through the bulk of the supper, especially after Orion mentioned Claudio had his own meeting that afternoon, and one he was much less sure about. The outline of that made both Isembard and Thesan laugh, though they didn't explain why they were so amused, just that Claudio had made a good choice there.

Thesan had come across something in some other bit of reading, a book to lend him about the Thirty Years War. Or she'd gone looking for it, because he couldn't imagine her picking that up just because. She was, on the whole, focused on astronomy in all its forms, the way he focused on martial magics, but he could also tell when she was acknowledging his own interests. She didn't hide it, anyway.

Mostly, though, they talked about the school and students. Orion could tell both Isembard and Thesan were talking around things, not just about the ongoing demands to manage food and people on top of teaching and running the school. And it was Thesan's first year as head of Horse House, and that was taking a lot of time. Besides all the school commitments, the orchards and the beehives were in her particular charge, because her family magics had a lot to say about both. Isembard of course had responsibility for all the protections. Compared to that, the single-minded work Orion and Claudio were doing seemed much simpler to manage.

Finally, though, they came to the pudding course and the relentless progression of time. If he was going to talk about any of this, he had to do it now, or give up the idea for ages. He had no idea when he could get leave again, the excuse for this one wouldn't do a second time. When the conversation hit a more or less pause, he blurted out, "Why is she doing that?"

Isembard leaned back, and then visibly kept his mouth shut. Thesan, however, leaned forward, the braid of her hair falling over her shoulder. "Cammie or - no. Hypatia, right?"

Orion nodded. "Why is she doing that?" He knew it wasn't a sensible sort of statement, and trying to explain it, even here, where they'd listen, made him feel even more stupid than usual. "I keep getting in arguments with her. Stupid ones. I don't mean to. They just sort of happen. And then I feel even more stupid." And that was revealing, the kind of thing that would get him killed in a fight. Only they already knew it. He'd said it enough to them over the years.

Thesan pressed her lips together. "Insert the usual comments about you not being stupid here to save time. We'll come back as needed. How do you get into the arguments? Can you give me an example or two?"

He gave her the last three. They'd been burning in his

mind. None had gone quite so far as both of them shouting at each other again, but it had come close once. The other two times, he'd got himself out for a walk and a smoke before he did anything even more unforgivable. He'd thought he was asking questions, he was more or less following her line of thought. Then boom, like an explosion he hadn't calculated properly, they were fighting.

Thesan listened through the whole thing without commenting, though somewhere in the middle, Isembard's hand covered hers. When Orion finished, his voice now down to a bit of a croak, he was holding back his despair at the whole thing badly. Isembard silently poured a bit more cider into his glass. Orion couldn't look up.

From across the table, Thesan said, gently, "Hey. Thank you for the examples, that helps a great deal. What do you think you're doing when you ask her those questions?" The thing about Thesan was that where he wanted to fight nearly everyone else, even Isembard sometimes, he didn't want to fight her. He hadn't much since Isembard had started visibly courting her, his fourth year, and Orion had spent hours trying to figure out why. She understood things Orion couldn't put into words. That was part of it.

Now he swallowed, then tried it with a bit of the cider, which helped. Looking at a spot in the middle of the table, the leftover crumble, he avoided meeting either of their eyes. "I want to understand. And she's really clever, isn't she?" Not like him.

"She is." Thesan paused, and she was choosing her words very carefully now. That was a horrid sign. "When you ask her why she's doing it like that, she doesn't hear you wanting to understand. She hears you demanding she prove she knows what she's doing."

She might have gone on, but there was a roaring in Orion's ears. "Those are entirely different words! A completely different sentence! Why would I tell her she didn't know what she's doing? She's the expert, shouldn't she know that?" His voice was a shout at the end of it. He'd pushed up out of his chair, and his heart was pounding in his chest, loud enough to challenge the shouting.

He managed a glance at the two of them. Isembard hadn't moved, hadn't got in between Thesan and danger, the way he could and did if there was an actual threat. So Orion wasn't even capable of being a threat, now. A failure all round in a way that made him ache worse, like he'd lost something he really was never going to get back. Even if the rest of him knew he never wanted to threaten either of them. He looked back down at his lap. "I'll go." It came out quiet and sullen.

"No, you won't." Isembard's voice cut at him, as sharp and lethal as anything he'd ever seen his mentor do. "We're not letting you go off in this state."

Orion wanted to argue, but he was fairly sure if he tried, Isembard would actually take steps. And Isembard was miles and decades better than Orion at that. Also, he'd sat between Orion and Thesan, and between Orion and the door, both at the same time. He had tricks Orion had never learned, and he had the clear-headedness to use them when Orion got stroppy. And all right, he was talking himself into not even putting up a fight now. He turned his hands and set them on the table, both in their gloves, of course. Yielding silently, because he couldn't bring himself to talk.

"Take a breather for a minute." Isembard's voice had gone much gentler now, and that was almost worse. "And then we'll let Thesan explain it to both of us."

It was the 'both of us' that got Orion to look up, wide-eyed and startled. Very deliberate, because he could see them now, the way Isembard had meant that, had set that trap and lure so deftly. Thesan was smiling, but she didn't look upset. He took another long sip of the cider, then a bite or two of the crumble on his plate, before he managed a careful, "Please, Thesan. Would you explain it so I can understand it?"

That got a warm, beaming smile from her, the kind he got when he'd done the perfect thing. Not that that made any sense either. "You've got so much better at getting yourself out of holes, Orion." She let out a breath. "Hypatia's brilliant, yes. But she's had a lot of people assume they know more than she does. And your questions sound like more of that."

"Why is she making it that weird? That's not what I'm saying! It's not what I want to be saying." Then his chin came up. "Did people do that to you?" His astronomy - despite her best efforts - was adequate to the necessities of the magics he used, but not much more. He knew he couldn't follow a good three-quarters of what she did when it came to her own research, even in summary. His only comfort was that he was fairly sure Isembard only understood about half of it himself.

Thesan nodded. "Did. Do. Well, a bit less at the moment, but that's only because everyone's busy with the war. I'm sure when the war ends, it'll start up again." She said it like it was the sun rising in the east or setting in the west. "I learned to deal with it a long time ago. So did Hypatia."

"You don't talk about it." Orion was turning it over in his mind. She didn't. She talked about what she was doing, why she found it intriguing. Thesan would save up tidbits that were also interesting to whoever she was talking to. With Isembard, it was usually warding. Some of the maths around aiming things with Orion. He could repeat the maths once he understood how they worked. With Claudio, it was sometimes a bit of applied theory. Thesan loved finding the kind of thing that let Claudio pull together several strands of magic and do something useful, find the people who knew more of what he needed.

"Frankly? It's boring. And talking about it with you two isn't going to fix anything. Usually. Can you trust me when I tell you what she's hearing?" Thesan had her hands on the table now, leaning into them a little, like the moments in her teaching when she was most caught up in things. It would be foolish in a duel, showing your hand - metaphorically - that much. But here, it made him more sure she meant it.

He nodded slowly. "What do I do differently?"

"That is an excellent and sensible question." She paused, obviously hoping the praise would sink in a bit, rather than floating on the surface, like it did. He didn't move, and she went on. "I'd like to learn more about that, is there somewhere I should start? Or, let's see. I hadn't come across that before, now I'm curious. If you know about part of it, maybe, oh. I've read this thing by Horatio the Eldest, but this part I don't know about. Anything that acknowledges she knows what she's about. You don't have to make yourself sound stupid. That's not actually required for this to work."

That last bit made his mouth quirk up, almost in a smile. "Good. Though, I mean. I'm doing a good job at that. And that's really going to help?"

"Make it an experiment. Take notes. Try it my way for a week, or half a dozen of those discussions, whichever takes longer. Let me know how it goes. We'll write back."

Orion swallowed, then managed to look up at Isembard. He'd stayed quiet all through this, not interfering, not arguing, not poking at the sore spots. Now he turned his free hand - the other had slipped into Thesan's fingers - palm up. "I am too old and too tired to argue you into this. So it'd be a lot easier all round if you do a touch of scientific observation. I bet Thesan's right, though. She usually is about this sort of thing."

"Not going to fight you." Orion said it mostly to his plate. "Know better." And he certainly wasn't going to do things that made Isembard more tired. He could read the ongoing exhaustion there far too easily. There was grey in Isembard's hair now, and lines on his face that hadn't been there two years ago. Even four months ago.

"Good thing, too. I did think your duelling had recovered a lot today. You gave me a good run for it. Whatever you're doing isn't, I don't know. Making anything worse." Hearing that was, honestly, a relief. Orion hadn't been sure how he felt about any of it, but he could trust Isembard's evaluation. More than his own.

He managed another smile and a nod at that before he looked at Thesan again. "If someone does that to you, tries to claim you don't know what you're doing. After. I mean, if there's an after for me? Can I punch them then?"

It made her crack into a broad smile. "Punching is generally not the way we resolve academic disagreements, no matter how satisfying. But yes, should it become relevant, I will let you know and you and Isembard can decide on proper measures." She was teasing him, they all knew that, but she was so gentle about it he didn't mind. "You had three things."

"You said that." He tried not to sound grumpy again.

"Here, I am cheating. Claudio told me what his mother told you." Isembard leaned forward. "Council isn't everything, you know that. And I know it doesn't matter."

Orion could feel his shoulders stiffen. And worse, his

hand ache. "Sir." He didn't mean to be stroppy, but he could feel it coming out. "I knew he would."

"You're right, there's no open seat immediately likely. But if you want to give it a try, I'll back you. Alexander will back you." He tilted his head, glanced at his wife, and then added, "Decent chance Gabe would consider it."

"Edgarton? He's made his priorities very clear," Orion pointed out. "Whatever he might say to Claudio today." He wanted to know about that, rather badly, actually.

"His priorities do in fact include tormenting Claudio's mother. With purpose," Isembard pointed out. "I've got my reasons for thinking he'd consider it. You don't need to decide anything right now, just - know that there are some options. Depending on what you want."

There wasn't anything Orion had to say to that, so he just nodded in acknowledgement. "Third thing?"

"You haven't told them about your hand. Not any details. Even Claudio." That was Isembard again, his voice now a lot quieter. "I've got a salve for you. Might help a bit. And a couple of bottles of pastilles you can try. Helps the aches and pains, non-addictive. We've got a package of things for you to take back."

"I keep the glove on. Except when I'm actually bathing. Used to it by now." He was, that was the worst of it. He'd got used to never feeling anything with his remaining fingers on either hand, because it drew attention to have one glove on, and one off. "I'll try the whatever." Knowing the two of them, they'd put quite a bit of thought and favour trading into it. It must have taken a while to sort out, if they were only bringing it up now.

"To sweeten everything, I'll package up the rest of the crumble, bar some for Leo, and you can take it back. And I've got a few things for Hypatia and Cammie from Ibis and Pross. Another bottle of decent brandy, some better soap, lashings of Linta's herbal tisane that's got a flavour besides green." Thesan offered it, immediately.

That one made Orion laugh. "Not a cow myself, no. Why do the herbals have to taste like that? Is it all mint?"

"No, quite a nice blend, and there's dried fruit in it. Here, let me go pack things up, and then you can go down and see if you can catch Leo before Isembard walks you back to the portal. He'll be pleased to see you. I'll take your patrol, love." She stood up, kissed Isembard on the top of his head when she had the extra height to do it, and then went off humming to the tiny kitchen tucked into their quarters.

It wasn't as if he and Isembard talked much once they were walking back the mile or two to the portal in Schola village. But it was comfortable, not talking, in a way Orion had desperately needed. Just as much as he knew he'd needed the awful, complicated, lancing conversations they'd had tonight. He hoped he could do something to make both Isembard and Thesan proud of him. Not keep messing up in the same bloody ways, over and over.

CHAPTER 16
CLAUDIO, APRIL 14TH AT VERITAS IN KENT

Claudio came out of the portal at Veritas unsure what he was going to find. Veritas was one of the great demesne estates, of course, but not one Claudio had ever been to before. He was met by a woman of middle-age, perhaps five or ten years older than Claudio himself. She wore an aggressively neutral medium grey jacket and skirt over a white blouse. It was a uniform without being any of the current uniforms. Her dark hair was up in a tight bun, none of the waves or folds of the usual hairstyles among the ATS, with thick-glassed spectacles on her nose.

"Captain Warren? Penelope Edgarton is waiting. This way, please." She turned, without waiting for more than a nod of acknowledgement from Claudio. They walked in silence, though as they got close to the house, he could hear a slight wheeze in her breath. Once they were inside, she headed straight for a hallway, stopping and knocking on a wooden door.

"Yes?" The voice from inside was a pleasant inquiry,

not the sort of brusque response that Claudio had often heard from many people when interrupted. He'd expected to be kept waiting. A Fox probably would have done, just to make a point, but of course Edgarton was no Fox, never mind his family would imply otherwise.

"Captain Warren, sir." She opened the door at some signal Claudio didn't sense. Gabriel Edgarton sat behind a long wooden desk, wearing country tweeds. He might have looked entirely at leisure. But two-thirds of the desk held more or less tidy piles of files, papers, and books arranged along it, as if he were working on five or six different projects simultaneously. It made the leisure a visible lie.

"Thank you, Mirth." The man behind the desk offered a warm smile. "No interruptions unless it's urgent, please."

"By the usual standards, yes, sir." She disappeared before Claudio could figure out if there was a slight hint of something that might be amusement there.

Edgarton stood up, making a proper gesture. "Be welcome at Veritas, and I offer hospitality in my father's name." It was a peculiarly neutral form of ritual welcome, the most impeccably neutral, in fact, calling as it did on both sides to honour those implicit and explicit expectations. It made it clear, too, that Edgarton was his father's heir, not the Lord here, with all that meant.

Claudio nodded, giving the expected reply. "I appreciate and honour your hospitality." He could match that formality, even if he hadn't quite expected it. Manners, yes, but Mother complained on the regular about Edgarton's informality.

To his surprise, Edgarton didn't sit down. "Coffee? Herbal tisane? Spot of wine?" It was four, and Claudio had been wondering all day if the suggested time was for the liminal nature of things, or something else. Edgarton went on as if he were reading Claudio's mind, and he could see why the rest of the Council thought he could. "I wasn't sure how long your question would take. We dine after sunset on Fridays, but that gives us some flexibility."

Given that they'd just moved onto Double Summer Time, near four and a half hours. Surely the man didn't mean that. The comment seemed to come out of nowhere, and Claudio felt his metaphorical footing begin to slide away from him. Claudio had expected thirty minutes, maybe an hour. Edgarton had no reason to do him any favours.

He cleared his throat. "Coffee, if you don't mind. Council Member." His mother would have been horrified to hear him addressed as Penelope. She considered the title of Council Member to be the greatest in Albion. This man disagreed with her on that and on quite a number of other things.

Edgarton could have offered half a dozen locations for this meeting. A meeting room in the Council Keep had too much chance of Claudio's mother. Claudio would have declined that anyway. But they might have met at one of their clubs in Trellech. He knew the Edgartons had a townhouse there. There was even Edgarton's office in among the halls of the Penelopes, though that was some-where else Claudio had never been.

Instead, Edgarton had chosen this office, which was decorated in shades of woodland greens and browns, with highlights of wheat-gold. It had a warmth to it Claudio hadn't expected, and a comfort. The desk chair was well designed, there was a sofa behind it, under the window, that looked pleasant to lie on. Bookshelves lined the rest of the room, obviously used regularly. Edgarton nodded, and turned to a small cabinet with a tray on top, pouring coffee into two mugs. "Black?"

Not offered any of the dairy or sugar ration, no. And he wouldn't ask. Though Edgarton didn't add any to his own cup, either. "That's fine, sir." Something in the response made Edgarton half-smile again. He gestured Claudio into the chair beside him, and took his own again, with no sound of a creak.

They sat in silence for about twenty seconds, before Edgarton took pity. Or that's what it felt like. "I gather you have something you particularly want to ask me about. I should tell you I am used to collaborating on consultations, but I do, of course, respect the necessary oaths on confidential materials or war secrets. And..." Here, the quirk of the mouth turned into a smile. "I will leave it up to you how much you wish to annoy your mother. Much as I consider that a hobby, these days."

It was not the done thing to lay it out like that. Claudio found him, honestly, as disarming as Thesan was in a number of Council social situations, though he came at it entirely differently. Perhaps from the same seed, though, of being so confident in their chosen work that the opinions of people outside of that didn't matter much. Edgarton had been one of the Penelopes for two decades. He was one of those who sorted out magical problems and unwove tangled magic. They fixed the apparently unfixable when other people's experimentation or greed or carelessness got beyond them.

Only, he would have thought that the Council itself would be included in Edgarton's work, at least these days. He was not sure he was spotting evidence of it on the table. Edgarton'd made a spectacular challenge for his seat in 1940. Claudio's mother had been - and still was - furious at how that had played out, though she wasn't foolish enough to be obstructive without justification. Whenever she'd complained about Edgarton - which she did quite regularly - she'd go on about a lack of respect for tradition.

Except, Claudio could tell, here and now, that was all nonsense. He could feel the traditions here. It was an ancient estate, stretching back to the Romans. He'd never been invited here before, and he was fairly sure Mother hadn't been either. But he could feel the roots of it, the comfortable certainty of it. The Council dances did their best to recreate this particular feel at each solstices, and the Edgartons lived and breathed it, so far as Claudio could tell. He knew Edgarton was good at his work, but the feel of the place and, even more, how Edgarton was acting, actually gave Claudio some hope that this conversation might be a help.

Mother would have noted every place where power rested, and every place it might flow. She'd have established her own station and role from the start. Edgarton was doing none of that, the very feel of the room was even. Edgarton had every right to turn this into a power play, with Claudio in the middle. Mother would have, if it served her goals, and it probably would. Edgarton apparently had no interest in even setting that up as an option. Claudio had no idea what to make of it; he felt almost as if Edgarton were speaking Arabic as fluently as Hypatia and Cammie did. He took a breath, and tried to match the mode as best he could. "It is surely not a surprise if I tell you it is quite a successful hobby." He wasn't sure, as it was coming out of his mouth, exactly what made him say that. Mother would be furious if she found out. For all it was entirely true.

Edgarton grinned, suddenly, a flash of real amusement. "I am glad to hear you say so. Before we get into your question, let me assure you the warding here is superb, but you are welcome to check it yourself. I can summon Mirth or someone else in the offices next door if needed, but no sound will carry."

"Mistress Mirth was very formal, sir." Claudio took a breath and trusted that flash of intuition again. "As I'm sure you told her to be."

"And you have excellent manners. Not that I'd have expected anything less. I do respect your mother's very real skills, for the record. And, of course, yours." Edgarton leaned forward. "Check the wards."

Claudio pushed back in the chair, standing. He knew people who were good enough to feel this sitting, lying, likely doing handstands. He needed his feet under him, his weight between them, to balance his magic against the warding. What he found was elegantly formed, smooth, done with certainty and experience. And he knew at least some of the signature behind it. "Professor Fortier?" He'd be formal here.

"Isembard and Thesan are both friends and welcome guests here. Besides the astronomy and the duelling, we do have children the same age." Edgarton was leaning back now, looking entirely relaxed, as if something in that had given him a key piece of information for a particular puzzle.

"He didn't say. Hasn't said. Beyond the ordinary sort of social comments." Claudio certainly didn't expect that Isembard and Thesan told him all they did in a day. That was ridiculous. It hadn't been true even when he'd stayed with them during summer hols, or brief breaks in his apprenticeship. They hadn't lied to him, though, either, as he thought back on it. Just let him make the assumptions that made sense at the time. Then Claudio sat, managing not to thump down in the chair, despite the way he was desperately off balance now. "And this is a different kind of duel, of course."

"To be fair, I think the third thing I said to Isembard when we met in more intimate conversation was asking whether he'd duel me. But yes. I was interested when you wrote to arrange this. We will have a much better time of it on our own terms, leaving all the usual expectations of how this should go to one side."

Claudio let out a long breath. "Sir. What form of address would you prefer, then?"

"Gabe, if you can bring yourself to it. Edgarton is fine if you can't. It does quite well in most circumstances." Edgarton leaned back, picking up his coffee.

"Erm. Yes. I know you've made all the oaths on secrecy, but the work, the thing I need to ask you about." Claudio couldn't figure out how to finish that sentence. He felt like a stripling schoolboy again, rather than a grown man who had some fair competence of his own to draw on.

"On the Silence, I, Gabriel Anthony Edgarton, swear and affirm to hold secret those things said here, binding them up with my other oaths." He said the ritual words lightly enough, but Claudio got a flash of enormous coiling power behind them. There was something that held the potent fear of any Silence oath, but had flashes of black and iridescent green and a sharp edge to it that Claudio had never seen before.

"Thank you, sir." Claudio let out a long breath. "Our project deals with, for lack of a better word, creating magical distractions. Things that the German magical folk would read as the movement of troops, planes, ships, all of that. I know that you have been working on related projects for years, and I could not think of anyone better to ask."

"Despite knowing what your mother thinks of me." Edgarton's mouth quirked up, as if he were very bad at keeping a straight face. "What would your father have made of me, do you think?"

That made Claudio laugh, almost despite himself. "Mother's frustrated and furious at you. Father would have wanted to destroy you." He sucked in a breath. "I'm beginning to think he wouldn't have succeeded, to be honest. And that..." Oh, this was heresy, by every form of belief his parents had taught him, but it was also true. "I think you might be right in what you're doing."

That got another flash of genuine smile. "I asked Isembard about you, when you wanted to see me. I know, of course, how well he thinks of you. And no one he speaks of like that has been a disappointment in my experience. You especially, though, I think. You and your chosen brother." He said that very gently and Claudio's hands clenched once.

Orion was with Isembard and Thesan, or at least had been today. Probably still was, getting time to talk to them that wasn't purely about the driving demands of their project. His brother needed that desperately, even more than Claudio did, and Claudio wouldn't permit himself jealousy over it.

"Sir." It came out in something that might have been a prayer, if Claudio had been an entirely different sort of man. But his family were not made for prayers, they were not made for the land magic, not in generations. They were made for the Council, in one form or another, and that was a complicated sort of power. He'd known that from the time he was toddling around, some of his first memories were of being taught how to behave among people who thought like that.

Here, he'd walked into some alternate realm. Not a Fatae realm. Claudio knew the wisps of what that tasted and felt like, if he got too close. But something else, and he didn't know how to weigh what his senses were telling him. "And that's why you agreed to see me?" He didn't want pity, not like that.

"If you had been many other men, I'd have met with you somewhere else. Maybe in my office among the Penelopes, or at the Council Keep, or perhaps the Trellech townhouse. I'd have given you the information you wanted. But it would be a very different sort of conversation. Isembard's good word meant I - hmm. I wanted to see what you would make of opportunities presented. Not just what, but how." Edgarton flicked his fingers.

"You have been respectful of me, which doesn't matter so much, and also been polite to Mirth, and respected the land, which does. You have the right feel in your bones, you don't assume you know what you're sensing. That's rare enough." He shrugged once. "You'd have made a fine Penelope, actually, I suspect, if you'd been allowed to make that choice."

Claudio couldn't breathe, couldn't move, at that. It was as if a bomb had dropped directly on top of him, and his mind hadn't realised he was dead yet. Edgarton had said it with that mix of weight and levity that had danced through this conversation, as if it were nothing and everything. It turned Claudio's world upside down. His father had disparaged the Penelopes, though he'd given them due courtesy in public. Mother had started out more neutral, but she found them - all of them, now - frustrating, and Edgarton most of all.

"They say you read minds, you know." It came out before Claudio could quite stop himself. "I'm fairly sure you do, now."

That got an open laugh, one like Thesan's, that invited him in. It wasn't mocking or humiliating or condescending. Then Edgarton spread his hands out. "I can suggest some reading in your infinite free time. When the war's done, if you'd like to consider a new line of work, we'd be willing to talk to you about what it would take. With appropriate modifications to the apprenticeship for what you already know."

Claudio found himself looking at a spot on the desk, near the edge closest to him. "Why would you even offer that?" He had no doubt that Edgarton had the right to make the offer. There had been no hesitation. But did that mean Edgarton had discussed him with other Penelopes? The mere thought was overwhelming.

"Because curious and creative minds are rather rare. Because you're not nearly as stuck up as you look. Because you've demonstrated a sufficient range of your skills. There's going to be a lot of dangerous magic to undo in the wake of the war, if we win it. We could use more competent hands for that work." A slight pause, and then a cheerful, "And all right, your mother would have to deal with a number of things she's refusing to think about. I'm quite sure that would be good for her. Eventually. But it'd be better for you, and for us. I care more about that."

"She thinks you have no ambition." Claudio said. He had to know that, Edgarton had to. "You have a great many, don't you. To reshape the Council. Reshape everything they touch. You touch."

Edgarton spread his hands out, palm up, a gesture of gathering in. "That's what we do. Penelopes. Unweave tangles so we can weave ahead some more. Besides, it's the best sort of puzzle, doing something that matters."

Utterly foreign to Claudio and to all his family, but Claudio could see some of the appeal. He took a breath, feeling his shoulders lift, then let it out. "I would very much like your help with our current puzzle. Now you've given me something to think about for months." He would too.

And he'd eventually talk it out with Orion, though he had no idea how to even start that conversation.

Talking about what he'd come for actually went remarkably smoothly. Claudio set out the limitations, both of the magical skills on their end, and the ones related to timing and materia available. Edgarton asked dozens of precise questions, about what they'd already explored, about what they'd considered and discarded, about how they'd gone at the conversations.

By an hour into their talk, Edgarton had got up and pulled a hidden blackboard out from behind one of the shelves, covering the window. He filled it with chalk to outline half a dozen different places to focus on. Claudio was kept busy scribbling down everything, hoping desperately he'd remember enough of what they were working through.

That was the thing. It wasn't just Edgarton lecturing, or telling Claudio what to do. Though if he'd done that, Claudio would have listened. He wasn't fool enough to ignore an expert at his best. But no, Edgarton led Claudio through it, piece by piece, explaining whenever Claudio didn't make a connection on his own. None of it was condescending, none of it made him feel bad for not knowing something yet. Like his father had, or his mother did. Instead, it was a constant sense of discovery, of bouncing ideas against others, and seeing what emerged.

Like Claudio had done with Orion, since his third year at Schola. Like they did now. Like the two of them were starting to do with Cammie and Hypatia if they could avoid getting into arguments. Going at it like this, Claudio felt he could almost grasp how to take this mode there, and make it work. Maybe. If he got unreasonably lucky. It was an entirely new way of looking at the world, though not, in the end, so distant from what Isembard had shown him over the years.

That one was going to keep him up at night for weeks to come, actually. How the influences ran, where they began. What would happen if Edgarton got his way, and remade the whole proud sharp ambitious Council into something more like this.

The two of them went on and on, through a clock chiming the hour twice more. Finally, Edgarton came up for breath. "Enough to be going on with?" Claudio's wrist ached. He had run out of paper twice and had been given two different chunks of loose paper shoved into order. "Write if you can't remember something, I can likely reconstruct it." Then he shook his shoulders out. "Stay for supper, or do you need to get back?"

With a start, Claudio remembered that Orion would be back himself, sometime. "I should..." Then he swallowed. "I wouldn't want to put you out. Or your ration books."

"I let Cook know we might have an extra for supper. Our home farm's still going well. It'll be mostly root vegetables from the stores, but that's fine." Edgarton said it easily. "Not a lot of us tonight. My parents, my wife, our two daughters." He glanced at a set of lights above the door to the hallway, as if checking on something. "Rowena, our eldest, is apprenticing with her mother. Avigail's a year from Schola, like Leo Fortier. She's looking forward to following our Anthony there. The food won't be fancy, but more good conversation."

Claudio took a deep breath. "I'd be honoured." Then, tentatively, he added, "Gabe." Edgarton - Gabe - smiled warmly, waved a hand to dismiss the wards with a precision like a brisk breeze. Then Claudio was shown to their dining room, with a quick pause in the library for a dozen books on loan and a bag to carry them in.

The supper that followed was exactly like eating with Isembard and Thesan. The meal was full of conversation, side explanations, and references to things Claudio knew and things he had no clue about. Gabe walked him to the portal after the meal finished, near enough ten at night. Claudio's head was spinning in ways it would take ages to make any sense of, and he didn't mind at all.

CHAPTER 17
CAMMIE, APRIL 15TH AT CAMP GRIFFISS, THREE MILES AWAY.

The dance was everything Cammie had expected, good and bad. What seemed like thousands of people crammed into two big halls near each other. There were two bands going, one in each hall, with the space between them a competing cacophony made up of two sets of music, and dozens of accents, some of them mutually unintelligible. To Cammie's right, she could hear someone whose first language had to be Scots trying to talk to someone with a deeply Southern American drawl. They weren't making much headway.

She kept a close eye on Hypatia. It turned out her sister had mostly missed out on this part of being an ATS girl by being in with magical folks. Cammie actually liked a dance. That was the thing of it. What she didn't like was having to navigate American assumptions about the colour of her skin and how her accent didn't match anything they expected. But the dancing was grand, once she got someone willing. She was delighted to give herself over to the joy of the music, and a change was as good as a rest.

That was how the saying went. And she was as human as the next woman. She liked being flattered.

The other thing she hated, though, was the expectations of the ATS girls at these things. Even though they'd put in a full day's work, they were expected to turn up clean and shining, lipstick and stockings - or the illusion of them - and hair all done to perfection. And then they were supposed to be cheerful and bright, chatty. But of course also not at all tawdry or letting the men get away with things they ought not to be trying. It was a balancing act Cammie was quite good at by now, but that didn't mean she wouldn't rather be doing something else. Charming a small group, for example, was much more her speed. Other than the dancing.

It had also been an odd and confusing day, and she was still trying to figure that out. Both Claudio and Orion had been gone most of Friday, all afternoon and late into the evening. They'd not got back until nearly ten. This morning, they'd refused to talk about it, maybe even with each other, just made the tea and got to work.

All four of them had made good progress, actually, though Orion kept looking up, opening his mouth, closing it, and going back to whatever was on his desk. Tonight, they'd both come along in the truck with the others from the camp, mostly secretaries, also ATS girls, but half a dozen other officers. Someone had pulled the men away almost immediately, leaving Cammie and Hypatia to sort themselves out.

Now, Cammie was trying to figure out how to get a drink, and then maybe a dance. All of a sudden, though, she saw an arm waving across the path before a bright ginger head was coming her way. "Cammie! It is you! Are you posted here, then? Do say it's true. I was wondering if you got sent northwest. No one knew where you'd been

posted." It was followed immediately by the kind of energetic hug Cammie tried not to give other people. It left her
breathless.

It took her a moment, then she managed to get Hypatia, who was looking alarmed. "This is Alice. We were in
training together. Alice, this is my sister, Hypatia."

"She said so much about you! And also not a lot about
you! You know how Cammie is." Alice went burbling on,
cheerfully talking about when Cammie had got someone
out of a closet she'd got locked in accidentally. And that
time with the sudden thunderstorm and all their washing
out to dry, and all the other stories of their training. All the
while dragging Cammie with one hand off to a corner by
one of the makeshift dance halls. There was a group of
other ATS women there. A couple were sitting like people
who'd been on their feet all day already, and the half a
dozen men looking for a dance did not appear to have
noticed that.

"This is Cammie! We trained together. She's grand.
You still dance, don't you? And this is - how do you say it?
Hypatia. Sister."

"By choice, my Mum's married to her older brother,
but, well. Near enough the same age, we get on." Cammie
offered the explanation, which sorted the puzzled faces.
Then she nodded. "I'd like a dance. Any of you fine
soldiers want to see what we can do?" One of them, a
dark-haired man, spun her out into a bit of open space,
and Cammie let herself fall into the music. She had to
concentrate, not just because of the uneven ground and
the competing bands, but because there were people all
over.

Her partner of the moment, though, was a fine dancer,
and once they got each other's measure, they began getting
a good bit more acrobatic about it. He didn't go so far as to

try a flip. There wasn't enough space for that, but plenty of fast kicks and playing off each other's steps. When the music came to the end, there was an arc of people standing back watching them, and a round of applause. Cammie made a bob of acknowledgement, held up the drink she'd been handed, and called out, "To a grand night on our feet!"

There were laughs all around, and the music picked up again. Cammie got about three sips before she got swung into another dance with barely enough time to hand the drink off to Hypatia. From there, she got glimpses, now and again, of her sister and the other women.

She moved from dance partner to dance partner until she was entirely out of breath. "Give me a minute, gentlemen. Even an ATS girl can't run forever on a few sips of beer." That got a laugh, and she made her way to the necessary to wash her hands and give herself a moment.

Or that had been the plan. But when she was in the hut, she picked up a scent, and it wasn't what she expected. It crossed over all the ordinary human scents. Cammie ducked out of the hut, around to the side, then considered her options. There was a nice dark corner there, a bit of a 'nothing to look at here' charm, and she could make use of that. A minute later, she was on four feet in the shadow of the building and the scrub grass, and she could figure out who that was.

She was fairly sure it was a 'who', too. Another shifter. What self-respecting mustelid would come this close to so many people if they weren't also one? She sniffed again. Male, and likely a weasel. Ah, well, stoats were bigger than weasels, and she'd take that advantage. She went off around the back edges of the building, trying to get the most recent scent and sign.

Here, here, no, not that way. Here. Here. Then

Cammie spotted him. Yep, him. Yes, weasel. He was sitting up on his hind legs, listening intently, as if to conversations in one of the nearby huts. She couldn't hear them, not where she was, but that didn't matter. A weasel listening like that meant nothing good, and she ought to know.

She considered her options. She could shift, but that would be enough noise to alert both this weasel and whoever was inside. The latter might be fine, but it might not be. Well, no time like the present. Cammie slunk her way closer, settled back on her haunches, and then pounced, coming down on top of the weasel-man with her teeth buried in the nape of his neck.

She couldn't get a really good grip. She wasn't trying to kill him, just disable him. He was, in fact, a little smaller than she was, in this form, and she used her length and weight to get them rolling forward, scrabbling. She wouldn't let go. He couldn't break free, though now, of course, they were causing plenty of noise. Cammie had a lousy sense of time on four paws at the best of times, and a fight always altered time, as surely as any bit of astronomical magic.

A tumble here, he tried to shake her off, then brush her off against the corner of a hut. She clung on, digging her teeth in. He tasted foul. She suspected some sort of unsavoury potions, on top of whatever else he did with his time. She didn't exactly have a goal here, just not to let him get away.

Before she could bring it to a standstill, just as she was beginning to get somewhere, there were hands reaching down and picking her up by the scruff of her neck. She lashed out, trying to get away, before she got leather gloves, a scent she knew, and she screeched in fury, striking out with her teeth. Worse luck, she got the edge of the glove, a bit into his wrist, before he shook his hand, and she went flying and somersaulting away.

The weasel was well and truly gone, though she'd got enough of his scent she'd know him again. Now she had two problems. First, she had to get out of sight long enough to shift back and redo her hair. And second, to figure out why Orion had been right there at exactly the wrong time. She let the motion take her rolling and bounding under one of the huts, along one edge back into a wood pile - mice, no time for mice now. They scattered. She kept going, hopping and weaving from building to building until she'd put distance behind her.

Her next job was to circle back to where the music was, and she did that bit by bit, much more slowly. It was unlikely anyone had been watching her. Also she was more fully into her summer coat, and well, she wasn't anywhere one might look for wildlife on the average Saturday. But if they could see her, they'd have seen her look like a stoat. For all their vibrant acrobatics, stoats also could be very patient.

She could be very patient. It took her another three songs or so, but then she was back near enough the latrines. Another two songs got her in position where she could come out. She'd managed to find where Hypatia'd got to. Dancing with someone, a slower dance, though there was plenty of space between them.

Cammie ducked behind a storage hut, made sure there wasn't anyone around for those crucial thirty seconds until she could layer another charm or three. She managed it, did the charms, and then spent a couple of minutes patting her hair back in place, checking her clothes, doing it all by feel and habit. At least getting dressed in the dark far too often had some virtues when it came to this sort of thing. Her lipstick was gone, but there was no helping that, and there were plenty of other reasons for it. She hadn't drawn blood except a few drops from Orion.

Right. Next stage of the stalking. Cammie strolled out past the end of the latrine, sliding into a group of people dancing, before she let the charms drop and joined in. A dance later, she turned up by Hypatia. She was about to say something, when there was a voice from behind her. "You two mind if we drag you away for the evening? We thought we'd walk back, no ride for a bit." Claudio's voice, smooth and even. It was the sort of false smoothness that made her sure something else had been going on, and she had no idea what.

Cammie turned. "Both of us?" She made it into pure innocence, and she thought it worked. Though it was hard to tell with Claudio and Orion, they were good at not showing their thoughts at all. Or, at least, Claudio was good at it, and Orion was good at looking grumpy regardless of what he was actually thinking. Though he was particularly so at the moment.

"If you don't mind. There's something we want to get an early start on in the morning." It wasn't an order, though Claudio could have made it one. He ranked both of them, and he was nominally in charge of this project. There was something in the absolute flat politeness that made Cammie give in.

"Of course. Hypatia, are you ready? Need to grab anything?"

Hypatia turned and looked Cammie up and down, then shook her head. "Everything I need." Both of them made the proper show and then the men walked them back toward the entrance to the camp, checking out as they left. The walk back was not horrid - almost pleasant - but the four of them walked in near total silence, as if no one wanted to attempt to make ordinary conversation.

CHAPTER 18
HYPATIA, LATER THAT NIGHT

Once they got back to their huts - their dark, too-quiet huts - Cammie grimaced and began working her way out of her uniform. "Do you think someone's going to come wonder at us why we're not at whatever the local church services are? Now they've remembered we exist? Or notice?"

"Ugh." Hypatia worked her fingers down her own buttons. "Do you have a clean shirt for tomorrow? I can throw yours in the laundry if you do."

Cammie nodded. "Do." She tossed it over, and Hypatia tucked it into the laundry bag with her own. "So long as I keep the jacket on." She eyed the shirt hanging up, which had an odd stain on it.

"What on earth did you get into with that? It looks like turmeric, of all things. Hand it over, let me see if I can get one of the stain removal charms to work." A moment later, Hypatia had cloth in her hands. She rummaged in her trunk and brought out her sewing and cleaning kit. "Can you look at my shoes? You're better with them."

Cammie nodded, changing into her nightgown with a

smock over it for protection before pulling out her shoe kit, grabbing both pairs of shoes. She settled down on the floor, spreading out the protective cloth to avoid getting polish everywhere. Hypatia let her get into it before she said, "Where were you, when you were gone?"

"When did you notice?" Cammie didn't look up, and Hypatia knew that was intentional.

"I was watching you dancing, then you weren't dancing, then you disappeared. I could feel where your stone was, near enough. About how far. I wasn't entirely sure that was going to work."

Cammie did look up at that. Then she swore energetically and at some considerable length in Arabic. Hypatia considered the warding and added another layer for good measure. "What happened?" she repeated, when Cammie's line of invective had run down.

"I need to figure out how to report something. We. Because I'm hoping you'll help." Cammie looked up, and Hypatia hadn't seen her look like that for ages. Near two decades, not since Cammie had started at Schola and been a lost little firstie. She'd done away with that look by the middle of October, and Hypatia hadn't seen it since. Though, to be fair, she hadn't seen Cammie in her apprenticeship, or her ATS intake, or a number of other places.

"Of course I'll help." Hypatia didn't have to think about that. She would. Whatever it was, she'd be right there. This one, whatever it was, disturbed Cammie, in a way that went beyond her usual flicks of intense focus followed by a burst of action. More than anything else, she wanted to know what had happened, and the fastest route to that was helping.

Cammie nodded, leaning her back against the bed frame, one shoe in her lap, as she worked on polishing it. "There was a weasel there. A shifter. Male, I'd know his scent now. But what was a shifter doing, skulking around a US Army base? In Richmond."

Hypatia was about to say something, opened her mouth to start, then snapped her teeth together. "You didn't, Cammie. Go after him, I mean."

"Bigger than he was." Cammie said it with the sort of stubborn bravado that Hypatia had honestly expected. Cammie liked a fight. Not like Orion liked a fight, though now she'd got that idea in her head she was going to have to analyse it properly. Why Cammie was fine, and Orion drove her up a wall, over a fence, down a tunnel, and into a well. "I did."

Hypatia sighed and leaned her head back against the wall, trying to figure out where to start. "So. You found a shifter eavesdropping. You don't know who, and you know for sure he's a shifter because you were a stoat at the time." She let out her own line of swearing now, the sort that Ummi would be horrified by. Ibis, too.

"Can't tell the men, because they don't know. I don't think Junior Commander Roberts knows about shifters. I pay attention, you know?"

"Since Ibis has been clear about what the military thinks of the skill. And more to the point, what they do with it." And Cammie was perfectly positioned to be turned into a combatant, in that particular and terrifying way. She could get into small spaces, she could defend herself quite well, considering. Small predatory land mammals were the most versatile when it came to combat. She'd heard Ibis's lectures, just as Cammie had. "Bloody hell, you like making things complicated."

Cammie's hands twitched before she dropped them in her lap, looking down. Not meeting Hypatia's eyes.

Hypatia frowned. "Tell it me from when you left the dancing. Which was grand, and you know it. I'd love to see you with someone you know." Cammie looked up at that, the sort of sharp look that was all stoat and not much woman, and Hypatia reconsidered a number of calculations. "Tell me the sequence first, then I've got something else."

"Bossy." It was an old teasing comment, without any heat. Truth be told, Cammie was the bossier one, almost all the time, but Hypatia was more often right, and they both knew it. "I was dancing. I took a break, I got a whiff of weasel."

"Less in the way of alliteration, more in the way of explanation, please." Hypatia hesitated, then picked up the shirt. She used the pipette in the bottle in her kit to dampen the stain with a few drops of potion, then call the charm to her fingers and work the fabric through them.

"Anyway. I was in the hut with the necessary, and it was strong enough there to get past the people being human." Cammie's shoulder twitched. "So I shifted, circled around until I caught up to him, and he was listening, really intently, to a conversation in one of the huts."

"Could you pin down which one, if you had a map?" Hypatia was thinking through the implications. Spying, that was what came to mind first, and that was a whole host of problems. "I have a sense which direction you went from where we were."

Cammie cocked her head. "Probably. Might take me a bit. Anyway, there he was, lurking. There I was, pouncing. I didn't actually want to kill him. I could have. It's much harder not to." She sounded entirely put out about it, and that, well, was never a problem Ibis had had to deal with directly. "Anyway, we were going head over tail. I almost had him, and then someone picked me up by the scruff and he got away." She waited a beat. "Orion. I bit him."

"You didn't. Oh, Cammie." Hypatia dropped the shirt

in her lap, and buried her face in her hands. "Good grief. Of all the people." Then she peered over her fingers. "You really bit him?"

"He deserves it, the way he's been treating you. Even if he didn't actually do anything today. Which makes me suspicious. Why didn't he?" Cammie crossed her arms, and where most women would have looked faintly ridiculous, Cammie looked just as fierce as when she had four feet. "Anyway, I bit him, drew blood, I didn't actually hurt him. I'm not that careless. And he dropped me and I took off. Took me a while, five songs, maybe half an hour, to circle back? And they came up and found us, almost immediately after that."

Hypatia closed her eyes, trying to think. "So. They were behaving oddly all day. Why were they over where you found him listening? Was he listening to them, do you think? And did they track you back, by the stone?"

"There would be an analytical paper in tracking sympathetic magic talismans through shape shifting, except, of course, that we can't actually talk about any of that. I certainly don't know if we can trust them to tell them. For one thing, you know what that sort thinks about shifters, almost all the time."

Hypatia let out a huff. "Yeah." She knew Isembard knew about Ibis, for reasons Ibis had never properly explained. And that both men were comfortable with it, enough that Ibis occasionally helped place small warding stones in places no human could reach. Cammie had done the same and quite a few times. She could climb far better than a hedgehog, and she'd helped place some warding stones up on the top of the castle, all along the curtain wall roof. But that didn't mean Claudio and Orion would be as reasonable. They couldn't take the risk. "And for the other, they were being decidedly odd today. Even before the part tonight."

"You were paying a lot of attention to them today. Especially Orion." Cammie said it almost casually. Too casually.

"Because he was being extremely odd. You saw him. He kept opening his mouth, and then shutting it. He didn't even try to argue with me once. Or monologue, either, though those are fine in moderation." Hypatia frowned. "It's not like him." She had kept watching him, though. Something about him was annoyingly compelling, like there was a resonance there that she couldn't make any sense of.

"Maybe he had a hangover. No. I can't imagine Thesan and Isembard would let him drink that much. Not without sending off a potion with him." Cammie picked up one of the shoes again, and the soft sounds of brushing and polishing resumed.

"I can see them letting him get drunk, if it might do some good. But you're right. They'd sober him up or send him off with a potion. And it was a Friday, Thesan had class after, so we can bet she didn't drink much." That was the thing about Schola. Anyone paying any attention at all, especially if they knew the professors as actual people rather than terrifying figures from adolescence, got to know their habits. "The crumble was amazing, mind."

"And he was generous about sharing that out. More than he needed to be." That was another example of the thing. Orion kept confusing her. It wasn't just the arguing. She felt she had a handle on that. It was the way the arguing got balanced by those gestures of sharing out a good moment, in a way men like him almost never did. Orion didn't do it with Claudio's manners, the way Claudio made the gesture into something graceful. Orion's offers were as likely to be gruff as elegant. Rough-hewn, for all he'd grown up in just as much privilege. Or so she assumed, anyway, given he held the land magic now, and he'd been his father's heir.

"You don't know what to do with him, do you?" Cammie's voice was quieter now. "He's doing his fair share of the work. They both are. They're not implying we ought to clean or keep track of things for them. They fetch the food most of the time, they do their own share of cleaning the workroom." None of which was entirely expected.

Hypatia took a breath. "No. I don't. I was thinking, earlier, how he likes a fight. Like you do, but not like you do, and you do not send me up a tree with it, and he does." She shrugged. "Not going to solve that one tonight. We do need to figure out something about the weasel. On the list of difficult, complicated men, he's the one to actually worry about."

Cammie nodded. "Write Ibis? I can do it in code in the journal first thing tomorrow. It'll be Sunday. He should see it promptly enough. I don't know what they're doing at that camp there, but there's an awful lot of them, aren't there? Thousands, and we didn't know about it until this week."

"To be fair, we've only been here a month today." Hypatia pointed out. Someone had to be the voice of comparative reason, and as usual, she was the one appointed, elected, and stuck with it. "Write to Ibis, and see if he can tell you who to talk to." It wasn't a great solution, but great solutions, even reasonably good ones, did not seem on offer. "And the men?"

"Not going to tell them. Not unless there's some compelling reason, and this isn't it. Besides. If Orion keeps being difficult, I'd like to keep my options open for being difficult right back."

Hypatia snorted at that. "When you put it like that." She hesitated. "I don't hate him. He's not like Virgil."

"Or much like what was his name. Cadwallader. Who was a cad. Don't you argue about it." Cammie had entirely too good a memory for Hypatia's failings when it came to romance. On the other hand, that was a traditional role of a sister, to be vengeful about such things on her behalf. Just, Cammie did get fierce and focused about it in a way that wasn't good for anyone. Especially Cammie. "What do you think of Orion?"

"Sublimely irritating. Fairly sure he practises. Come on, I need to rinse this out. See if it takes the stain with it. Can I put the shoes out to air now?"

Cammie could tell when Hypatia was done talking about a topic, at least. She stood, then brought the shoes out to where they could air out nicely in the front room. By the time Hypatia had rinsed out the shirt and hung it up with a bit of a drying charm to help it along, Cammie was wriggling her way under the covers and reaching for her book. It had, in fact, been a long day. And there was more of that to come.

CHAPTER 19

ORION, THAT EVENING IN THEIR SLEEPING HUT

Orion made it into the hut without losing his grip on his emotions, mostly by shoving them ruthlessly aside. He'd had plenty of practice with that all his life. The dance had been too much, in every way he could think of. Bouncing along in a noisy truck, with a horde of chattering men and women, only three of whom he knew at all, had been a poor start. Then there'd been the competing bands, the people shouting over them, the way the music had reverberated against the metal roofs of the huts.

He'd taken some of the pastilles Isembard had given him. A moderate dose, but it had helped in ways he didn't have a name for. Orion had read the labels, but he knew well enough that Isembard wouldn't give him anything addictive. Except, well. The low grinding awareness of being broken and the dull ache of his hand had lifted. It meant his head had more space for everything else.

Not that it had been much use that evening. No one had wanted to dance with him, not that he'd expected that.

Here, he didn't even have the women who would hold their noses for a chance with a Lord. Certainly no one who'd choose to be with him without that.

There were far more men than women, anyway. Cammie had looked grand, but he was nowhere near her skill level, hadn't ever been. And Hypatia had been sitting with a knot of other women. It wasn't like he could have gone and interrupted without making it something notable. He'd had to peel off, after a bit, to find a bit of quiet, and that was when it had all got worse. When he'd noticed something off, but couldn't figure out why, or what, or who.

Claudio came in the door behind him. "Pour you a glass." It wasn't a question so much as giving Orion the chance to object.

He let out a huff of breath. Orion had checked the potions and pastilles Isembard had given him. Moderate alcohol was fine. Though Isembard knew him, it wasn't like that hadn't already been accounted for. "Please. Do we still have some of the whiskey?"

"I'll see." Claudio went over to their makeshift drinks cabinet and bookshelf in the front room, and Orion continued down the hall, frowning. Both his hands hurt, and he was going to have to make sure he knew all of why. And he couldn't think of a way to do that without Claudio getting a look. Animal bites could fester fast, he knew he'd lost sensation along the edge of his mangled hand, and if he'd been bit there, he needed to know. He called over his shoulder, "Can you grab the first aid kit, too?"

Then he was slowly pulling off his jacket, hanging it up, as if taking care now would mean his hands were both all right. There wasn't much blood, but he could see a few spots on his shirt. He'd have to figure out how to get that out. He was peeling out of the shirt when Claudio came in, a glass in each hand. Claudio set them down on the tables by each bed, not saying anything.

Orion swallowed. "Need your help for a minute, do you mind?" His voice near cracked on the last word, and he had to look away.

"Of course. What with?" Claudio's voice was even, the sort of deliberately even that meant he was worried, and not saying anything about his worries. He was shoving them all aside the way Orion shoved his anger and frustration and pent-up demands.

"The stoat got me. Need to check it didn't get my left hand." That probably wasn't clear enough. "The parts I can't feel well." He didn't want to think about diseases, most of them weren't likely, surely. Not in Albion.

"Oh." There was silence, then. Claudio was a bit behind him to the left. Then, carefully, like the moment was something fragile that could shatter, Orion heard, "Let me know when you're ready." There was the sound of Claudio bustling around a bit, taking off his own uniform bits, jacket, shoes, then the rest of it. Orion knew those noises, of buttons and cloth moving against cloth. He kept himself focused, facing the bed, not least because the shirt buttons were taking him forever tonight.

Finally, though, he couldn't put it off. He left the shirt on, open over his undershirt, for the moment. Orion went around to his trunk to pull out the small wooden case Isembard had given him and set it on the bed, before he toed off his shoes and hung up the shirt. Wouldn't do to have it in the way. "Can you manage a light?"

"Of course. Where do you want me to be?" Claudio had, in fact, got everything off, and he was just finishing shrugging on his pyjamas. Orion sighed, and settled near the head of the bed, one leg tucked up. He put the wooden case from Isembard by his hip, and the first aid box in the middle of the bed. "Here." He gestured at the foot. He'd known this was inevitable. Orion hadn't wanted to do this tonight. But life always picked the inopportune moment, he'd found.

A moment later, Claudio was sitting, more or less facing him, and he'd cast a charm light, tapping on the wall to hang it up and light up the bed properly. The blackout curtain was all properly closed, but Orion glanced around instinctively to check one more time. Then he took a breath and pulled off the right hand glove and liner. "That's the one I felt. Salve and a bandage?" It was just a scratch at his wrist, where the glove had ended.

"Glad you're taking precautions." Claudio's head bent over as he checked for the right tin of salve and a bit of plaster to bandage it. There was a queer note in his voice all of a sudden.

"Something the matter?" Orion didn't know what he was asking, but he did, really. He knew Claudio had his own ghosts, ones he hadn't been talking about, just like Orion did.

"Lost someone. It's been a bit. Before the last project. Infection. They took his arm, eventually, not soon enough. He didn't make it." Claudio didn't look up. "Wasn't magical, but I kept wondering if..."

"Yeah." Orion had seen plenty of that. He knew the limitations of magical healing perfectly well, that it wasn't a simple matter of a Healer snapping their fingers and fixing it. He was proof positive of that. Even if they hadn't been able to replace his fingers, that kind of fantasy magic could have done a great deal for what was now a mess of scarring.

But they did have a much better chance with infection,

with gut wounds, with all sorts of other injuries, if a Healer got to it fast enough. He held out his hand, silently, keeping still while Claudio went to work, cleaning it out with one of the washes, drying it, dabbing the salve, then adding the plaster. "I just see the tooth marks there. It drew blood, but no more than a hint of a scratch, not deep."

It was the first time anyone had touched him, skin to skin on his hands, in ages. Since the Temple of Healing. And like he had last night, Orion felt the ache of it. Then, without looking up, he made himself go on, taking his hand back to pull off the other glove, carefully. Once it was off, he set it down on the bed by its mate, though here the two and a half fingers were still full. Then he pulled off the liner, he'd need a clean one. He braced himself for Claudio's reaction. Better Claudio than anyone else, but it would still be a reaction.

There wasn't one. Just quiet words, Claudio's most even and deliberate voice. "May I touch you, turn your hand so I can see all of it?" Orion nodded, eyes still fixed on the stretch of bed between them. A moment later, Claudio's fingers were under his, first steady, then lifting slightly, to get a better look with the light, then twisting gently to one side, then the other. "A bit of irritation, but I don't see any signs of a bite. More like the glove was rubbing. May I touch and show you where?"

Orion managed another nod. Then there was a light touch along his skin, on the outer side of his wrist, where the worst lump of scarring was. That was normal enough. But if they'd gone this far, well. Orion cleared his throat. "There's a bit of salve in what Isembard gave me last night." He couldn't quite ask, but it was hard to get it in the right spot himself. The angles didn't let him see well. Or maybe it was that he found it so hard to look at his hands now, at all.

"Which one? Blue label or yellow?"

"Blue." The simple exchanges helped. A minute later, Claudio had applied the salve, slipped it back in the case. "Anything else from here?"

"The blue pastilles. Two of them, if you don't mind?" His hands felt leaden now, heavy, though Claudio had lowered the left down when he'd finished with the salve, letting it rest on Orion's knee.

"I see Isembard was very thorough about what you might find useful." It had, for just an instant, a note of frustration before Claudio kept going. "How are they doing? Besides the cooking."

Orion let out a long breath. "Thesan's working on something complicated. Took the Official Secrets Act oath since the last time I was there. But she cooked. It was, I really needed." He broke off. "I wish you could have come too." Because he knew Claudio ached for that, too. "I felt like I could breathe, for once. And these things. They do help. Or at least I think mostly help." He lifted his right hand. "That's tonight. Can we come back to that?"

"Mmhmm." Claudio didn't say anything else for a moment. "Edgarton - he told me to call him Gabe, and I managed it by the end of the evening - wasn't anything I expected, at all. Turned my head upside down." That, now, brought Orion's chin and gaze up, searching his brother's face, now terribly worried.

Claudio looked embarrassed, almost. That wasn't the right word, but Orion didn't know what the right word was. Shaken, rearranged, shy, uncertain, like someone had just added a whole other dimension to his world. When Claudio began to talk, Orion realised just how true that was.

Claudio was better at laying out a proper report than Orion was, and he did it unflinchingly. He must have been thinking through this conversation all of today, what parts mattered, what he needed Orion to know and, more importantly, to understand. When Orion realised what it meant, what Edgarton had offered, almost blithely. As if it wouldn't throw - well, a pair of fighting weasels into the midst of everything to do with the Council - he rocked back, feeling everything stiffen up along his spine. "He didn't."

"He did. Not that I can do anything about it right now. But he wants me to think about it. What I want to do. Loaned me some books." Claudio let out a breath full of shudders all the way out. "The hell of it is, I want to say yes to him. I know I'm probably going to, when I can. Much as Mother will hate it."

"Isembard said he thought Edgarton might back my challenging for Council, if I wanted. How much do you think they coordinated last night?" Orion offered slowly. He was cautious not because of who he was saying it to - Claudio knew his secrets, even if they didn't talk about it. Like he knew Claudio's. But because it would overset everything they'd both been taught to be and to do. And how they were supposed to do it.

"I've been thinking about that all day, and I can't bloody tell." Claudio let out a half-laugh, then stretched over to grab Orion's glass and hand it over, then grab his own. "Here's to the three of them, at least, being up to Alexander's standards."

That made Orion laugh. He'd have snorted the whiskey out of his nose, but he'd not yet quite taken a sip. "To that." Then he took a long swallow, feeling it burn on the way down, leaning into the sensation. Without meeting Claudio's eyes, he added, "Next time there's a challenge, if I can, I think I'm going to try. Might not get anywhere, but."

"But you won't know until." Claudio shifted on the bed. "Here's the thing of it. It was like having dinner with Isembard and Thesan, only different. Gabe had clearly warned his parents, his wife. Probably his children. But it was warm, it was comfortable, it flowed, it wasn't awkward or stilted or formal. Just a conversation. Some of it I understood, some of it I didn't, but that was fine too. They explained most of it."

"What sort of things?" Orion moved his foot a little, then decided he could manage to finish undressing. "Stay where you are. Let me put things away." He left his glass on the bedside table, put the first aid kit and the case of potions away. He silently turned to swap trousers for pyjamas and all the rest, pulling out the soft cotton gloves he slept in.

"Well, for one thing, their son - he's at Schola, a year ahead of Ursula. He's in Bear House, and none of them even seem to mind." Orion could read that one as Claudio meant it. One was supposed to want to be in Fox. All the best people were, from the best families. They had both been, with all it meant and implied and obligated them to. "Been on the house bohort team since his second year, which Gabe finds baffling, and everyone else was teasing him about?"

"His parents are Fox, both of them, aren't they?" Orion asked, hanging up his trousers to air.

"But Gabe was Salmon, Rathna's Seal, and so's Rowena, their eldest. Likely enough that the youngest will be at Schola with Leo, but they don't know for certain yet. She's not twelve until May. She's sharp, though. She had lots of questions, and they did their best to answer every single one."

"Not in tutoring school?" That was another difference, then. Orion moved to sit back on the bed, grabbing the whiskey as he sat, and then beginning to work around to putting the cotton gloves on.

"The one they wanted for her's too near the coast. I didn't get a chance to ask about the other two. We got off on a tangent. Well. A lot of tangents." Claudio ran his hand through his hair, obviously chewing on saying something specific.

"And you want to see where his invitation goes." Orion frowned. "Despite your mother? Because of your mother?"

"Both." Claudio let out a rueful sort of laugh. "Definitely both. She'll be furious if I do, but." Claudio swallowed. "I think he's right. I think she needs it. She has no clue what to do with him. He doesn't look at power like she does. Like most of us do. And I think, maybe, I want to learn more about why. What it's like to live like that. Not always worried about doing the wrong thing."

"Not doing the right thing well enough." That was the thing with the two of them. Orion worried about being wrong. He felt he often was. And Claudio worried about not being good enough, even though anyone could look up competence in the dictionary and see his face.

"That." There was another hesitation, then Claudio said, as if it were just another part of the conversation, "Do you need to sleep in the gloves? Don't feel you need to on my account."

He hadn't left them off for more than a few minutes since Before. Long enough for his skin to be washed or dry, no longer. Not when anyone else was around. Orion looked down at his lap. "Need, no. Have been, yes. Even when I was on leave, in my own rooms."

"Oh." Claudio shrugged, once. "Just needed to be clear." Then he went on, leaving Orion with nothing to grab onto about what he should do now. "What happened tonight? By which I mean, why on earth did you pick up that weasel?"

"Stoat. Black bit on its tail." Orion frowned. "Maybe her? About the same size, a male stoat would have been bigger. I'm pretty sure." He let out a huff of a breath. "The dance got to be too much. Too many people, too raw in my head?" He didn't have good words for this, he never had. "Even watching Cammie dancing."

"I didn't expect that." Claudio agreed. "Not the way she is working. It was, I don't know. Acrobatic. Precisely on the beat, the rhythm of it, knowing exactly what she was doing. Makes me wonder what she was like, running signals in real time."

"Terrifyingly competent," Orion said, immediately. "Hypatia wasn't dancing, though." Which he'd paid attention to, of course, because after the conversation over supper, he'd been coming back over and over to what Thesan had explained. "Anyway. Quieter bit of the camp, and then there comes, I don't know. Weasels. Stoats. Whatever. And I don't know." He looked away, staring at a bit of wall. "I wasn't in my right mind, really."

"Most people in their right minds don't put their hands where the sharp teeth are, no." From anyone else, it'd have been cutting and hurtful, but Claudio didn't mean it like that.

"I'll do better next time." Orion said it to the wall.

"Does better mean less being bitten, less going to dances, less something else?" That one had more of an edge, the part where Claudio pushed him to put words to things that no one ever talked about.

"Could do with less being bitten." That part was easy enough. "Maybe also less dances. It was too many people. I'm not used to that many people. Noise. I was, now I'm not. Lost it all pretty fast."

Claudio shifted, as if he were going to reach out and touch for a moment. "You've had a hell of a time the last six months. It's not that I'm surprised you're still going, I know you? But a lot of people wouldn't be. A lot of people wouldn't have insisted on going to a dance they could have skipped, for one thing."

"Didn't want them getting hurt." Cammie. Hypatia. It sounded a bit sullen in his ears, and he didn't quite mean it like that, either. "It's so damnably hard to know what to expect. Mixed company like that. In Greece, at least we didn't have much in the way of dances. It's a lot easier when you're just at war, all the time. For me, anyway."

"That's the thing, isn't it? They're all there because they're going to be at war, sooner than later. The things we're working on, most likely, not that anyone's actually told us. But why else, thousands of fighting men, all sorts of skills - a lot of unit badges I'd have to look up - if they weren't part of the planning?" Claudio leaned back on one hand, drained the rest of the glass. "There's something wrong there. Also, I hope, a lot of things that will go right, but there are deep waters. I don't understand them."

"And that's why you wanted to come home, right away." Orion finished his own glass, then stood. "Let me go rinse them out?"

Claudio handed over his glass, and Orion took his time washing them out and setting them to dry before he came back to the bedroom. By the time he did, Claudio was in his own bed, under the covers, back to thinking ferociously. Orion snagged the cotton gloves, pulling them on, then taking the two pastilles that were waiting for him before getting under the covers himself. "Night." Apparently, they would not be continuing the conversation further at the moment. That was fine. Forcing it never worked for them. They'd sorted that out long ago.

"Night. Tomorrow's another day." Claudio's voice was distracted. Orion just nodded, pulling out a book and settling into read. He was hoping to lose himself for a bit in a story that had nothing to do with war or confusion or pain or especially weasels.

CHAPTER 20
CLAUDIO, THE MORNING OF APRIL 17TH

Monday morning, Claudio considered his approach carefully. To be precise, he'd been considering it all through Sunday. Orion had seemed a tad less overwhelmed by then, though he'd also gone out for a long walk in the park by himself. They'd otherwise spent it much as they'd spent their Sundays thus far: mending their uniforms, polishing their shoes, and writing and proofing reports. They'd barely seen the women, other than dropping off their meals, but Claudio had heard their hot water running a couple of times. That echoed through the pipes, and of course the rather pitiful water heater was inside their own soundproofing charms.

Now, on Monday, he felt he'd given everyone plenty of time to wake up, get some tea and food into themselves, and settle into the work of the morning. As the other three started coming to natural pause points around the same time - they were more or less on the same schedule now - he cleared his throat. "Tea and talking through some things?"

A general murmur met him, followed by Hypatia and

Cammie ducking into their hut to wash up and grab tea, while Orion did the same. Claudio gathered his notes, such as they were. He'd spent Orion's walk yesterday working through the pile of commentary he'd scribbled down while talking to Gabe. In the cold light of a new day and a new week, away from the warmth of that office, he knew he'd missed important pieces, somehow. He'd have to muddle through.

Another man might have paused and thought about how his father would have done it. Or his mother, since Mother was, in this case, actually the better model. Most of the time. Claudio, on the other hand, was the sort of son who wanted to do better, and somehow never quite met the standard he thought he should. No one said anything about it, ever. Except Isembard, who was kind but clear about the places he could improve. And Gabe, Friday evening, had been much the same. That would send him on a spiral, wondering how much they'd talked about him before Friday, or how much they would now.

By the time the other three came back, he'd got a firm grip on his reactions, and more importantly, the kettle was singing. There was the usual fiddling with the teapot, letting it steep, and Orion sharing around a few more of the biscuits from the package Thesan had sent back with him. It wasn't until they were sitting with their tea in hand that Claudio cleared his throat.

Orion was instantly on the alert, watching closely now. Claudio offered a smile, though he felt it rather weak. Not at all as reassuring as he wanted to. "I'd like to talk through what we're doing in more detail. Or where we're aiming. I had a very productive conversation on Friday."

"With?" Cammie leaned forward. She'd pulled her chair to the side of Hypatia's desk.

"Gabriel Edgarton." Claudio made himself say it as

clearly and neutrally as he could. "He's been involved for some years on a project for the Council - from before he made his own challenge. It's related to coordinating the magical responses of Albion, of people in various esoteric orders in Britain, and so on."

Hypatia nodded. "And as such, must also have as good a sense as anyone does of the magical techniques in play in Germany."

"Emphasis on 'as anyone does', because honestly, it's rather a lot of guesswork. We don't have good sources there, we do know they've changed approaches and permissions on a number of things, back and forth. Astrology, for example, for all they've mostly been focusing on the parts that aren't so much about locational and chronological magics, more personal charts and all."

"Right. Fair enough." Cammie leaned back, and somehow that was even more directly challenging a posture than her leaning forward was. If Claudio had more attention to spare, he'd be thinking about analysing that, the way her body language was often not what he expected, or read differently than it would in someone else.

"I know we've all been investigating different parts of this, but I feel like it's scattered. Not that that's anyone's choice. It's not as if we've been given any sort of adequate information for planning. But talking through things with G - Edgarton, I think I have an idea how we can look at bringing it together." That, also, was not at all decisive. His parents had modelled what leadership in the Warren family looked like, decisions clearly made, which others carried out. One did one's own part, of course, but at a higher level.

Claudio wasn't sure he could do this other thing, of setting out the options, working through them collaboratively. But he knew he wanted to try. It might well be the only way forward. Each of them off in their own little field wasn't doing well enough. And the count here wasn't power or social hierarchy games, it was saving lives. Maybe preventing an invasion here, as well. He had to set all those assumptions aside, all the things his parents had shown him again and again, and their friends and allies. Do something else.

And hang onto the slender, delicate thread of hope that the something else actually worked.

"What did you have in mind?" Hypatia set her teacup down. He'd learned that meant business for her. She never drank anything near her materia or her notes.

"I think we need to go back to first principles. What our assignment is, and what we can reasonably deploy. Fundamentally, we know there will be an attack this summer, on the coast of France. Other people - some of whom we report up to - are busy laying out information that will suggest to the Germans that the attack will be in one place, when it is going to be another. The idea being that the more we tie up their forces in the wrong place, the better all round. Simultaneously, can we help hide the movement of the actual troops, until it's too late to do anything about it." They'd all heard this before, but Gabe had pointed out that laying out the problem again sometimes shook something loose. "Anyone have any additions to that before we talk about the options?"

Orion opened his mouth, then closed it. Claudio waited, because it was a one in two chance Orion had something to add, when he worked around to sharing it. Hypatia caught that, but she went ahead and said, "I'm wondering about the resonances."

"Go on?" He'd talked some of that out with Gabe, but it wasn't Claudio's expertise, and apparently not really Gabe's, either.

"If we want to pull attention there, there is, there are two options." She let out a huff of breath. "The easy one is geological. The chalk cliffs of Calais are the same cliffs as Dover. Magically and geologically speaking. Cut in half by the Channel."

Claudio smiled. "That's a good place to start, certainly. And that means it's easier for us to get the materia here, of course."

"Seeing as how it doesn't rely on sending people to do things in enemy territory, even if we could find someone and get the results. There are samples in various places, I'm sure the Penelopes or the Portal Keepers can lay hands on some." Hypatia's chin came up, and Claudio suddenly felt she was reading his mind. That described Gabe and his wife, of course, though not only them. He just nodded, he hoped encouragingly. "And?"

"Give me a minute on the other. I need to look at a map. Cammie..." She diverged into Arabic. It wasn't anything Claudio could begin to follow, and Cammie got up without a word, going to pull several maps out of their flat storage, coming back with them. She sat again after clearing her own cup and papers from her sister's desk.

"Orion, did you have something?" Claudio glanced over at his own brother.

"Thinking about it still. I'm not sure I've got the right end of the stick about it, a bit of history." Ah, and he'd not want to be told he was wrong, not by these two.

"Fair enough. Cammie, anything on your end?" It was Claudio's job to keep things moving along.

She shrugged, once. "The part I've been working on has to do with figuring out how to read some of the references. What kinds of information could be conveyed, or should be avoided, that sort of thing. And helping Hypatia with the maths." Hypatia snorted, ignored Cammie, and rummaged in her desk drawer for a compass and protractor, laying a piece of tracing paper over the map and making various marks.

There was a silence then, before Claudio cleared his throat. "I've been trying to figure out how to. There are various of the martial magics around targeting, drawing attention or making it hard to focus. We'd want one on the site we're trying to lead them to, and one on the advancing troops, obviously. Or at least the former. There are risks in hiding your own troops from each other."

Orion shivered suddenly at that, then stood to go pour some more tea, without asking if anyone needed to be topped off. Claudio swallowed his desire to apologise, drawing more attention to it certainly wouldn't help right now. That was a topic for later, in private. Probably also briefly. "I was thinking, though, I keep coming back to the symbology."

From behind him, Claudio heard, "Oh?" Orion was at least talking. That was good.

"The putative army that's attacking at Calais is the Fourth, as established. Their badge is the white boar, King Richard's badge, though admittedly the head alone, not the full boar as King Richard used it." Always King Richard the Third, when not further clarified, in Albion. "You brought it up, when we got the briefing, and I can't stop thinking about it. What it means that it's a boar."

"That's - look, I don't have an actual idea here, yet." Orion came back slowly. "But I'm wondering if there's some historical battle that might be relevant. Give us ideas."

Claudio opened his mouth, but Hypatia got in first. "That's part of the idea I'm working on. Possibly a different application, though." She made a neat pencil mark on the tracing paper, then added a couple more lines.

"Here, have a look. This is Calais, here. This area's all chalk coast, then it turns into sedimentary rock. Along here, where they're actually aiming, more limestone." She was avoiding saying the name. They could all fill in Normandy anyway, they'd been in the same briefings. "But I'm thinking there are a couple of techniques - you may know more about them than I do - where we could draw on the resonances of a battle. Agincourt, here." Then she hesitated, and Claudio was suddenly very glad he'd told her about Hector already. "And, pardon, Orion. The Battle of Vimy Ridge, from the last war, here."

Claudio looked to Orion, who spread both his hands out, palms up in their gloves, with a muted, "It happened. It is part of history. Go on, please."

She traced a line, darkening the pencil mark deliberately. "For good measure, there's Dunkirk, here. All that emotion, all the myth-making about it, those are things we can use to counterweight the pull we're setting in place."

"Oh!" Cammie exclaimed, bending her head over the map and blocking Claudio's view of the details, not that he was crowding the women right now. "I'd have to do some research, but there might be something with the language we could use. Evocative, you know what I mean. And of course, using the particular battles - plus whatever else we turn up - to create a shape that would draw interest. Huh. That's a really interesting problem."

She sounded - well, rather like Claudio had, on Friday. Fascinated by the challenge, almost able to forget for a little that what they were doing was about war and death for someone, if not immediately for them.

"All right. That seems like a good start. We'd have to figure out how to represent a large enough body, the way the magical signatures run. That's partly my job, and Orion's, I think, but there are a couple of different ways we could go about it, and I'm not sure what would work best here." Here, though, he was on ground he knew better, metaphorically speaking. He'd never actually been to that bit of France. He wondered if it would have made things easier, but Father hadn't left Albion since he became Head of the Council, and Mother hadn't travelled since she married, either, not outside of Albion. Maybe if the war came to an end, he'd insist on the chance to see more places, somehow.

Orion pulled his chair closer, making a couple of suggestions about the ways that a large army felt in terms of magical signatures. The women both knew the theory of it, but Orion had all the theory and also a great deal of experience, in Greece and in other places, before.

He'd even been informative about Agincourt. At length, he'd gone on about the assumptions of that battle, before pulling himself up short. "Oh, wait, I'm doing that thing again. Going on about it. It's not helpful right now."

Hypatia had tilted her head, as if peering over glasses she wasn't wearing. "Actually, it might be." She'd asked him a couple of questions about the positions, about the advantages of each side. It got her another twenty minutes of explanation, but she was nodding along, making notes as Orion gestured, before claiming a couple of small objects from the desk to lay out the map.

She actually had a far better understanding of military thought than he'd expected, given her background. Once Orion ran down a little, Claudio got in the question. "You also interested in military history?"

Hypatia had shrugged. "Ummi's family comes from a border town, Kom Ombo. My brother's inclined to Hetheru. I've always been remarkably fond of Sobek. Where we come from, he is her husband." Claudio must have looked lost, because she said, tidily. "Crocodile-headed, Lord of the Nile, tutelary god of the Army." She added something in a language he didn't understand at all. She took a breath, and before either of the men could say anything, she added, "Some people consider him evil, like they do Set, but that's wrong. He's an avenger of wrongdoers. There's certainly plenty of wrong being done, and we could use some avenging, don't you think? And he's also associated with the fertility of the land."

Claudio had no idea what to say to that - his family were not remotely inclined to religion. Orion wasn't much better there, but he did have a question or three about what that meant, what kind of avenging might be of interest. From there, Hypatia shifted to various discussions of skirmishes and cleverness from that side of her family's mythology, then back to their actual plans.

By the time they took an actual break for lunch, they had a solid dozen ideas to work on and put into play, and a number of half-formed ideas that needed more time. Claudio didn't feel like he'd done it with anything like deftness, but he thought he perhaps hadn't entirely shamed himself here. Or Gabe's assistance, and that was perhaps more important. He'd have to write a note in the journal tonight, making it clear the new approach was doing some good.

CHAPTER 21

CAMMIE, APRIL 18TH BETWEEN TWO CAMPS

On one hand, it had taken the various higher ups remarkably little time to come to a decision about what Cammie should do. On the other hand, no one had actually provided either direct instruction or logistical support. It was, in fact, rather a trick for her to get three miles down the road from Camp 020, in blackout conditions, on a Tuesday evening, without someone noticing.

If she left Camp 020 on two legs, they'd pay attention to how long she was gone and when she got back. And no sensible woman would go for a walk in Richmond Park after dark by herself. Not because it was particularly unsafe, but the bombing had picked up again after a fortnight's break. She didn't want to get caught out away from shelters if the sirens went. And it wasn't as if she could wander into Camp Griffiss's air-raid shelters as if she belonged there. On four legs or on two.

There'd been the sirens last night. Nothing had fallen terribly near them, it turned out. But she couldn't just wait for a clear night. It wasn't as if the Germans announced them, and the ones that had no air raids were generally miserable to be out in.

She was under instruction to see if she could get herself to Camp Griffiss as soon as possible, learn what she could, and report back. Was the weasel there? Was it the same weasel? Could she figure out who he was? The questions were, honestly, somewhat implied, and they came through at least three or four layers of obfuscation of exactly who and where she was.

If people were more sensible about shifters, she could have got herself brought over to Camp Griffiss for some signals work or consultation or something. Probably. It wasn't unheard of, and Alice would have been glad to see her and would have vouched for Cammie's level of skill. If Cammie weren't at an even more secret posting, she could have wrangled it herself, probably.

She'd been very fortunate in a different way, though. Ibis had taken her information seriously. She'd coded it for good measure, of course. He'd let her know he'd be in touch one way or another once he'd passed it along. And then Ibis had updated her regularly, as he heard back. He'd put himself between Cammie and risk, probably half a dozen times, without making any mention of it. Not that she hadn't been sure he would, given Mum.

From a slightly rough start, and certainly a number of nights where she'd been up late worrying he was going to change things with Mum, they'd settled into this dance. She and Ibis respected each other, loved each other, not quite as daughter and father, but more like an uncle, maybe. He'd never tried to replace Dad, and the more Cammie saw of the world, the more grateful she'd been about that.

At any rate, that didn't solve all her problems, but she was well aware he'd prevented quite a few more. Her job now was to get to Camp Griffiss, see what she could find out, and report the relevant parts back. Without hinting to Claudio and Orion what she was up to, why, or how many feet she had while she was doing it. Which meant she was going to keep walking, under a moon that was waning to new, without attracting any attention. That, at least, she had charms for. She'd cut through the houses, then down along the Thames, over the bridge, then through the last rows of houses. Once she got close enough to the park, she found a copse of trees and shifted.

Like a sensible stoat - and a sensible woman engaged in a spot of authorised investigation - she took a minute to get her bearings. She could smell the camp, the mix of human smells, cigarettes, all drifting on the wind. No weasel, not here, anyway. Cammie made her way along, keeping to the shadows. The charms she'd used to avoid detection on two feet should have carried through on four, but no one had ever actually done a rigorous study of the matter that she knew of. She'd have to propose that to Ibis for when they both got some time free at the same point.

She and Hypatia had planned the strategy of this out last night and first thing this morning, talking through it quietly. There was the main plan, and then there were the branching alternate plans, depending on what challenges she found. She had her papers and authorisations in her pocket, because if she did get picked up somehow, they might be a protection. Or not, but better to have them. Cammie and Hypatia had come up with a cover story that might just barely hold about a particular despatch that she was delivering.

Cammie made it halfway around the outside of the camp, up to the north-east corner, where it let out onto more of Bushy Park, when she scented the weasel. This was an older smell, but not so old as Saturday. Last night, probably, maybe Sunday. It wasn't as if anyone wrote up actual guidebooks on how stoats perceived the world. Just the handful of more or less reliable guides for shifters that Ibis had copies of, and several dozen more deeply dubious ones. However, Cammie wasn't new at this, and so rather than following that scent immediately, she went on and continued her circuit.

Another fifty feet along, she got a much stronger line of scent, the sort that suggested the weasel had come this way in the past few hours. She went on, down to the road that cut through into the camp, and the gates at that side. When she didn't come up with anything of use, she back-tracked and followed the weasel. This part, oh, this was fun. Hunting always was. Working out signals and codes was a kind of hunt, and she was also superb at that. But this was a hunt of nose and tooth and claw, not just of her brain, and doing it with a purpose was even better.

She stalked the scent, following it as it moved from building to building, pausing here and there to listen and look and gather up any other information she could. Technically spying, but in point of fact, currently covered under her existing oaths. Finally, she got the scent to a spot under a large building, some sort of fuel depot. The smell of the gasoline and other fumes drowned out anything more like weasel. And the floor would be concrete or cement or something of the kind, and that didn't hold a scent well either.

She considered her options, and decided on a circuit of several of the huts, the sort that looked more promising for conversation. She'd come alongside the third one - the first had snoring, the second the ordinary sounds of someone mending and complaining about the chill. The third, though, had officers playing cards and chatting, so certain no one could overhear them.

They did not enunciate, or rather, their accents blended and got muffled by the metal of the hut and the thin walls. She missed words here and there. What she could pick up, however, was useful. This was where a large portion of the force that would be attacking Normandy in the coming months was stationed. The First Airborne Army, if she had that right, and then Army forces from Britain, from the United States, from Canada. Some Free French, she heard a few references to that. The officers she was listening to were easy enough, not new to one another. They didn't say much of note, but it let her put the masses and masses of men forming up here into context. This was only some of them, too.

Cammie stayed there for a good half hour, before giving it up as not worth further time. She made another circuit of the fuel depot, and managed to pick up a scent again. This time, she could follow it back out, a slightly different route that cut out north, along to the northern bridge, near the old Sheen Palace and the portal. Her feet were going to hate her tomorrow, but here she was, and there was information to be hunted down. And an insufficiently weaselly weasel.

Deliberately, and on four feet, she made her way along to the portal, keeping the scent in her nose. At times like this, she wished she'd managed to come up with some sort of useful second form, maybe an owl or a corvid or something of the kind. Wings would be very useful, given the uneven ground and the bits of glass people ground into small bits without any consideration for a mostly-harmless woodland mammal.

Well, all right. Not actually at all harmless, but a woman could pretend.

The scent stopped at the portal, of course, and she didn't have the skills in reading where he'd gone. She could, however, shift back, write it all down, and give an estimate, within an hour or two. And she didn't think the Sheen portal actually got all that much traffic. It didn't have anywhere for a mail drop, for one thing. That likely meant whatever mail went through it was delivered to someone's house in the town, and only got put through if there was something to send. Not like London or Trellech, which had someone on duty near all the time, and bins and baskets ready to go.

That part, though, she could leave with Ibis and whoever he was reporting to. They could get the Penelopes on it if they wanted. Thinking of them made her consider, then find a bit of woods and cover to shift back to two feet. She rummaged in her pockets, and managed to find a couple of corked vials for samples, and she got a bit of the dirt that had smelled most of weasel. Likely where he'd shifted himself. Out in the open, tsk. He was either quite brave or quite foolish. Almost certainly foolish.

She wasn't going to get any more tonight, so it was time to begin the long walk back to the gates of Camp 020. A quarter mile out, she shifted back to four feet, and then went and bided her time. Cammie could get through the fence if she had to, but she wasn't sure if it would be obvious if there was a noise at the wrong time. Not even her, but one of the guards catching some flicker of movement or scrape of stone or branch.

It turned out to be more useful than she'd realised, though. As she crept in closer, waiting for her moment, she heard a couple of the soldiers on gate duty talk quietly. Gossiping, actually. They were talking about people in the camp, though at least they'd be able to see any of their officers coming. Good thing, too, since they were gossiping about some of the men Claudio had had drinks with, who'd come along to the dance on Saturday.

Then, the conversation went sideways. "You know anything about that, um. Who is it, Captain Sisley?"

Her ears pricked up. Nearly the rest of her, coming up on her hindquarters, ready to dance forward, but she held herself in check. "Not much. Heard some gossip - not from Captain Warren, someone else - there was some sort of family mess. He got invalided out, six months ago, maybe, and turns up at home, his wife's thrown him over, there's a baby on the way. Or that's the bit I heard them talking about. That she had the babe, he'd divorced her."

"He almost punched Biggs." The first man said that almost reverently, as if Biggs could stand to be punched. Cammie considered adding him to her list of people worth finding an excuse to bite, which had a rotating membership much of the time. "Would have, if Captain Warren hadn't turned up."

"Biggs probably deserved it. I heard from Sherman that he heard that Biggs said Sisley needed two girls to keep him sweet." Definitely a candidate for biting, then, at least for further investigation. "Feel sorry for Sisley, even if he's stand-offish."

"Well, all four of them are. Even the girls. Especially the girls. And besides." The second man shrugged. She couldn't get a good look at their faces, and their voices were quiet enough she couldn't sort out who was who. "Officers, them, too. Even if Gates is friendly enough."

Of course she was. It was more fun that way. Certainly more informative. "Wonder how she puts up with Sisley. Takes all sorts, I suppose. And I bet they didn't get much choice in who's in there, just like us."

"How'd you end up here, anyway?" They wandered off onto that topic, and a minute or two later, there was the sound of a car coming out. They pulled the gate open, she scampered through on the far side of the car, and was well inside before they closed it again. That just meant making it back to her window, in through the gap and past the blackout curtain, landing on her bed.

Hypatia looked up, raising an eyebrow as she shifted back. "You were ages. It's gone two." She was curled up in bed. She'd almost certainly been dozing, but the light was still on. Cammie reached up to make sure the curtain was back in place.

"Had to get to the park, detoured by the portal, then had to wait on the gate. I'm surprised it's only two, honestly." Cammie sighed, but she couldn't let herself fall asleep. "I've got to write it up and code it properly. I'll take it to the front room."

"How're your feet?" Hypatia was frowning. Something in Cammie's face must have given her away. "I've got some good salve for that. I could also set up a footbath."

"We don't have anything big enough, do we? I'll soak tomorrow. Salve and one of the pain potions, I guess." Cammie stretched, hearing her back crack, then something in her shoulder. "Ugh. And I didn't even get in a mouse."

"We've got some cheese and biscuits from the last package, and I kept a flask of tea hot. You go set up at the desk, I'll rummage." Hypatia stood up, pulling on her dressing gown. Cammie changed into night things, it saved doing it later. She took her journal, her code book, and her somewhat battered self out to the front room.

It was nearly four when she finally got to bed, with Hypatia curled up on her side deeply asleep. Cammie had done a day on less sleep, but that didn't make this any fun. She'd have to double check all her work tomorrow. And come up with another excuse for why she wasn't out on her usual walk.

CHAPTER 22

HYPATIA, THE MORNING OF APRIL 19TH

Wednesday morning, Hypatia was up before Cammie, not that that was any sort of surprise. She got the kettle going, heated up some of the porridge for breakfast. While the bread was toasting on the stove, she rummaged for one of the good jars of jam Pross had sent along. Cammie came out twenty minutes later, not quite limping, and looking horrid. Though at least dark circles didn't show much on her face.

Hypatia held out a mug without saying anything. Cammie nodded, sank into the other chair, and sighed. When she'd drained half of it, she looked up. "Potion?"

"We've only got two, and Ibis wasn't sure when they'd get more of the alertness ones." Hypatia had checked their stocks while Cammie was out last night.

"And it's not like we can ask the men if they've got spares. Ugh. I'll try without, if I can't, I'll come take one. Is it a materia limitation or something else?" Cammie asked.

"Materia and someone with enough skill to make it. You know the stamina ones are tricky if you don't want all the side effects. And the people with that sort of skill have dozens of other things they need to be doing." 'Side effects' ranged from damage a badly done potion could do to the heart or brain, to the smaller but essential things, like being able to sleep for the next day or two. Anyone with any real knowledge of alchemy had plenty of horror stories. Ibis had quite a few from students trying to stay awake to study for exams, and taking the wrong sort of thing or bodging something together themselves.

"Right." Cammie drained the rest of her mug, handed it back with a hopeful expression, and picked up her plate. "I'd give a lot for a proper full English sometime. Not that anyone's getting much of that. Even the people with home farms."

"No. Not multiple sausages, not eggs, not butter on decent bread. Though the black pudding's all right, still." Hypatia refilled her mug and passed it back over. "So, what should I know?"

Cammie poked at her food, which made Hypatia sure she was indeed very tired. Cammie generally had an excellent appetite. "Found the weasel's trail, tracked him back to the Sheen portal. That's what I was writing up. I'll run it up to the gate to go to the London address and then the portals. With any luck, they can figure out who went where from Sheen. And I got some samples that have his scent, so they should be able to test it against him if they can get a short list of people."

"And you're sure it's a him." Hypatia wrinkled her nose, thinking. "Why, do you think?"

"I don't know. I can think of a dozen reasons he might be snooping around. From what I heard last night, those are the troops doing the actual invading. Not our fake, the one we're covering for. Being a distraction for."

"That many?" Hypatia frowned. "Thousands, we thought."

"I didn't hear a number, but seeing the camp, I don't know. Six, eight thousand? Depends how packed into the barracks buildings they are. And we know it's not for long. Less than two months." Then her brain caught up with the maths, if a bit more slowly than usual. "Forty-eight days. Just under seven weeks."

"Which is why we ought to get a move on." Hypatia said, finishing her own plate, and scraping it clean into the bin that would go to someone's pigs. "I mean in general, with our implementation. You've got ten minutes or so before we need to walk out the door."

"At least getting to work is quick." Cammie worked on her food a bit more before going on. "Anyway. He could just want in on the epic battle. Some people still like that sort of thing, dreams of heroism I mean. I can't see why. He might have been spying, though everything Ibis has heard, and everything Giles has too, suggests that there aren't any German agents in Britain who aren't, well. Here, or being held somewhere else."

They'd talked that through, and it was the best explanation they'd been able to come up with. That, and a few things Claudio had heard over the weeks. Some of the people who were prisoners here had been cleared enough to be given the freedom to work in the garden. Some had permission to use the library and recreation room, or even cook for themselves sometimes. Not that any of the four of them had met any of those men - all men, they thought. It was one more reason to keep the four of them away from the general staff spaces most of the time.

Orion was still none too happy about it, but he'd simmered down to quiet discomfort after several rounds of arguing with Claudio about it. Thankfully, the fighting had always happened when he'd remembered to use charms to keep his voice from carrying. From what Hypatia had gathered, he didn't like the dishonesty of it, keeping people in case they might be useful, not treating them as proper prisoners of war, with the usual protections. She was not sure what to make of the way he was so furious over principle, even while she suspected he was probably right to be.

Hypatia nodded. "But still, half a dozen reasons someone might be spying, and I'm sure I haven't thought of all the variations. What else?"

Cammie shrugged. "Honestly, he's a weasel. It's entirely possible he might just want to get on the fight somehow, even if it is on a grander scale than teeth. Not that we're known for being good at taking orders, weasel-kind."

"I was thinking you were actually being remarkably obliging about doing what the mysterious They were telling you to do," Hypatia said, as mildly as she could.

She got a toothy smile back. "I wanted to find out what he was up to. And I don't know yet, but at least I got to find out a bit more. Every little scrap counts."

"Why are men like that? Wanting to be in on a fight? Or being, well." Hypatia jerked her elbow at the wall that backed onto the other hut. "Them."

"They have been remarkably easy-going, considering. Even Orion. He only argued with you, what, twice so far this week?"

"You missed twice last night. Though that was more academic wrangling, he was taking issue with the citations in what I was reading." Hypatia frowned. "He actually had some good points, and isn't that irritating of him?"

Cammie had picked up her fork to take the last bite or two of her food. "What sort of irritating?" She raised a finger. "I heard some gossip last night. About him, about his ex-wife, about the fact he almost punched someone. Because of us, if the gossip was right. I don't know how accurate any of it is."

"Almost punched someone?" Hypatia had been about to stand, and she sat back again.

"Biggs, I presume Captain Biggs? Someone Claudio had drinks with. Because he was implying that we were keeping Orion sweet, is what the guard last night said while I was waiting for a chance to get through the gate. Gather Biggs is not the sort of man who wants to be alone in a room with us. Because he'd do something unfortunate, and then we'd have to do something about it."

Hypatia grimaced. "Oh, that sort. And Orion—" They weren't keeping Orion sweet. That was not remotely their job. Both of them had the sense not to take that sort of thing on, given Orion's moods. Besides all the other reasons they wouldn't ever do that. Honestly, if anyone had that job it was Claudio, anyway.

"Almost punched him. Apparently Claudio came along at the right moment? Or at least that's what it sounded like. I don't know what to do with them either. They're entirely polite to us, they're respectful, except for Orion wanting to argue about everything. But he argues with Claudio, too."

"Not so much with you." Hypatia pointed out. She'd been keeping count, actually, and she couldn't begin to tell why that bothered her. Why she noticed it.

Cammie's head came up. Then she stood, turning to scrape her own dishes and leave them to be washed when they got a chance. "No. What do you think of him, beyond the obvious? I mean, for one thing, I'm not sure he dares argue with me. Even without him knowing about the biting."

Hypatia opened her mouth, then said, "Not right now,

Cammie, right? Besides. We don't have time for that." She felt sort of like squirming as she said it, an uncomfortable weirdly hollow feeling she didn't know how to explain.

"Long list, then?" Cammie grinned. "Can you do the dishes, while I - um. No, I need to take something for my feet. Ugh. I'll soak them in the tub over lunch." Five minutes later, they were in the working hut. Cammie started setting up her typewriter and began to settle into work.

Orion and Claudio started the day out quietly, but by their mid-morning break, both of them were eyeing Cammie warily. She'd yawned half a dozen times, and she'd been working more slowly than usual. The problem with working with observant men was that they noticed things. That was also, in fact, irritating. At least at the moment. Neither of them actually said anything, but they kept watching.

Once they all had their tea and a biscuit apiece, Claudio cleared his throat. "Rough night, Cammie?"

Her chin came up, her back stiffened. Claudio said, his voice careful, "Lots of reasons for it." When Hypatia looked at him, he looked a bit haunted, actually. "I've got a sleep potion, if it's dreams. Plenty to share. Or an alertness one, though I'd not take them on the same day."

"That's generous. We've only got the two stamina left in our kit, and I didn't want to use it unless I had to." Cammie let out a breath. "The sleep one, though, tonight, if you're sure."

"Of course. And, well. I can ask Mother about a round of additional potions. She'll complain, and I know materia's dear on some of them, but we'll see."

"Let me know on the materia, Ibis might have some sources or some to spare. For a good cause," Hypatia put that in. Claudio's eyes went wide for a moment, then he nodded. "Share round."

The rest of the tea break was quiet chatter. Afterwards, Cammie went back to her desk, working things out by pencil and paper. She'd been working on a coded message with magical implications. Or at least Giles and a couple of other sources thought it might be relevant to upcoming troop movements, or who might spot them.

Hypatia was up on a stepstool, getting a large volume down from the top shelf. It was larger than she expected, slipping in her hands, and she leaned back just a little too far. She could feel herself falling. All of a sudden, there was an arm at her back, one at her hip, steadying her, until she got her feet under her on the ground.

It wasn't until she turned to see who it was that she realised it was Orion. He'd stepped back as soon as she was on her own feet, his hands now tucked behind him, as if something in that touch had been far too much. He took another half step back, hands still behind him. "Pardon."

There had been something there, that somehow, absurdly, she'd relaxed when he caught her. Her heart was pounding with the shock of it. Her head might be in a minute. But at the same time, he'd been right there. "Please don't apologise. You saved me from a nasty tumble."

"You all right, Hypatia? Sit maybe?" Cammie's voice cut through, worried. She had a point, and Hypatia stepped back.

"Orion. Thank you. You have excellent reflexes." It seemed a banal thing to say, but something in it made him duck his chin, eyes not meeting hers, then make a gesture at a bow. He didn't say anything further, just retreated to his own desk again.

Hypatia settled at her desk, willing her nerves to settle.

It worked as badly as that always did. She looked up a couple of times, once Cammie had poured her the universal balm of tea, to find Orion watching her. Not staring, just paying attention to where she was. It was a tad unnerving, but it wasn't as if she'd complain. Not today.

CHAPTER 23

ORION, THE MORNING OF APRIL 22ND

Orion rolled over in the bed, hearing it creak, and rubbed his face. The inside of his mouth felt like it was covered not just in fuzz, but in outright hair. Pretty much everything ached, not just the parts of him that usually did. He rolled flat on his back, letting his eyes close again. Ten seconds later, the sound of the alarm shut off, and ten seconds after that, Claudio was pressing a small vial into his hand. "Drink that, or you'll be impossible today."

Orion's mouth quirked. He had been invited to a game of cards with a couple of other officers stationed at the camp. They'd plied him with alcohol to get him to talk a bit more about who he was and where he came from. But the Pact was far stronger than any alcohol. Even whatever it was they'd been drinking, which shouldn't have had the name of whiskey. Or the beer they'd started with, which was not at all up to standard.

He pushed up enough on his good hand to drain the vial, then set it on the table beside the bed before sitting up. "Thanks."

"Self-preservation." Claudio had turned his back, starting to pull his clothes together. There wasn't any heat in the comment. "Learn anything useful?"

"Not really. Let me think through it. Nothing obvious. Who knows if I'll piece anything together?" Orion shrugged, and then got himself upright once he felt the potion start working. "How many more of those do we have left?"

"Counting out how many nights you can get?" Claudio glanced over his shoulder. "Better you than me. How much did you win last night?"

"Just the right amount, tactically speaking. Enough they'll invite me back to see if they can win it back, not so much any one person will hold a grudge." He stretched, feeling his neck and shoulders pop. "And as for the reasons it was a good idea." He shrugged, careful at first. "Let me check the journal."

Orion thumbed through his journal. Two messages from Mother, one from Aunt Violetta, and then there were the bombing reports. "Nothing much in our lands, it sounds like. That wasn't what got me in a mood, then."

"Not the most useful of your arcane magical skills. Like Isembard and his knee before it's going to rain. There might be some bombs, but who knows where?" Claudio shook his head. "Glad there wasn't anything there, at least. How do you feel about food?"

"Toast," Orion said. "Nothing much."

"Right. I'll get that going. And tea." Always tea when he had the chance. Claudio went off to the front room, and Orion took his time washing up and getting dressed. By the time he had himself together, uniform on properly, Claudio had tea, toast, a scraping of jam, and his own porridge all ready. As they moved over to the working hut and settled into the needs of the day, the headache behind

Orion's eyes had settled into a dull ache at the back of his skull. Much more manageable. His hand ached, but that was the usual. Perhaps the usual with a side of rain. He wasn't experienced enough to tell yet.

Orion had his own work to do - he was sorting out calculations about how much materia they needed to do what the others were planning. Some of it was sympathetic effects, which would be a strain during the invasion itself, but wouldn't need nearly so much pragmatic preparation in advance. Some of it was things that might get brought into France via various illicit routes beforehand and deployed by people on the ground there.

Those, they had to put together early, and they had to look entirely ordinary. Tea bags, small pastilles of herbs. Nothing that would be too dangerous if someone were caught with them, or made to take them. That meant figuring out how to divide the necessary ingredients and carry them separately.

He'd been set to do the sums about how much they needed, of which things. If they couldn't get the materials - or the materia - they'd have to rearrange their plans. Again. Cammie could likely have done the sums much faster. But she was working on an analysis of information, something that made sense to her and was complete gibberish to Orion. To be fair, he was almost certain it made no sense to either Claudio or Hypatia, so at least he wasn't alone with that one. Claudio had been busy with reports and picking up materia deliveries and making nice with people who didn't want to talk to Orion anyway.

It didn't help that the two women seemed to be working on an entirely different sort of level than he was. Or than he and Claudio were. They were as much in sync as anyone might want in a duelling partner, but Orion couldn't figure out for the life of him who they were

duelling. It didn't seem to be Orion and Claudio themselves. But every so often, Hypatia would stand and slip a
scrap of paper on Cammie's desk. A few minutes later,
Cammie's hand would cover it and draw it over. She'd look
at it, maybe raise an eyebrow or move her hand in a way
that might or might not have been a signal. And then
they'd both go back to work.

If they were having a conversation like that, it was very
elegant. Orion wanted - well, part of him wanted - to sit
back and admire the dance they were doing, even though
he was sure he wasn't actually meant to be the audience.
He was sure they were working on something they hadn't
shared. He was sure they had some reason not to share.

Well. Some reasons. Both women were unstinting in
their actual work on their assignment. They stayed up as
late as Orion and Claudio did, reading and making notes.
They did their fair share of the ordinary chores. To be
honest, they probably did more than their fair share of
keeping the supplies organised in the workroom. Fetching
the food was not a hard task, it didn't take thought. And
now Orion had figured out how to place himself with the
rest of the officers, even fetching the food wasn't as dire.
He didn't mind seeming like the Boar, rougher around the
edges than Claudio, but good for an evening of drinking
and cards and rustic amusement.

Orion kept finding himself watching Hypatia, most of
the afternoon, a second or three here or there. The way
she moved her fingers stung, but it also kept drawing his
eye, the way she was quick and sure in her movements. She
didn't waste motion. That was something that reminded
Orion a bit of Isembard. Efficient, that was partly it, but
she didn't have any of the little anxious fidgets a lot of
women had.

Like Decima did. Decima couldn't sit still even if

someone bribed her - and weighted her down - with rather a lot of jewellery. She'd been - she was, it wasn't as if she were dead in the literal sense, just dead to Orion and his family. Orion stopped and gathered his thoughts. Decima was rather like a hummingbird. It had made Orion twitch before the war began, and far more once he'd been in combat. He knew that her movements weren't a sudden threat, at least not that way, but good luck telling his reactions that.

Hypatia, in contrast, was almost soothing. Also very annoying. How could she go on being that steady and calm and consistent? But she just kept working, as if she didn't notice him watching, didn't notice him looking away, didn't have time for anything but the project at hand. Orion sighed, perhaps a bit more loudly than he'd meant to, and went back to his own work, checking the maths a third time for certainty.

That work at least took him through the morning tea break, through luncheon, through the afternoon, though he was flagging by the end of it. When they finished, he and Claudio went off to fetch the food, dropping it off without much conversation. Orion sank into the chair in the front room once they'd filled their own plates. "I don't get it."

"Don't get what?" Claudio grimaced, then checked something, a small card that had been stuck on top of the meal tins. "There's a package at the front gate. Want me to go get it? Addressed to both of us."

"I can go. Walk would do me a bit of good." Orion still didn't feel settled, and wearing himself out a bit more physically wouldn't hurt. Then he said, "Or a walk in general." It'd be light out for ages, yet.

"I'll keep your food warm for you. Get the package on the way back. Take your journal, just in case."

Orion nodded and went to change into running gear. He got himself let out the gate, picked up a steady jog. He spent the next hour alternating between the jog and a faster run when he had a bit of space, pushing himself far enough he was breathing hard, over and over again. By the time he circled back to the main gate, he was damp with sweat, aching in different ways, and he might be tired enough to sleep well tonight. Or as well as he could.

The package was indeed from Isembard and Thesan. Few people would address something to both of them. It was compact, easy enough for Orion to carry, but it had the sort of heft that suggested substantial food, maybe another bottle of something to drink. Somehow, they both had impeccable timing about that sort of thing, though the last package had been only a week ago. He missed being out and fighting properly, in a lot of ways. But the chance to get packages, to see them now and again, that was a good reason to be back in Albion.

Claudio was reading when he came in, one of the dense books he'd been working through, complex theory. He had reading glasses perched on his nose, though he avoided wearing them around other people unless he had to. The light in here wasn't good. There wasn't a good angle for it, was part of the problem. And of course, at the end of a long day, things got fuzzier.

"Package. Let's open it up?" They got the small crate open with a touch of magic and then unpacked the contents. Two tins of biscuits made out of fairly coarse flour, a large bottle of whiskey, a potions case with half a dozen vials and bottles. There was another bottle of something for Orion to try, now he'd reported the way the first set had worked. And then a couple of books, for what pleasure reading they could scrounge up. Another military history for Orion, and a mystery for Claudio, who liked that sort of thing.

Once they'd put everything in its proper place, Orion sank into his chair. "They aren't telling us something. I'm pretty sure." The jerk of his chin made the antecedent clear, the other hut.

"You too, then?" Claudio frowned. "About us?"

"I don't think so. They're good, they're disciplined, I mean. But they weren't paying us that sort of attention," Orion said, after thinking it through. He'd noticed that, earlier. "So what aren't they telling us, and why?"

"Some other sort of mission? Something additional in this one - no, they'd be paying us more attention, how we were taking it." Claudio rubbed his face. "I don't know how I feel about being outside, not worth fussing over."

Orion tilted his head. "Not your usual position in things, I suppose." He kept the bitterness out of his voice, but of course Claudio knew where that lived most of the time. Then he frowned. "I was - I don't know, somewhere in the back of my head, I was assuming they must have some reason."

"Normally, you'd be wanting to get it out of them. Pronto." Claudio visibly had to stop and think about that. "Huh. You know why?"

"No." Orion grimaced. "And that part is decidedly annoying. I don't think it's anything that's in, what's the word, opposition to this project? The oaths we took would make that hard, but also they're just..." He turned his hand palm up. "They're frustrating, but they're competent, and they do their work. If we were in combat, I'd trust them behind me." He hadn't put it like that before, not even inside his head, but as he turned it over, he could tell it was true. "That, also annoying. Actually. I don't know how that happened."

"Or when?"

"Or when." Orion closed his eyes and rubbed the bridge of his nose. "I should go to bed. I know it's early, but."

"But you could use the sleep, and maybe we'll all get a solid night in." Claudio nodded. "I'd like to just read for a bit."

Twenty minutes later, they were tucked into their respective beds. Orion had applied salve externally and pastilles internally. The book was enough to hold his interest for a good two chapters before he fell asleep to the quiet sound of Claudio turning pages.

CHAPTER 24
CLAUDIO, APRIL 25TH

By Tuesday morning, Claudio was utterly convinced something was going on. He was also utterly at sea about what to do. If it were some other mission, something the women couldn't talk about, asking wouldn't get anywhere. And it'd be rude, too. If it were something about Orion and Claudio, and the women were as competent in this as they were in other things, it still wouldn't get them anywhere.

They hadn't broken their oaths. That would be obvious. Whatever they were doing wasn't against their oaths. Not against the one everyone made on the Pact, not against the specific ones for this assignment, not against any others they might have made in their lives. Q.E.D..

Claudio felt like he was stuck in one of those logic puzzles. The one where one guardian tells the truth and one tells the lie, and there was only one question to figure out which path led to death, so the other one was clear. And he'd never been particularly good at those puzzles, honestly. Father had enjoyed them, much as he'd enjoyed crosswords. He'd seen them as a sort of bloodless battleground upon which he could triumph on the regular. Claudio had never had that gift, and he certainly couldn't ask Mother about it.

The hell of it was that the women were being utterly, unambiguously, correct. They did their work exceedingly well; they kept their focus. If Cammie had been yawning a bit more than ideal for a day or two, well, it wasn't like Claudio and Orion could throw stones there. Orion hadn't got much else out of the other officers at the camp. Neither had Claudio. They'd just managed glancing connections long enough for a game of cards or darts in the recreation hut at pre-arranged intervals. Presumably so they wouldn't run into others here.

Now, of course, Orion was increasingly on edge. Some of it was that his divorce decree would be final in two days. But Claudio thought more of it had to do with the coming obligations for the land magic. He didn't talk about those much, though before the war, Claudio had often been a guest at Fairlight for them. Orion had a great deal of practice not talking about a number of topics.

Among a number of the demesne lands, May Day was one of the more hedonistic rites, and of course, that would rub everything raw again for Orion. From all Claudio had heard, Decima had not been particularly well liked among the magical families of Orion's lands. But she was very beautiful, she could bring herself to making the proper show of things a few times a year, and that did go over well in the pageantry.

Now, though, Orion was still short on patience, and that was going to make things difficult. The general rites involved garlands, and a chimney sweep dressed as a green man, leading into the dancing, the maypole, and all that. It would be a lot of smiling and being welcoming and shaking hands and admiring babies and small children.

None of those were particularly Orion's gift at the best of times.

It wasn't even as if Claudio could go along. Junior Commander Roberts had made it clear, in last week's report, that Orion could take the portal on April thirtieth. He had permission to sleep at Fairlight, and come home after supper on May first itself. No longer, no additional guests, and of course no talking about where he was posted or what he was doing. It would get the rituals done, but it felt stingy and scant. That was the opposite of what everyone needed, this far into rationing and food shortages, and with a desperate need for a good yield on every harvest planted.

All of that meant several days of an increasingly cranky brother, a day or so without him, and then whatever the aftermath looked like. None of that appealed. Not that there was any way out of it Claudio could see. Mother had written to see if he could get leave to visit for a day or two, and of course he wasn't even going to try. He couldn't see any point in it. He certainly didn't want to hear her complaints about Edgarton. Gabe. Or slip up in talking about him, and Claudio was more than tired and worn enough to worry he might. Mother was fearsomely perceptive when she chose to be.

None of that was getting their work done. He'd spent the last hour pulling together the notes for a report, couched in suitable language to be shared with the non-magical. It was all about an untested method to fool radar into thinking there was something there when there wasn't. Also he'd gone on about something that might mimic the effects of a large number of men in a given location. Roberts had assured them they wouldn't need to demonstrate the efficacy, so long as they weren't asking for anyone else to deploy them.

Finally, though, Orion tapped him on the shoulder. "Talk it through?"

"Yeah." He was exhausted. He could feel the stiffness in his shoulders, and the way they were around his ears. "Tea?"

Five minutes later, they were settled in chairs - well, Cammie was on Hypatia's desk. They had tisane and biscuits, courtesy of the package from Thesan and Isembard. "Right. What we've got right now is something, but the more I write it up, the more scant it feels. We can simulate effects near Pas-de-Calais thanks to the sympathetic magic effects. Is that something we need more people for, Hypatia? Vitality and all that?"

"It depends how much area we want to cover, and for how long. I can probably manage a few hours. It's fiddly work but not as draining as it sounds? If you're willing to lend vitality, either of you - I know Cammie is - then we're probably looking at six or seven hours capacity, or shorter bursts." Hypatia considered something on her desk, a sheaf of papers. "That's a fairly conservative estimate, but I'm assuming the same range of air raids we've had the last month or so, which is to say some, but not every night."

"Isn't the weather going to play into this? If it's clear enough for them to give the signal to go, it's also clear enough for planes overhead." Cammie pointed out. "On the other hand, it might mean we have RAF cover."

"The timing depends on if they've got someone on the ground, magical enough to investigate." Orion said, hooking a crate with one foot and propping his boots on it. "Doesn't it? If they might have someone nearby, we want a constant effect." Then he tilted his head. "Do you have thoughts on the air support?"

Cammie shrugged once. "You heard Junior Commander Roberts, there are plans for bombing raids in various places that could include drops. Though of course, we'd need either something triggered by the bomb it's attached to, or that drifted down in the aftermath. And neither of those would do to simulate troops on the ground."

Hypatia clucked her tongue once to indicate she wanted to break in, and Cammie stopped before saying anything else. "We need a delayed release. Get them dropped just after the bombs, then trigger them. We'd need to sequence it, and that will be the tricky part, but I should be able to map them if we set up unique significators in the design."

"How long will that take to do, people and materials?" Claudio asked.

"How good are you two with needle and thread? The easiest way to do it would be a small fabric pod. Something like a carved clay talisman bedded in dried herbs and other materia, in a little linen bag." Hypatia tilted her head. "Probably its own parachute. Drop it out of the hatch when the bomb goes. Whatever makes sense. We just need it in approximately the right place. We'd want fired clay, but I bet Ibis could get it done for us. Schola has a kiln."

Claudio nodded. "Make up your list, then, and we'll see what we can get. Variations on the materials, if possible."

"Of course." Hypatia's tone was a trifle crisp, but she'd earned that. Claudio recognized belatedly that he was being overbearing again, in a way that both wasn't useful and wasn't needed here.

"May I?" Orion cleared his throat, leaving Claudio glad of the interruption, honestly. "I had a thought. About what we're signalling." He turned a hand over. "Isembard sent along a new book - well, new to me. I was reading about the Battle of Towton." He didn't quite make it a question.

"Not really one for battle history. Though that's one of the Wars of the Roses, yes? Notable for some reason?"

Hypatia reached out to nudge Cammie in the ribs. "Let him talk. That's the one where Norfolk came at the last minute, isn't it? It ended up as a rout of the Lancastrians. Henry fled to Scotland with a few nobles, Edmund IV properly took over. Thought to be the largest battle on British soil, though isn't there some question about if the numbers are exaggerated? 1461, then."

"See, someone appreciates history," Orion said, rather gleefully, needling Claudio now. Not that Claudio much minded. Knowing earlier battles was a great part of Orion's speciality. And particular interest, honestly, even if this war was nothing like the last war in a number of ways, and the Great War had been new on a dozen fronts.

"I appreciate history. Just not usually the battles." He leaned back. "Go on, explain your idea, then."

"The thing I'm reading goes on about the Yorkists taking advantage of conditions. The wind in their favour, particularly. They had more range than the Lancastrians, who were shooting into the wind."

Hypatia saw it quickly enough. "So they could hit the enemy without worrying about returning arrows. For a bit, anyway. Right. And here?"

Orion leaned forward, elbows on his knees. "Where's our advantage? Excellent pilots and bomber command." He nodded agreeably at Cammie. "If we put it to them as some sort of targeting or marking device, would that do?"

"Probably. So long as it doesn't look like much or take them more effort. Cramped quarters, already a lot to keep track of, in a bomber. But that should be manageable. What happens if someone finds one of them on the

German side, or it gets blown off course?" That was directed more to Hypatia.

"I should be able to set it - we can test. Orion, you were off for a day for May Day, right? Can you bring one with you if I set that part up? We can see how it links to a map. Or two or three, I want to test some variations."

Orion sucked in a breath. Claudio watched his shoulders hitch. "Sure." He said it mildly enough, but there was a note in his voice about having been caught off-guard by the question. "How big are we talking?"

"Probably the size of a pocket watch or so. I can bulk them up if more weight would do." She shifted position slightly. "You're sure they're doing deception runs, planning on it?" Claudio was caught off guard by Hypatia's question, but it was aimed at him.

"That was implied, yes. I don't think they'd change the routes for us, or tell us what they were in advance, but we could give them a list of where."

Cammie pushed herself off the desk and went to grab a couple of the maps. "But if they're bombing near Pas-de-Calais to cover for Normandy, then they should be aiming at what we want. We'd need to figure out what we're triggering in which order. How many can we coordinate, Hypatia, do you think?"

"It's the question of figuring out which one is where. Ugh. Colours would do it, but that's limiting. Numbers would be ideal, but getting them to show up on a map is a trick."

"Markers that light up as it gets closer to the right place? We'd have to play hot or cold with each one, but it would give us more range." Cammie came back with the maps. "We mostly want near the beaches, presumably, but then working inland. But we won't know which packets we can deploy where until they've come to rest. We'll lose

223

some to the Channel, or I don't know, a dog finding a new toy. Or a later bomb."

"Right. And I don't know the calculations for that. How many to assume we're going to lose?" Hypatia ran her hand through her hair. "That's not my sort of maths."

Orion shrugged. "Ask Isembard. Or I'll ask Isembard. If he doesn't know, I bet Alexander does, and Alexander will answer him promptly enough."

That, now, was a clever thought, and it was the sort of tactics Orion was best at. Once he was aimed at something, he got it done. It was one of the things Claudio had always appreciated about his brother. "All right. You write it up for Isembard, Orion. Cammie, can you do maths on what we need for materials once Hypatia gives you a list? And Hypatia, can you work out multiple materia options, and the sequence we'd need for enchanting them? I can help with that if it's not too complicated, but it's a fairly straightforward linking charm, yes?"

"More like four links in the chain, but no, the charm's easy enough if you know Fossey's Fifth. Or Ninth, but I prefer the Fifth, and in this case, I think it will work better with chalk and limestone. It's a more oceanic sort of feel."

"As you wish." There, that would keep them suitably busy, productively busy, for a good bit now. And Claudio would find it easy to make a report and some proportionate requests once they'd sorted out the practical details.

CHAPTER 25

CAMMIE, THE AFTERNOON OF APRIL 30TH

Sunday afternoon, Cammie went out for a walk. As she was coming back, she saw Orion heading off down the road, too far away for conversation. And besides, he had the sort of purposeful walk of someone going to do something he didn't much want to do. She wasn't the right person to help, but she could at least avoid making things worse.

And besides, he didn't know she'd been the one to bite him. It made conversations awkward now, on her side. She'd come to think that Orion and Claudio had been in the wrong place at the right time, or whatever the proper phrase was. That it was chance, not something nefarious. But that didn't actually help much. She still didn't know if she could trust them with knowing she was a part-time stoat. Nothing since that dance had made it clear enough she could.

By the time she got back to their hut, she saw Claudio sitting on the wall, his feet not quite touching the ground. He caught her movement and waved a hand, encouraging her over. She went, but raised an eyebrow, the sort of posture that suggested she wasn't at his beck and call. "Orion's off to the family estate. Hypatia said she'd be busy with something for a bit. Give her until half-past before you go in, if you don't mind?"

"Some sort of resonance work, then, probably," Cammie said. She was used to that.

"You don't mind being kept out of your hut? You're welcome to use ours if you need the necessary or to wash up or anything." It was a very civilised offer, and a thoughtful one, which was more or less what she'd come to expect from Claudio. That was something that had been nagging at her quite a lot, actually. He was much nicer to her than he ought to be, by the usual standards.

"I'm fine, but thank you." Cammie considered her options. "Why are you sitting out here, then?"

Claudio shrugged, one uniformed shoulder moving up and down evenly. "A bit at loose ends. Orion's gone for the night. I have work to do, as always, but I don't need to do it quite yet. And it's an unusually pleasant bit of weather." It had got near enough to seventy in fact, the last time Cammie had checked, with plenty of sun. Claudio hesitated for a moment, then added, "To be honest, I feel like I'm getting away with something when I'm not busy all the time. Enjoying the weather."

That was also a sentence Cammie did not know how to handle. She tilted her head. "Mind if I join you?"

"It's your wall as much as it's my wall," Claudio answered, affably. "Please."

Cammie settled herself, feet dangling a couple of inches above the ground. "You're not like I expected." Might as well be straightforward about it. Stoats were capable of deception, but none of those skills worked in an actual conversation.

"How so?" His voice stayed pleasant, even slightly

amused. "You aren't either, for the record. Either of you. In a good way, I should be clear."

"Oh, now we're going to have to talk about that." Cammie leaned forward. "I suppose I should go first, though."

"You did start the conversation with that," Claudio agreed. "But if you'd rather defer, lady's choice."

Something in the way he said that, the emphasis on 'lady', caught her ear. "What does that mean to you, then? That kind of manners."

"Ah." Claudio leaned back a bit. "You know my family, the public parts."

"Only child of two Council Members, your father was Head of it for more than thirty years, he died - I'm sorry about that - what, twelve years ago?" It had been a visible pivot point in Albion, more so than who was First Minister, or led most of the departments of the Ministry, the courts. About as important, as she counted it, as who was the head of Schola. Or arguably the other of the Five Schools, but Cammie knew perfectly well where her priorities were. She tilted her head. "Brought up with expectations."

He winced. He actually, visibly, winced. Cammie had not expected that at all. Then Claudio nodded, slowly. "Quite a lot of expectations." He looked off, down the road, as if he could see Orion there, somewhere barely in view. "Orion understands a lot of them. He grew up with a number of the same ones."

"Excellence?" Cammie suggested. That was a common one for families like the Warrens. Though excellence was too weak a word, from what she'd seen. Perfection, unreasonable perfection, that was their standard.

"Excellence. No failure, not ever, not in anything. If I got a good mark at school, the question was why it wasn't better. It was easier with Isembard, outside of class. I wasn't actually expected to beat him. Orion, yes, and that's a hard go. He's a terrific duellist. Better than I am, several ways around."

"And how good are your skills in self-evaluation?" She made the question reasonably gentle. Which was to say, not terribly. Gentleness was not actually one of her skills, and she knew it. So did most people around her.

This time, it made him laugh. "Decent. Mostly, that's Isembard and Thesan. Isembard held himself up to impossible standards for a long time. He's learned a lot, since the last War, he says. And teaching, teaching taught him a lot. Seeing the range of skills when you're not right in the middle of it trying to figure yourself out."

"And dealing with all the other parts of it. Drama and gossip and your body not being the same one day to the next." That was, technically, more true of her than most people, but she had also actively and vigorously pursued shapeshifting. She had only herself to blame, there. Besides, she hadn't got a start on it until halfway through her fourth year at Schola.

Claudio grinned, chuckling comfortably now. "Right. And in our case, lots of people who said they wanted to be our friends, and who wanted the connection, a bit of the shine to rub off on them. Or the skill, or the nepotism." Claudio shrugged. "Orion's always been loyal and true. He'd do much better in a world that still had proper chivalry, honestly. He wants - not that he'd say this if you asked him - a feudal lord to look to for instructions and his own people to take care of. Now, he's stuck in this place where he has all the responsibilities. But there's the Council above him he's supposed to aspire to, and yet, he can't bring himself to be loyal to them. Not that way, the way the loyalty wants to run in him."

"He's loyal to you, though." Cammie spoke the words

slowly, spacing them out, her thoughts racing. "He's angry, so much. Not at us, but you can see it."

Claudio shrugged. "He's got a fair bit to be angry about. His - his injuries." Claudio's voice caught there, but he didn't add anything on. "His ex-wife. The situation he finds himself in. That we're fighting a war where he can't just launch himself into battle anymore. He was reading that military history, the one that got him on about Totham, again. He'd do well, charging in, being the last bastion between an oncoming army and the king or a prince, or some key symbol."

"Huh." Cammie thought about that a bit. "Does he hate being here, then? Working on something like this?"

"To be honest," his voice took on a confiding tone. Cammie was more than sharp enough to know he was doing it deliberately. Whatever he said next he was doing as part of a larger strategy. Not that she'd let on to him she knew that. It wasn't how the hunt was made. "He thinks we're all much smarter than he is. All three of us. It makes him want to reach out and scratch or fight or nip. Only that won't do any good, and he really is mostly civilised. Doesn't even leave his socks and pants lying around in the hut."

That last sentence did make her laugh. "Is that the measure of civilisation now? I do think we could have slightly higher standards."

"Oh, that too." Claudio shrugged, but he was smiling and looking more relaxed now. He had a nice smile when he let himself show it. "Anyway. Our sort of people, it's more about alliances than friends and loyalty. Orion finds it dire. I play those games better, but I like knowing who has my back. I like that about you and Hypatia, too. It's good, knowing other people do that."

"Different reasons," Cammie said. "We don't have

those expectations. Mum and Ibis want me to do well and all that, but they've been glad enough for me to set the standard and decide where I'm doing it. Maths and codes, and Mum has no head at all for them."

"You're far beyond my own skills," Claudio agreed. "I don't know much about Magister Lefton."

Cammie nodded once, letting her feet swing slightly. "You didn't know much about Penelope Edgarton, either. And you still went and talked to him."

"I knew enough to know it needed to be him, and not someone else. Mother would hate you calling him that, by the by. She thinks being a Council Member is the pinnacle of everything. And on one hand, she's not entirely wrong. But he's rubbed her fur the wrong way from - well. Before he challenged. She doesn't understand him. She wouldn't understand you or Hypatia, either, I suspect, but she'd find it a lot easier to manage. He keeps being, well. Visible."

Then he got a peculiar look on his face. "And he got me, too. When we talked, the way he used the formality, the expectations." Claudio seemed amused rather than offended.

Cammie giggled at that. "And we're usually off with our noses in our work. Easier to ignore." That much was true. She didn't much want Silvia Warren's attention anywhere near her, thank you. It seemed stultifying at best and actively repressive at worst. Only, presumably, Claudio cared something for her. "So, is she going to be furious at you? Or whatever that looks like in your family."

It got a huff of noise. "A certain kind of disappointment, some sharp remarks, probably. I'll play it as wanting to get information he had, and seeing if I could figure out what he's about, what his goals are. If I get lucky, I'll pull that off well enough."

Cammie blinked several times, because that was

certainly not a mode of dealing with one's parents she understood. "Pardon, do you do that often?"

"Often enough." He made it seem like bowing out of the summer garden party, or making up an extra at table for a dinner invitation. Also not things Cammie had a great deal of experience with, actually, beyond the more informal sorts. "That's the thing. She expects me to be up to that sort of plotting all the time. Leveraging information and resources for some larger goal. She usually is, Father certainly was. I'm not sure Father ever took a break from it."

"And you?" Cammie wasn't sure how they'd got on this topic, and now she was almost fascinated. "And Orion?"

"Oh, Orion's lousy at this sort of game. If he says something, he probably means it. If he doesn't say anything, he might be plotting, but it's more about lobbing artillery shells than something that's pure subterfuge. Shells are not, in fact, at all subtle."

"There's a truth," Cammie agreed, shivering once, despite the current warm weather.

"Something other than air raids?" Now Claudio wasn't looking at her, but carefully off toward the hut.

"A couple of times. I was over in Paris, doing signals work in the field, the magical side, until just before Paris fell. We got out by the portal, but, well." She didn't like to think much about it. "I'd rather be over here. I'm probably more use, too, honestly."

"You're quite a lot of use, and I hope you know it." Now Claudio had shifted into his I-am-a-leader voice, as she'd come to label it. Buck up, good job, onward ho! Except, under all that, she was coming to think he actually meant it, as much as he meant anything else he said.

"Don't put on that voice with me." Her own comments came out sharper than she meant to. "I mean." She swallowed once and tried again. "I know you mean well. And you do the bit quite thoroughly. But you don't need to do it with us so much."

Now Claudio swivelled around, looking at her for a long moment, twisted at his waist. "Either of you?"

"Either of us. Hypatia's like Orion that way. She knows there are all sorts of things other people are doing, but she doesn't bother with spotting them herself, most of the time. Let her do her work."

"And you?" The man was sharp.

"I want a target I can get my teeth into. I want to do my bit to end the war. And," Her voice caught, and it slipped out before she could stop it. "I want Duncan to get through it alive and enough in one piece." Because she knew the numbers for the RAF, he did too, and until he was done with the current round of combat missions, each one could be the last.

"Ah." Claudio let out a slow breath. "That's quite a bit of help. About both of you. And I hope for you, too?"

Cammie might have said something else, but just at that point, Hypatia stuck her head out the door of the hut, and waved twice, before disappearing inside. "That's my cue, isn't it? But yes. We'll have to do it again sometime. Nice bit of wall, nice bit of chat."

Claudio hopped off at the same time Cammie did. He didn't offer her a hand down, just sketched a ridiculously formal sort of bow, mocking himself cheerfully. "At your pleasure, then." Cammie grinned at him, letting her teeth show to see what he did with that, and then went off, not quite skipping, to see what Hypatia needed.

CHAPTER 26
HYPATIA, MAY 2ND AT SCHOLA

"**A**nders, don't think I don't see you. Sharp objects away on the stairs, please." Ibis paused, where he was looking out the door from the Head of House's rooms. "Oh, bless, Jessamary. Are you around for a bit? Can you get them to keep it down to a dull roar? Thanks. And can you find out why Anders had an awl out?"

There was a murmur from the girl he was talking to. She was one of the fourth year prefects. Hypatia knew the name but wouldn't have known the girl by sight. Ibis had another exchange or two with students going by, then closed the door and came inside.

Hypatia had turned up at Schola at half-eight. She'd spent two thirds of the day in the library, tucked into one of the study rooms with about fifty books, pulling references for specific things. When she got back tonight, she'd cross-reference against the available materia lists. Now, though, it was mid-afternoon, and she wanted to pick her brother's brain. Ibis was looking about as tired as he usually did at this point in Floralia term, a month or so after the equinox break. Now they were properly rolling rapidly into the end of the school year, and the spring always brought out high spirits.

"Pross will be up when she's closed up the shop. And we should have quiet for a bit, everyone will settle down until food. Or as settled as they get. Can you stay for supper? Susanna wants to see you if she can."

"I can. I just need to be taking the portal by eight or so."

"That does well enough. Supper and a bit of a family chat after, then. I'll make sure to set an alarm, get you back down to the village in good time. Or we could eat down there, if you like." His mouth quirked up. "Not a problem to get permission of her Head of House." Seeing as that was also him, which was sometimes awkward and sometimes much easier all round.

Susanna was currently in a multiyear project to convince both Ibis and Cammie to teach her shifting, and they were holding out until at least her fourth year. It wasn't that the magic was necessarily complicated in the ways that meant waiting was sensible. Rather, it was that teenagers were not sensible, and shifting magnified the kind of trouble available at least twenty-fold. Probably a hundred-fold, given what she knew of Cammie, though some of that might be particular to Cammie.

"Oh, that would be novel. Not a problem on the rations and all?" She rubbed her nose. "I'd rather just us, and not all the questions, actually. I'm out of practice of a lot of people."

"Several places are running on the restaurant scheme. Nice basic meal, you can only get one serving of meat or fish or whatever per person. But it's quite good. Excellent fish and chips, as always, and I'm betting you're not getting that much at the moment." And eating in the village would limit Susanna's pleading, which suddenly seemed like a lovely idea.

"If you are trying to guess where I'm actually posted, no place in England is all that far from the ocean, technically speaking." Hypatia grinned. "Still not giving you specifics. But I do want to talk a couple of things through with you. Wards up?"

He snorted. "Teach our grandmother to suck eggs." Despite that, he checked them, sending a flash of magic that made the warding flare up gold and turquoise for a moment. "How's Cammie? Any news on the mysterious weasel? And your peers on the project?" Ibis said the last one carefully, and Hypatia made note of his tone. Ibis settled into the chair, crossing an ankle over his other knee. Then he tugged his journal over to write something. "No reason to make Pross come up here. We can meet her there. All right. All the logistics are done for the moment."

Hypatia grinned. "Can't have messy logistics," she agreed. "Cammie's in clover. There's more signals work coming in. She's also working on how to put things that might get picked up with the right labels, which I gather is just her sort of puzzle." She looked at her brother for a moment. "The weasel, first, thanks for that. Putting yourself in the middle. She takes more risks than I'm entirely comfortable with."

"Still." Ibis nodded. "I know. And I'm glad she told Pross a little of it. That I don't want to get between. I know better." Cammie's mother was generally mild and even-tempered. It was something of an interesting question where Cammie's ferocity had come from. But Pross was fiercely protective in her own way. Certainly, she was prone to worry. "We just got a note that it had been handled." She lifted a finger.

"And?" Ibis leaned forward.

"We don't know for certain, but did you see that notice in the Trellech Moon that Adrastos Rix was declining all invitations for the foreseeable future?"

"Which is a certain equivalent to gardening leave, rather. Legal matters still unspooling, don't want them near anything sensitive. I read that as house arrest, for the moment, bound by oath, but I couldn't figure out for what." Ibis twisted his palm up. "He challenged for the Council when Gabriel Edgarton did, but I don't know much more about him than the usual public sort of thing. Not posted overseas, though."

"Anyway. Cammie can't tell for certain without smelling Rix in person, but it seemed plausible. If you hear anything like that?" Ibis nodded, but just gestured for Hypatia to go on. "It doesn't explain what he was doing there, and I suppose any actual trial will be quite secret. But no one's tried to get in touch?"

"Not about that. Half a dozen other things, yes. Cammie's particular skill with her nose, no. Did she really bite Sisley?"

Hypatia grinned. "Not very hard. I mean, she drew blood, she didn't actually do much damage? Mostly, she was really annoyed she got interrupted. You know what Cammie's like when she's on the prowl."

"I do. And I'm glad you're there with her." Ibis rubbed the bridge of his nose. "It's going all right? I mean, properly? They aren't being awful to you?"

There was that odd note in his voice again, and Hypatia tilted her head. "How about you tell me what you're actually worried about? We do not have time for the usual roundabout discussion, not if you want to get this out before Pross wonders where we are, or Susanna barges in. We've got what, an hour at best? And other things to talk about." There, she'd laid it out nice and neatly, as was proper here.

"It's Sisley, mostly. I don't know anything against Warren except for his parents, and not the way that might be meant." Ibis looked up and frowned. "Did I ever tell you much about the excavation, when I met Pross?"

"That there had been some mess with the Research Society. It got rather nasty, when you were out at the dig site. But you told me I should focus on my end of year exams. And then you didn't come back to it."

"To be fair, we were both busy actually working through the dig, and you were too, and there wasn't any real privacy." It had been tents in the field, for some of it, and half a dozen other people working on the site. Also a lot of mud, Hypatia remembered, the way the dirt got everywhere and stayed. "It was Lord Sisley - the current one's great-uncle - who was head of the Research Society then. Also a plagiarist and a backbone of an entirely questionable esoteric society that turned out to be pillaging other people's magic, though we didn't know that at the time."

Hypatia straightened up. "No, you did not mention that. Though I remember the trial going on. He had the title stripped, put under house arrest, somewhere else in the family holdings, not Fairlight." Ibis raised an eyebrow, rather loudly. "The demesne estate. Of course Orion's mentioned it. Or actually, Claudio has more, now I think about it."

"You see my point. But yes. The title went to Matthias Sisley, who'd been on the Council for quite a while at that point. And then he resigned due to ill health, died maybe six months later, and that left Orion Sisley to take it on." Ibis rubbed his face. "I know Isembard thinks well of both of them. Sisley and Warren. But I've never been able to figure out why beyond the obvious connections. And every-thing I know..."

"What did he think about shifters? Orion's great-uncle?" That was the crux of it.

"Well, he almost tried to kill me. There was a snake shifter involved, terrified his secret would come out. What do you think?" Ibis stood up, abruptly, visibly agitated, going to stare at one of the pictures on the wall, a scene of an Egyptian temple draped with festive decorations. Hypatia folded her hands in her lap and stayed put. No sudden moves, no distractions. That was the only kind thing right now. Also likely the only one that would get her more information. "The snake was white and posh, for the record. Sisley was willing to blackmail his own sort. Or throw him away if that seemed useful."

"I argue a lot with Orion, and he hasn't ..." She frowned, suddenly putting something together. "He's shouted back. But he's shown no sign of wanting to hurt me. No flare of anger that seemed dangerous. Frustrated, yes, upset, certainly. But not edged like that." She found herself wanting to defend him, and she hadn't expected that. Ibis certainly hadn't, he had that slightly startled look, rather more hare than hedgehog.

"That doesn't mean much. There's a first time for the claws and teeth to come out." Ibis said it, sounding exhausted now, as if there were some old wound that ached.

Hypatia went on. "And Cammie had a conversation with Claudio, Friday night. After Orion had gone off to Fairlight. She says Claudio says—" Hypatia stopped "I know that's a questionable rhetorical chain when it comes to evidence, but I trust Cammie. Specifically, I trust Cammie to have accurately repeated her knowledge without unmarked editorial comments. I mean, come on, she's in signals, that's what she does."

Ibis's shoulders shook for a moment, then he turned back. "You are relentless. I can't find a hole in that. And?"

"She said Claudio talked a lot about how Orion wanted very much to be loyal, that he'd have done much better back before the Pact in a lot of ways. You know, a feudal hierarchy where he was responsible for his people and he had someone above him to be loyal to. And now he's got half of that, but it's shaky and uneven. And he was out of the country fighting for the last few years. That can't possibly have helped any of the land magic."

"No, not as I understand it. Even if he'd known it was coming. Isembard worries a lot about that, as his brother's heir. It comes up when we're having a drink, on the regular. Because he's here, not there." His hand twitched open. "All right. Or it's not, but I'll allow as how Orion is not his great-uncle. That doesn't mean he's safe."

"Brother." Hypatia felt her chin come up. "There's a war on. None of us is safe." She saw him about to interject and forged on. "Not in the sense of bombs and air raids and the threat of invasion. But in the sense that none of us who's fighting is safe to be around, sometimes. I know I'm not." She hadn't said this much out loud to anyone except for Cammie. Who was also fighting, and who was made for it, body and soul, far more than Hypatia was. To be honest, far more than a lot of people.

Ibis let out a loud huff of breath. "All right. You've worked with him. I haven't. And Isembard is generally a good judge of character. Though I never had either of them in class, and that's fouling my feet. Helena was still teaching the fourth and fifth years when I started. You'll let me know if there's something I should worry about?

Promise me?" He sounded so much in earnest about it, the way he had when she'd been in school, that she nodded.

"I will. And Cammie's right there. Unafraid of biting when it's called for."

"What a world it is where that's a comfort. Good grief." Then he paused, catching the sound of one of the clocks. "We've got just about an hour before Susanna shows up. We should get to work."

By the time her niece showed up, right on time, they'd spread out books all over the table in the study. There were stacks eight or nine titles high on the floor. Hypatia's notes were covered with scribbles and commentary to come back to later. She wasn't quite bowled over by Susanna's running hug, but it was a near thing. She helped Ibis put things away again. Susanna was chattering along a mile a minute about her classes and the latest school gossip, even before they set off for Schola village and supper.

CHAPTER 27
ORION, MAY 5TH

Claudio had gone to collect their mail and drop off several pieces. The notes included a request for Junior Commander Roberts to come for a meeting so they could show her their specific plans. They'd worked to standards, they had examples made of most of what they had in mind. And they had mockups for the rest, where they were waiting on materia still.

Orion was walking back and forth, over by his desk. He knew it wasn't reasonable of him, that he should sit down and do the ordinary thing, but he just couldn't. It hadn't been so bad before May Day, but now every moment he wasn't doing something else, it itched at him. Not an outside kind of itch, where he stood a chance of doing something about it, but an inside sort of itch, where nothing helped. His uniform was bothering him, and his shoes.

Mother would have said he ought to be on his land, maybe even barefoot for a bit. She might even be right, but that wasn't an option. He'd barely made it through the obligatory rites without snapping at everyone there. Orion had stayed civil and polite, and then he'd gone back to his bedroom at Fairlight - the Lord's chambers, with only a few of his personal items out.

No pictures, of course, bar the one of his parents early in their marriage, holding him. They'd looked almost happy. Sometime, if he lived through the war, he'd figure out more art from the attics, or maybe change the curtains out, or something. He'd had everything pulled off the walls and packed away after Decima had been thrown out of the house, and he hadn't replaced most of it. He wasn't that man anymore, whatever he was now.

It wasn't just the buildup to the climax of their work, either. Though that was certainly getting to him as well. He'd always found the anticipation the hardest part, knowing that he was going to be called on to be brave and steadfast and committed, but not yet. Doing those things wasn't the problem for him, it turned out. But knowing he'd need to, in a future he couldn't quite pin down yet, often almost did him in.

The women had been giving him a wide berth since he got back. Hypatia, especially, and he kept noticing it, over and over again, little ticks and twitches that made him wonder if she was watching him carefully. But why would she? Claudio mentioned he'd chatted with Cammie a bit more, the kind of easygoing comment that made Orion a little envious that Claudio had that, while he'd been off doing a duty he wanted to do better than he had.

Much the same as he felt about fatherhood, honestly. He'd spent half an hour with the children, but they were both shy of him. They were painfully uncertain of what to do with him, or what it meant that he was home so briefly. Aunt Benedicta had hurried them off after the conversation had stalled for the third time, with comments about getting along to their tea. He didn't want to be the sort of father who saw children for twenty minutes before someone else took them over. He didn't want to be the sort of Lord who appeared for the rites and then was gone. The war made him that, and all his life before the war had made him that too, and he didn't know how to change it now.

Orion told himself sternly that that was not his current problem. He couldn't do anything about it for a bit, not really. The realities of time, space, geography, and his current binding oaths meant he couldn't. He had to go forward with the plans for this deception, even if mostly what he'd been useful for this week had to do with having opposable thumbs and an ability to stab himself with a needle repeatedly and keep trying. Hypatia had said it was a help, but she'd done it in exactly the sort of tone he couldn't read. Claudio had gestured for him to keep at it, so he'd ploughed forward.

He was about to say something when Claudio came back in, frowning at a letter on the top of the stack. "For you, Cammie. And for you, Hypatia. And there's one for you, Orion, but I didn't know you were talking to Watts outside the journals."

"I wasn't." Boethius Watts had gone into some line of Intelligence work, the kind of thing he couldn't talk about. He liked Boethius well enough. They had regularly got a drink together when they were in Trellech. He was sharp, a great eye for patterns, and he didn't mind the fact Orion lost track of conversations and went silent for minutes if someone didn't nudge him. And he had a mutual interest in historical warfare, so he didn't get bored when Orion got going on that, not like most people. "Hand it over? Wonder why he didn't write there."

Orion broke the seal as soon as the letter was in his hands, feeling the magic give way. Meant for his hands in particular, then. He unfolded the paper, read the scant five lines of text, and then shivered hard before swearing. Mostly under his breath, nothing that would be coherent, but he couldn't stop himself. He could feel the anger rising up in him. Not just anger, there was desperation there, and despair and misery, and knowing that what that letter said was going to hurt and hurt and hurt.

He lost time then. He didn't know how much, except that his voice wasn't raw and his face wasn't soaked. Orion couldn't bring himself to look up, and he couldn't be so cruel as to let Claudio just read the note. All he could do was hold up a hand, a single finger, to indicate that he'd be a little. Maybe a lot.

Time wavered again. He could hear the clink of someone putting a cup of tea down, then Claudio's flask, the silver shimmering as he added a glug of brandy. By the time that was done, the tea must have taken a little, Orion could begin to pull himself together enough to explain. "Rodin Petroff. Parts unspecified, no chance of getting his body back."

He heard Claudio swear behind him, though he was going for a different set than Orion favoured. Claudio's hand came down on his shoulder. Once he'd swallowed his own emotions, he heard Claudio's raspy "Do they know?"

"That's what Boethius wanted me to do." Orion clenched both hands, heard the paper wrinkle. "He shouldn't have told me as much as he did. But." But sometimes you passed on a thing privately that couldn't go in the official notices. And Isembard had a right to know this. Both he and Thesan did. "Bloody rotting hell."

It was only then that he realised the two women were still there, that they hadn't left. He'd have heard if they did. The door creaked, and it was exactly the kind of sound his body wouldn't let him ignore. It had too much of the shifting whistle of a shell to it. Orion forced himself to take a breath, to release the paper in his left fingers and set it down, before he looked up, feeling his jaw clench.

They were standing a good ten feet away. Hypatia had her hands folded in front of her. Cammie had one hand on her back, it looked like. They both looked solemn but mostly uncertain what to expect. And they deserved at least a brief explanation, because both he and Claudio were going to be useless for at least the rest of the day.

Orion felt Claudio's hand on his shoulder tighten, one squeeze. It was a signal that Orion should go ahead if he wanted, then. That Claudio wasn't going to stop him. Right. If it were done, best it were done quickly. "Rodin Petroff was my year at Schola. Also in Fox. He and his family got out during the Russian Revolution. He was the oldest boy to survive."

Orion let out a puff of air. "He had a hard time of it. Especially a few years later, when it started getting into more complex magical work. And he was one of Thesan's Time and Place students, did really quite well on locational magic." He gestured with his left index finger, the one that moved most reliably, at the letter. "Boethius is in Intelligence. I don't know more than that."

Hypatia nodded once, then she said, her voice having the resonance Orion always associated with the best rituals. "A thousand of bread, a thousand of beer, a thousand ox, a thousand fowl, a thousand alabaster and linen, a thousand of every good thing. May his name be remembered." It wasn't a form he knew, but it was one he could understand, and certainly acknowledge.

All he could do was nod. Claudio cleared his throat. "We should, one of us. It's going to tear them up. But we can't get permission, can we? Fast enough?"

Hypatia's voice cut through. "Don't ask. Go. You've got

permission to see them already. They're on the cleared list. We'll cover for you." There was something resolute there, not just resolute, but the sort of thing that made ancient statues in far-away places stand tall after millennia. As if this were a principle of the world that would not be broken, not under her watch.

"How?!" Orion's voice cracked in the middle of the short word, and he just kept going. "I'll have to sign out and back in. They'll know I'm gone."

"Thirty minutes to the portal, what, forty to get up to Schola? The same coming back, plus whatever time you spend there." Hypatia's voice was even.

Cammie followed right up. "If you're not confident in your concealment charms, I can meet you on the road and do them again coming back."

"And how will you get out?" It didn't make any sense, even more than things usually didn't make sense, but Cammie had her hands on her hips and her stubborn face on.

"Me to know," Cammie said. "But I promise I can do it. Not much risk to me, even."

Orion blinked and found he couldn't focus on her. "Both of us?"

The women exchanged glances, a silent communication. "I'll need to do a quick talisman." Hypatia said. "But yes. Don't ask how, please. Just. Can you trust we can do this?"

He wanted desperately to believe they could. He'd seen enough of both their sets of skills that it wasn't impossible. Even though what they were talking about wasn't in their ordinary line of magic, at least as he'd understood it. The hell of it was, he did trust they meant it.

The worst that would happen if he got caught would probably be a dressing down, some sort of sideways discipline. He didn't care much about his rank; they weren't likely to pull him off this work until after the invasion. And it wasn't like they had a lot of leverage over him in Albion. The Council would consider this a right and proper use of magic, honestly, because whatever else they did, they understood this particular kind of loyalty and honour. Might not have it themselves, but they were smart enough not to get in the way.

Orion let out a huff of breath. "Right. What do you need from us?" That turned out to be several strands of hair, eventually a bit of spit and blood. Hypatia did a dozen things with bits of clay, hardening them with charms until it was like they'd been fired in a kiln. Orion had at least been able to write to Isembard and Thesan, let them know they were coming, that they'd want to clear the evening.

Then, the four of them set off as if on a walk together. Orion and Claudio made straight for the portal up at the old Sheen palace. They got through to Schola village promptly and were in Isembard and Thesan's quarters half an hour after that. It hit them both tremendously hard, as Orion had known it would, the way he'd seen parents crumple at the news of a child's death. The way something had cracked, unmendable.

It took a long time for either Isembard or Thesan to say anything. Claudio had poured drinks, had kept them filled, and the two of them just sat and waited. They were there, as much as anyone could be. It was hell to go to war. But Orion thought, as he had before, it must be even more of a hell to see your students go off to one. To know that some number, possibly some great number, wouldn't be coming home, or would come home so changed as to be unrecognisable.

Finally, slowly, the stories started. The simpler ones,

first, then the more complex ones. Helping Rodin find his feet, in a culture and country that he didn't know. Orion hadn't realised that Thesan had arranged for his apprenticeship. She'd pledged that he'd be a good fit in some complex trading of favours that he didn't begin to understand. Or that Rodin had helped out, the summer Leo was a babe, just being around and an extra pair of hands. Rodin had been skilled from helping take care of his younger siblings.

The stories broke his heart into even smaller pieces, and there was no helping that. He and Claudio didn't leave until well past midnight. When they got down the road near the camp, Cammie was waiting silently in a dark cloak, with a makeshift dark shawl for each of them. Instead of bringing them in through the gates, she led them down the road a little more. They stopped at the fence nearest their hut, and she more or less opened a gap in the fence to let them through.

It shouldn't have been possible, and she made it happen anyway. Orion was still thinking about that, about how whole-heartedly both Cammie and Hypatia had stepped in to help, when he fell into bed still fully clothed.

CHAPTER 28

CLAUDIO, MONDAY MORNING, MAY 8TH

Monday morning, Junior Commander Roberts turned up with no warning at ten. Claudio had been useless on Saturday, and frankly on Sunday, too. Though it made less of a difference on Sunday, which was given over to various necessary chores and mending and cleaning rather than work that required his brain. It wasn't just the alcohol or the grief; it was something else that weighed on him and pulled him down every time he tried to catch a breath.

At least when Junior Commander Roberts showed up, the lurking fear of what kind of trouble they'd be in stopped prowling. She'd opened the door briskly. "At attention."

All four of them had stood, of course, properly formal with sharp salutes. She made them hold it for quite a long time before she shook her head. "I'm disappointed in you. Also furious. What did you think you were doing? Were my orders not sufficiently clear?"

None of them bothered with demurring. Cammie had been fairly certain the gate records wouldn't be a problem, though she hadn't explained how. You couldn't ask how you'd tripped up, though. It's not like people told you. Claudio straightened his shoulders, preparing to take whatever consequences there were. No one spoke, and Junior Commander Roberts cleared her throat. "I expect an answer."

It should have been ridiculous, honestly. She ranked them, but she was also a decade younger. Somehow, though, she brought all her force of will to it, in a way that Mother would have smiled on. Unless it was aimed at her.

Claudio began with the briefest explanation he could think of. "It was a family matter."

"Surely not." Junior Commander Roberts began circling the four of them, which made every hair on the back of Claudio's neck prickle.

"We made oaths on the project, ma'am. We did not break them. We wouldn't be standing here if we did. The people we visited are on the approved list, and we did not speak of the project. It is a family matter." Claudio corralled his voice into something clipped and proper but unyielding.

"You're not blood related." She inhaled sharply. "Nor to the people I'm assuming you visited."

She didn't know then. That was interesting. Claudio didn't budge, and he hoped none of the other three would. He couldn't exactly look at them, though, never mind signal.

"Family comes in a number of forms, ma'am. A matter of honour. And sheer human decency." Claudio fought to keep his voice even and steady, and also not to say more than was actually necessary.

"I had half a dozen notes last night about this, all of which demanded my urgent attention. And then I had to arrange things so I could come out here this morning."

Junior Commander Roberts walked behind them, around to where Cammie stood. "Are you going to do that again?"

Claudio held still and steady, as steady as he could. "I very much hope we won't need to." She could press him to a promise or an oath, and they both knew it. He hoped she wouldn't think of it.

"Don't." That was hard and flat, then she brushed her hands together. "Consider yourselves duly scolded, because it's not as if we can replace you, it's not as if the usual punishments make any sense, and—" She cut off. "Where are things."

That, at least, got them back on a much more even keel. All four of them had thought she'd likely be coming round sometime in the next week or two, to work out the final arrangements for deployment. Some things were better handled in person, and her being able to see and touch the working models was, in fact, helpful. People had such odd ideas about what an object of a given diameter was actually like, it turned out.

"These are meant as distractions?" She tapped the clay balls. "Explain how they work, please?"

"Each ball has a talisman inside it that links up to a marker. We can align the markers on a map - this one will do. One at double the size for this area would be even better. I've got notes with the specifications that would work best." Hypatia picked up the answer smoothly. "Then you move the token here to the place on the map where it shines brightest, and it tells you where the ball that matches it. Sympathetic magic, if you follow."

"This thing is like that other thing. But surely there's more to it than the clay?" Junior Commander Roberts frowned, looking at the model they'd been testing with a token and a map of the immediate area.

"Herbs, a few resins for binding, suffumigation, a

couple of somewhat less arcane rituals than might be." Cammie said it lightly, as if testing the waters. "How much of the theory do you want us to get into?"

"Mostly, I'm interested in how resilient they are, and what happens if one of them breaks. The practical parts." Junior Commander Roberts found a chair, peering at the example model.

Hypatia took over, explaining the work, and Claudio refused to get in her way. "We expect to lose some of them. One lands too close to a bomb, or goes into a bit of deep water, or someone rolls over it in something heavy. The hope is to have enough of a spread to anchor a trigger point for effects. Claudio explained, I believe, how magic has a sensory component, how people who are familiar with it will recognise the density of the magic in play. An army, even if it's not magic, pulls a lot of that weight with it. Fear, excitement, anticipation, all of that has a magical context as well. What we're doing here is simulating that and creating a place we can create an effect."

"And the links allow you to know which item is where, so you can trigger them in the correct sequence." Junior Commander Roberts tapped the token.

"Just so. They might end up in an unexpected order. We'll lose some. There are other unanticipated events. Once we know where they've landed, we can plan a progression, triggering them in time with an invasion force. We should be able to use them for the feel of an army, magically. By that, we mean the signature of that many people and tanks and weapons. Possibly also at least a hint of illusion, suggesting shapes and movement."

"That seems impossible." Junior Commander Roberts seemed entirely unaware of how she sounded. Claudio wasn't nearly the expert that Hypatia was, but he had enough - especially after her explanations and their trials - to be sure she had a solid idea. "From just a few clay balls."

"Sympathetic magic theory. Take one thing, use it to affect another thing. Do you know your history of longitude?" Hypatia had settled back to lean against the desk.

"What does that have to do anything?" Roberts sounded peeved now. "Vaguely. Something from my school days, I can't remember."

"It's an example of the doctrine of sympathy. A somewhat ridiculous one, but that's true for a lot of history, really. They were trying to solve the problem of longitude. How to know where you were, how to take measurements at the right time, to match up with the angle of the sun in a given location." Hypatia paused to check everyone was following, then went on. "The idea was that you had a wounded dog, the knife that did the wounding, a ship, and the powder of sympathy."

"This seems like one of those riddles about getting a wolf, a sheep, and a cabbage over a river. Go on." Roberts waved a hand.

"You wound the dog with the knife. Then you put the dog on a boat and give the knife to someone on shore with the powder and a reliable way to tell time. Each day at, say, noon, he - it's always he in this story for some reason - puts the knife in the powder. On the ship, the dog yelps, the captain makes the calculations, and you can determine longitude. It's all silly, except that the powder of sympathy is a real thing. Not quite in that form."

"I've never actually known when you all are pulling my leg. The whole thing with the land magic, for example. Surely the rituals don't just make everything better. There are still floods and famines and all that." Roberts did step back to find a chair to settle in. Claudio's, not that he was going to argue.

Orion opened his mouth, then closed it. Good. Hypatia glanced at him, read something in his expression, and then said quite mildly, "The usual line of argument is that things would be rather worse without the rituals. And that's the trick of it, isn't it? We can't run a proper experiment on all the variables. You get one go at each season."

"Now, that's going too far," Roberts said, irritated again.

A beat behind her, Orion's voice cut across. "Ma'am." It wasn't deferential at all, and Claudio couldn't find himself willing to object or to gesture at Orion. "You acknowledge I have some sense of the land magic, yes?"

"Yes." Roberts answered that a trifle slowly, taken off-balance by something in the moment. "I can't really say anything else, can I?" It showed a modest amount of good sense.

"Hypatia is entirely right about the theory here, and I want to extend it a bit more. We do the rites, repeat the rites every year, if at all possible, because it gives us a rope to pull on, to brace against. How else do you think we're getting through years of war, turning over the land to agriculture, cutting down timber, people in military camps all over the place?"

Orion's voice got fiercer as he went on, and Claudio blinked once. He'd known the land was running deeper in Orion, but not how. Or how much. That was new. Possibly new to Orion, too, the way his mouth was twisting at the corner.

"And?" This was the rock meeting the hard place. Junior Commander Roberts' voice was cut glass.

"What we're doing, in part, is acting on the sympathetic magic of the land. Like this, you tend the connection you can touch, access, and it spreads out from there. These talismans, they'll be in their places for a bit, before we activate them, think of them like seeds, sending out roots. Do I have that right, Hypatia, from what you were saying last week, the bit from Pitten and who was it, Allegory? No. Allegant."

Hypatia took a moment to blink at him. "Allegant Major, yes," she agreed.

"I had a look at it, blast, I can't remember which day now. You took his theory a few steps further here. Using the extra herb as a stronger identifying linkage, rather than just the inscription."

"Well, the inscription might get damaged." Hypatia settled into the conversation more comfortably now. "If the herb's still there, embedded into the clay, it's one more layer of interwoven magic. If one doesn't work, maybe the other will."

They went on like that, batting ideas back and forth, for a good five minutes. Roberts didn't interrupt them, but she did ask a question here or there, and listened to the answers. Finally, though, she cleared her throat. "Right, all. Don't sneak out again. If there's something urgent, at least let me know, so I can handle it on my end. This part," she waved a hand, "is entirely beyond me, but I think I can put the right sort of thing in my reports. Make yours on Sunday, please, and let me know about materials requests." She swept out, barely leaving them time to salute.

Once the door closed behind her, Claudio let out a breath. "All right. Break for lunch and then get back into it?"

There was a general murmur of agreement, and Cammie and Hypatia disappeared through the door to go to their hut to wash up a bit or do something else, unspecified. Besides talk it through, which was certainly what Claudio and Orion wanted to do.

"You all right? Give me a minute to tidy up, and we

can go to the canteen?" Not that Claudio needed to tidy, much. But it was an excuse to take a moment and check in.

"Sure." Orion turned away. "Did I overstep just now?" He didn't look up.

"With Hypatia? No. You were backing her up rather nicely, actually. I assume that's the effect you wanted?"

"She's right. She knows what she's doing. It, I don't know. It bothers me when people don't see that. And people don't, apparently." Orion turned around. "And I didn't want to make her angry, you know how it's been. But I wanted..."

Claudio said, before he could stop himself, "You wanted her to know you were at her back."

There was a long silence, a very long one. Then Orion said, gruffly, "Let's go get the food."

CHAPTER 29

CAMMIE, MAY 9TH

"I still don't understand it." Hypatia was tucking her hair up in a Victory roll, rather than just braiding it.

"Define your antecedents, please. There, my bed's made, I have evaded your peeved looks for another day." Cammie finished straightening the pillow at the head.

"Beds are eternal." Hypatia pointed out, shoving a hair pin into the roll, angling it and then reversing it to twist the hair tighter and hold better, before she pushed it all the way in. "Neheh, not djet." That was the ongoing roll of cycling time, the minutes and hours, days and weeks, seasons and years, rather than those things that echoed outside of that rhythm.

Cammie, mind, was used to this argument. "If it were djet, it'd be a sarcophagus, and that does not actually seem terribly comfy. Anyway. I have made my bed. My clothes are tidy. Can I have breakfast now?"

Hypatia made a shooing motion. "Put the tea on, would you? On your way out?" It was the day their laundry got picked up, which always led to a bit of chaos.

And needing to be in uniform a little earlier, so they could stick the laundry out on time. They'd been scolded last week for going out without their jackets, even though near no one was going to see them. Cammie started the kettle heating, grabbed both laundry bags, and hauled them out to the road to wait for the truck that would pick them up.

It was brisk out, but not otherwise unpleasant. The camp was fairly quiet at this hour. Cammie mostly wanted to settle in to her work. They were making good progress now. It felt almost buoyant, especially after they'd made it through Junior Commander Roberts' gauntlet of disapproval yesterday. Which reminded her of what she'd wanted to talk through with Hypatia, now she'd slept on it.

The truck came by. "You today, not Ward, Cammie?" The man in the back had his cap on, tufts of brown sticking out.

"I'll tell her you asked about her. She's making our tea." Cammie helped heft the laundry bags up onto the truck. It amused her that they asked about Hypatia now too.

"Your sweetheart still all right?" The man leaned over. "I mean." He gave a little twitch of his shoulder.

"Last we heard, yeah. Nothing new since Saturday." Cammie had got a letter from Duncan around lunchtime. It was a proper long one, and she'd promptly refused to go to Saturday's dance in order to read it thoroughly and write back. Not that she'd wanted to go much. Hypatia had pled a headache, and the men had been just as glad to stay put. They couldn't get away with that too often, Cammie suspected. But there wasn't another dance scheduled now until, well, after what they were all working toward, and who knew what'd happen from there.

"Good. Here we are, ma'am. Clean things back on Thursday." He signalled at the driver, and the truck went off again, slowly given the bumps in the road. Cammie brushed her hands off and went back to the hut.

"All good?" Hypatia looked up. The kettle had just started to sing. "Couple of minutes to tea. The porridge and toast's nearly done." She doled that out into the meal tins. "Jam here."

"One of them asked how you were. Greg, he's rather sweet." Cammie hung her cap up for the moment.

"Which one's Greg? I can't keep them all straight like you can."

"Brown hair, sort of sticky-out ears?" Cammie said. "His brother's in Bomber Command. He worries too." She considered, snagging one of the knives to apply jam to her toast. "Also, I think he might be a little sweet on you."

Hypatia frowned. "How do you figure? I mean, what makes you think that?" It was the expression she got when the world really didn't make sense.

Cammie tilted her head. "What does, I don't know. The step before flirting look like to you?"

"I haven't had tea yet! That's a terribly hard question." Hypatia tapped her fingers. "I'm not good at it. The flirting."

"No, you got into all the relationships I know about because you were in the same place at the same time. They had the good sense to notice you're amazing. And then the bad sense to be awful about it when you weren't the shiny and new thing in their lives. No staying power, that's the problem." She signed along as she spoke. Both of them were fluent in it because they'd helped Ibis with negotiations with the merfolk who lived around the island of Schola often enough. There were always bits about fishing rights and the ferry route, never mind whatever else was going on in the local ocean. This time, Cammie's fingers ended in quite a crude commentary, a definite sagging and impotence implied.

"Cammie! You shouldn't." Cammie had always had a rather more earthy approach to the body and its functions, even before the stoat was a thing. Hypatia always found it a bit much, and normally Cammie didn't tease about it. It wasn't kind.

"Why not? It's just us." Cammie then went through a series of jokes, each one bawdier than the first, her fingers moving along. Part way through, they shifted into bits from *Lysistrata*, never solely crude but entirely suggestive. It was a good thing they didn't have tea yet. Hypatia would have snorted it, and that was unpleasant at the best of times. Then Cammie turned around to pour the teapot's contents into the waiting mugs. "Cheers."

"You're impossible." Hypatia shook her head, drinking first.

"I am, in fact, entirely possible. I am here, for one thing. And for another, it's quite possible to get me in bed, if you're the right sort. I mean, not that I have with anyone but Duncan since there was Duncan, but on principle."

"Fair." There was Hypatia not asking about it. Again, still. Most of the time, Cammie appreciated that, because it wasn't as if talking would change anything. And it wasn't that Cammie didn't maybe want a future with Duncan, if they got to have a future. Better not to talk about it. Or think about it too much, beyond the pleasures of the moment.

Only his letter, Saturday, had touched on wanting something more. Looking toward the end of his second and final round of combat flights, before they'd assign him somewhere else. He was able to let himself think about that, and Cammie couldn't, not quite yet. It made writing back tricky.

But at the same time, every day got them closer to that. Teaching and training, or moving planes around, could still be dangerous, but it wasn't the horrifying odds of combat.

"Talking, I guess. Having things in common." Hypatia finally came out with an actual answer. That was good. And a grand distraction when Cammie needed one.

"Right. Do you think about the content of what you're talking about? Some things being more intimate than others?" Cammie sat down and tucked into her food.

Hypatia snorted. "Cammie, love, I'm an Owl who's seen other Owls. I don't think we've known how to have a conversation that didn't have footnotes, at least to start." Cammie wasn't sure if Hypatia had noticed that Orion certainly wasn't an Owl, but he cited like one. Claudio didn't, interestingly enough, though he'd tell you where he'd learned something if you asked. Orion stuck it out ahead, like a flag, some signal to indicate he knew what he was saying.

Cammie also wasn't saying that she'd noticed Hypatia seemed to be enjoying that particular kind of wrangling. Orion had changed how he went about it, remarkably thoroughly, in terms of what he asked and how he put things. She was not at all sure why, and that was a scent she did not have time to track right now. Which was a little irritating. But Hypatia had relaxed into it. Cammie was pretty sure her sister hadn't consciously noticed, and if Cammie brought it up, it'd make everything awkward. They were far too busy to deal with that kind of awkward, and besides, it seemed a waste when everything was going better.

"All right. So. Among some people - um, most people who aren't Owls, I suspect - you start with general topics. The weather, the adorable dog that's visible, a bit of comment on something someone chose. Then maybe you move into talking about a book, or something they made, food, drink, object. Though ideally without insulting their taste or sense of colour, that does not get you anywhere good. Even if it's true." Cammie took another bite of toast, swallowed, and went on. "And then you get into more personal things. Stories about your life, the not so sunny parts. The things you're less sure about. The things that are more intimate. From there..." She set down her spoon, her fingers dancing through a decidedly intimate set of signs.

"How do you even know those? I'm sure Ibis didn't teach you." Hypatia shook her head. "They can't come up that often, surely."

"Mum did, actually. I won a bet with her. That was what I asked for." Cammie was still incredibly smug about that. "She was blushing the whole time, but she taught me everything she'd picked up. They're apparently rather curious about how humans do things. They do see what students get up to, when they've found a bit of quiet on the beach, with no one apparently watching." It wasn't often she got one over on Mum, and this one kept delighting, over and over again.

"Huh." Hypatia had told Cammie that her actual experience of the physical sort of thing had been fine. But it hadn't left her with much desire to do more of it, or learn the different ways it could be. About most other topics, that would have cued her sister that perhaps, everything was not fine. But close as they were, Cammie had not figured out how to point out that perhaps the sex in Hypatia's past had not actually risen to the level of fine.

Cammie felt she'd nudged enough for the moment. In kindness, Cammie left her to finish her food in peace, then took the tins to wash them out while Hypatia did a last round of tidying. Right at nine they were at work. Cammie was sorting out information that had come in overnight, Hypatia working on the talismans, and the men helping out at various stages of the process. Claudio actually had quite a nice touch with the charms for hardening the clay properly. Hypatia had trusted him enough to hand most of that over.

The day went on like that, steady and unsurprising, until later afternoon. Someone came and asked for Claudio, in specific, some matter of a report to someone or another, and Claudio excused himself and went off. He had to make those, sometimes, and better him than anyone else. Cammie had a strong sense that whoever Claudio reported to didn't think much of ATS girls and their skills, and Orion would lose patience five minutes in. That wouldn't be good for anyone.

Most of her attention was on her work, of course it was, but she'd noticed Orion seemed to be in a better mood today. He and Hypatia had talked all through lunch, about something he was reading, mostly. Cammie had worked through it, glaring at them over her typewriter as she worked on notes. Finally, they did the proper thing, took their meals to the other side of the workroom, and put a sound charm up for the rest of their meal.

Now, Orion kept glancing at Hypatia, as if he were trying to read a language in a script he didn't know. Hypatia didn't know what to make of it, she kept looking up and back down. Finally, coming on around half four, she looked up. "Orion, do you have a minute?" she asked. "Something you said at lunch, um." She frowned. "The thing about, it wasn't Towton. Something about magical implications of the landscape, um. The one that had a moor?"

"The Battle of Hedgely Moor." Orion perked right up. "Yes?"

"Can you explain the magical bits in that to me again? Oh, come over here, pull over your chair, it's no use shouting. And Cammie will glare."

"Can't have that." Orion shook his head. "Um. Here?" He set the chair at the edge of Hypatia's desk. Cammie snorted, and went back to her work, which was mostly checking a bit of encoding, then typing the next bit of it, piece by piece.

Hypatia nodded. "You were saying there was something about the landscape. The nature of the land? I'm sorry, I don't quite remember it."

Apparently she'd said the right thing. What she got was a good five minutes explanation of the landscape, the use of geomantic magical theory to bounce some spells off the local land. Then quite a bit about how one of the commanding officers had been Earl of Northumberland. He didn't come from the longtime line, it had been awarded to him a few years before that. Which made something of a difference to the land magic.

Cammie didn't pay attention to most of it. She was more listening to the rhythm of it, the pace of the conversation, the way they were tossing ideas back and forth comfortably.

A bit of it rose in Cammie's awareness then. Hypatia was talking again. "So, was he drawing on what's the word, knowing what the land magic ought to be like, even if he didn't have the direct connection as he ought? That's clever, I wouldn't have spotted that at all."

Orion's face lit up. "I think so, yes. Did you read Macklebight's monograph on that?" Then, before she could say anything, he stopped and said, "Oh. And you're beautiful. Did you know that?"

Cammie put her pen down, didn't bother to cover the typewriter, and pulled silence around her like a cloak. Now was a time to be somewhere else. Keeping an eye out, certainly. But the look on Hypatia's face told her more than enough. That Orion had completely surprised her, but not in a bad way. Not in a way that Cammie needed to bite him for. At least not yet.

CHAPTER 30
HYPATIA, THAT AFTERNOON

"Pardon. I'm what?" Hypatia blinked several times, as if it would clear her ears instead of her eyes. That didn't work. She saw Cammie disappear out the door, almost soundlessly, then she was looking back at Orion.

"You're, um." Orion actually flushed. She hadn't expected that at all. "You're beautiful."

"What am I supposed to do with that, then?" Hypatia wanted to resent him for putting her in this particular awkward position. It was awkward. If she said yes, well, they were going to be working together, flat out, for the next month or so. If she said no, exactly the same problem, just a different kind of difficulty.

Orion let out a long breath. "I didn't mean." Then his shoulders straightened up. "You are beautiful. And clever, and fearsomely sharp, and extremely good at your work. Watching you do the talismans, today, it made me sure of that. The way you're combining the pigments and the herbs. Being so careful about the inscriptions, all the ways any tiny variation might affect them. All of that. But I won't bother you about it. If you don't want."

Still her choice, then. Hypatia didn't entirely know what to do with this. If someone had asked her last night, she'd have said she wanted no part of trying and failing at a relationship again, or whatever else was on offer here. Which, come to think of it, was entirely unclear at the moment. Except, apparently, compliments. "What did you expect, when you said..." She took a breath and forged on. "When you said I was beautiful. What did you think I'd say back?"

He looked even more abashed. "I actually hadn't thought that far ahead? I'm sorry, my tongue got ahead of my sense. I, that happens to me sometimes. Though more often my fists than my tongue. It's true, though, it's absolutely true. Not just that you're beautiful, but that you care about what you're doing, you keep giving it your best. I've been a pest, more than enough. There's no reason you should want anything more from me." He stood up, hurriedly, though he didn't yet step away.

Hypatia didn't move, but now she was reading as much about him as she could, the way he stood, the way he spoke, the way his magic felt. There was something eager in it, not quite like a puppy, but with some of that hopeful energy. Something she hadn't had before, in a whatever it was she might call her relationships.

He was expecting her to say no. That was the heart of it. He was expecting her to turn away from him, maybe kindly. That they'd never talk about this again. She took a breath, because she didn't have nearly enough information. "I would like, I think, to hear a more developed idea of what you're offering." Possibly with citations, though come to think of it he was remarkably good at citations for a Fox.

That clearly took him aback, enough that he took half

a step away from her, then braced himself, as if offering himself up for an exam of some kind. "It's been ages since I did this. I'm out of practice." Then, without more than a breath, he went on. "I can't take you out for supper, I'm afraid, and arranging for flowers or sweets might be rather a trick. Whatever dancing we could get to would have an audience, the kind with music, I mean, and I'm not sure I want that. But I really am quite good in bed, given the chance. I made rather a study of it when I was younger."

"Just offering the bed?" Then she snorted. "We don't exactly have a lot of bed on offer, actually."

"Suspect we can make do, about the bed, at least to be going on with. If we can get some privacy." He let out a grunt. "Not that that's easy, either. No idea when Claudio will be back, and Cammie..." He suddenly craned his neck around, certain she was listening.

"Cammie took herself off a sentence into this. She has more sense. She also thinks it'd be good for me to find someone who treated me decently. I suppose the experiment at hand is whether you're up to the task." Hypatia wasn't at all sure what she was getting herself into here, though framing it as an experiment, not anything she was committing to, felt plausibly manageable.

Orion didn't hesitate. "I'd be glad to prove my skills, then. Um. Your hut, if Cammie's not there?" There were very limited choices here, and Hypatia could trust Cammie to stay out of the way.

"My hut, and we can start with a bit more talking about what you have in mind." Hypatia pushed back from the desk, the chair squeaking. Orion started, then turned around to get the door. No visible touch, not in public, they both knew better. She could feel her heart pounding in a way she'd never felt before, not about anything like this. Air raids, certainly. Other risks, absolutely. Never about the idea of someone getting her into bed. She was relieved, though, that she knew the hut looked its best right now.

A minute later, they were through the door of her hut, and Orion gave her space. She closed the door behind them, added a locking charm on it, and glanced at the window to make sure the blackout curtains were still down. No one could see in. He stood maybe two feet from her, into the middle of the cramped front room, not reaching for her. His cheeks were flushed, his breathing was a little shallow, just like hers. And when she looked him up and down, the uniform didn't hide as much of his interest as it probably should have. That, now, was an entirely different sort of thing for her. Her past lovers had taken a while to warm up to the idea.

"What may I offer?" He kept his hands tucked behind his back, as if to make sure he didn't do anything she didn't want. She leaned back against the wall, considering.

"What would you like? If you could choose. I don't know - I'm not used to talking about this."

"Oh, it's much better if you talk. At least I think so. For one, you get to anticipate the things you've talked about. I like that very much." It brought a purr into his voice. "It's - it's been a while for me. So you know." There was something there, a deep hurt, that he let her see. Just for an instant, not long enough to measure or map it, but the way it cut a jagged line through him.

"And you're still willing to try?" Hypatia's voice dropped to a whisper. "I couldn't do that. Hadn't done that. And I don't think my last was like yours."

"I do hope not." His voice was sharp for a moment. "But that's the past. This is right now. I'd like to make you smile first. You've an amazing smile, when you do it properly. It makes your whole face change. I want to hear you laugh. That's like bells. I suppose that's bad poetry, but it's true. And then I want to see if I can make you moan. However that works out best."

It hit her, after a moment, that this was all about her. "And for you?"

He shrugged, as if that were not at all relevant right now. "Whatever you permit. If that's me talking and never touching you, I'll manage. I'm used to taking care of my own needs in private, after."

Hypatia had to think about that, had to parse out what it actually meant. Then she shook her head. "That won't do. If we're, if we're trying this experiment, you have to get something out of it too. Not just my reactions." There. She wanted to be fair about it. She wasn't sure what to do otherwise. Hypatia had always assumed, expected, that his pleasure, whoever 'his' went with, would be the louder one, the more obvious one.

"May I kiss you?" That came out lower, a purr of something powerful and entirely potent. All that force he normally kept controlled was suddenly bubbling up to the surface, but it excited her to see it, that he was letting her see what he cared about. That what he cared about, inexplicably, seemed to be something involving her. "Close up?"

She could still say no. She knew that. Hypatia could have said she had no reason to trust it, but the thing was, she could. Orion, for all his crankiness and all his moods, certainly all his arguing, had been reliable like that. If someone told him to stop, he did. "Yes."

An instant later, he was right there. He'd stepped forward, bracing his left forearm on the wall behind her, the other coming - still gloved - to cup her cheek. His lips met hers, gently, at first, then pressing. She didn't know what to do with the eagerness and the desire on display, then he brought the rest of his body closer. Hip leaned against hip, one leg along hers, warm and solid. She could feel the ridge of his desire against her stomach, absolutely undeniable. Then her mouth opened to his. Here was his tongue, pressing and yielding, in and out, in a movement she was quite sure he wanted to demonstrate in other ways soon enough.

She whimpered, letting her head arch a little, giving into it. It was nothing like she'd expected, not this morning, not last month, not for years. He wasn't controlling. That was the mystery of it. He just moved, the way Cammie danced, trusting the moment, leaning into it, and encouraging her to follow him. For all the hesitation she'd seen in him at other times, he was absolutely certain of his skill. It made her wonder what it looked like when he was duelling, doing the magics he'd trained for near all his life.

Finally, he pulled back to let them both catch their breath, his eyes watching her avidly. "You've done this before?" It wasn't really a question. She hesitated for a moment before nodding. "Then you know what you like." He seemed pleased by it. An instant later, he caught something, what must have been a change in her expression. "And what you don't like. Can I go punch him later?"

The sheer idea of it made her want to laugh, in all the best ways. She threw her head back, rolling against the wall, and he was ravenously nuzzling at her neck without saying another word. This time, his right hand came down, resting against her ribs at the side, not quite touching her breast. He slid his hand down to her hips, so he could arch against her more. He pulled back one more time, murmuring a charm, then in her ear, he said, "Contraception?"

She'd kept it up, even though it hadn't been needed. But it did make her cycles easier to manage. She'd told herself that was the reason. She nodded once. "Not a problem. I use one of the charms." It would be a sore spot for him, she realised, as soon as she said it. "I can confirm it?"

Orion pulled back far enough to meet her eyes, and then he nodded just once. She had to bring her hands together, to do the confirmation charm, repeating the words clearly, so he could be sure what she was doing. The light formed, just where her womb was, about an inch out from her body, glowing the pure gold that made it clear the charmwork was solid.

He dove back into kissing her again, then rocked his hips into her, making the wall shake behind her. "Tell me what you want. Tell me what you're feeling, can you?"

Something in the question, the fact he so clearly wanted to know, wanted the information she might share, made her want to cry. Hypatia shivered once, trying to summon words. It was terribly difficult, for all she was usually good at words. "I'm wet. I want, I want..." She swallowed hard. "Show me. Show me what you mean. About making me moan. About your skill."

That made him near frantic. There were fingers working on undoing his jacket, discarding it over one of the chairs, then to loosen hers. She'd never done this in a uniform, and there was something delightfully taboo about him peeling her out of it, bit by bit. She managed to kick her shoes off just as the jacket slid down her back, and he bent to get his own boots off. Then he had an arm around her, guiding her back down the hallway into the bedroom. "Which is yours?"

Which what? Oh. The bed. She nodded. "Wall." He steered her that way,

"What I'd like, very much, is to get your skirt down, get your blouse open, and let you feel me, how I'm hard, so hard. Against the wall, if you will, to start. I can't wait, I don't want to wait. I don't want you to have to wait. I want to show you how good it can be, when there's nothing but the sex, nothing but me making you moan, and cry out. To start."

It was like nothing she'd ever done. Never at all. All her previous had been, well, they'd involved a bed, being horizontal, and reasonably civilised about it. For all he was being so careful about permission, this was absolutely primal. It burned like fire and made her want to come closer and closer to it like a moth. For a moment, she didn't know what to say, and he just held back, waiting. Then she nodded. "Show me."

Orion's eyes lit up his whole face, like she'd given him a tremendous gift he'd never expected to get. All his birthday and solstice gifts come at once. His hands fumbled between them, loosening his trousers, then working on his shirt, until it hung open and he pushed the trousers down to step out of them. Not his pants, quite yet, he was turning his attention to her now. His fingers fumbled a couple of times, but she didn't want to discourage him.

Hypatia did wish she wasn't wearing the uniform underthings. The ATS girls always referred to them as passion killers. The knickers were plain dull khaki, and her brassiere wasn't any better. Both went horribly with her skin, too, in a way that felt even more like an insult. It didn't seem to slow him down at all, as he pushed first her skirt and then her knickers down. She managed to fiddle behind her back and undo the hooks.

Seconds later, she was standing, naked, her back against the wall once more, and him right up against her. One hand, still in the glove, came up her stomach, then cupped one of her breasts. "You're beautiful." He murmured in her ear, then nibbled at the lobe. "I, are you …"

"Am I?" She was more or less sure what he was asking,

but she didn't know how to answer it. A moment later, he cursed under his breath, and then he was pulling off one of his gloves with his teeth, finger by finger, to loosen it. He glanced around for just a second, then tossed it on the trunk facing her bed. His hand, his bare skin, immediately came down between her legs.

She couldn't have told anyone what he did in the next few minutes, or even how long it was. Hypatia knew she was moaning, that his fingers were playing her like an instrument. She knew she had flung herself into the moment, in a way she had almost never done before in her life. She was trusting that she'd fly and that he'd see her safely to the ground. Her head rolled back against the wall as his finger slid inside her, testing her readiness. Then, finally, he was nudging her legs wider, taking himself in hand. For a moment, they hung there, something hot and heavy and damp pressing at her entrance, both of them knowing there was no turning back.

"May I?" Even right then, he managed to ask. She could only nod, and an instant later, he was sliding in, smooth as could be, filling her up. She cried out, overwhelmed by it. His hands were all over her body once he was seated. The one with the glove pulled one of her legs up to brace around his hip, leaving her balancing on the other foot and pressed against the wall. His hips rocked into her, over and over, in a rhythm that started out urgent and got more and more so. His other hand teased her breasts until his head bent to kiss and suck at them. That did her in, and instants later, she was clenching around him, shattered with pleasure.

Before that eased at all, he had picked her up, still deep inside her, twisting and tumbling until they were on the bed. He surged into her, riding through the climax, bringing her to another one, her legs coiled around his body, her hands all over his back. It went on and on for eternity, the best kind of eternity, until finally he whispered a charm, thrust three more times, and flooded her. His head and shoulders arched back as he bellowed. As he finally began to slow, he was kissing her again, a needy kiss, like he didn't want to lose the moment. She didn't either. She wanted to be here forever, now, to figure out what this was, and if it could happen again.

CHAPTER 31
ORION, IN CAMMIE AND HYPATIA'S HUT

Orion lay there, stunned. That had been so much more than he'd expected, in every possible dimension. Now, here he was, lying on a narrow bed. He'd slipped to one side as soon as he could. He had manners. In bed, probably, more than anywhere else, because the ones for bed made sense to him. Now, he shifted, nuzzling at Hypatia's shoulder, urging her to curl up against him.

She, somehow, miraculously, did so. She didn't pull away; she didn't break the moment. Her hair had come mostly loose, black strands coming out of what had been a roll at the back of her head. She lazily reached up, pulling a couple of hairpins out, and then waving them vaguely. "Table?" Her voice was muzzy.

Orion could do that. He reached, dropping them on the table next to the bed. There were other things on it, he made sure not to drop the pins there. Then he brought his hand back, letting his fingers play along her spine and nuzzling at her exposed shoulder. Orion could do this for hours, for days. He didn't let himself think about longer than that. Whatever moments he could get, he wanted.

When they were both breathing more easily, he kissed the curve of her shoulder. "Successful experiment?"

It made her laugh, and he wanted to do that again and again. "Mmhmm. Might need further data collection."

Oh. She. Orion swallowed hard. "You mean that? You can decide you'd rather not, later."

Hypatia pushed up a little on her elbow to look at him properly. "Your evaluation of your skill was quite accurate. But you left out your, mm. Devotion to the outcome." She let her own fingers move down his hip, and he could feel himself starting to recover an interest again. It had been a very long time since that had happened. "I'd like more. Now. Soon. Probably also later. I don't know how we make that work."

He let out a huff of a breath. "Not my preferred environs for a seduction, I admit." He rocked a little against the bed, then got his shoulder at a better angle. That reminded him to take inventory. His hand was actually not throbbing more than usual. He'd been a tad worried he'd banged it in the process and hadn't noticed. The rest of him felt fabulous, in a way that he hadn't in ages. Like he was alive again, properly, instead of blighted. He then had the sense to glance around. "Though you've made it pleasant in here." There were brightly coloured wool blankets on the bed, a turquoise one under them, and deeper blue on the one that must be Cammie's. There were rag rugs and a few comforts that weren't just practical.

She snorted, and tugged one of the pillows more under her head, watching him now. "How long had it been for you?"

Of course she'd ask. And it was a reasonable question.

"It's May. My leave in 42, that was October. Whatever that is." He couldn't make the numbers go in his head yet.

"Eighteen months." Hypatia leaned to kiss his cheek very gently. "I'd be no good at punching her, but I want to."

With eleven words, she laid him entirely bare. He couldn't breathe. All of him froze up, stuck, in a way he knew and a way he hated. That this damage was as visible to her as his hand was. She didn't fuss at him, not like Mother did in those moments. Certainly not like Decima had been, all cutting comment and ridicule. She didn't even touch him more, like she knew perfectly well it would be far too much.

He could feel her, the way her weight made a dip in the bed. Her breath warmed the air near his face, the scent of her that wasn't the ordinary issued soap but something with herbs. Neither of them moved, for what seemed like forever and more than that. Finally, he managed to come back to himself enough. "How much do you know?"

"The bits I caught in the papers. A little from what Claudio said, here and there. He worries about you a lot. I'm glad you had someone to worry." Her voice was very soft now, and that was perhaps even more confusingly attractive.

"Oh." He closed his eyes. This wasn't a conversation he could have while looking at anyone. With his eyes closed, he could pretend she wasn't looking at him, at least a bit. "It was bad." He could see it, behind his eyelids, now.

There were the flashes of the way Decima had been with her lover, the kind of raucous abandon she'd discarded with him once they were actually married. How she'd seen him look and seen him understand in that moment that she'd set the whole thing up. He'd walked out, because the only other thing he could have done was violence, the kind he'd never recover from. There was maybe barely enough real Fox in him to care about his reputation and stop. Orion had gone on and on, over hills and down roads, until he'd ended up over ten miles away. He'd had to beg a ride back near enough to Fairlight in the blackout, talking his way through two stops by the Home Guard.

Hypatia didn't say anything at all for a long time. Then, carefully, she spoke, as if each word were an oath full of magic. "I don't know what we are, what the future holds. I'll probably hurt you. I'm lousy at people. Ask Cammie. But I never want to hurt you like that. No one should." He opened his eyes at the last part of that, watching her now, and she was entirely in earnest. "I'll make oath on it, if it helps. When I can figure out the wording."

He shook his head immediately. "I don't need that." Only, as he said it, he knew it to be at least partially a lie. He needed something that he could be sure about, and he could be sure about an oath. Maybe other things, too, things he couldn't sort out in his head right now. Claudio would have ideas. Isembard. That made him snort, all of a sudden.

"Mm?" It was a gentle sort of inquiry, and he leaned first to kiss her again, taking his time with it, letting himself fall into just being with her.

"I was thinking about what Isembard would say to that. He's - he had a history as a playboy, before. He's the one who made it clear if I were going to do that, I should learn to do it properly."

"What does that mean, then?" Then she half-smiled at something, but gestured for him to go on.

"Be honest about what I'm doing, what we're doing together. That I shouldn't make promises I can't keep or don't want to keep. I shouldn't lead people into expectations. And I should absolutely see to my partner's pleasure, before my own. It's the decent thing to do." His mouth quirked up. "And also the logical one, if I want more chances."

That last part made her throw her head back, laughing. She didn't hesitate at that. He liked that so much, that she let her pleasure show. Even if whoever she'd been with before obviously hadn't appreciated that remotely enough. "Ibis warned me off you. In general. I have no idea what he'll think about this. Not so much you in specific, but he's got issues with your family."

"My great-uncle, I'm hoping, not anyone closer in?" Though that was quite close enough. "I don't know all the story there, but enough."

Hypatia nodded once. "I decided I'd make up my own mind. And besides, it's not like I had a choice in who got assigned here."

True enough. And somehow, despite what she'd heard and what her brother had told her - entirely reasonably, given the history - she'd still said yes to him. There was a miracle, not that Orion actually believed in miracles. "Why did you?"

"Can't resist a properly defined experiment?" That, now, he was sure she was teasing him a little, the way her eyes crinkled at the corners. She was making it obvious enough he could be sure. "You asked. And then you kept asking, kept checking. And it was fabulous." Her hand trailed down his hip again, then dipped to brush against his cock, testing. It, of course, was interested in that line of inquiry.

"How long was it for you? And please, may I punch him?" Something flickered on her face. "More than one him."

"More than one. Neither of them did much to make it good for me. It wasn't bad. I thought it was fine. This morning, at breakfast, I was arguing it was fine!" She exhaled in a puff of breath. "It was not fine. They didn't hurt me, they didn't force me. They just didn't, I don't know. Care much about what it was like for me, beyond the basics."

"Can't have that. I will punch them if I get a chance. Or something else. I know all the sorts of charms boys get up to, making trouble. Pebbles in their shoes. Everything tasting of mint or something. Besides the ones that are about them not being able to get it up for ages."

It made her snicker, just at the thought of it. "Don't. They're not worth the trouble." Her hand moved down his leg, then she was wriggling to get a little closer, more skin against skin. "I like you touching me. Like this. Just easy. Though I liked the other too, the needy parts."

He let out a slow breath. "I like the skin, too. It's been..." Now he really couldn't count. "A very long time, for much of that. Being like this."

Orion saw her eyes shift, a glance at his hand, where it rested against her ribs. "You wear the gloves all the time? Usually?" She could still feel his fingers on her back of course.

"Both of them. It feels odd to just wear one." He swallowed. "It's ugly. The reason why. And it's protective."

Something in what he said made her shift, pushing up on her elbow again. He thought she was going to say something. Instead she leaned in to kiss him, the sort of kiss he'd given her. It was all about intensity and focus, about being right there in the moment, where there was nothing else but wanting this. About the particular intimacy of kissing. Bodies could do all sorts of things, but kissing was about the heart, he'd always thought. Or at the heart.

He let her push him back, until he was lying on the bed, back pressed up against the wall. When she finally pulled away, she braced on one hand, and he realised she could see both of his now. "Protecting yourself from the words and the looks and the assumptions." She sounded offended by that. For a moment, he thought she was offended by him. Then she went on. "People are so stupid and selfish and awful, about all the wrong things. I like you touching me. I bet I'd like it even more with both hands. But that's up to you. It's always up to you. Like you say having sex in the first place is up to me. I could change my mind any time."

Her logic laid it out, straight and inarguably perfect. He couldn't breathe again, his vision blacked out slightly, like he couldn't process what he was seeing and do anything else. Then, carefully, he sat up, twisting a bit to face her. He wanted to be able to move, if he needed, to scramble out of the bed and, well, probably hide in the bathroom. His clothes were strewn around the floor. Then, carefully, he pulled off the left glove, then the liner, leaving them on his thigh.

She was watching his face all through it. When he had the glove off, he nodded once, and she looked down. He couldn't have done this without showing Claudio, he knew that. Since then, he'd managed to leave the glove off, here and there, when he'd just come out of the bath or when he was letting the salve soak in. The scars looked better than they had. They'd healed a bit more with the new salve, not so pink and red and obvious.

Hypatia didn't move, she certainly didn't say anything. He could feel her looking like it was a weight. Then, so carefully it was like she was doing deadly alchemical work, she asked, "May I?" He couldn't meet her eyes, but he nodded once. Her fingers - delicate, skilled, precise, all the things he'd noticed over the weeks - came up to rest against his palm. Then they spread out, his hand resting on hers, the tips of her fingers against his wrist. She might even be able to feel the way his pulse was beating, like he was a trapped rabbit.

"What parts of it hurt?" Most people would have asked if it hurt. She assumed it did, and of course she was right.

"The, um. Where the pinkie was, most." The scarring there was worst, an untidy sort of worst that pulled and bound. "If I hit it on something. The fingers in the glove help protect it a bit."

"Then I'll be careful. You be careful too. I don't want you hurting on my account." Now, finally, she met his eyes, briefly. "I do want you touching me. Will you? Please? With both hands, if you're willing?"

She made the question into a hope, into something she wasn't at all sure she'd get. It made it possible for him to say yes to it, not automatically retreat. Orion looked down at her. She'd settled on the bed like a queen, reclining at her leisure. Her hair was loose, long and beautiful, her skin was flushed, her nipples hard. That wasn't just the room, he was sure. He nodded once before considering his options. He wanted to spoon her, honestly, to arch into her from behind, but that was more awkward for the touching. The question was if he was brave enough for the other.

Then he thought about what it would be like, him on his back, her riding him. He'd get to see her in her pleasure, he'd be able to touch her with both hands, she'd have the freedom to move as she liked. That, if she was willing. He shifted a little more toward the middle of the bed. He tugged the pillow under his head, reaching to tuck the glove in safety on the table on top of the hairpins. "Will you ride me?" She blinked, and he added, "Punch them for that, too. You straddle my hips. I have my hands free. You have your hands free, and you can set the pace. And we can see each other properly."

She lit up at that, and moved quite swiftly. She settled on his thighs, her fingers dipping down to begin to stroke him to proper arousal. Not that he needed all that much encouragement. He took a breath, and then rested both hands on her, one on each hip. Orion slowly let his thumbs stroke, feeling the warmth of her skin, how the two hands didn't balance and somehow it didn't matter right now. All he needed was this moment to go on forever.

CHAPTER 32

CLAUDIO, THAT AFTERNOON, OUTSIDE
THE HUTS

Claudio came back from the centre of the camp, running his hand through his hair. That had been an entirely unnecessary meeting, a matter of show and making a bow of obligation, rather than anything actually useful. Claudio knew how to do that. He'd always known how to do that. He'd been brought up to do it from infancy, because Father certainly expected it.

Now, he opened the door to the working hut to find it empty; the lights gone dark. That was odd. It was past five, now, so it was possible they'd gone to wash up or for a walk before supper, or something of the kind. Still. He'd expected someone to be around. He ducked out, closing the door behind him, to go back to his own sleeping hut.

Coming around the corner, he saw Cammie appear like she'd been bending down behind the wall for something. Then he blinked, and she was sitting, her feet dangling. She gestured him over, the one-handed 'here first, please' sort of wave.

He went, because, for one thing, she probably knew

where Orion was. As he got close, she patted the wall. "You'll want a seat."

"That doesn't sound good?" Something in her tone was unusual, and he couldn't make sense of it. Though reading the tone from four reasonably ordinary words wasn't exactly easy.

"I am waiting for additional information. You should be too. Or you might tell me useful information?" She craned her head, then frowned at something.

Claudio didn't know what to say to that. It was, on the surface, a reasonable sort of comment, but he wasn't sure what to attach it to, precisely.

The curtains in the window on the women's side shook, then again. Cammie sighed. "Oh, my. I suppose it's going well, then? The sound charms are actually quite good, but of course, we didn't think about the building being not as sturdy as it might be."

There was a sudden sinking feeling in his gut. Claudio cleared his throat, not sure what answer he wanted here, or what answer he was dreading. "What's going on, then?"

"Orion told my sister she was beautiful. I ducked out for the next part. I'm not a voyeur. Well, more to the point, she knows how to make my life miserable if she wants, and that's no fun. Why give her cause? Anyway. They came around into our hut maybe four minutes later, she signalled that she was good with where things were, and I sat out here to make sure of it."

Claudio frowned, feeling like he was missing a step. Possibly several steps. "Together. They're not, um, arguing?"

"Engaged in passionate something?" Cammie was still watching the hut carefully, and he was sure she was counting the way the curtain moved. "Details currently unspecified."

"Wait. He said she was beautiful? And she was all right with that?" Definitely, he'd missed a step. It was catching up to him.

Cammie absent-mindedly patted his hand without looking at him. "If she hadn't wanted to go off with him, she'd have let me know."

"What could you have done? What would you have done?" Claudio didn't think that was the question that needed asking here, but he was still working around to those.

"Oh, I'd probably have bitten him. Somewhere sensitive." She sounded entirely blithe about it. She hadn't moved her hand, and that felt reassuring, somehow, that he wasn't entirely alone in his confusion. Even though, actually, now he thought about it, she was the one instigating all the confusion. Narrating it. Naming it. Whatever he wanted to call it.

"Biting seems rather specific?" It did, too. Orion would talk about punching people, but it really was mostly a placeholder. He meant doing something unpleasant enough they'd notice and change their ways. Claudio was fairly sure Cammie actually meant biting with teeth.

"Yes." She didn't expand on that at all, and when he glanced over at her, she had an entirely amused smile on her face.

Someone ought to be amused, he supposed. At least theoretically. Then he looked back at the hut, as the windows gave a decided twitch. "And you're sure you're not worried?"

That got a longer silence, and the hut didn't move at all now. Which could also be worrisome. He felt entirely out of his depth here in what signals actually mattered. "Insufficient data for analysis." Now her voice was brisk, the way she was when she was working. "Oh, I'll take pity on you, spell it out." Now there was the amusement back, front and centre. "He said she was beautiful. I'm fairly sure that whatever they're up to is an extended interaction at this point. With a fair amount of their clothes off. Probably off. You can do a whole lot without actually stripping. I should know."

"Cammie!" Claudio craned his neck. "What if someone hears you?"

"They won't. I took care of that already." Now she finally moved her hands, brushing them together. "I'm guessing you've never had the sort of thing where you've ended up in a hayloft or a broom closet or something like that. Because that's the spot you have and if you don't get into each other right now, there's no chance later?"

Claudio felt himself flush. "Not really my line of things, no." He hesitated. "The delicate dance of negotiating a spot of adultery at a house party, yes. Though there are a lot fewer of those by the old rules than there used to be, even before the war. The thing about going off riding and meeting up in some isolated spot, yes. Ideally that has a folly or a shepherd's hut or whatever the local variation is, so you have a roof over your head. Timing things so you both happen to be taking a trip to the same part of France, yes. Goodness, fancy running into you."

The last one made Cammie laugh. "I mean, that's Ibis and Mum, sort of, except they were on a research trip." It lightened her mood a little. "Right. So I got out of the way because I know what it means to be able to leap on the moment. And I'm fairly sure Orion had an idea how to make the most of the limited options for location. You'll notice they're not in your hut. That would be rude." The last bit was mock-prim, and it made Claudio laugh.

"Can't have that, no. He is considerate. I just— I don't know what got into him." He kept staring at the hut, as if it would tell him something new. It had stopped shaking, at least, and he couldn't decide if that was good or bad. "Do we knock?"

"No, we do not. One of them will come out, eventually. If they're, oh, another half hour or so, you and I can go fetch supper and bring it back and leave it in your front room. Think of it as keeping up unit morale. Does that help any?"

"It doesn't! I mean, yes, if things go well for them and keep going well for them, that would. Gods know Orion could use a bit of—" Now every word Claudio could think of was too crude to say here and now, to Hypatia's sister.

"He's a man who needed a bedding, and she's a woman who's needed one. Gods bless her." Cammie said, amiably, at least showing a way through that problem. "I don't know all of his reasons, and I don't even know all of hers. She doesn't talk about some of it. But I was fairly sure, from the gossip, he's at least showing her a good time."

"I didn't think he'd ever, I don't know, want to look at someone. He's been, I mean, they've been working together, arguing with each other. There's that kind of getting to know. But he hasn't really suggested anything like that." Claudio waved a hand. "The kind of thing that comes out in 'you're beautiful'." Then he nodded. "He does. I mean, Isembard made sure he knew how to be decent about it. A fling. Or…" No, he couldn't put words on that either.

"A fling." That was Cammie's voice when she was measuring out signals information, decoding a dozen things on the fly. "We definitely need more data."

They sat in silence for a good bit, then Claudio wasn't paying attention to the time at all. They could go get supper anywhere between six and about eight, and the change in the light would tell him enough. It was comfortable, at least, to be quiet with Cammie. She was letting her feet swing, but otherwise she wasn't fidgeting. She was staring intently at the door.

Both of them saw the hut start to move again, a different sort of motion this time. She glanced at him and then laughed. "I think that means it's going quite well. A second round, do you think?"

Again, he felt himself blushing. "I— how do you make it?"

"There was just enough time in there for a bit of a chat. Recovery." Then she peered at him. "It's something people do, sometimes, when they're short on time, and don't know when they're going to get a chance."

"Your Duncan?" It came out before Claudio could think better of it.

It wasn't really possible to see if she was blushing, at least not unless she went quite red. But she nodded, her curls bobbing. "We make the most of the time we get together, throw ourselves into it. Maybe after this is over..." she gestured at the working hut, this time, "You can meet him. He and I, we match each other in being on the hunt. And he's a fine dancer, he is. Vertically and horizontally." She snuck that last one in, watching Claudio's face as it clicked for him.

"I'm not so used to, well." Claudio shrugged, not quite looking away. That would be cowardly. "I didn't much want to play the field before I married. Not like Orion did. My wife did her duty, but she wasn't much interested in more than that with me. With anyone, I'm pretty sure I don't have Orion's problem that way."

"And there's the war, to keep you from feeling desperately lonely for the moment." Cammie's voice had gone softer, but there was an edge inside it, like a curve of a fang. She added, more quietly, "I'm sorry. That seems rather awful to live with."

There was a thing he absolutely hadn't wanted to name, but it was true enough, and had been true for a while. "I knew what it would be like. Enough. I said yes, and I knew what that meant. Our agreements, I could find a lover, if I wanted, but I've never met anyone I'd want to ask." Orion knew that, Isembard and Thesan knew, they worried about him. He'd never said it to anyone else. Saying it to Cammie was its own sort of ache, but he would never dream of even suggesting such a thing to her.

"I hope you do, sometime. Someone to have a good time with, in bed or not. Besides Orion."

Claudio felt his mouth quirk now. "I hope you'll be around. And Hypatia. I've got to like both of you. You make me laugh, remarkably often."

She might have preened then. "Good. We'll keep doing that." She considered the pace of the hut's movements. "Shall we go grab supper so it's here?"

"Sure." That took up a good twenty minutes, maybe a bit more. Three separate people wanted a word with Claudio. Just as they were coming back, the door to the hut was opening, and Hypatia was peering out. She waved at Cammie, who promptly took two of the food tins, and said, "Later!"

Orion came out a moment later, not quite slinking. It certainly wasn't shame he was wearing, but a wary sort of caution. Claudio tsked. "Supper. Come talk, yeah? Drink?"

"Drink and a smoke, if you don't mind?" Orion went through more of them than Claudio did, on average, though neither of them smoked as much as many soldiers. It did odd things to materia on the one hand. And, on the other, they weren't in combat and didn't need it for either nerves or hunger nearly as much as some. Claudio let

Orion get himself settled before he took his own seat. Finally, Orion looked up at him, and it was that glowing delight that Claudio hadn't seen in years and years.

Neither of them said anything for a good two minutes. Finally, Claudio asked, keeping his voice as light as he could. "You treating each other right?"

"Did my very best." Orion eyed his glass, took a good swallow of the brandy. "I— she's amazing. Beautiful and smart and sensible and willing to try things she had no reason to think would work out well, and I don't even know what I want, just more. A lot more."

There were many reasons Claudio should disapprove or should worry or should point out the challenges to their actual mission here. This was absolutely not something Junior Commander Roberts or her superiors would approve of, nor would Ibis Ward, nor would any number of other people. On the other hand, this was his brother, and his brother should be happy. "So Cammie and I should figure out a way to give you both a bit of privacy, then? And, um, charm the hut a bit more solid? The walls move in certain circumstances."

It took Orion a second to realise what that meant, and then he buried his face. "Both of you saw that?"

"Cammie did first. She had to explain the implication to me. And to be fair, the walls are, what, plasterboard?"

"I'll figure out some charms. I know most of the trench reinforcement ones." Then Orion started laughing, a rolling, easy laugh, like nothing Claudio had heard in ages. "Yes. I'd like more with her. More time. More conversation. More sex. More whatever it is she's willing for. If you'll help."

Claudio took a breath, let it out, and reached out to pat Orion's arm, once. "Of course, brother. Of course."

CHAPTER 33
HYPATIA, THAT EVENING

Hypatia couldn't quite look at Cammie for a moment. Part of it was that everything seemed much brighter right now, louder and shinier and perfect and overwhelming. The rest of it, of course, was that she knew some of what Cammie would say, but not remotely all of it. Instead, she nodded over her shoulder. "Talk before food?"

Without pausing to check, she went to fling herself on the bed. They'd remade it, done the cleaning charms. She wasn't rude like that. And especially when Cammie hadn't seen Duncan in months and months, it was not nice to rub it in her face more than was actually necessary.

Hypatia stretched out on the bed, which somehow now had entirely too much room in it. One stretch of an hour or maybe two, she wasn't actually sure what time it was, shouldn't change it that much. And yet, it did. She wanted a warm body right next to her. Skin to skin, an arm around her. The sex itself had disarranged everything she'd assumed in her head. The quiet afterwards had done so even more, honestly.

Orion had been entirely truthful when he said he liked talking about things. Once she'd collapsed in a sated heap on top of him, she'd slipped to one side. He'd gathered her to curl up with her head on his shoulder, left hand resting along her back, and just talked. Some of it - about her beauty, mostly - was fairly incoherent and certainly insufficiently calibrated by external standards. The rambling, though, it didn't come out in the ways she'd heard before from men who'd wanted something, but mostly with details he'd noticed. And he'd noticed rather a lot of those.

She hadn't stopped him. For one thing, she hadn't wanted to, even if she couldn't quite believe what he was saying. And for another, there was something about being there that she hadn't known she'd wanted. He was much stronger than her previous lovers, for one thing, with broad shoulders and muscles he knew how to use.

Hypatia might have, back in her school days, dismissed that as not her type. Turned out it was. Sometimes early data was utterly wrong. Or at least in this specific case. It would need more investigation, if they could. When they could.

But then he'd gone on, talking about nothing very much in particular, just being there in the moment. Small things he'd noticed, a half-forgotten reference he'd gone to some trouble to look up two days ago, what he was currently reading. They hadn't taken terribly long like that. She'd known Cammie would be outside and it was getting on for supper. But they'd had enough time she'd been able to lean into it, enjoy it, and roll around in that feeling.

That just made her sigh. It all felt like a dream, and she was ill-prepared for this sort of dream. She heard Cammie come in, and the distinctive creak of her bed, then the sound of her shoes hitting the floor. "Talk to me, would you?"

"Tell me what you see first. You're the one who reads code." Hypatia flopped onto her back. She'd put on enough of her uniform back on for dignity - the skirt and blouse and underthings - but it felt more constrictive than usual.

Cammie laughed. "Put on your dressing gown or whatever. We know you're not leaving the hut tonight, yeah?"

"True enough." Hypatia hesitated. "Were you going off hunting?" Then she hurried to add, "Not that I was going to ask him to come back over. Just."

"Maybe you'd like a little time on your own? Sure, I can go out for a bit more." Cammie stood, then came and dropped Hypatia's dressing gown on her, covering her face. "Change. Then talking. Then I'll leave you alone to be dreamy and write..."

Her voice cut off all of a sudden. "Write?" Hypatia pushed herself upright, then standing. She paused to blush at a particular patch of the wall. Then she set to work hanging up her uniform for tomorrow, putting her shoes aside neatly, and shrugging into a nightgown and dressing gown.

Cammie had settled on the bed again, now cross-legged. She shrugged. "You're awfully dreamy. Some people would be writing out names. Possible names." She said it quite gently. "Gods know, I've got a couple of pages I won't ever show to anyone in my notebooks here and there."

It made Hypatia sit down on the end of her bed with a thump. It wasn't like that. Probably. Certainly, neither of them had committed to anything other than a desire to have madly passionate sex sometime again in the near future, if they got the chance. "You got all that from a couple of minutes?"

"You weren't just in here for a couple of minutes.

What, an hour and a half? And two rounds, I'm guessing, enough to make the hut shake."

That, now, that was a distraction. "It did what?" Hypatia could hear the pitch of her voice rising. "The hut? Oh, gods." She fell back on the bed. "Moving? Enough you could... what did you see?"

"The curtain twitching, and the shake of the hut. I'm sure there are charms for that. Claudio saw too, though I had to explain to him what he was seeing. Not a man who's ever had a quickie in whatever bit of building was handy." She sounded sorry for him. Hypatia heard that much, though she was fearfully distracted by her embarrassment.

"I didn't mean. Gods. He's going to be..." Hypatia rubbed her face, as if scrubbing at it would make the red go away. Which was not how that worked, blood vessels being what they were.

"No one else saw. Claudio wasn't angry. Worried, I think. And there are certainly some consequences for all four of us, not just you two. So we should talk about that. What you want out of it. Under what conditions I get to bite him. Again." When Hypatia managed to look at her sister, Cammie had leaned her elbows on her knees, chin in her hands. "Claudio thought that was a very specific sort of threat."

"Were you threatening my—" She couldn't say 'my lover', though it was an entirely true statement. Or at least it was true in the past tense. It was not true in the present, either the simple or continuing forms. Hypatia was not currently having sex with him. She was attempting to have a conversation with her sister. She hoped there was a future tense that applied, but they had been unspecific about that. They'd had to be.

Now, of course, her mind wanted to skitter across and contemplate the chasm between what they'd been doing and Lady— no, she couldn't even put her name in there. Though actually, it didn't sound horrible. Lady Sisley.

She shook her head, then reached for a bit of ribbon to braid it up for the night. It at least gave her something to do. "Orion? Did you threaten Orion?"

"It was, in this case, a hypothetical threat. I said that you'd signalled you were good with whatever you had in mind, and that if you hadn't been, I'd have done something about it. Which would likely involve being bitten somewhere sensitive."

It made Hypatia wince. "Please don't. Especially his hand. Just. Please."

Cammie cocked her head. "Then we're going to need to talk about it. The implications. Even if there are a lot of variables you're going to say you don't know yet. Relationships are not actually made up of solvable equations most of the time."

"Besides, you're the one who's much better at maths. You and Orion." Which just got her in a full circle again. Good grief that was going to take some getting used to. Every single one of her thoughts went to him like the purest example of sympathetic magic she'd ever had in her life. She was an expert in this, thank you. She did not need the infant version of the demonstration.

Cammie went on when Hypatia didn't say anything else. "So. Topics to be discussed. What kind of schedule you'd like for the hut. What I get out of making it easy for you, besides sisterly devotion. To be fair, you've got a fair bit to draw on. What that means for the work." She then steepled her fingers. "And whether we tell them about the stoat."

"You don't have to. You never have to. You don't know if they're safe to tell." Hypatia leaned forward. "Don't do that because of me."

Cammie met her eyes now, deliberately. "If you get serious about him, and he finds out later, it's going to hurt him no end. Also, if he's awful about it, better to know about it sooner than later. Before you get," she paused and considered, "more attached."

Hypatia flopped back on the bed again. "Why do you have to be right all the time?" She was, too. "But if it's awful, what does that do to the assignment here? We can't stop now. They couldn't get anyone else in time."

"We don't have to solve it immediately. If they are decent about it - and they've been surprisingly decent about a number of other things, so I'm not actually ruling it out - they'd understand if we held off until after the invasion." Cammie was thinking aloud, partly, but that was how they worked.

"They would. Probably. But you know what— I mean, he has good reason to hate someone lying to him. Even if it's for good reason." Hypatia sighed, lifting herself to sit facing Cammie, her legs to one side. She was still getting used to how her body felt at the moment, honestly, it was as if the entire arrangement had been altered. Part of what she wanted tonight was to soak in a bath, probably. "Could we sound out Isembard about it, maybe?"

"He knows about Ibis," Cammie agreed. "And he knows about me. It'd have to go by portal, not journal, it's not the sort of thing I'd trust in the journal. I'll write something up, you can add whatever you want, and we'll see what he says."

"That's fair. And sensible. We'll get a bit more information. And you can use the weasel as an explanation. Not the details, just that you got the scent of something out of place." Hypatia felt a bit better now.

"And if, well, if the topic comes up, in a way that I could duck, but it'd be weird later than it did, I'll make my best judgement. How's that?" It was an exceedingly generous offer on Cammie's part.

"You are the best sister." Hypatia frowned. "I mean. I don't even know what we're doing. Besides both being clear we would like another round or three, if we can. The physical part was..." Then she laughed. "I was wrong this morning. Previous experiences were not actually fine. My charts are all mislabelled. It'll be a bit."

Cammie threw back her head and laughed at that. "I wish you much pleasure in the process, then. I rather liked how he looked at you, actually, the bits I saw. Like he hadn't expected to ask, certainly hadn't expected you'd say yes. Like you were something he wanted very much, but not in the rude, awful, possessive way, but to treasure."

Hypatia sighed. "He was, it was just. He does have a lot of skills. And he knew he had them. He doesn't when it's knowing things, mostly, had you noticed? He keeps giving sources and citations, like that makes it clear he knows things? I'm going to have to think about that more."

"They'd both have made good Owls, actually, if they'd been allowed to be. Even though Orion keeps going on about Richard's Boar, so that too. Like he's putting on the show of being one." Cammie considered. She stood up, suddenly, beginning to rearrange into suitable bits of her uniform to go out hunting in. Blouse and skirt, mostly, though she checked the stone was in her pocket. "What do you like about him, then?"

That was a challenging question to answer. "I like his loyalty." She hadn't tried to put a name on it until now. But she did like that. "He's not going to make a promise he can't keep. And that probably means no promises, for a good while, at least. Except that we'd like another round, sometime. I think..." She let out a huff of breath. "I think that's what we can have right now. Work first, work and magic and maybe saving lives with it. After the invasion comes off, then we can figure out what's after that." She couldn't think that it wouldn't. That way lay utter despair. Also spoiled magic, wasted supplies, and a lot of time and energy that no one could recover.

"Right. It'll be interesting to see how you two are when it's work. And Claudio knows, I'm sure they're having their version of this conversation just over there." She gestured with her chin at the wall behind Hypatia. "Anything else?"

Hypatia couldn't look at her sister for this part. "His passion. He's alive, fierce about it, and I don't understand it, and I want to. But he didn't think I'd like him. That anyone would like him, not like that." Hypatia understood the feeling, and she still didn't have words to talk about it. "I maybe should ask Ibis about some of the Hetheru devotions, though that would tip him off. Beauty and passion and love, all coming out."

Cammie snorted. She didn't follow the same sort of practice there, or faith, but she certainly knew the basics of it. "It would in fact tip your very intelligent brother off that you've fallen for someone, at least as far as bed. I'd ask Mum, but that's just adding a step." She shrugged. "In due course, maybe. In the meantime, I'm glad to clear out for a couple of hours every few days if we get a little break. A long walk, or maybe Claudio will let me borrow a chair in their front room." Cammie considered, pulled the hairpins out of her hair, then put her hair back in a tight knot at the base of her neck, stabbing the hair pins in to anchor it. She was definitely planning on a hunt then.

"Going for rabbit?" Hypatia asked cautiously.

"Mmhmm. If I can get one. If I'm not back in an hour, feel free to eat my supper." Cammie turned. "Leave the window cracked if you go to bed. But I bet you'll be up a bit." Now she was just teasing.

Hypatia smiled, and didn't argue. "Supper, bath, dreaming a bit, yes. Shoo. It's near enough twilight. Good hunting. Come home safe."

"Always do." She knocked on the window frame softly, twice for luck, then touched her fingers to the lips and the frame. She was feeling a tad more superstitious than she did sometimes. She'd picked that one up from Duncan. Then she was furry and on four legs, with almost no transition. Hypatia got up to give her a hand out the window and waited until she couldn't hear a sound on the wall on the far side. Then she went off to heat up her supper and consider her life and her choices in rather more detail.

CHAPTER 34
CAMMIE, THE NEXT MORNING, MAY 10TH

I n one way, it was helpful that their Wednesday abruptly got much busier than they'd expected. Junior Commander Roberts wrote a note in the journals almost as soon as they were in the working hut. She let them know that additional information was coming by despatch later that morning. It meant they had an hour or two, maybe three, to finish up the other things on their desks, get themselves in order, and prepare for a new onslaught of demands and documentation and work. Status of that work, unknown, of course.

Cammie had spent those hours finishing off her notes on several points. She'd been helping Hypatia cross reference likely locations for the talisman drops, what names might be used, or how they might be referred to. She'd also been working through some folklore, to see if there were any other places where they could draw on the resonances beyond the battlefields they'd already talked about.

There was, actually, a fair bit of folklore to work with, but Cammie was mostly sure those were Fatae, and it was best not to mess with the Fatae. Particularly the sorts that turned up with names like Ech-Goblin. Those looked like white horses strung with bells that wanted to lure you onto their back for a small spot of drowning. If she wanted that, she could get it from a kelpie without crossing the Channel.

Except, of course, that the kelpies weren't supposed to do that sort of thing anymore, given the Pact. She did make a note to ask Mum later why kelpies were described as black horses, more or less, and the Ech-goblin was apparently white or ghostly. Though the similarity of the name was a thing, as well, the kelpies were sometimes Ech-uisque or a couple of other terms that began with 'ech'. There was likely an academic paper in that. If there wasn't already, she could think about writing one.

And it would be a nice topic to wrangle over with Mum that was not about the war, how Cammie was, how Duncan was, and how Hypatia was. Or any other topic where Mum would be entirely too perceptive for comfort. Cammie kept a stash of that sort of question for good reason, and several of her standbys were getting a bit worn. Twice, people had published about them, which was fine when it came to academic expansion of knowledge, but annoying when it came to Cammie's need for reasonably neutral engaging topics.

Of course, she was also keeping a watchful eye on Orion and Hypatia. Mostly Orion, because he was the one she was dubious about. Twice, Cammie looked up to meet Claudio's gaze. He was doing the same thing. They'd smile, go back to watching their respective siblings and their work, and repeat at intervals.

To be fair to them, both Orion and Hypatia were actually focusing on their work, and at separate ends of the room. Hypatia was checking their supplies, so that whatever the despatches brought, she'd be ready to make orders. Orion was busy with some logistics planning about what kinds of army they should be pretending to be. It seemed to suit him brilliantly, he kept thinking of dimensions that Cammie had not considered properly. He'd obviously studied a great deal of martial theory, magical and otherwise, and not just because he found it interesting. Specifically, as he'd explained it, how much metal in the forms of tanks and artillery they should be impersonating with the talismans.

At half-ten, there was a knock on the outer door. Claudio stepped out, and they could hear the conversation clearly enough - thanks to the sound charms - from the inside. He stuck his head in. "Despatch at the gate, I'll be back in a minute." Then he disappeared, leaving the three of them in the peculiar limbo of army service. The mode of waiting was all about being about to be exceedingly busy but not quite yet.

Cammie felt rather sorry for the despatch riders, honestly. Most places, they'd get to come in, have a cuppa and a bit of something to eat, maybe wash up. Here, they got turned around at the gate, and had to go right off again to whatever the nearest other base was. Not Camp Griffiss, that was American. Cammie wasn't sure where the nearest British base was, actually.

Twenty minutes later, about the point where Cammie was considering going after him, Claudio came back, a thick bundle of papers wrapped in brown paper in hand. "ATS, very curious about the camp. They wanted me to stick around until they were sure she was gone," Claudio said, putting it on the table and rummaging in his jacket for his pocketknife. "The camp's a bit nervous, I think, in general."

"We still don't know much about what they're doing, or how that's involved with what we're doing. Check the charms?" Cammie suggested, generally, pulling out a sheaf of paper for notes. Orion went around the corners of the room and did that. And he did both checks. He was diligent about that. He had one to make sure their charms were still working, and another to make sure no one had planted something that would let them overhear.

Cammie would have said the second wasn't at all likely, but she could in fact think of a couple of ways to do it. Sensible people checked regularly. One or the other of them ran a check any time there was any concern, and every couple of days otherwise. By the time Orion came back, Claudio had the packet of papers open, and he'd pulled up his chair to the main work table they used. The files were divided up into five groups. Hypatia sat next to Cammie, across from Orion, which meant they would be looking at each other, but also that Cammie could kick her ankle if needed. That would do fine.

"One for each of us, it looks like, and a general file." Claudio flicked through his, quickly. "Looks like mine's additional information about diverting attention from the actual invasion, mostly. Orion?"

Orion was skimming through his own folder. "Similar." He frowned at something. "I hope they know what they're doing with the tanks. There's a geological report here. I'll need some time with it."

"Mine's mostly information for the illusion work, more details about the timing for the bombing raids, and where we might be able to get things dropped. Quality time with the map for me." Hypatia flipped through a couple more pages, then nodded. "Plenty of coordinates, though."

Cammie was frowning at hers, then she flipped back a few pages and read through again. "I am going to need a lot of time, I think. This looks like intercepted messages, including what I'm fairly sure is esoteric coding. You know how awful alchemical language is at the best of times for obscure symbolism. This looks like it went through at least three languages and a side of automated decoding that transposed characters a few times."

"Can I help with the alchemy?" Claudio offered it a little cautiously. Cammie hadn't threatened to bite him, after all. "It's not my speciality, but I know most of the theory and references pretty well."

"Sure. I'd appreciate another set of eyes. It'll be a bit." At that, they split up to their own desks. Cammie put up a little bubble of silence around her own space. If someone disturbed her, so help her, she would bite them. She fell into the work easily enough, and then she stayed there and stayed there. People moved around the room. She was fairly sure they came in and went out. Finally, she was aware there wasn't enough light, and that her neck was complaining loudly, and she was starving. She'd got through the whole stack, she at least had a sense what she was dealing with, now.

Cammie sat up straight, hearing her neck crack twice, and then blinked. Claudio was settled in a chair, reading something that looked like a research book from this distance. He was leaning it on the table now, but he was watching her. Cammie grimaced and ran her hands back to tuck her hair in. "Keep you waiting?"

"I figured I'd make myself handy here. Hypatia's working on something in your hut. Orion went out for a run and he's currently buried in an obscure bit of military history magical theory? I do not begin to follow it, but I'm sure I'll have an hour explanation coming as soon as I ask. I expect cross-references to King Richard's boar, given everything." He didn't seem bothered by the idea at all. Certainly not any more than Cammie minded the equivalent lecture about whatever eddies and byways of sympathetic magic theory her sister had come across recently.

"They really are both like that, aren't they? Not that either of us has room to throw stones. Maybe a little about the hour of non-stop information. I try not to do that to people unless I'm sure they're interested." Then Cammie's stomach grumbled again. "How late is it?"

"Getting on for ten. No wonder you're hungry. You worked right through supper. I kept yours for you, it's there. Keep-warm charm and all."

He'd brought it in here, which meant either Hypatia didn't want to be bothered for a bit, or that Claudio wanted to talk. Possibly both, it could always be both. "You're saying eating it here would be smart?"

"Can't have you fainting from hunger, can we? That's no good for your code-breaking." He flicked a finger at the piles of paper. "How much of a tangle is it?"

"I could definitely use your help - tomorrow, or the day after - with the alchemy. There are a number of phrases I'm fairly sure are encoding things twice over. Once in the encryption, obviously, but then the message itself has things that mean things to the individual people, but wouldn't to an outsider. There are some curious repetitions, and I think they're too frequent for chance, though. That's lazy code work. Giles would not approve. I also do not approve."

A moment later, Claudio stood up, then gestured at the central table. "Eat here? I've got a bottle of beer for you, if you like."

"Gods, yes. Please." She hadn't realised until that moment how much she wanted a beer. Cammie stood with a few more creaks, stretched, and then claimed the comfiest of the worn chairs at the table. Claudio set down the meal tray with a slight flourish. That did not match the food - mushy peas, mash, and some sausages. But it smelled better than the average canteen meal here usually did, and she frowned at it.

"Hypatia doctored it up a bit. She says you'll think it has actual flavour now. I gather you two do a bit of that?" With that, he eased himself into the chair next to her, kitty-corner around the table.

"Mum and Ibis sent along a lot of dried spices. We both like a bit more spice than some. Not that that's hard in lots of Albion. Those are dried peppers in the mash, and garlic, mmm, and she did something with a bit of mint in the peas." The sausages, mind, were one of the reasons she'd done a proper hunt last night. She got particularly cranky on the limited meat rations. Sausages were at least half filler it seemed, these days. She took a bite, then tested the peas, and sighed. "All right. I earned this."

"Long since." Claudio agreed. "And extra today. And I swear, Hypatia and Orion are not making the cottage shake."

"Hasn't been time to do the charms, has there?" Cammie snorted, though mostly she kept eating.

"Orion has some in mind. He'll do both cottages. Though I think for private time, he'd rather be in yours than ours. He was going on about the colour and the furnishings this morning."

"It's not our fault if you men choose darker colours." She considered. "I'm guessing that oxblood burgundy, mostly. All the Fox House implications, none of the Council assumptions, and there's plenty around in oxblood."

Claudio had the decency to flush. "Rather, yes. It really goes better with wood panelling than plasterboard. And we've got navy blankets." Then he added, quickly. "You're welcome to come make use of our front room whenever they - um."

"Don't know how to finish that sentence, then?" Cammie chuckled, taking a sip of her beer.

"No." Claudio rubbed his face. "There's so many things that could go wrong. Also, some that could go right, but I don't even know how to talk about that."

"How's he, then?" Cammie thought it was only fair Claudio go first. She was still eating, after all.

"Not terribly coherent, but exceedingly happy? I haven't seen him in this good a mood for years. Since before the war. It's not just the sex, though obviously, that's a help."

"If it were that easy, a lot of men would be more cheerful than they are," Cammie agreed. It made Claudio snort.

"That'd take cooperation from women, and I'm rather sure you all have standards." He went on after a moment. "I think he's really missed touching. Not the thing you're thinking, just ordinary touches. And whatever else she did, she handled that fine. I was worried it'd get fouled up somehow."

"He's careful about the gloves. She didn't tell me about that. But she was dreamy as all get out last night, and humming this morning, and I also haven't seen her that happy in ages. So as long as it lasts, right?"

Claudio's chin came up, but he didn't comment on that. "What's Ibis going to think? I gather there's some history."

Cammie knew the story, but it wasn't one she could talk about. Mum had told her more than Ibis had. She'd also been clear Ibis didn't like talking about it. Mum didn't either, but Mum had a very accurate evaluation of the kind of trouble Cammie could get into if she didn't know things. "I don't know, honestly. He's going to be really cautious about it. It was Orion's great-uncle that was the problem."

"And he's dead now, and turfed from the title before that. The courts were very thorough." Claudio grimaced. "That whole mess was right when Orion was finishing school, and I don't think they told him half of it, so you know. Shooed him off into his apprenticeship with a very traditional sort who didn't let him out for events for six months."

Cammie snorted. "Works for some, apparently. I wouldn't have stood it that long, glad no one tried with me." She'd actually spent a fair bit of time being Giles's eyes. Then she'd worked with a number of other people he knew on both maths and cryptography. All through, though, Giles had made sure she had time to go out and do other things. "All right. I'll see if I can figure out more about Ibis. If Hypatia's happy, and I take her side, though, I'm..." She stopped. "I won't say he'll come round. He's as stubborn as the rest of us, and more prickly on average. But there is a point at which he stops actually arguing and just grumbles quietly in the background, and we can prob-ably work round to that promptly enough."

"You have a lot of confidence in your ability to do that?" Claudio sounded queer. Not as if he disbelieved her. That would be different. But as if he wasn't sure what to do now, none of the maps worked anymore.

"Enough. Hypatia's got different leverage than I do. Two on one's not fair, but it also is. Mum knows enough to keep out of some things." Cammie sighed and eyed her food. "Look, can you give me a pocket lecture on the alchemical metaphors to start with, so it's in my head before I go to bed? I know the red lion and the white eagle, obviously, but what else?"

"Oh, sure." He leaned forward, then pulled out a

notepad to scribble down some ideas, organising before he started. She appreciated that. Cammie was, in fact, exhausted, and she'd likely fall into bed as soon as she got back to her own hut. Getting terms in her mind before that would be a help.

CHAPTER 35

ORION, SUNDAY EVENING IN CAMMIE AND HYPATIA'S HUT

"**B**efore anything else." Orion cleared his throat. "Here. I hope you like them." He sounded rather like Claudio had, when he'd been walking out with Kensa. That was back in their school days, all stammers and earnestness. Hypatia had just drawn him into her hut, closing the door firmly behind him, then down the hallway into the bedroom. He brought out his hand from behind his back, and waited.

"What - this is beautiful! Are they paper?" Hypatia looked down at the four paper bellflowers in a little paper folded vase. He'd folded the paper himself. It mostly relied on the thumb and index and middle finger for that, and he'd managed smoothly enough after a couple of practice attempts.

Four petals curled down from the centre, and he'd tinted each of the four individual flowers a different colour. One was a deep blue, another purple, one a brighter magenta, and one a glowing pink. The last two even went rather well with the rag rug, actually. He hadn't been sure about that at all. "And what are you intending to say with these, please?" Her eyes met his for just a moment.

"You needn't read them in the language of flowers, if you don't want." Now he really was on the edge of stammering. Bellflowers were often read as everlasting love and constancy, though the colours on these changed that. "Choose the one you favour, if you like." It felt like she could shatter him into pieces, with a comment about them. The flowers weren't much, far less than he'd wanted to give her. It was absolutely the sort of thing Decima would have sneered at, and then made into a story used to mock him for months.

It made her go still, her hands cupped around the paper of the vase. Then she set it down very carefully, as if she were afraid it would break. "Are you a romantic, Orion?" As soon as she said it, Hypatia's hand came up to her mouth. "I mean. I don't think anyone's done anything like that for me. Personal. Where it's time and skill, both."

He reached to take her fingers in his. "I wanted to give you something beautiful and colourful. Like I said Wednesday, I can't do any of the usual things between rationing and our duties." He coughed. "I did think about finding a book you'd like, but I'd ask Isembard and Thesan, and they'd ask Pross, and that seemed entirely too odd."

That, now, made her laugh. "Fair enough. And whatever we are - besides, I hope, in bed in a few minutes - that's a particular step. Asking my sister-in-law about books." Her hands were free now, and she twined them round his neck. "Did you make them?"

"Learned from someone whose mother had a whole thing about teaching children by making things with their hands. A very popular theory, I don't know, someone in the 1850s? I don't remember the name, but the paper is lovely.

Magic for the colour, of course, and to attach the stems, glue makes them bend oddly."

"Show me how, sometime? Can you make other things? Not now. Sometime." Something in her interest made his heart beat faster, certainly made the rest of him even more interested than he already had been. Orion let his own right hand drift to her waist, then paused. He pulled off the right glove, then the left, depositing them both on the table by the flowers for safety. It felt decidedly odd and strange, but in a way that made him feel absolutely alive, here and now.

She turned to put them on her dresser, moving a small metal box, with the lid open. Her fingers brushed against it. Orion didn't know whether to ask about it or not, but then Hypatia turned. "My Sobek shrine." There was a tiny hesitation, then she picked it up, to show him a malachite crocodile on a resin river, blue as a perfect sky, the bank along one side dotted with what he recognised as specks of materia. Not that he could name any of it, or would dare to try except that he thought some of it was eggshells.

He swallowed hard. "What does that mean to you, so I don't get in the way?"

"He's Lord of the River, of the fertility. I was thinking, after our first night, after Cammie got out of the way for the rest of the evening." She closed her eyes, blushing. "Some texts talk about him as violent, aggressive, fierce. A crocodile, after all."

Orion didn't know what to say to that, though some of it cut near to the heart of what he thought about himself, in his worse moments.

She went on, without needing him to say anything. "But like I said, he defends the innocent, avenges. And sometimes that's what's needed for new growth." She opened her eyes to watch him now. "There's a lot there that reminds me of you. And the way you are fierce about the land, even when you're not talking about it."

It made his breath catch, and he absolutely didn't know how to say anything. It wasn't a moment for words. Then his arm was around her waist, drawing her against him to kiss, then pulling back before kissing, over and over. Bit by bit, they managed to get their uniforms off, deposited into a jumbled, mixed pile on the floor.

He was glad he'd cast that all-too-necessary charm again, to keep him from going off entirely too early. The way Hypatia gave herself over to pleasure this time kept bringing him to the edge. It wasn't any single thing she did, it was the combination of everything. He still saw and felt far too many of those moments of hesitation, as if she wasn't sure what was right in the moment. But then she'd venture a touch or give herself over to the sensation, and her reactions were everything.

They fell onto the bed in a dance of entirely mutual exploration. He couldn't bear not to watch her, and that rather limited their position choices. Once she was ready, he settled between her legs, her knees around his waist, and slipped in. At the moment, it was all about letting her arch and moan and find what felt wonderful to her.

He wanted this to last. He wanted her to feel what it was like when all the raw desire in him boiled over, how she could ride and delight in it. She certainly enjoyed making him groan as she moved and twisted, her body absolutely on display for their mutual pleasure. He left marks along her shoulder and collarbone, but not too far up onto her neck. Charms could do a great deal, but no sense taking chances with someone seeing something at the edge of her uniform collar.

Besides, there was plenty of her body to kiss and suck and worship. It wasn't a word he'd used before, even in his head, but it felt right here, before he reached the point where there was no space for thought at all. He brought her off first, rather triumphantly for the second time, then his own need overwhelmed him, and he couldn't think of anything else.

He had just enough strength in the aftermath to rearrange, spooning around her body, her back to his chest. He'd dreamed about this for days, and now, here he was, all that skin touching and his right hand settled between her breasts. He was quite sure they'd have another round before he had to get dressed, help her tidy up, and go back to his own hut. Best of all, they didn't have to rush, they still had plenty of time. He let his thumb continue to brush her skin, just now and then. His other hand was up over his head, mostly covered by the length of her hair, which was beautiful too.

Somewhere in there, he let out a sigh, and she wriggled a little against him. "Penny for your thoughts?"

"Enjoying this, mostly. You, right here." Orion kissed the back of her shoulder. "Do you mind that I marked you up a bit, I think?"

"We've salve. You've no idea what Cammie gets herself into sometimes." Then she swallowed. He could feel that. "I mean."

"Dancing, for one. Swing dance seems to me like near enough a combat sport, the way she goes at it." Orion offered it as a truth, but now there was a thread he'd spotted of something Hypatia was nervous about. He wasn't going to press, just notice it.

Giving her the out had been right, though, because he could feel her relax a little. "With a partner she knows,

316

she's stunning. She took to it like they'd invented it for her. She and Duncan are absolutely magic together."

Orion nuzzled a little more at her neck, because it was right there, and it needed a bit more attention. "Is she all right with this? It's got to be hard on her. And on Claudio."

"You'd know better about him." Hypatia shifted slightly, before deciding against twisting so she could look at him. "He seems very stoic about things, on the whole."

It made Orion laugh, and he tried not to be too loud in Hypatia's ear, which mostly meant resting his forehead against her shoulder to muffle a bit. Then he squeezed her tight. "Stoic's not the word. We're both raised to a particular role, and he's so much better at his than I am at mine. He wants to do well, too. He's convinced he's not, but he keeps on trying to meet his own standards, even if they're utterly unreachable. I admire him a lot for that."

Now, she did twist, so she could peer at his face as he looked up. "And you?"

Of course, Orion didn't really have an answer for that. Then, slowly, it came to him. "I want to do something that matters. Something where I made a particular difference."

"This will." She was absolutely confident about it, and for a moment, he couldn't understand why. "The work we're doing here, the four of us. It should be a dozen, really, and we're still making it work, and if we're right, it could save thousands of lives. Change the course of the war. I don't know, all sorts of things."

"I'm glad it's just the four of us." That was by far the easiest thing to start with. "Claudio hasn't talked a lot about up north, but I get the very strong impression it was one of those 'too many cooks spoil the broth' problems. Everyone getting in each other's way. That's what I like about it, here. You and Cammie know how to work together. Claudio and I did."

"And the four of us seem to be doing quite well. Cammie's brilliant at what she does. I'm, I don't know. Creative, but not as sharp as she is. Claudio's got a dedication that won't stop, like you said. His standards, his expectations, and in a project like this, that goes a very long way." Hypatia kissed his shoulder now, before letting her head fall back on her pillow again.

"And me?" His voice didn't quite crack at the end of it, but it was a near thing.

"You keep showing new sides of yourself. Let's, mmm. It isn't just the fact you gave me something, it's the fact you thought about what you could give me that I'd like, despite quite a few limitations. And then, even before that, you'd picked up the skills to do it. You keep surprising me with the things you know or you've read, and it's not like I'm not well read, and my family isn't." The last bit from her was deeply amused, actually.

Orion nodded. Again, he wasn't sure what to say. Part of him wanted to talk about how he always felt stupid, except with just a few people. He knew he wasn't, not really, but that didn't change how he felt. But that wasn't a conversation for right now. "I like things making sense." There, that was a good way to put it. "I like people who explain things. Not just what to do, but how it works, why you do it that way. Claudio's great at it. Isembard and Thesan, of course. The flowers are like that. He was making them when we were behind the lines, an evening where there wasn't much to do, but we had scrap paper. There's something about making them out of near nothing that appeals."

"Sometimes, I think that's what we're all doing in our lives. Taking something and turning it into an entirely different thing." Hypatia paused, then asked, "What was it like for you, spending time with people who hadn't come up through Schola? The families you knew?"

That was a question no one had ever asked him. "Oh, gods. So confusing. So many things I didn't know, a lot more than usual." He remembered what that had been like during the first months in his original unit. "It wasn't just the fighting parts, they taught us that. I went through training with everyone else. But what people's fathers did for work, the fact their mothers didn't, or did very different things than I'm used to."

"I suppose Claudio's mother is not the sort of thing that's common in the non-magical." Hypatia agreed. "Women are in a lot more roles, professional roles, than used to be, even there, but it's still a fight."

Orion nodded. "Hobbies. I still do not understand cricket. Rugby makes a lot more sense, or football. Not that I've done more than a bit of pickup play. Rugby's actually rather like certain styles of bohort play. I just have to remember not to use magic. And the goal of the game is simpler. Instead of half a dozen win conditions, you just have one. Score points by getting the thing over the other team's line."

It made her laugh, nestling against him, her body shaking with it. "That's your version of swing dance. It was the music and the literature that got me. Not that I was entirely ignorant, but the things they cared about a lot, I'd heard less, and all that. It made me feel like I could never get my feet under me."

"Which is why this particular assignment, for all of the hours and the restrictions, and all that, is in fact a bit of a relief. Not just being with Claudio." Then he arched a little against her. "We still have some time. May I interest you in another round?"

"You only have to ask once." She arched a little. "How do you want me?"

So many ways, not that he could put any of that into words, and not that he was going to try right now. "Like we were a few minutes ago, me behind you? I'd like to see what you think of that." As she turned over on her side, facing away from him, he let his fingers wander down her body, just soaking in the moment.

CHAPTER 36
CLAUDIO, NEXT WEDNESDAY, MAY 18TH

Claudio had thought that they were all running headlong, desperate to get their work done, with no time to spare for much else. Orion and Hypatia had managed a bit more time together on Tuesday. But they'd managed it only by working through lunch and supper, eating while they caught up on reading, and working to nearly ten at night on the Monday. Claudio had spent Tuesday catching up on his own reading and research, desperate to find a few more references they could use.

Wednesday morning, though, one of the soldiers brought over a letter, even before Claudio went to get the mail. It had the green seal and ribbon that marked it as being some official document from Trellech, but Orion couldn't see the seal itself. That meant it could be the Ministry, the Courts, the Guard. It could theoretically even come from the Penelopes if they actually went in for formal documents with sealing wax, which seemed unlikely. Not unless the sealing wax did six other interesting things, anyway.

Claudio glanced at it, starting to open it, then pulled his hand back, stung. "Pardon, Cammie. This is for you."

She'd taken it, opened it quickly, and skimmed the contents. "I'll be gone tomorrow. Probably just for the day. I'll write in the journal if it will be longer." She held up a hand. "Don't ask."

Neither Orion nor Claudio asked. Orion had the good sense not to want Cammie annoyed at him. And that had been before Claudio had conveyed the odd and precise comments about biting. He held up both hands. "Wasn't going to."

That evening, over supper, he'd seen the two women having an increasingly tense conversation through their window while he was reading on the wall outside. They'd pulled back the curtains in their front room for a bit to air things out, but of course the soundproofing charms meant he couldn't hear anything.

Orion had come out, then blinked at the window. "They're upset, aren't they?" Checking in with Claudio's read of the situation was something Orion did, and things went better when he felt he could.

Claudio had nodded slightly. "I don't think at each other, though. See how they're leaning towards each other? There's Hypatia's hand on Cammie's arm. They wouldn't do that if they were fighting." Having to spell it out made him feel a little better, but he hadn't been able to make any more sense of it than Orion had. And he hadn't got a good look at the seal before it bit him. They had been forced to set it aside, as one mystery they couldn't solve, not without at least one of the women being willing to help. Orion wasn't going to press Hypatia about it either. That would foul up everything, and he knew it, even without Claudio warning him against it.

Cammie had been gone before the rest of them were

out and about, and she didn't come back until well after eight, looking exhausted. Hypatia had kept herself busy in the working hut, and it wasn't as if Orion was going to leave her alone with it. Claudio wouldn't either, and he'd stuck around to see if he could help, at least until someone told him to go away.

When Cammie came in, though, Orion's head came up immediately. Claudio couldn't tell why, just that there was some key information there. Then Orion raised his hand, the sign of 'let me talk'. Claudio just nodded once.

Cammie strode over to her desk and flung her uniform jacket off, though it was not actually terribly warm out. Her hair was coming out of her bun, and she pulled her equipment out. It was all the short furious gestures of someone who wanted to attack and fight and didn't have a target.

Orion knew a lot about that. He lived that mood pretty much every day. He circled around in front of her desk, where she could see him, not getting too close to her. Then he turned his hands palm up. "Do you need a fight to get it out of your system so you can do anything else? We could figure something out."

Cammie's chin came up. She stared at Orion for a long moment. It was an aggressive sort of stare. It seemed intended to put its target on notice that it was a mouse and this was an owl, and there was only one way that fight went. Orion held his ground, and one part of Claudio's mind began analysing the not-duel before him. He was fairly sure Orion could handle himself if needed, even though Cammie was exceedingly competent in other ways. Probably. It was quite a stare.

Then she let out a huff of breath. "You don't know what you're asking."

"No. I don't. But you're upset, and you're my..." Orion

stalled, as if sorting through and discarding several words. "Friend. What do you need right now?"

She didn't move for a long moment, a dozen heart-beats, maybe two dozen. Without moving, she asked, obviously aiming at Hypatia, a string of something in Arabic. Probably Arabic.

Hypatia stood up, brushing her hands together, and then tucking her current work into the desk where she could lock it away for the night. "Come to ours, would you? Cammie, go change first. You'll feel better for it."

Cammie stood, just as abruptly, stalking out without any comment at all. Once the door closed behind her, Claudio cleared his throat. "We'll give you a minute or two, clean up in here, and come bearing the decent brandy and biscuits?"

Hypatia nodded once, without looking at Orion, and then she was out the door after her sister. Claudio pushed back from his desk as the door closed. "You all right?" Orion was standing there, staring after them, his hands out, as if he didn't know what to do now.

"I'm not sure." He swallowed, reaching to rub his fore-head, and now Claudio could see a bit of sweat. Orion reached into his jacket for a handkerchief.

"What did you get when Cammie came in?" That, at least, seemed like a question that could be asked, instead of all the unanswerable ones about how Orion had kept his self-control like that.

"I know where she was. Not why, not on which side. But she's been under the truth-telling enchantments of the Courts. And it was the Trellech Court, not soc-and-sac or anything." Orion finished mopping his face and jammed the handkerchief back into his jacket. "I've done it myself often enough now."

It wasn't a magic Claudio knew, not that way. The

Lords of the land could call it, in certain circumstances, if their magic were strong and well-trained enough, if they were on their land and had due cause. The first two weren't a problem for Orion, and the latter two had come up a few times before the war.

"Oh." He should say more. Claudio knew he should. "That's a thing, isn't it? Only way we're going to find out more is go talk to them."

"Hah. Not sure that's going to help, but you're right. Here, you take that side, I'll do this, make sure everything's settled up?" Orion was already in motion. He put away the materia, locking files in compartments in the desks, then making sure the wards closed behind them. It was all the small things that had become habit in the last weeks. They paused in their own hut to discard their own jackets, both of them sensing it would be better to be less formal. Claudio grabbed the brandy and their mugs, and Orion snagged the biscuit tin.

When they knocked next door, Hypatia opened it. "Best come back. There's not much space here, is there?" The front room theoretically had space for four, if one didn't mind standing, but not if any of them wanted to move or gesture. The bedroom had a bit more. And seating for four, between the beds and trunks. It wasn't as if Orion hadn't been back there.

Claudio took in the room, since he was seeing it for the first time. There were bright colours, unlike his and Orion's beds. They were covered in turquoise and blue. Rag rugs on the floor made the place look positively comfortable despite the plasterboard walls and the uniforms. The bright paper flowers on one of the bedside tables next to a little decorative diorama of a crocodile made it more purposefully cheerful.

Cammie was perched on her bed, changed into a skirt

that was a deep red, and a matching cardigan. He'd never actually seen her in anything other than uniform, not in all the weeks there. Hypatia still had most of hers on, but she discarded the jacket and pulled on a turquoise cardigan that matched her blanket. As she settled next to Cammie, she gestured at her own bed. "Might as well sit there, or the trunks if you'd rather." She clearly didn't think Cammie was a threat, or at least not to Hypatia herself. There was still something fierce in Cammie's expression, that made Claudio unwilling to generalise too far.

After a moment's hesitation, Orion settled on Hypatia's bed, nearer the pillow, leaving the foot for Claudio. Claudio carefully set the brandy down on the empty spot on the bedside table, set the mugs on the ground after a moment, not wanting to invade Cammie's space. He sat. It was entirely awkward, and it got more so as the silence went on.

Before it got entirely intolerable, Orion burst out with, "It's like a cartoon of a deeply confused tea party in *Punch*. Though I'm not smart enough to come up with a funny caption."

That broke the tension a hair - Hypatia managed a smile. But they also couldn't quite ask what was going on. It was for Cammie to say something, more or less. Finally, after one of those silent conversations with her sister, she crossed her arms. "Will you take oath on not sharing what I'm going to say while we're here?"

Hypatia blinked, twice. Not the question she'd expected, then. Not it was any help in figuring out the topic they were about to swear to. Cammie lifted the fingers on one hand off her arm. "Nothing that conflicts with your current oaths, unless you've made some I don't think you have."

"How are we supposed to answer that, Cammie?"

Claudio said, really quite reasonably under the circumstances. "Does what you're telling us have to do with national security? Does it cross your own oaths? Does it put someone at risk?"

Quickly, quick as gunshots, Cammie replied, "Yes, no, yes."

Claudio felt the footing slip away under his feet. Before he could ask anything else, Orion was right there. "Does Hypatia know what you're going to tell us?"

That got a nod before Cammie added, "Well-spotted. She does, all except what actually happened today. Which I would tell her either way, whether you hear it or not."

Orion pressed a little further. "Who's at risk? You? Someone else? And have you made any oath about telling anyone else?"

Cammie half-laughed now. "Definitely not slow in your logic. Me, yes, at risk, but not just me, and I'm not telling you who else. And no, I wasn't asked for an oath. Besides, you were there for the part that might have been touchy. You just didn't know it."

"All right, now you're completely speaking in riddles." Claudio said, leaning forward a bit. "I want to know, please."

Orion was right behind him, and then both of them were making oath - this was a fairly simple form, the kind they'd both made enough times, even before the war. Cammie waited until they were done, then she lifted her chin, proud and steady like a famed warrior out of legend.

"Today, one Adrastos Rix was on trial for espionage. He was nosing around Camp Griffiss a few weeks ago. I spotted him, couldn't identify him at the time, but reported him to the proper people."

"Rix?" Claudio reacted first. "I had a bet on he's in Intelligence. Some right to snoop."

Cammie threw back her head and laughed at that. "Not anymore, he's not. Didn't know how to keep his nose to himself and he made the mistake of doing it at an American base. He's lucky he didn't get handed over to them directly, honestly."

Orion frowned, piecing things together. "But he was tried in Trellech. It's the truth-telling charm. I know how it feels. You had it on you. And the summons, of course. If you'd reported it to the Army or whoever, there wouldn't be any of that."

"It is a good thing you took the oath, honestly. You'd keep gnawing at it." Cammie said that in one of those tones Claudio knew Orion would have trouble reading. He thought it was a bit of praise, but wrapped up in something complicated. Now, he just nodded, because it was a true enough sentence.

"If it was something you spotted, and it had to do with Camp Griffiss - during the dance?" There were only so many times they could reference. Claudio blinked. "Is that why there was something about them tracking through the portal?"

"Yeah." Now Cammie shifted, not relaxing, but subsiding a little from rigid attention. Claudio took his cue and leaned forward to pour some brandy and offer it. "I'm sorry, I should have realised, when you both went out to Schola, that they might be still."

"How could you have known?" Claudio asked. It was a reasonable question.

Orion half-stood to offer them both biscuits. He was watching Hypatia now. She was still wary, but whatever Cammie was, Hypatia was more like a nervous rabbit. No, that wasn't quite right, either. A rabbit would be prey. More like an owl, observing from a distance, or some other raptor, not down in the fray. "Are you all right, Hypatia?"

She looked up at Orion, and there was a tiny smile on her face. "I will be in a bit, I hope." She then glanced at the room and stood to pull her trunk to the space between the beds. "Put things there, would you?"

That was not an informative statement at all, but both Orion and Claudio knew better than to ask about it or to protest. "Right. Go on then, Cammie? Biscuits and brandy as needed. This isn't a night to stint." Claudio tried to be encouraging about it, and he felt he might not have succeeded sufficiently.

CHAPTER 37

CAMMIE, IN CAMMIE AND HYPATIA'S HUT

Cammie tried not to squirm. It wasn't going to help anything. This was the sort of conversation she found frustrating with two feet, because the rest of her wanted to handle it differently. On the other hand, most conversations did not actually improve with teeth and pouncing unless what she was going after was a complete distraction from the topic.

It was the best chance they were going to get to tell the men about it. She had their oath. At some point she was going to have to take the leap. Hypatia had added a couple of layers of protective charms in here before they came in. Of course she had. And the men hadn't actually tested for anything, not that Cammie had spotted. It was a particular kind of a dance and a duel, and they'd see how it turned out.

The day had left a foul taste in her mouth, though. It had been long, the sort of long day that had been mostly tedium interspersed by moments of raw anger and frustration, and needing to keep a complete lid on it in public. She had been one of the early witnesses. She'd given her testimony under the truth-telling oaths to the judge and officers of the court, but not in front of Rix or his solicitor. Hers wasn't the testimony that made the case, it turned out. It was simply the information that had allowed them to realise there was a problem. A different category, that, and it meant the court had been glad to grant the petition to keep the source of her information private.

But of course, then she'd needed to sit through the whole thing. Ibis had offered to come meet her, but it wasn't actually easy for him to get away from Schola for a day. Also, she thought that would have tipped the audience's hand that there was something odd going on. If she was there in her ATS uniform, all proper, assigned nearby, it was one thing. If Ibis had been there, there would be implications.

She wished he had been, though. She'd hoped she could maybe sidetrack by Schola for a couple of hours. But the case ran through lunch, through supper, and to about eight at night. They had only brief breaks for sandwiches on awful bread and weak tea from the canteen. Cammie leaned forward to snag one of the biscuits, because Orion was right. It wasn't a night to stint.

A bit of biscuit, a bit of brandy, a fair dollop of bravery, and here she went.

She glanced at Hypatia, nodded once, and then she shifted. Four feet on the bed, before she reared up on her hind legs. It had been a long day. But for her, the shift always brought a surge of vitality with it, as if all her magic were now compressed into a smaller space, overflowing. Both men had stood, near leapt up, but they weren't trying to move toward her - or Hypatia.

After a moment's consideration, Cammie prowled her way over to her sister's lap, then up onto her arm. There were paintings of women holding ermines. There'd been quite a fashion for them in Albion after da Vinci's more famous one had become known. Ibis had been joking for a while that he'd attempt one of the two of them, if he ever had time when Cammie was properly in her winter coat. Hypatia automatically lifted her. Cammie settled one paw on Hypatia's shoulder, able to peer at them better.

There was a long pause, both of them standing, not moving, their jaws dropped open. It was actually hilarious. Once she was sure they weren't going to do anything suddenly, she launched herself off Hypatia's shoulder. She twisted and arched until she landed on the bed, then bouncing up and throwing herself into the air again. They didn't fascinate like rabbits did. Probably.

It did get them to sit down, both at the same time, the bed clanking a little. Hypatia said, without moving, "Cammie, they're not rabbits."

Big sisters never let anyone have any fun. Cammie did stop bouncing though, lifting up on her haunches to sniff now there was more information. Neither of them had called any magic to them, at least not to cast, though there might have been a bit of a protection ward in there. She wasn't as practised with those, on average, the kind that were produced in a second. Maybe they'd let her hone her skills with that now. Neither of them had reached for her. And neither of them had said anything at all.

Hypatia's voice cut into the silence. "May I ask, please, how you feel about shifters in a general way, and what that means for us, in the specific? When you manage to get your tongues back, trust Cammie to make a show of it."

Orion managed to gather his wits up first, though he kept his hands in his lap. Someone - well, probably Isembard, really - had trained him well, when confronted with a bit of decidedly twisty magic that wasn't currently danger-ous. "I, um." Not that it was a very coherent commentary.

"I'm not sure that I've ever known I've met a shifter." That made Cammie snort, one of the sounds that carried across well in both forms.

A beat later, Claudio offered, "Your particular emphasis on biting now makes a lot more sense, I admit." Then his eyebrows went up. "Wait. Was that you at the dance? Who bit Orion?"

That was going to need her shifting back, and she did, as smoothly as she'd turned furry. She'd put a lot of time and practice into the transitions, and right now she was glad of it, because it was a tremendously good trick. It made both of their eyes widen again, when all of a sudden, there was Cammie, on the bed, skirt smoothed down over her knees.

Cammie took her time answering. "I wanted to get at Rix." She wasn't going to apologise for it. It wasn't as if she'd had a lot of options at the time, even if she hadn't been interrupted in the middle of a hunt. Well. She could maybe apologise a little, or Hypatia would be cross, and they couldn't be having that. "I didn't mean to hurt you, though. I just wanted you to let me go so I could go after him."

"Rix is. Wait." Orion rubbed his face with the glove, then rummaged for a handkerchief. "I am about ten steps behind here."

"Let me see if I can summarise." Claudio looked almost amused. "Cammie is a stoat, yes, not a weasel? And you've been able to do that for quite some time."

"Not the sort of thing I picked up in the last six weeks, no." Cammie agreed, grinning toothily. "We've been a trifle busy."

"And when we were all at the dance, you realised that someone - um. Another shifter. Was there? Rix. Who is also a, um?"

"I did. He is a weasel, for the record. Stoats are bigger, by at least a little, and you may properly admire the black spot on my tail if you are very good at some future point. He was being sufficiently unweasel-like that I noticed."

Hypatia cut in here. "She is ridiculously vain about her fur. Don't encourage her. There'll be no living with her at all."

"And you've - obviously - known too. About all of it?" Orion frowned. He reached to pour out a swig of brandy in two of the mugs, handing one over to Claudio before holding up the bottle. Hypatia leaned forward with both of theirs, and he filled them up a bit more.

"I've known Cammie was a stoat near as long as she's been one. Minus a couple of hours, I think. About Rix since we got back from the dance. She can tell the rest of that, though. She was there for it."

Cammie took the mug, clinked it against Hypatia's and lifted it. "To people being willing to listen. I appreciate it, and I'm sure Hypatia does." She then tilted her head. "You haven't said what you think."

"That's because I'm bloody well not sure what to think." Orion said, all of it bursting out. "I know what the usual line on things is. Don't trust a shifter. They're not really human, they're disposable." That cut a little too near some of what Ibis was worried about. "But you treat it as if it's just a part of you."

"Well, I would," Cammie pointed out. "It is. No sense lying about it. Not telling people, now that's sensible, for all the reasons you just said and about three dozen more. Even before the part where a lot of people really like ermine fur, and owls are a problem, people have very odd ideas about the wildlife around them, and good grief, rat poison, don't get me started about rat poison."

At least three things on that list were also not at all

what they expected, and Cammie enjoyed that too. She would make her own fun, as much as required.

Claudio was chewing on more questions, the way he had of going along quietly before coming out with something sharply incisive. This time was no exception. "Do other people know?"

"Really, that's quite a demand." Then she took pity on them both. "Isembard knows. You can talk to him about it if you like, just make sure it's just him or Thesan who can see, no one else. I've helped him with getting some of the stones for the enhanced wards up on the roof, more than once." Then, after a moment, she added, "He gave us a letter for you. If we told you."

She let that settle there, right into the middle of the conversation. There was a terribly long silence, then Orion started laughing, the sort of full-throated laugh that went on and on. After a moment Claudio joined him, a bit higher-pitched. When they subsided, a little later, Cammie raised an eyebrow.

Orion coughed, then managed a sentence. "I wrote to him, actually, because I wanted to do something nice for Hypatia." He gestured at the paper flowers.

Cammie laughed. "And we'd written around the same time, it must be, asking him about your attitudes to shifters." She giggled then. "Oh, that must have made him wish for the ordinary follies of students." Then she got back to business. "Do you have questions?"

"Lots, actually." Claudio had caught up. "About shifting, I mean. You're right about the attitudes, of course you are. And I, for one, understand why you didn't let on. Though I'm glad - honoured - you felt you could tell us." Orion didn't say anything, and after a moment, Claudio added, "Your turn, you."

Orion was chewing on his lips. "You spotted Rix. And

under the circumstances, I don't mind the bite, I suppose, though I'd rather not in the future, if it's all the same to you."

"Keep treating my sister well, and I will save my bites for rodents and rabbits. Or at least not you." Cammie agreed, amiably. "I did. I got some advice on how to report it. Saying 'Golly gee, I'm a shifter, the nice sort, and I saw something I can't verify, just take my word for it' goes over so terribly well. And I didn't know who he was, then. I just had his scent. I'd have known him if I'd spent much time with him, probably, but I haven't."

She hadn't fully mapped how that worked, she just knew that sometimes she recognised people from their scent long before anything else registered. "Anyway, via channels, I got told to go back to the camp, see if I could pick up any more information, and report back. He'd been there again, this was the Tuesday, and within the last few hours. I traced him all the way back to the Sheen portal and then had to come back here."

Orion saw some of the problems with that much faster than Claudio. "That's what, three miles either way, plus the leg from Sheen. As a stoat?"

"Two legs, most of the way, thank you. Thankfully, the clothes come with me." Ibis had made very sure to teach her that. Not everyone learned it, the most available of the useful books didn't include it. And of course, there were various other ways of turning shape, curses and family magics, and all that. Not all of them brought clothes or the contents of their pockets along. "But I'd still have stood out if anyone had spotted me."

"It, um. Explains why you were tired that week. Not only doing all of that, but hiding it from us, too." Orion half saluted, and it wasn't at all a mocking gesture. "You pulled it off quite well. And what, then, you got him as far as the portal, and then couldn't find out where he'd gone?"

"Yeah." Cammie sighed, then leaned forward to grab a second biscuit. "It came out today. They tracked him back from that, then they followed him for a bit, and caught him. He'd wanted more of a role in something big, and he thought that was the way to get it. Not very military-minded of him."

Claudio's chin came up. "Always thought he was a bit of a weasel. Wait. Now I have a lot of questions. How do people become something specific? Is it, I don't know, a choice, or is it chance, or ..."

Cammie put her head back and laughed. "Don't ever let anyone tell you you're not just as much of a swot as an Owl, Claudio. Ever. Our sort of swot, mind. You ask the good questions." She waved her hand, then stopped, because the biscuit threatened to crumble. "There are theories about that, but most people agree it's an aspect of personality. If you learn it sensibly - I did - you can guide it a bit. But being a stoat felt right, and other things didn't, so much. Though I admit I thought about a rook or some-thing like that. One of the corvids."

"You can. People can turn into birds?" Orion blinked. "I thought that was just stories. The security implications alone."

Hypatia settled in, shifting to lean up against Cammie's side, more relaxed now. "Not that many people can shift. Birds are hardest, I understand, because it's a lot of differ-ences, all at once and flying is very different from walking. And birds are hilariously top heavy, if they don't manage themselves. Mammals are easier, birds are hard. Reptiles seem to take a particular kind of mind, from the bits I've learned. I don't think anyone's ever successfully done an insect. That's way too different from human, but maybe

I'm just wrong. Sometimes ocean creatures, I mean, you know your selkie lore, though selkies themselves are a different kind of shifting."

From there, they settled into a remarkably congenial conversation about the nature of shifting magic. Cammie carefully slid around exactly where she'd learned, only that she'd been told to wait until she was in her last year of school before she tried. It was most successful for people between sixteen and twenty. Ibis had a theory about people old enough to know themselves well enough to come back to two legs and hands and thumbs, but more malleable than an entire adult.

They went back and forth for a delightful wrangle about taking clothing with her. And that Hypatia could sense the magical talisman when she had it in her not at all accessible pocket. After a bit, Cammie changed back, so they could watch the process. Also so she could bound around the room and let her tension out, before permitting the men to pet her carefully. They had the good sense to admire her fur properly, and not to touch her in the wrong places, which in four feet meant tickling, mostly. It's not like she had shame in that shape.

Eventually, though, they ran out of biscuits, had gone through as much brandy as they should, and it was getting late. The men made their farewells, and Hypatia walked them out to the door, almost certainly to get a kiss from Orion in the process. When she came back in, Cammie was changed and under the covers.

"All right then?" That was the thing that mattered. If Orion really wasn't going to be awful.

"Yeah." Hypatia turned away to gather up her night-dress, braiding her hair up. "Thanks. For taking the risk. It was getting to me, and I didn't want it to, and I didn't know..."

"And you wanted him to know. I'm glad they took it well. I bet they'll have more questions, but that's just fun." Orion hadn't quite asked about the hunting, though she'd let a couple of comments drop. She rather thought he'd want to know more about how that worked for her. And Claudio was made of questions about the whole thing, every aspect of it, including bits Cammie hadn't really thought about for years. That was all right. From here, they could let it unfurl more comfortably. She wriggled down into the bed, making it as much a nest as she could. "Long day. Sleeping now."

Hypatia snorted. "Night, you. I'll wrangle breakfast in the morning." With that, she dimmed the lights a bit, and Cammie fell asleep to the quiet sounds of the hair brush and then Hypatia's book.

CHAPTER 38

HYPATIA, SITTING OUTSIDE THE HUTS ON JUNE 1ST

The next two weeks flew by in a haze of long hours, restless sleep, and tremendous pressure. There were snatches, here and there, of something that wasn't pouring everything they had into the final painstakingly detailed preparations for their part of the invasion. Those, however, mostly involved laundry and other essentials, rather than anything more enjoyable.

They'd not even had much time to talk about shapeshifting. Both men had individually told Cammie - and repeated it to Hypatia after - that they continued curious, and would love to talk more. More to the point, they mentioned they'd dropped a note to Isembard and Thesan. They'd been promised a little more reading material of the sort that could be shared, when time and energy allowed. Cammie actually didn't mind talking about it much, but it wasn't kind to make her do all the explaining from the beginning. Hypatia was glad both men realised people were a limited resource when it came to being a library.

Twice, Hypatia had managed a pair of hours in private with Orion. Those had happened when both of them were too frayed to do much more than fall into bed and enjoy what they could. Certainly, she didn't want to start any sort of conversation. She couldn't think beyond tomorrow when it came to whether she had a clean uniform, never mind anything else. She mostly wanted to curl up with him, to lean into his touch and the presence, and not ask it any questions at all.

It was very unlike her, but these were - as the radio and papers kept reminding them - unprecedented times.

But then, slowly, their preparations started coming to an end. She'd have a tremendous amount of work to do once the invasion began, of course, but most of the talismans had been dropped by now. She'd mapped their locations and tallied up the ones that had been lost or destroyed in transit. There were plenty to do what she needed, she was fairly sure. Plus she'd managed to get a fairly good anchor from two of the great battlefields. She thought she could push against those echoes for some quite evocative effects.

Orion was also, she thought, somewhat in limbo. He'd been a tremendous help getting the materia together. When he didn't have the skill to make something himself, he was quite good with an inventory and laying out what she needed so it would be ready.

He didn't get pushy about thinking he knew something he didn't. She'd noticed that now that she was paying such close attention to him. He'd throw out citations like a wall of thorns and roses. The more she listened to him, though, the more she understood how he wasn't trusting his own knowledge and intelligence and understanding of the world. Not that she was going to bring that up either right now. That was the sort of conversation that took months or years, not days.

Hypatia kept thinking about what Cammie had said,

about how Orion thought everyone was smarter than he was. All four of them were smart, clever, competent, all of that. But Orion's was a different kind of it. She could see how he'd think his sort of smart didn't matter. What kept catching her attention, though, was how often he saw something needed, and wrestled with it until it was sorted. A crocodile's attack, or the charge of a smarter sort of Boar, not an Owl's precision.

Cammie, though, was still working flat out. Signals work never stopped, ever, but this was more than that. She was sorting through material that had already gone through half a dozen other hands. Cammie wanted to find references that might allow them to tailor the magic they produced to be exactly what the Germans expected to see, rather than a best guess. Claudio spent half his time helping her translate the obtuse magical references - or finding someone who could consult. He spent the other half split between reporting on their doings and keeping everyone else out of their way.

It was queer, too, the way the rest of the camp was. They were all going about their ordinary business, from what little she heard, and what Claudio passed along.

But by June first, the Wednesday, all the parts she could do were as done as they were going to be until the fifth. Or maybe the sixth. The weather was a tremendous factor here. She didn't know all the details - she was no meteorologist, and truly competent weather workers were extremely rare. And it wasn't as if anyone was telling her the specifics. But they had been told, in a flying visit by Junior Commander Roberts, that the timing would depend on a number of weather conditions. If it didn't go off on the fifth or sixth, they'd have to wait another two weeks for the tides to be any use.

And it wasn't as if the weather had been helping. The

middle of the month had been cold, not that Hypatia had particularly noticed. Then, it was as if some switch flipped, and the weather not only got much warmer, but much wilder. The twenty-ninth of May had been tremendously, miserably hot in London and Richmond. Later that day reports had come in of devastating hailstorms up in Yorkshire and Derbyshire, and reports of over five inches of rain in a matter of a few hours. The thirtieth, two days ago, had been hot as well, unseasonably so.

Hypatia gave up, that afternoon. She was good for nothing, everything was itchy and uncomfortable, and she knew she was distracting Cammie. That wouldn't do at all. She went off to change her blouse again, then rather listlessly brought a book out with her to sit on the wall behind their huts. She didn't want to go too far in case she was needed for something, but she didn't want to be inside, either.

Perhaps twenty minutes later, Orion came around the corner of the hut, bee-lining it for her. She saw, of course, because she wasn't doing well with reading either. She'd been over the same five pages a dozen times now, and none of it stuck. Hypatia tucked her bookmark in at her page and blinked at him. "Yes?" It came out peevish, and she didn't mean that at all.

Orion tilted his head, looking her up and down for a moment. "May I join you, or would you rather be alone?"

"I don't know what I want." That, on the other hand, came out rather like a toddler. And goodness, she thought she'd left that far behind her.

His mouth twitched slightly. "I have a guess about some of what you're feeling, then. If you don't mind, I'll join you?"

She blinked at him, knowing it was the sort of thing that got described as owlish. Nothing made sense, and her head was aching a bit now, with absolutely no good reason for it. She was sitting sideways on the wall, her feet up on it. Orion sat with his dangling off one side, not touching her. They were at least nominally visible here. And if they went back to her hut, well, for one thing they'd get distracted. That wouldn't be helpful if they could lend a hand. And for another, whenever Cammie finished up, she'd want to wash up and change. She couldn't do that if they were doing all sorts of energetically passionate things in the bedroom. It was very annoying, the whole thing.

Orion cleared his throat when she hadn't said anything. "May I tell you what I think you're feeling?"

"You don't, you know. Generally." He was actually surprisingly polite about that, unlike a lot of people she'd known, both men and women. She always thought it seemed tremendously rude. She might not know what she was feeling, after all, but it wasn't as if people who weren't in her head had any better idea. Generally speaking. Cammie made a lot of good guesses due to long knowledge, and so did Ibis, but that wasn't the same thing at all, and besides they didn't push about it. She really was scattered now.

She caught the flicker of his hand in the leather glove, one of the sigils for a privacy ward that would muffle anything they said from a few feet away. Then he twisted, watching her intently.

"The waiting is the hardest part." His voice was entirely earnest now, a low rumble she hadn't heard from him often. "When you know there's going to be a battle, and you know more or less when it's coming, but it's not here yet. You're not alive yet, you're not dead yet. You're not whatever happens next. You're stuck, in tar or honey or a bog or whatever other name you want to give it, and you can't do anything."

Hypatia frowned. She hadn't thought of it like that, she'd been thinking about it like not having done enough, that there should be more she should be doing. "But why are we waiting? I mean, they told us the basics, but I don't understand the timing at all."

Orion's laugh came out like a bark. "Don't ask the easy ones, do you? I don't know the whole of it, but it's going to be a combination of things. They can only land the big tanks and equipment in some places. They're going to want, ideally, a full moon to see by, clear skies. Light winds or all the boats and things will get blown about. Low seas, which is all about the tides. And more than a week or two out, you know about the moon, and you've got a pretty good guess at the tides. But the other two are all luck and favour and guesswork, mostly. Even with knowing a lot more about the weather now than people used to. And you want the tides at a particular time of day, too."

"Huh." Hypatia had to think about that for a bit. "And if they can't - when they thought, what happens?"

"Put it off. Maybe two weeks. That would get you the tides, but not the moon, obviously." That was rudimentary magical timing, never mind anything else. Of course she knew that. "You know how it is with magical timing, probably better than I do." The twist of his mouth was more relaxed now, a bit of self-mockery that he did quite often.

"Come on, you know a great deal more about some of it than I do." She nudged his leg with one of her feet. "You mean it about the waiting being hard?"

"Hardest part for me. It's a lot easier to be brave and press forward when there's something right in your face to be brave about. Cammie's got the same feel for it I do, I think."

"She does like to get her teeth into things. And she's

got more practice at working to a point, a crescendo, whatever you call it."

Now he was laughing. "A climax, if you wish."

That bit of innuendo made everything snap into place for her, the way she felt unsettled now, and the way she'd felt that first time with him. She wasn't sure how things were going to go but certain it was going to rearrange her world. She leaned back on her hand, because she didn't dare let someone see her lean forward. She wanted to kiss him, and that wouldn't do at all right now. "Oh." Then she was laughing along with him. "You are brilliant. Putting it in a way I can make sense of much better."

He let her settle down into amused chuckles before he went on. "Claudio doesn't understand the battle thing either. And I can't really use this particular explanation with him, not the same way. But that's the thing. It's all building, then there's a point where you can't control it and you shouldn't, and it's all about rolling along with how things come out in the moment." He leaned a little more toward her. "If you do that, if we do that, I don't think we'll be far wrong. And it's certainly easier to follow, as a guide, than most anything else. So long as we keep within our actual orders."

"That's always the trick, isn't it?" Hypatia said. She looked off toward the working hut. "Thank you. I was thinking I was going completely wrong, that I was going to foul everything up, or I don't know... something worse. Hurt Cammie or you or Claudio."

"It's going into battle. And your magic's going, even if we're over here on this side of the Channel. So's mine. And I'm sure Cammie's working hard for a dozen reasons, but one of them's named Duncan. Claudio just..." His shoulder twitched. "Claudio can't let himself fail."

There were volumes of things to talk about in that last

sentence, and it wasn't Hypatia's business to pry. Except that Claudio was her friend now too, even aside from how he mattered to Orion. "We should talk about that sometime. Not until after..." She waved her hand at the hut and its implications. "See if Cammie and I can think of something to help."

"Oh, there are a couple of things that might. I don't know." Orion didn't explain. "It can keep for now. Shall we go see about grabbing supper, for when they come up for air? You can make sure I keep out of trouble." He held up both hands immediately. "Not that I expect you to be my keeper. That's unfair. Besides, it should probably come with hazard pay."

That made her laugh. "You've been much more mild the last few weeks." Now she was teasing right back, and it felt good to be doing that, not prickly and irritating. "Let's. And see if we can cajole one of the cooks out of a bit for an evening snack."

CHAPTER 39
ORION, EVENING OF JUNE 5TH IN THE WORKING HUT

The tension was not just palpable; it was a great weight, sucking all the air out of the room. The worst of it was, they'd been like this for a day already. Originally, the plan had been for the invasion force to cross the Channel on the night of June fourth. Worries about the weather had pushed it back a day, but that had meant they'd barely had time to sleep and eat before they were up again.

Orion scanned the room, over and over. It was a different kind of battle awareness than before, different than what he'd learned duelling. Oh, a lot of it carried over. There was the soft gaze that took in the movements at the edges of his range of vision, rather than a hard focus on just one thing. His ears near swivelled at every small noise, whether it was a scrape of a pencil on paper or the rasp of one of the talismans being moved or triggered somehow. Like Cammie as a stoat, as if some piece of that were just slightly transitive.

The women were doing the bulk of the work of it, too. Hypatia, in particular, and they'd been keeping it up for

348

most of yesterday, as well, with Cammie spelling her sister while Hypatia napped. There was all sorts of detritus around the sand-table now, scraps of paper and stubs of pencil and bits of clay. There was more of that around the big map table they'd set up in the middle of the room. Claudio was kept busy clearing things away when they were used up, without jogging anyone's elbow.

Orion swallowed against the tension, feeling it boil up in him again and again. He couldn't let it out, not the way he'd known. It wouldn't do any good here, for one thing, and it could do a lot of harm. Most of his part in the active invasion was already aloft, charmed into the slips of reflective material cascading down from out of planes. Or so he hoped. Anyway, they wouldn't know if it had actually helped until sometime, well, later.

Claudio had pulled away, perching on a desk, his journal open on his knees. He was flicking through pages, likely enough looking for the news. Orion circled around him, cast a charm to muffle the sound so they wouldn't disturb either of the women, and cleared his throat.

"Anything?"

"Duncan's squadron's on the move, I'm pretty sure." Claudio tapped a passage, which just had a hint of it, couched in the language of Roman omens. It wasn't a very good code. Honestly, Cammie would tear it to pieces in minutes and rightfully so. But it was in a journal message that only a handful of people would have received, one of Claudio's more obscure connections. "Do we tell her?"

Orion looked up, watching the way Cammie was moving. Her also being a stoat made a lot of things make more sense, honestly. When she was on the hunt, she was absolutely terrifying. It was all in the way she moved around the space as if every foot and hand had a job, and it was doing it precisely and perfectly. As he watched, she stepped back to pivot past Hypatia, moving one token on the map. She leaned to cast a charm to check a reading on the sand-table. Then she flicked her hands up in a couple of quick patterns for Hypatia to see on the return pass.

"I'm fairly sure she knows. Look at her." Orion was not the one who was good with people. But he had been watching the two of them - well, more Hypatia, to be fair - closely all day. He considered their various options. "Can you go fetch some food? I'll keep helping."

Claudio nodded. "Good idea. And I'll grab another set of stamina potions." There were risks, taking them too often in succession, but Orion knew that Hypatia knew the risks. She'd take them, anyway. He would too, as needed, though hopefully he and Claudio could spell each other.

Claudio slipped out, and Orion let the sound charms drop again. He circled in to grab a couple of pieces of paper that had floated to the floor, so neither of them would slip. As he straightened up, he took a step back, as Cammie went charging to the sand-table. "We lost thirty-two and seventeen. And I'm seeing indications there are forces moving up toward the coast, to the east."

"Bring up, what is it? Eighteen, then. No, twenty-one." Hypatia called it out. "I'm going to need to figure some-thing else out. Give me a minute."

Orion could see her now. It wasn't just her in the moment. It was the thing he'd talked about with Isembard, the gift of seeing the branching paths, just for a second. It wasn't anything so simple as seeing the future. That was an uncertain and unreliable gift, and he didn't actually want it. This was more about seeing the range of what might happen. It was about being able to put brackets on either end so that energy could be conserved and prepared to be ready where it needed to be.

Here and now, it wasn't like it gave him answers.

Generally, it didn't. But it did mean that he took two steps to the left, and brought up his hand under hers, palm to palm. It was the opposite of the usual way people did that, but it let her be the one to choose what she took in more easily. She stopped, like a great ship easing into port, then blinked at him. He let the vitality flow out of him. A second later he felt her open to it, a charge that wasn't at all electric or magnetic, but had some of the quality of both.

She held still for perhaps thirty seconds before she pulled her hand back and twisted off to the map. That much he could do, bolster her own magic. She was burning it off as quickly as anything he'd ever seen. She was doing, as far as he could tell, the equivalent of running half a dozen duels at once. Or maybe like someone going down a line and playing twenty opponents at chess at the same time.

In a different world, one where the magic had the support it needed, it wouldn't just be four of them here. It would be twenty or thirty, with support staff to manage the maps and bring the drinks and run messages. As it was, it was four of them, they were going to need to drive forward and see it through, whatever it took. He could rage about the limitations and the way they'd near enough been hamstrung later. Now was for doing things.

Hypatia had launched herself back into it, shifting five or six or eight tokens around, telling Cammie what to watch, then moving over to the sand-table. She was doing a complex set of illusions combined with using sympathetic magic to help bog down a tank here. Or she'd add a bit more flooding there, whatever would make it harder for them to manoeuvre. Granted, even if they heard about the actual attack at Normandy, it wasn't as if the German Army could transport itself across half the northern coast of France immediately. Every bit they could do would help, though.

Somewhere in the middle of it, Claudio came back, and they settled in to the ongoing work. Dawn came and went, then noon, and then finally at around four, Claudio got a notification in his journal. He was half-drowsing, the sort that meant a great deal of jerking awake at every little sound. He flicked through the pages. Cammie and Hypatia were still at it, on their third stamina potion, plus who knows how many gallons of tea. "We can stand down. More info coming tonight or tomorrow. I'll keep an eye out."

Neither woman slowed. Orion stood, pushing himself upright. Every bit of him ached. He could only imagine how they felt. He came up a couple of steps behind Hypatia. "What do we need to do to leave it for a bit?" He spoke as clearly as he could, but she started. Orion repeated. "We can stand down. You need bed."

She was about to argue, then her hands were leaning on the table. He got an arm around her before she could pull everything down. "Part of the battle is stopping at the end. Resting. C'mon." He hefted her up into his arms, glanced over his shoulders to see if Cammie was coming. Claudio had offered her an arm, much more the usual way a gentleman used that word, and they made a little procession around to the women's hut.

Neither bothered undressing nor doing anything with their hair. They just kicked their shoes off, tossed their jackets aside, and fell into bed. Hypatia, at least, did not fall flat on her face. Orion frowned, then said, "Moment. Something to take first."

Claudio was already ahead of him, meeting him at the door of the hut with two more potions, restoratives. They wouldn't make it all better. That sort of magic had costs too, but it'd mean restful sleep, not plagued by aches and nasty dreams, and they'd wake less sore whenever that happened. He handed Cammie hers, and she drained it without asking.

Orion perched on the other bed, awkwardly in the four inches between the edge and Hypatia's hips. "Not going away until you take it."

"Promise?" She blinked up at him, her eyes barely focusing, and he got the vial into her hand.

"Drink that, sleep. We'll talk more when you're awake again. Claudio and I will keep an eye on things." They were competent to run backup, and Claudio had already drained another stamina potion himself and gone back to it. "Time for me to sleep, too."

Five minutes later, he was in his own bed, though at least he'd got all his clothes off and pyjamas on. Merciful exhaustion claimed him then, and he didn't care about the world for some hours to come.

CHAPTER 40
CLAUDIO, THE EVENING OF JUNE 6TH

C laudio was sitting alone in the hut when there was a knock on the door, a rapid knock. It wasn't the other three, for one thing. If any of them stirred in the next six hours, he'd eat his desk and everything on and in it. It wasn't one of the camp's soldiers. That sounded different, and they superstitiously avoided this hut, anyway.

He came to attention, standing and taking the dozen strides to the door. "Who is it, please?"

"Roberts. Do let me in. I don't have much time." Her voice was muffled, but entirely recognisable.

Claudio opened the door, standing back and saluting. "Ma'am."

Her gaze swept around the rest of the room. "Your others?"

"Sleeping, ma'am. We were running from about noon on the 5th through to three hours ago. Relying on private stocks of stamina potions, but they'll need a bit to sleep it off."

"And not you?" She nodded once, sharply, and added. "At ease."

Claudio relaxed a hair. "Keeping an eye on the information coming in, and making notes." He caught a flash from the sand-table. "Pardon, just a moment." He wasn't asking permission. This was too important for that. He just nodded and made his way over to the table, grabbing his notebook and pencil on the way, making a note of the light that was flashing. A large mass of metal near that point, almost certainly a tank bogged down somehow, that was a help. He finished the symbols that would remind him of what to tell Hypatia later, then set the notebook down.

"That was?" Junior Commander Roberts was standing with her feet a foot or two apart, in that easy elegance that went well with the ATS uniform.

"Likely a tank bogging down in the mud, or something of the kind." Claudio said. "I'm assuming you're here because you want a report of some kind, faster than the usual."

It made her snort, the way he'd gone directly for it. "Well, yes. My seniors on the non-magical side are currently very pleased with themselves. But they do not understand that you all just did the magical equivalent of storming a beach under steady fire for more than a day. With far less cover. Everyone is all right?"

It was the first personal note of concern he'd heard from her this entire time. To be fair, their conversations up to this point had been brief, to the point, and entirely focused on the work. She'd mostly left them alone to do what they saw fit, so long as they could justify the materials and the direction. He wondered suddenly if someone had explained to Roberts what they'd done, sometime in the last twelve hours. "It's a little hard to tell yet, but we—" His voice caught.

Centuries ago, born to his sort of family, he'd have held power that was all about the land magic, but not at all in the way Orion did. He'd have led armies into battle directly, the sort with horses and swords, rains of arrows, blood on the field and staining the rivers. It would have been brutal and he'd likely have died younger than he was now. But he'd have had his feet under him, doing what he'd been bred and trained for.

Now, here he was in a flimsily made hut, in a camp that felt increasingly artificial by the day. They were a bare hop from London and yet galaxies away. He had his people to take care of. But, for one thing, they were generally quite good at taking care of themselves. And second, it wasn't like that now. Whatever slight advantage he'd held over them, both rank and experience, that had long since evaporated. But they were his people. Orion had been since Claudio turned fourteen. But Hypatia and Cammie too, and not just because Hypatia made his brother so happy.

Claudio did have the skills not to let any of that show on his face. "They gave their all. Far beyond all. I did too, and when I can collapse, I'll be just as badly off." But he wanted to give them as much time as he could. With any luck, Orion would be up in a few hours, and he could hand things over. But he wasn't going to wake either of the women if he could possibly help it.

Roberts opened her mouth, closed it. "What can I arrange on a practical level that would help?"

"Food. Restorative drinks. More tea. We completely ran through everything we had there." Claudio frowned, counting vials in his head. "Also our potions, though if one of us could go round to the portal tomorrow, we could get more. That would be a help. I can get you a list inside an hour."

"I can likely arrange a courier for that. Someone suitable." She frowned. "Ongoing damage?"

It wasn't as if Claudio could tell yet. He thought not. He thought that somehow, Orion had kept both Hypatia and Cammie going long enough. They'd both shared vitality just before it would be a crisis. But it had been a terribly long stretch, with almost no break. No, now his mind was spinning out again. He pulled his thoughts back. "Can I ask why?"

It caught her oddly, and then she coughed. "You're an interesting mix, the four of you. You've done excellent work. I'd—" It came out awkwardly, the way Orion would have said it. "I hope you don't take any lasting harm from it, any of you."

"I'll let you know. But food, some ongoing potions. Not doing anything like that again for a bit." Claudio was feeling his way here, what his mother would have done, what his father would have gestured at. Roberts had never hinted, not in all their time here, about what happened after this invasion.

"Ah." Now her mouth quirked up. "We're going to have additional information coming in. If things are successful over there, perhaps needing people on the ground, investigation and making things safer, magically. You needn't decide about that now. And it's going to be hell to send ATS girls over there. That's an entirely different sort of challenge. But you know as well as I do that they've got options most don't."

Claudio grunted. "So you're saying we might have more assignments coming." All of a sudden, he felt a rush of certainty, and he didn't question it. "I'd like us to stay together, if we can. If they're willing, but I'm fairly sure they'd also prefer that."

"We can certainly take that into consideration." She

flicked her fingers at the sand-table and the maps. "Monitoring for a few weeks, at least. And whatever other advantages we can gain around Calais. After that, likely some work with more of the little talismans, to be able to bring effects ahead of the main force of the army as it moves. Yes, I know, you'll need more materials. Work up a list as you get a chance in the next two days, the amounts for different numbers, and I'll see what I can get for you."

"Ma'am." It was the thing to say at this moment.

"And some leave, of course, once things quiet down. Not this week, but perhaps the week after, or the one after that. A week's leave, likely, especially if you can do some light monitoring from wherever you take it."

Ah, now that would be an interesting challenge, but the materials for the maps and talismans were all portable. The sand-table wasn't, but Claudio was fairly sure Hypatia had samples of all the bits of chalk and limestone from specific places left. "I'll see, ma'am, what the options are. We could all use a leave, to be sure. At the same time, ideally."

Roberts nodded once, crisply. "I'll see about getting a hamper here tonight. Spare you canteen food." It'd be a trick with rationing, but she must have some resources. Though, for that matter, so did Claudio.

"You might check with the home farm at Fairlight if they've got spare. Or Schola, you'd want to talk to Helena Trembley, Linta Argonne, or Thesan Wain. Any of the three of them can tell you what they've got at the moment." And all three would understand why he'd suggested it.

She raised an eyebrow, but just inclined her head. "I'll see. If there is one, I'll manage a note in the journal before supper. Spare you the walk." She then looked around. "Anything else I ought to know now?"

"We're proud of how this assignment came out. We

hope it was a great help, and we respect the bravery of the men on the ground - and of all those involved in the planning." It was the proper thing to say, and he would be damned if he neglected it.

Her mouth twitched up again. "I'll pass that along appropriately. At ease, Captain. You did good work, all of you, and I'll be making note of that as I can."

With that, she wheeled around. Claudio barely managed to get the door open for her before she was out. She cut across the camp toward what Claudio glimpsed as a waiting staff car.

Claudio waited until the car pulled away then he stepped back into the hut. He let the door close and the warding come up behind him as he sank back into a chair. Two hours later, there was a notification about a hamper coming. An hour after that, he was barely keeping his eyes open when the door of the hut opened and Orion came in. He looked rumpled, but more awake.

"Potion? You shouldn't have."

"Natural stamina and a touch of the land magic." Orion replied. "I'm ..." Then his mouth cracked into a smile. "I was about to say I'm not stupid. And I'm not. But I'm still so tired that's funny. Does that make any sense?"

"Glad I don't have to talk you through that. You're not. You've never been. The women?" Claudio gestured at the chair.

"Still asleep, I'm sure. I didn't risk checking. Cammie probably wouldn't bite me. She's likely too tired to shift, if I have that right. But I don't intend to test her reflexes." Whatever else was true for his brother, he sounded remarkably content, actually. Odd, that it took an invasion for that, well, and a romance, but Claudio would take it.

"We should have a hamper coming through by courier in an hour or so, if you can keep an eye out for it. Keep my journal. Junior Commander Roberts was arranging for someone to get it from the Sheen portal. No, I don't know how." Claudio leaned back, feeling the exhaustion get him now.

"Did she write?" Orion considered his options, but he didn't sit, instead starting to work through some of the ordinary daily stretches.

"She came. Quite pleased with us, I think, a little worried we'd done ourselves harm in the process, actually. Leave in a week or two. If things settle down, all four of us."

"That'd be grand." Then he frowned. "Solstice. Blast. I'll have to figure out solstice. If I can do the offerings and whatever, the Council ones."

"You don't need to figure that out today. And who knows, maybe that'll be the week we can get leave. We can sort it out in a day or two, when we've all slept and can ask better questions."

Orion laughed, amused now. "Not in any hurry to go deal with your mother, no," he admitted. "Even at a distance and with all the formalities."

"Well. There you go, being sensible. I don't much want to deal with her, but I don't have to go make my formal offering, either." Claudio ran his hand over his face. "Can you take over here?"

"Go, go. I should be good until at least one of the women can take over. What's happened that I should keep an eye on?" Orion made his way to the sand-table. Claudio gathered up the notebook, showing him what had changed so far, and the couple of places he'd been watching in particular. He'd got enough of a sense now of something shifting in the magic, even if he couldn't entirely figure out what.

Five minutes later, Claudio had fallen into his own bed,

barely in time. He could feel the lassitude and exhaustion near drown him, as the last of the stamina potion wore off. He'd nearly cut it too close, he'd done that enough before and found himself hours later in some curled up position half wedged under a desk. It was neither good for his dignity nor his neck. He fell asleep on that thought, and whether he cared about the dignity part any more.

CHAPTER 41
CAMMIE, JUNE 8TH IN THE WORKING HUT

"Someone still feels guilty." Cammie looked up from her desk, rolling her head and hearing all the cracks and noise of tense muscles complaining. She'd been bent over her work for, had it really been three hours? Figured. But now there was noise at the door of the hut. Claudio and Hypatia were bringing in a new good-sized hamper.

The work of a signals expert was never done, and now the traffic was including at least something about the invasions at Normandy. She was still picking through for anything that might let them judge how successful the efforts at Calais had been on the ground. Most of those were in codes Cammie couldn't crack on her own, but some of the information came through things like radio sources. Those weren't to be trusted, of course, anyone could say anything on a radio.

Orion had been working on the calculations for materia so Hypatia could go over them. He'd been as caught up in the work as Cammie had been. Now, he stood up, and moved to open the hamper's latch and peer at.

"This came from Fairlight. Bless them. Mother came through, or someone did. But yes, it was the special courier again, so everything's newly packed."

He knelt, going through the containers. "A lot of things in stasis, plenty of makings for salads, something fresh. And what looks like an amazing amount of berries, that will brighten things up. Raspberries and strawberries, both, and it looks like some jam, too, with honey. The hives must be doing well."

"Better than they had been?" Claudio asked. "They might like having you back in Albion. The bees and everything else."

Cammie caught the moment where Orion almost said something dismissive and then stopped. He pushed himself back so he could look at Claudio. "Do you think so? That me being, I don't know. Something different matters that much?"

"Happier, brother. The word is happier. Both in general, in specific," Claudio waved a hand amiably at Hypatia, who'd taken up a place leaning by the door. "And we did excellent work the past months, and you know it. And how that makes you feel." Claudio glanced around the room, meeting Cammie's eyes briefly. "How it makes us all feel."

Cammie pushed away from her desk to come over and peer at the hamper. It wasn't exactly the food she was most interested in, but rather the way it smelled. There was something honest about it, something legitimately joyful, and that was a change after months of institutional smells. Everything had felt heightened for her the last couple of days. Before she could say anything, though, there was a knock on the door.

Claudio blinked, but then went outside for just a minute, maybe. Less than that, just long enough for a few muffled words to come through the door. "Regular mail. Cammie, for you."

He handed the envelope over immediately, and Cammie could instantly see Duncan's handwriting. He made his 'a' with the long diagonal running down to the bottom left. It was readable, but distinctive. She tore it open, feeling several sheets of paper inside, different dates at the top as she spread them out, suddenly frantic. There were reasons for a packet of letters like this, all at once, and some of those reasons were horrible.

Then she managed to get to the top sheet again, seeing yesterday's date, Duncan's handwriting still. Then the first word, 'dancer'. He was the only one who'd write it like that as a pet name. Before she could figure out what to do next, someone was pushing a chair up. "Sit before you fall." That was Claudio, not Hypatia, but it felt much the same, someone she trusted, having her back. "Everything all right?"

In other times, in other places, Cammie would have snarled. She could feel herself, the way there was that edge of feral tooth and claw, just barely under the surface. But she knew better, and besides, this was a friend. It smelled like a friend.

Her fingers fumbled with the sheets, but then she made herself focus. The current hunt was for what the paper said. That was all that mattered, reading through Duncan's hand. She traced it, her finger under the lines, moving quickly, even with the quirks of his handwriting. He'd been part of the invasion, more than a thousand flights had been made in the course of a day or so. He'd come home safely. They'd only lost eight planes, which put it in perspective, exactly how much they'd done and how lucky they'd been.

Come home safely, and he had only a few more before

he'd done his second two hundred and he was done. When they'd take him out of combat missions, and have him do training, or moving things around in Britain, or something else. He loved flying, that's how he'd ended up in the RAF, but the war had worn on him. She knew that, even without all the actual and many dangers. "He's all right." She flicked through the pages again. "Give me a minute, please?"

"Of course." This time it was Orion's voice. She heard other small sounds around her, nothing to worry about. Someone putting the kettle on, someone else nudging a small table near enough her elbow. Before she'd finished reading, there was a mug of tea there, a small bowl of the raspberries, a scone. She let them sit, until she'd gone through all the pages, each of them, swallowing them down in a way she hadn't known she needed.

"Duncan's all right. He was flying, on D-Day. He's got four more, likely, then he's done for good. No more combat flights." If she repeated it enough, maybe it'd feel real, properly so. "He'll have leave when that's done, a couple of weeks of it, while they figure out where he's going."

"So you'll be able to see him. There's a good reason to arrange our leave at the same time, isn't it? We can come up with whatever timing excuse we need for the thing. Probably wanting another week or so to see the aftermath through and document the results." Claudio gestured. "Eat something, would you? You looked shaky."

If most people had said it, she'd have grumbled. She didn't like to be nagged. But Claudio was right, and when she looked around, the others had claimed little treats as well, a bit of a momentary celebration. It wasn't champagne and a night out on the town, but it would do for the moment. "You don't mind?"

"Nah." Orion shrugged. "They've got to figure out

what to do with us too, and I'm not inclined to rush that. There are phases to a war, or a bit of a war, and I don't know all of it, not like some people do. But I want them not to rush us into the next thing. So drawing out our reports, dotting the is and crossing the ts, that's all to the good. We spend some time highlighting - um, what was it you were saying, Hypatia? Last night?"

When Cammie had been working late on the signals and also giving them some time. She couldn't figure out, even now, which had been the actual thing, and which had been the excuse. But they'd needed it. She wouldn't begrudge them the comfort of it, and Claudio had kept her company. He was actually getting quite good at sorting out patterns in the words himself, at least at spotting which bits needed more investigation. Anyone could decode something known. It was the gift for spotting the important parts before decoding them that couldn't be taught, only encouraged.

Hypatia took her time answering, as if she'd half-lost the conversation. Unsurprisingly, honestly, Cammie was clear that Orion was very determined to be distracting when he had the chance. "There's a whole line we could take in the write-up about the resonances, and the bits about playing with the local history, as much as we can. Though, mind, there's plenty of history to play with, and enough of it's available to us with some library access."

That was a good point. And it would mean they'd continue to be useful. Claudio had, of course - well, of course he would, even if most people wouldn't have - shared that he'd already asked about them staying together. They made a good team, for all Cammie was inclined to be more solitary by nature, in the long term. Doing her own thing, Mum said, and Giles, and most others who knew her. Now, though, she just nodded. "I can help with that. Make it sound good." She finally leaned back, hearing her back creak again. "What does that mean right now?"

"Means you take a break. A good long one, not just enough to eat. We could have a nice meal. Heat some of this up in, say, an hour, and then you could take the rest of the evening and go do whatever it is you want on four feet."

If she were well fed, she wouldn't much want to hunt, but that was a problem she could sort out later. Scout out some options for some other night, maybe. Cammie felt her mouth twitch into a smile. "Fair enough. You're ..." She stopped and started that again. "I'm responsible, I promise."

"I know you are." Claudio didn't stop there, though. "But you and Hypatia pushed yourselves hard. You know it, we know it, with any luck by the time we get all our reports done, the higher ups will know it. We should certainly have had, oh, five times the people working on it, plus support staff, and not having to duck around in the canteen. Private sleeping space, even if Orion and Hypatia would want to share."

"If we'd had more people, they wouldn't be, almost certain." Cammie pointed out. "And I don't know the formulae for it. I'd have to ask Giles, he'd think it a fun problem. But we probably got more done because it was just the four of us, because of the added benefits of I don't know what you call it. Mutual lust, admiration, amuse-ment." She lifted her chin at Hypatia, who was about to object. "Don't say it's not the first, or I'll get specific."

Hypatia held up her hands. "Forget the idea." She agreed, but she was laughing. "You're right, though. It would have, if we'd had more people, gone differently. But I don't know that that's better. You spread things out more, when there are a lot of hands in the mix. And lots of kinds of magic. Whatever else, we never really argued a lot about whether ideas were worth trying. Just someone kept wanting citations." She twisted to look up at Orion, who had settled into standing just behind her chair. "Keeping me on my toes."

He laughed, easily. The whole thing had been good for him, honestly, best for him of the four of them. When he'd first shown up, there'd been all sorts of things tangled up and fouling him up, and now they weren't. It wasn't as simple as the sex, though Cammie thought sex was actually a pretty good thing to try, with that sort of tangle, for about six reasons. It was that he had more confidence he was doing some good, something that mattered. That felt like a fine thing, actually, even better than the triumph of the invasion.

Now Orion was smiling. "So. Look. It'd actually be convenient if we could work out leave for over solstice. I've got obligations, but we could work that out. Meet up as soon as I'm done with the necessary bits."

Cammie considered. "There's the Solstice Fair, still." The agricultural fair, the one for Albion, had continued through the war. Too many people had traditions that tied tight in with the harvest that started there, and no one wanted to mess them up. "There are dances, this year, I bet."

"Ah, now, that's a thing to aim for. I want to see you dancing when we're not worried about where we are," Orion said. "I could stand to learn a few things."

Hypatia snorted. "I am only a barely adequate dancer. Warning you now, because you seem to have expectations."

"That's the thing about dancing. A skilled partner makes everything better. And I'd like to give it my best." Cammie certainly heard the undertone, the implications there, even if she wasn't entirely sure Hypatia did. Or, for that matter, as she watched him, if Orion had realised it until it was out of his mouth.

"I can give you some lessons. And something to watch, if Duncan can get free by then. Chances seem decent. Do we look for rooms up there, or whatever, or go from, I don't know..." She made the offer partly so Orion wouldn't keep being snarled up.

"The Schola portal's still fine. Maybe aim at staying there, other than whatever Orion needs to do at Fairlight?" Claudio suggested, almost off-handedly. "I can see if there's space."

Thesan and Isembard would be wrapping up for the year. They usually didn't migrate to their estate in Essex until the week after solstice. "It's not like you'd put them out. They've two beds spare, still. And Mum and Ibis can put us up, sure, or there's one of the guest rooms. Write, would you, and see what's sensible?"

"It'll give us all something to look forward to. And people to be around who won't be..." Claudio didn't want to go home to his family. That much was clear, and Cammie wasn't going to pry about it. He'd told them enough, mostly not in words, and she saw how Orion watched him. Not restful, certainly. That sort of stay would be full of expectations and spikes and little digs.

"People who know what it's like to have been at war." Hypatia's voice cut through clearly. "And you need that. We all do. Even if we weren't in the middle of it."

"Ah, now that's a philosophical argument for you. Our magic was." Orion picked it up smoothly. Cammie laughed, finished the last crumbs of scone and the solitary raspberry, and then charmed her hands clean before going back to her notes. An hour more, and she could then really use a break.

CHAPTER 42
HYPATIA, JUNE 11TH

B y Sunday night, they had begun to relax into a new normal, whatever that meant. Cammie was out for the time being, and then intending to settle in the other front room with Claudio and chat. Or curl up with four feet whenever he got tired. To give Hypatia and Orion a whole night together, she'd made that clear.

Hypatia had kept watching Claudio. She couldn't decide if he wanted something more with Cammie, or if he'd already decided it was hopeless, and that Cammie's friendship meant a lot. Especially if he didn't mind a stoat in his lap from time to time. For all Cammie was fond of choices in many other ways, she was absolutely devoted to Duncan, and Hypatia knew that, too.

But it wasn't as if she could ask about that kind of thing, unless someone gave her an opening, and neither Cammie nor Claudio had.

Now, her position was also quite cosy, but in an entirely different mode. Hypatia was on her back, her hair loose, blanket pulled up over her hips, with Orion's hand along her ribs and between her breasts, keeping that more or less warm. Even if very little of it was actually covered. His left hand, and that was a wonder for her to delight in, that he was somehow no longer shy of letting her see or feel it. Somewhere in their countable number of nights together, he'd shifted from determination to comfort, almost without notice.

Except she'd noticed. Not just now, she'd spotted when he'd stopped pulling off his gloves like an act of war, when he'd left them off longer.

His thumb moved a little, just enjoying the touch. "Penny for your thoughts?"

Hypatia wasn't entirely sure he wanted them. "Which ones?" Then she swallowed. "I was thinking about Claudio. And the way he looks at Cammie sometimes."

"Like a thing he doesn't get to have? Not that she's the thing, but that kind of - she's very open with her affection, isn't she? When she's comfortable." Orion's thumb and index finger just shifted slightly against her skin. "He won't, I mean. He knows there's Duncan."

"I am not sure anything could divert her from Duncan. At least for the moment. But I'm sorry it's hard on him." Hypatia let her eyes half close. This was an easier conversation to have if she wasn't looking anywhere.

"Like it or not, he's used to things not being easy. Doing things the expected way. Even if I think he'd be a lot happier if he could find someone in agreement with his marriage, he could just enjoy being with." Orion shook his head. She could feel it.

"What's she like, his wife?" Hypatia knew the outline of it, from what they'd said.

Another of those twitches of hair on her shoulder. "Not horrible. She does her bit, she cares about their kids, she's a more involved mother than a lot of people of our sort. But she doesn't like things much. Near anything, as

371

far as we can tell. Books, a little, but not the same ones as Claudio, which - actually, it's sort of surprising there isn't more overlap."

"I'm assuming not the sort of daring novels." Hypatia said. "Morally improving literature, the other possible direction?"

"Morally improving literature, and also very dry family genealogies and memoirs? So many of them are interesting only to their immediate relatives, but she seems to read a lot of them, no matter how excessive the prose."

"I can't see that producing a lot of conversation, no. And Claudio kept busy, even before the war." Hypatia offered it a little cautiously. "With what?"

"Magic, mostly. Varying kinds, but he's best at pulling different pieces together. His mother expects him to challenge for a Council seat soon. There's no reason not to, except the war." There was a bit more of an edge to his voice now. "I don't know if he will. I'd help, if he did."

"And you?" Now they were on thin ice. It was as if she could hear it shifting and moaning under her feet, just barely avoiding the crack of it and the tumble into frigid water.

"So." Orion started, then stopped. "There's a thing. Before that."

"There is?" Right, now they'd gone off the map, properly. Hypatia could only ask questions, really.

"Would you come home with me? To Fairlight for solstice?" They'd made a good argument for getting that week off as leave, maybe a fortnight, depending on how things went. If they were to keep working, they needed more materia stocks, and someone had to make those happen. They'd absolutely earned some recuperation time. Cammie desperately wanted and needed to see Duncan. And Hypatia wanted to see her family, too.

She didn't answer immediately, and she felt Orion's fingers still. Before she managed anything else, she got out, "I don't want to say the wrong thing. Give me a minute."

To his credit - to his very great credit - he didn't press. He didn't dismiss the idea she could say a wrong thing. He gave her the space to think out not just what she wanted to say, but the implications. "I'm not answering you yet, but can you tell me what you're wanting, there?"

"I don't know." Orion pushed up on one elbow beside her, she opened her eyes to find him leaning up, watching her intently. "But I'll know more if you're there. And you said yourself, about the land. Maybe you need to see if I measure up there, properly. No one will be awful, I'll make sure of it. I'll have to go to the Council Keep, the afternoon of it, to make my bow and give in my records and all that. But I don't have to stay very long. Mother would do it, but it would look bad if I turn up on leave the next day. Or people know I am."

"Can't have that. All right, so that part isn't me, right? That's very public." Hypatia also did not remotely have a frock that would do, or even a new enough uniform without mending for such a place. Though probably she could sort something out with Thesan, who did have spares of that sort of thing in her wardrobe. And who would be there herself, almost certainly.

Her mouth quirked up and Orion's index finger brushed the corner. "You had a thought? And no, you don't need to come to that part."

"I was thinking I didn't have the right sort of frock. And that Thesan probably did, and also that's probably not a conversation we want to have yet. Because of Ibis, as much as anything else."

Orion nodded, slowly, like he was thinking through the ramifications. "If I could have anything, I'd like you to come home with me. See the place. See what you think of it, at dawn on solstice morning. It's beautiful, I can promise you that. Meet my mother and my aunts." Then, carefully, he added, "Maybe my children? I don't know what you think about children in general, never mind specific ones. And I'm not very good with them."

"You've barely been home since they were born, right?" She'd worked it all out a couple of weeks ago. She had the dates she knew about and the ones that were easy enough to rummage through the gossip in the journals about. "I like many children. Not all of them, but my niece was lovely as a little one. I've got plenty of practice being amusing. Or ignoring the screaming, both, when it's not mine to sort out."

That made Orion laugh, surprising himself. "That's a knack I definitely don't have. I'm always sure it's something I did."

"Oh, no. Some of the time they're hungry or too tired to sleep or something's wrong and they absolutely don't have language for it. Susanna picked up bits of sign. Ibis is pretty fluent in it these days." Hypatia thought Orion would have enough to make sense of that.

"He's the one who talks to the mermaids around Schola, of course. And Pross seems like the type to learn anything she can." Orion said, demonstrating once again that he was not at all slow on the uptake.

"And sometimes it's just really useful - across a room, or when it's noisy. Hordes of rampaging students, it's really handy to sign across the common room or whatever. Anyway, Susanna picked up some of it early, enough she could let us know which thing she was screaming about at the moment, more often than not." She shrugged. "And your mother? And your aunts, what will you tell them about me coming to visit?"

"That you're my colleague, my friend. That you're brilliant." He hesitated. "Saying I've fallen for you, hard, that I
want..." He stopped. "I shouldn't say that."

"Say it to me, would you?" Hypatia was watching now,
very carefully.

He couldn't quite meet her eyes, but she was used to
that now, with him. He wasn't ignoring her. It was that
looking and talking together were too much. "I think what
I'd like is to see what you think of the place. And me, when
I'm there. When I have, what's the word? That uniform
on. If you could like me there, want to be me with there,
like we are here."

Her breath caught, because that was as honest and
frank a declaration as she'd likely get. They'd both been
dancing around anything in the future, at all. She'd
thought it wasn't on offer for all sorts of reasons, starting
with his ex-wife, going on to the gossip, and the fact she
very much wasn't from the sort of family his would
approve of. Not that there was anything against them,
exactly. "You'd, something, longer?"

Now, he rolled against her, one leg over hers, not quite
pinning her in place. She could have wriggled away or
pulled back, and he'd have let her, but she didn't want to.
"I want everything I can have with you, everything you'll
let me. I don't know what words go with that. But I am
happier. I want to stay happier. I want you to be there, to
be happy with. About. For. With." He swallowed, looking
frustrated. "With, most of all. All of those words. I'm
making a mess of this."

"You don't have citations for it, love." She'd used the
endearment a few times before. It wasn't the first, but now
it rocked him. A moment later, she got her left hand up to
cup his cheek. "And it matters if I still want that with you
when you're there. All the formal on, all the expectations."

There was a long pause, utter quiet, then he nodded. "I hope you'll want me then, too. Like I am there. But I don't know that yet." Then his mouth quirked into a bigger smile. "No citations. We'll have to do our own research, I guess."

"I am, it turns out, entirely available for that sort of research proposal. Lay out the parameters, then. When do we go? Where do we go? What do I expect?"

It made him laugh. He stretched out against her again, tugging her now so her head was on his shoulder. He was keeping her warm with his arm and his chest, one hand on her hip, the other brushing the top of her breast. He explained, bit by bit, what he had in mind. That they'd go out there the night before, he could show her the land, a nice walk or ride, whichever she preferred. Meeting his mother and his aunts, that was part of it, an informal supper.

The next morning, they'd get up before the sunrise, and see the sun up. There were rituals for the land, talking to the bees. He'd go off to the Council Keep for the afternoon for a few hours. She could hide with a book or three, or explore their library, or whatever she wanted. When he came back, they could walk or ride or sit and talk or whatever made them happy. Made her happy, especially. She'd have her own rooms, but ones where he could join her, if she liked. The next day, they could go off to the Midsummer Faire and have a grand time, meet up with Claudio and Cammie and Duncan, most likely.

When he was done, she nodded. "First, I do like. I'm rather curious what it'd be like in a bed that's not near enough a cot, and that doesn't creak when you look at it wrong without muffling charms. I'm game. It helps to know what to expect." She considered. "I should see Ibis and Pross before that, but I could come out that afternoon, the Tuesday? It'd give me a chance to pack up some other clothes, not a uniform, too."

"I have got quite fond of you in your uniform. But I suspect I would be even more fond of you not in a uniform. Certainly, curious about what you wear when you've the choice." His fingers traced down the line between her breasts, as if imagining undoing a series of buttons. "Bright colours?"

"Bright colours, and decidedly less drab underthings." She snorted. "Not that you'd leave those on long, either."

"Probably not!" Orion sounded cheerful about that prospect. "Now, though, you're not wearing anything at all, and Cammie did promise we could have the night. I like that idea, too, waking up next to you. With more space."

"Mmm." Hypatia wriggled. "Enough talking. More touching."

With a laugh, he pushed her onto her back again. She rolled with it, letting him begin to be rather more active about the whole idea, while contemplating what she wanted to do in turn.

CHAPTER 43

ORION, JUNE 21ST AT THE COUNCIL KEEP

Orion had tried not to fidget during the necessary obligations at the Council Keep. He was in uniform, which itched at his neck, but at least he was used to it, and it would explain why no one had seen him about for months. Possibly help keep people from too much nasty gossip, though he wasn't sure anything would do that. Here he was, with Mother. Or rather, she was talking quietly with various of the other older women. They were Ladies and dowager ladies and various others of that class, making pleasant commentary and leaving him well out of it.

Mostly, they were asking about Achilles. Mother had handed Orion a letter as soon as he got to Fairlight. It was a month old, battered around the edges, but his younger brother was doing well, or had been then. Or as well as anyone could be, fighting in the desert.

Orion had been able to read between the lines, but he hadn't figured out how to explain to Mother what the reality was like. It meant he had to tune out her amiable comments to the other mothers and wives. They needed to feel all right about things. Forcing the reality on them wouldn't actually help. Certainly not today.

There weren't many men of his age here, and he'd expected that. Claudio had made excuses to stay away. He didn't want to deal with his mother, and Orion entirely supported that. He didn't want to deal with Silvia Warren much either, though all she'd likely do to him was glare. She was up at the front of the hall now, as the procession slowly moved. Each person presented their offering to Cyrus Smythe-Clive before moving down the line of the Council with a nod. She was a couple of people down from Smythe-Clive, with Mabyn Teague, then Alexander Landry - in Albion for a wonder - then Silvia. Gabriel Edgarton was down near the end of the line.

Mother, at least, had been decent. Orion wasn't sure how to read her reactions, honestly, though he thought perhaps she was a little startled. Whether it was at the fact he'd brought anyone home, who it was, or something else, though, he couldn't begin to tell. But she'd been cordial to Hypatia, not stuffy, making her welcome last night. Mother certainly hadn't commented on the fact Orion could easily get from his rooms to Hypatia's by way of a back stair.

She hadn't commented, even to him, about the fact he'd slept there last night. Having a bigger bed was absolutely delightful, both awake and asleep. He'd woken early that morning with Hypatia nestled against his shoulder. They hadn't needed the space at all. Orion had just lain there, looking up at the ceiling and wondering about his life.

He wanted more of that. A lot more of that, whatever society said, whatever gossip said, whatever the war demanded. Orion wanted days of waking up with someone who enjoyed his company, who - now they'd worked out that argument thing - enjoyed debating with him. Who expected him to keep up with her brains and her wit and her speed of thought. He seemed to be doing a decent job of that, actually.

He absolutely wanted more time in private with her. He'd had lovers for a few months at a time, in his Before, and sometimes the sex had got a bit better as they knew each other more. With Hypatia, it had started wonderfully, but he suspected there was quite a bit more to come.

There were all sorts of things they hadn't had space or time or enough privacy to try, where their need and urgency had got in the way. He wanted leisurely mornings with her, long evenings where they could take their time, where they could play with toys and oils and charms. He'd been practising a few of those, getting used to doing them the way his hand was now. Sometime soon, he'd try them with her, if he got the chance.

If she was willing to keep seeing him, being with him, whatever that looked like. He didn't want to pin her down, and besides, he didn't even really know how to talk about it. He knew asking her to come home for solstice was a start. She could see Fairlight in one of its best seasons. The gardens were gorgeous, and she liked the things that came from gardens and fed her magic.

Tomorrow, they'd go off and join up with Claudio and Cammie and the mysterious Duncan. They'd be in public, most of it, at the Midsummer Faire, but they could enjoy themselves. Cause a different kind of gossip, maybe.

The rub of it was that he didn't know how to talk to Hypatia about what happened next. So long as they were assigned together, without much supervision from above, it was easy enough. But he knew how much of that was a chance of good luck, that they could slip from hut to hut without anyone noticing them, even without magic. That Claudio and Cammie both were agreeably amused and willing to make time for them. Cammie especially, since she was the one getting turfed out of her own space for it.

The marriage to Decima had largely been arranged by their parents, the way their sort of families did. It meant that now he didn't even know how to ask Hypatia about it. Whether that was anything she wanted at all. She'd never been married, never been serious about anyone. He knew that much. He wanted to punch her previous partners for how they'd treated her, but that was an entirely different problem, and he probably wouldn't. Set up an opportunity for Cammie to bite them, maybe, but that seemed possibly not good for Cammie's health.

That train of thoughts got him through the tedious bits of the ceremonial portions of the afternoon. Each person only had to say a few sentences, but with two hundred and something, it took a while, no matter how brief each person was.

He had his records, his token of the harvest of the land. No manchet, this year. Mother had noted it used the finest filtered flour, butter, eggs, and milk. Given rationing, that was not a particularly politic move. Instead, he'd brought a jar of honey from the hives, wrapped up to glow when the light struck it. Getting the token right was always a trick. It was supposed to be form over function, but of course the look of the thing mattered as much as anything else.

They'd edged slowly up and around, and when they were about ten people back, he saw Silvia looking his way, her eyes narrowing. All of a sudden, he had an idea, and he wasn't going to stop to think about it. "Mother, could you hold this for a second?" She turned, took the jar and the rolled up scroll, without asking.

Orion took a breath. He was going to do this, no matter what a bad idea it might be. It felt like it wasn't; it felt like something he had to do. This was the kind of pull he'd felt a couple of times in his life in battle, where it had maybe saved him.

Then, deliberately, he tugged off first the right glove, then the left. He'd not had his hands bare in public since Before, not even with his mother. He tucked the gloves into his pocket, folded properly, then reached out both hands. "Thank you, Mother."

She didn't say anything, but a moment later she put her hand on his arm and squeezed once. Orion was watching the rest of the room. Oh, Claudio's mother had seen. She was absolutely furious. He caught a hint of Alexander Landry's expression, which looked as if he was signalling someone, quite subtly.

He handed over the jar and the scroll to Smythe-Clive without any comment there, then made his way down the row. Landry shook his right hand firmly, murmuring. "You'll want to tell Isembard yourself, I'm sure." Orion did, yes. Not that he was sure how to, or when. Isembard and Thesan were in a mesh of couples waiting out the formalities. Too many people for Orion to talk about this, and it included Edgarton's wife.

Two greetings done, and here was Claudio's mother. She offered one hand, palm down, as if even touching him was anathema. He made a show of bowing over her hand, bringing his other up to half-balance it, in the more European mode. She did not quite jerk away, but it was a near thing. His mother, just behind him, followed up immediately with some comment he didn't hear, smoothing it over.

By the time he got down to Gabriel Edgarton, his heart had begun to stop pounding. Edgarton offered his own hand, then covered it with his left, encouraging Orion to do the same. He leaned in and murmured, "Glad to have company in my particular hobby. A drink, perhaps, while you're on leave. We might get a chance at the Faire?" Orion blinked at him, but nodded, once. He'd have to ask Claudio about that tomorrow, what else they'd been writing about.

Once they were through the line, Orion nodded and smiled at a few people, but he was ready to leave as soon as it was marginally polite. His mother tsked, but nodded. "We'll talk later." He thought she wasn't upset at him. She didn't make the faces she usually did when she was upset but not letting it show to others. And it wasn't fair to have done that and not warned her, but he'd only had the idea a moment or two before doing it. Now, he nodded, and went back off to the portal. He came out at the Fairlight portal, a little down the road from the main house, and walked briskly back up.

When he came up the front steps, their butler opened the door. He was quite getting on in years, now, but had insisted on staying through the war to see the place ran smoothly. "Magistra Ward is in the garden, my lord." There was a tiny hesitation, as if he wasn't sure what Orion would do with the next piece of information. "With the children and Nanny."

"Oh. Thank you, Briggs." He hesitated for a moment, but the day was warm. Orion was home. He could bloody well be informal if he wanted to. "Would you take my uniform jacket, make sure it makes it back up to my case? I expect we'll be out there for a bit."

"Of course, my lord." Briggs stepped back, taking the jacket. Orion loosened his tie and went through, past the marble foyer, down the hall, through the drawing room, and then out the double doors onto the terrace. From there, he could see nothing for a moment, and then little floating brightly coloured bubbles rose from behind the garden hedge. Bubbles and laughter, which wasn't a thing he'd heard much here recently.

He came down the steps from the terrace and called out. "Hello?"

A hand came into view in the gap in the hedge, Hypatia's hand. "Back here. We're having a good time. Come join us?"

Orion took long strides, coming around the corner of the hedge. He found Hypatia sitting, knees pulled to one side, on a blanket on the grass with both Melchior and Sybil. She was wearing a frock from before the war, all turquoise fabric that made her particularly radiant.

Melchior looked rather absurdly like Orion had at that age. He was six - no, seven now - growing out of childhood roundness and taking on more of his own shape. Sybil was in a sensible sort of dress, not the frills Decima had insisted on when she paid attention. She was reaching up to pop one of the bubbles when she saw him. She hesitated, and he did too, then he spoke softly, as if it might break whatever spell Hypatia had cast. "What's this, then?"

"Do you know this charm? It's great fun, and it's a beautiful day for it, the colours in the light. Come, let me show you. Making bubbles is easy enough, it's getting them to do the colours brightly enough that takes skill, and I'm quite sure you'll get it. A variant on Thellar's Inspiration. You remember we were talking about it last week?" He did, though they'd been using it in an entirely different context, using it to deflect magic and spread out the damage, a warding application.

Now, though, he took a breath. "Where should I sit?"

Hypatia turned to his children. "Where should he? Should he sit there?" She pointed at the bench on the other side of the garden, where the nanny was amiably knitting. They shook their heads, laughing. "Should he sit here?" She tapped the top of her own head, and that got more laughter. "Should he sit there?" That was a bit of bare ground nearly in the hedge, and they shook their heads, a little more solemn. "Here? Or maybe here?" She pointed at the two more or less open spots on the blanket, one between her and Sybil and one between the two children.

They looked at each other, and then Melchior said. "Here is good, please." Between them.

Orion nodded, like it was a great surprise. He would have been happy next to Hypatia, but he'd have wanted to touch her, and that wasn't something he knew how to explain. And now Melchior was looking up at him. He nodded. "There is excellent."

It wasn't until he sat down that he realised his hands were still bare, the gloves still in his uniform jacket. Hypatia raised an eyebrow, and Orion said, because he couldn't not, "Edgarton's glad to have company in his hobby." Then he took a breath, holding out both hands. "Show me the charm?"

CHAPTER 44

CLAUDIO, JUNE 22ND AT THE MIDSUMMER
FAIRE

Claudio found himself standing by one of the corner of the fenced ring as the long day turned into twilight. During the day, the ring had been used for horses and other exhibitions, with the pavo field beyond stretching out into the growing shadows. In the last hour, they'd laid out a dancing floor, and the musicians were tuning up. He'd found a corner away from people. Oh, he wasn't alone. The Midsummer Faire was too busy a place to be entirely alone.

Claudio had been feeling unreasonably out of sorts since Monday. He shouldn't have been. He'd been staying with Isembard and Thesan, up in their rooms, and Cammie had been down with her mother and Ibis.

There had been a surprising amount of excellent food, though most of it was vegetables out of the garden, the things coming into abundance. And eggs, since the hens kept laying in amounts suitable for students who were gone for the summer. More than anything, there'd been conversation, without a need to guard himself.

Claudio felt like a coward when Isembard and Thesan went off for the Council obligations. Isembard was his brother's heir. Garin Fortier was on the Council and someone had to tend to the Lord's duties. And Thesan usually paired Alexander for the dancing that opened the ritual portion of the day. All good reasons for them both to be there. Orion had to make his bow, but Claudio hadn't felt able to face his mother.

He hadn't seen her face to face since they'd started the project, and he'd learned what she'd said to Orion. Oh, he'd have been able to restrain his impulses, keep his face perfectly acceptable, and do all the proper forms. He was, after all, his parents' child. But he wouldn't have been able to talk to her ever again, not without that wall in the way.

And maybe, sometime, he'd want to. Not right now. All of it meant that it was easier to stay away, even if it were also cowardly.

He'd thought, until this morning, that Cammie hadn't noticed. She'd certainly had plenty of distractions. Duncan had turned up Monday evening, when they'd been waiting out on the crest of the hill up to Schola's keep. She'd flung herself into a run, a bounding leap that owed quite a lot to her shifting form. This tall man, auburn hair cut to uniform length, had picked her up and swung her around.

The trick of it was Duncan seemed an honestly good chap. He was friendly, the sort of friendly Isembard was, curious about the world. Duncan might talk a tad much about aeroplanes for Claudio's current knowledge, but he had every reason to. And gods knew Claudio could go on about magical theory far beyond most people's tolerance. He laughed, but in a way that brought people into the thing, he seemed easy going.

It meant that Claudio had forced himself to put whatever he felt about Cammie that way aside. At least, all the ways that weren't about her being his friend, sister to Orion's chosen partner, and terribly skilled in her own way. She was not for him, but she'd made him realised he did, perhaps want that. That there was, absolutely, more he wanted than the properness of his marriage and the distance from his children, and all the formalities.

The longer Duncan was there, the more Cammie relaxed into it. Trusting he'd be there, the way Hypatia and Orion had been coming to trust each other. Claudio knew what it looked like, because he had that with Orion, and no matter what else, he knew what was steady.

Other men might have worried that Orion's romance would have changed things with Claudio, put space between them. But the thing about Orion was that he was as loyal as the day was long. And through the night, and to the next dawn, over and over again, once he'd decided on it.

Not that Claudio hadn't worried about him yesterday. They'd barely had time to talk about it when Claudio had met up with Orion and Hypatia this morning. Just that Orion had pushed Mother, in ways she deserved to be. He had, exceedingly literally, taken his gloves off, and made it clear what that meant.

If he'd had space and time, Claudio would have been crowing, because Orion had backed Mother into a corner. And two others of the Council - Alexander and Gabe - had both been clear enough about their approval. It was going to make things interesting, even if it'd be a problem for Claudio. Well, for Mother. Claudio was very clear on his priorities here, and Mother was a grown woman and could decide for herself.

It was while he was on that train of thought that he heard a voice, a couple of feet behind him, carefully measured not to cause too sudden a reaction. "A moment, Claudio, if you're not busy?"

Claudio twisted around, seeing Gabe Edgarton standing there. He had his cane out, not putting any weight on it. He was wearing the sort of country tweed he seemed to like in his off hours, a pointed sort of informality, even if it were one entirely suitable for the setting.

"Of course. There's plenty of fence. We could find a bench or something if you like?"

"Oh, in a minute I'm going to invite you to come join us at our tent, over there." Gabe nodded at a pavilion halfway along the large arena, lit by charmlights, and exceedingly brightly coloured, even by the standards of the day. About half the row was lit up, various of the Lords and Ladies hosting gatherings full of what food and drink they could arrange. Good wine, likely. Pulling things out of the cellars put down years ago both scored social points and wasn't limited by rationing.

There was conversation, and of course a great deal of plotting. Most of the pavilions went in for two or three colours, that one had at least five, and all shining in a bright chaos that somehow worked together. "Isembard and Thesan said they'd let Orion and Hypatia know. Give you all a bit of a place to set things down."

Claudio raised an eyebrow at that and waited. He didn't say anything and he didn't need to. He knew Gabe knew how to do this, the way Claudio's family did, even if he didn't usually.

Gabe laughed and came up to lean against the fence, folding his arms. "Orion made quite a statement yesterday. Have you had a chance to talk about it?"

"Not in detail, but that he—" Claudio had to pause and think how to put this.

"Oh, he's joining me in my hobby of tweaking your

mother's nose. I'll tell him, when we get a word, that if he wants to challenge again, I'm glad to help. And Alexander, too. Whether or not he's successful - and who knows, he might well be - I think it'd be good if he made the point of trying." Then Gabe cocked his head. "I'm not sure if I'd have said that before he got invalided out. I don't know much against him except that he's occasionally used his fists a bit more quickly when he'd needed to be specific about a problem than is entirely desirable in a Council Member. People will provoke us, remarkably often, even given all the stories that get passed around."

That made Claudio laugh. "No one has ever accused my mother of being too quick to use her fists, mind. Or my father." For all Father had, in fact, been a competent duellist by Council standards. Isembard thought, on the whole, Claudio was absolutely his equal and likely a fair bit better, and Claudio still didn't know how he felt about that.

"She needs, I don't know. Unsticking. If she sorts herself out, I'll stop rubbing her nose in the need for it." Gabe shrugged, apparently entirely at peace with the fact he might be jousting at this particular windmill for a long while. "Ah, there they go."

The music had finally started, and Claudio could see Cammie and Duncan over on their side of the dance floor. They started out simply enough, getting a feel for the floor under their feet, but within a minute or so, they were starting to get elaborate. Other couples around them were too, but they migrated to a bit of open space, and then the fun really got started.

Claudio could see Cammie's grin, the flash of her teeth, and then Duncan was swinging her around his body. She landed on both feet with a bounce and flung herself into the rapid steps again, perfectly on the beat. She spun in and out, always perfectly aware of where he was, as the moves got more and more incredible. The other couples around them were trying to match them, and all of a sudden, Claudio heard Gabe snort at something. Gabe didn't explain, and it wasn't like Claudio could tear his eyes away.

From there, it just got more ridiculous, and all of a sudden, Claudio could see just how the dance and the stoat went together. He'd have to tease Cammie about that properly when they were in private. He was sure Hypatia would help. Now, she was flying over Duncan's shoulders, landing with a jump before getting flung into the air again. The other couples, a couple of them got more height, but something about it wasn't quite the same, and Claudio was trying to figure it out when Gabe spoke again. "The others are using magic to look more impressive. Cammie and Duncan aren't. Well, not more magic than they are on the average Wednesday."

Before Claudio could think of anything else, the words came out. "Show me how you know." Then he swallowed. "Please."

"That's the first steps of an apprenticeship, you know." Gabe didn't linger on that. "Of course. Anything I can teach you, I'm going to. We both know that." Then, he launched right into the explanation. He was using a charm to let him see how people were drawing on the magic, how it was running in them, for lack of a better term.

"That'd be hell to duel against." Again, the words came out before Claudio could guard himself, not that he actually wanted to, just he was supposed to.

When he looked over, Gabe was laughing. "So I'm told. I don't cheat, that's no fun at all. But I do use every single tool at my disposal. No reason you shouldn't learn to do the same, and do something interesting with it." From there, he went on, laying out the flows of the magic in the dance. He paused here and there for a particularly acrobatic move, or the way Cammie was grinning fit to shatter into starlight. When the music finally slowed down, shifting into something made more for intimate whispers for a little, Gabe waved a hand. "Come to the pavilion. We can have drinks. And theory."

"What else am I saying yes to, if I do?" Claudio knew he should be cautious. He'd been trained all his life to wonder what the unspoken cost would be, because there was always going to be one.

Gabe laughed. "No obligation, without a clear negotiation. I do hope, very much, that in the not too distant future, we'll be able to go across the Channel and untangle a lot of things. That we can serve in the ways we can help and others can't. That's for later. I like teaching. I don't currently have an apprentice." Then his mouth quirked up. "And every single one of my family will thank you. I'm a terror when I'm bored."

Claudio snorted. "Fairly sure you're so busy these days that there's not much chance of that." But he nodded, and they went along. Within minutes, they had Thesan and Isembard, who'd done a bit of country dancing earlier, but weren't going to attempt anything more energetic now. When the musicians took a break, Claudio felt a sigh of relief when Orion and Hypatia, and Cammie and Duncan, all came back chattering. There was Orion's hand on his shoulder for a moment, checking in, Cammie was crowing about how good that had been. Hypatia was teasing her about how no one else on the floor could keep up with her, except Duncan.

"Did you know they were using magic to try?" Claudio slipped it in there, to everyone's delighted laughter and demands for an explanation. He gave Gabe every credit for it, of course, but Gabe just leaned back and laughed, not grabbing for any of it. As if he'd set that whole thing up.

Maybe Claudio's life was going to look very different in a few months or a year. If so, it'd be nothing like what his mother thought he should have, and that might be a wonderful thing indeed.

EPILOGUE
HYPATIA, APRIL 14TH, 1945 AT SCHOLA

Hypatia had known this was coming. She knew her brother and his particular anxieties and obsessions. Not that they weren't well-founded, most of the time. But she'd hoped that nearly a year would ease some of them. Now, though, the world was changing again. Armies - more than one of them - were advancing steadily on Berlin. There was every reason to hope the war in Europe was actually coming to an end.

When that happened - and she could think of it as when, now, not if - their work would be changing. Gabe Edgarton had made it clear he could use skilled hands to sort out and map damage in the previously occupied countries. Likely France and maybe into Belgium and the Netherlands, given the combination of their language skills and their magical skills. Maybe Germany, but Cammie and Hypatia would stand out in ways that might not make their work easier. Americans would mostly do better there, honestly, less confusing. People took Americans for what they saw, where they'd be suspicious of the mix of Cammie and Hypatia's voices and their skin.

At any rate, they'd had two days at Fairlight, after that conversation with Gabe, and they'd also got leave to come out to Schola for the weekend. Orion had wanted to see a demonstration match, a mix of the top bohort players from all seven houses, playing together in ways they didn't normally get a chance at. That was a treat, even if they'd been able to get leave more frequently since last June.

The conversation had wandered to a bit of quiet, and Hypatia was just thinking about what else to talk about when Ibis spoke again. "What are your intentions, then?"

"Ibis. You're not Father." Hypatia sighed. They were going to do another round of this. Ibis had been remarkably mild, and Hypatia had been thanking Pross at intervals for that.

Orion, though, leaned back beside her. "There's a lot of work to be done, still. Overseas now, figuring out how to undo some of the damage from the war. The damage here is - there's a lot of rebuilding needed, but it's not magical damage, mostly, the same way." He spread his hands. He was wearing the gloves. "Make ourselves useful, mostly, in the near future."

"And the more distant future?" Ibis was leaning forward now. It was the sort of pose that made her think of a hedgehog's spines coming up and into play, part protection and part something that forced space, whether or not that was wanted.

"Are you asking about Hypatia? About the Council? The land?" Nine months ago, Orion would not have taken it so lightly. Somehow, now, though, he could play with it. He didn't take quite everything as a personal attack.

Or, she realised suddenly, this was the battle he knew he was going to have, and he'd just been waiting for the other side to show up. Now it was here, he was somehow entirely relaxed. He'd said, back before D-Day, that the waiting was the hardest part. Here he was being right again, about something that couldn't have citations and tested evidence.

Ibis cleared his throat. "All three, if you're offering."

"If I am able to get back, I intend to challenge, next time there's a Council seat. I don't know what will happen with that, but that's not the point. It's making the attempt."

"Do you actually want to be on the Council?" Ibis could - and did - parry that one quickly.

"Want's not the right verb." Orion's voice was deceptively casual now. Hypatia knew how complicated he felt about it. "I was bred to it, and there's part of me that doesn't want to let my family down. The more decent parts of it, anyway."

Orion didn't talk about his father a great deal, but it was clear they'd been close without ever talking about it. Hypatia had even come to like his mother, who had been entirely unsure what to make of Hypatia herself at first, so it was at least mutual. They were now unified in their feeling that it was good when Orion was happy. Let's keep doing more of those things. Orion shrugged one more time. "I think if I don't try once more, I'll always wonder what would have been different if I had. And I think I could do some good with it, as things are now."

That was well put, and it made it rather opaque whether that was about Orion's injury, his divorce, his blatant adoration of Hypatia, or something else. He considered and went on. "And Hypatia enjoys Fairlight. My children think she hangs the sun and the moon and the stars. Perhaps because she always has some new treat or charm to show them, and—" He paused. "I'm very glad of her help with that. More than I can say." His voice got a little shy at the end. It wasn't something they'd talked about, just something she did.

Hypatia did like them - especially now they were getting more comfortable with her. Orion did a lot better when someone helped show him how to be with children. How they changed, over time, but she'd been around enough for Susanna to have a sense of the way things could change, sometimes apparently overnight. When it came to the land, well, that was a whole new set of sympathetic resonances to learn about. But she knew how to learn. She did like being on the land, and from everything she'd been told so far, that would go a long way.

"And Hypatia?" Ibis pressed on.

"It has seemed a bit premature to propose formally, the kind of thing that goes in the society papers. There is still a war on, and while it wouldn't be a scandal if I married again now, a little more time won't hurt there. We know the truth of things, my mother knows, my children, you and Pross, my aunts." He nodded. "And your daughter and, of course, Cammie."

Nobody could keep Cammie out of it with a tall fence, a stick, and a number of rabbits for distraction. As they'd proven several times over now. Not that Cammie hadn't been entirely reasonable about things. It helped they were now working out of research digs a bit further into Wiltshire, with a cottage for each of them and a refinished barn for a workroom. It had been much the same sort of thing, distractions and protections both, but in varying forms. They had continued having to think through the possible permutations of need in advance and then deploying them. Duncan had been able to visit regularly, now his leaves were much more scheduled and routine. He'd been doing well as a trainer. His pilots had better luck than many.

Ibis nodded slowly. "You're not asking my permission, then."

"No, sir. As Hypatia says, you are not her father, and I gather in any case that it's your mother I ought to properly be approaching. I do have a letter ready to send, but we thought better to sort things out with you first. And I have no idea when we might manage a trip to Egypt."

Ibis ran his hands over his face, and Hypatia knew then it was going to be all right. "I appreciate the sop to my dignity. You're sure, then, Hypatia?"

"Very." She put her all into it. "I don't need the show of it. And really, we should write to Ummi and let her decide how she's feeling about it, before we actually get married. If things really do work out, the war ends. Maybe she can come out here for a season."

That made Ibis make a delightful face. They loved their mother, but admittedly some days or months or years, that was a tad easier with more distance. On the other hand, it would make a delightful festival. Ummi would almost certainly have a lot to talk about with Cammie - languages was a thing they had in common - and with Alexander Landry, among others. That was a problem for a different time, though.

Now she waited to see what Ibis did next. He took a breath. "If you're sure this is what makes you happy." Then he did his best to glare at Orion. "If you hurt my sister, you'll regret it."

Orion said, with a straight face. "You'd have to beat Cammie to it, sir. And she already threatens me about once a week on average. I think she has a list. She's never quite repeated the same threat twice. Though I admit they often involve biting."

There was a moment where Ibis went completely still, and then he smiled, a real and honest smile. "Ah. In that case, I'll leave it in her capable teeth. Now. Is there anything you two can talk about, from your work, or should we find entirely other topics to be getting on with?"

Hypatia beamed, and now she could settle in against Orion's shoulder properly and relax. All was good, all was right, inside five minutes citations would be flying. And tonight, she and Orion could have whatever sort of pleasure they liked together without needing to be in a rush in the morning. With any luck, the world would have more space for relaxed pleasure in the months to come. For the moment she'd take every scrap of it she could get hold of.

Ibis might finally be convinced that whatever else Orion was, he wasn't his great-uncle. They'd got their plans out in the open, and they could sort out the formalities when it made sense to do that. Everything in its season.

If you enjoyed *Illusion of a Boar* and would like to read more of this series, please sign up for my mailing list to get all the latest news and fun extras.

Your reviews (on whatever review site you use) are much appreciated, too!

Read on for more historical details about *Illusion of a Boar* (and a few bits of history that didn't make it into the book).

AUTHOR'S NOTES

Thank you so much for joining me - and our four protagonists - on a journey into a very particular part of history. My thanks go out to Kiya Nicoll, as always, who particularly improved this book by commenting on a number of Orion's aspects.

If you'd like to read more about Claudio and Orion as students, they're in *Eclipse*, which takes place during the 1924-1925 school year and includes Thesan and Isembard's romance. Cammie first appears in *Magician's Hoard*, her mother Pross's romance with Ibis. She and Hypatia appear briefly in *Chasing Legends*, a novella that takes place over the winter hols at Schola in 1926 found in the *Winter's Charms* collection.

Other connections and places characters appear can be found at my authorial wiki at https://www.worldanvil. com/w/albion-celialake. It also has timelines, maps, and other useful ways to find characters in the various books where they appear.

The more I learned about the history behind Operation Fortitude, the more fascinated I got. To the extent that information was relevant (and available), I've used the historical details, some of which involve some odd coincidences. I'll start with the general notes, and then talk about specific chapter details or characters as they appear.

Starting with the actual history, **Operation Fortitude** was a deception operation aimed at confusing the German army (and Axis powers generally) about where the invasion that would be D-Day might happen. The people running the operation wanted to draw attention away from Normandy and toward Calais, and they used a wide variety of methods to get there.

Joshua Levine's book *Operation Fortitude: The Story of the Spies and Spy Operation that Saved D-Day* is a great overview, with so many fascinating stories, a number of them so unbelievable I felt I couldn't reference them briefly and have anyone take the fiction seriously. As Junior Commander Roberts mentions, most of the people behind that were public school (Eton, with a few from other places) and Oxford men.

There were actually two Operation Fortitude projects, one in the north (based in Edinburgh, where Claudio started out) and one in the south, mostly coordinated out of London but with various pieces taking place across the south coast. By this point, they were fairly confident there weren't German agents on the loose in England (they kept walking into pubs and trying to order beer at the wrong time of day - or just plain turning themselves in). A number of them agreed to be double agents, using their radio transmitters to convey information, including whole networks of fictional people they'd recruited in key locations. Levine's book describes all of this if you want more detail.

It made sense to me in Albion's context that someone, eventually (it was a very secret project, but there was, of necessity, some coordination with other people), would realise there should be a magical component. Which is where our four come in. There aren't a lot of resources, similar to the non-magical operation, which seems to have been running off of typewriter paper, attendance at dinner parties where someone could have a quiet word with key figures, and someone keeping the details of all the cover stories straight.

As Orion notes, one of the key aspects of the plan was to talk about the movement of the Fourth Army, which did not exist as a functional force in World War 2, but which was notable for its actions in the Great War, twenty years earlier. They did indeed use a white boar as their badge, a symbol also strongly associated with King Richard III, who has a very specific role in Albion's magical history.

The **Auxiliary Territorial Service** was staffed by a tremendous number of young women. Cammie and Hypatia's experience with their fellows in that service are drawn from a variety of memoir sources, especially Barbara Green's *Girls in Khaki: A History of the ATS in the Second World War*. If you've heard about the ATS recently, the late Queen Elizabeth II served as a mechanic in the ATS during the war. Women might be despatch drivers or mechanics, or many took on a wide range of secretarial and clerk roles. Some also took on much more technical roles like signals work. Others took dangerous ones, like staffing artillery batteries and anti-aircraft fire.

You can find a range of footage on YouTube. The 1943 feature-length film *The Gentle Sex: the great film story of life in the A.T.S.* was the last film directed by Leslie Howard before his death. It follows a number of ATS girls through their training and work, with some romantic storylines. Many of the extras were ATS members.

As Cammie notes, first, they were often referred to as "ATS girls" regardless of age. Most of them were between 18 and 29, depending on the year of the war, with some older women involved in training and supervision. Besides all their own work, they were expected to spruce themselves out and turn out to be sociable and friendly at dances to keep morale up. The comments about the beige uniform underthings being called "passion killers" come from multiple memories in Green's book, as do Cammie's comments about the issued mattresses.

The historical battles are pretty much all as mentioned in the text. All of them have other history attached to them, none of their stories are simple. The geology is also as mentioned, helped by the fact that the chalk and limestone cliffs at Dover are in fact the same geologic formation as the coast around Calais, part of a massive much older ridge that has since been worn down by water. **D-Day** itself has of course had extensive coverage in books, documentaries, and memoirs. What various characters discuss about the **RAF Bomber Command** (both statistics and flight information) is drawn from various historic sources.

Finally, I'll talk about specific parts of the camp in individual chapters, but **Camp 020** was the main camp holding German and German double agents. By 1944, there was not much active interrogation going on routinely, and most of the people there had been there for some time. It turns out to be quite difficult to get a map of a camp the British government kept secret throughout the war and well after, so I have taken a few liberties with placement of items like our protagonists' living space. It does explain some of the unusual arrangements, where you might want people isolated in different ways than the usual setup for the huts, or have slightly more private sleeping and living space for people there briefly.

Other details - the main house, the garden space, the recreation spaces - are drawn from memoirs about the camp, including extensive notes from Lieutenant Colonel Robin "Tin Eye" Stephens, who ran the camp. He vocally refused to use physical torture (though there's some counter-evidence), but there is documentation in multiple sources about psychological methods (including having the lights on all the time and sound isolation) used to convince prisoners to talk. By 1944, a number of the longer term residents did have some of the freedoms described - garden patches, time in the recreation rooms - but it was still a highly secret camp.

Our four are based there because they couldn't be in London, and this was the other main location for information key to Operation Fortitude. The camp was also located a modest walk from General Eisenhower's residence while planning the D-Day invasions, and 3 miles from Camp Griffiss, headquarters for that planning. **Richmond Park** is a historical park, and the **Old Sheen Palace** no longer exists, but would almost certainly have had its own portal for transportation.

Onward to the specifics!

Chapter 1: There were a wide variety of **huts** in use by this point in the war. I'm deeply grateful for a dissertation by Karey Lee Draper, *Wartime Huts: the development, typology, and identification of temporary military buildings in Britain 1914-1945* (University of Cambridge, 2017), which gives detailed information including dimensions and materials. Having plumbing in the hut is the unusual part, but not entirely unheard of. They were generally heated by wood stoves, with an ablutions hut nearby for toilets, washing, and showers.

Chapter 3: As Orion mentions, he was fighting in the **Dodecanese campaign** in the Greek islands, which was about to get rather worse. His younger brother is in the campaign in North Africa, which had a number of challenges around communication, supplies, and the natural environment.

Chapter 5: While doing the early research for the book, I came across a fascinating photograph from English Heritage in one of their articles about **Operation Fortitude**. It shows a group of eight men - and one woman - sitting around a large wooden table in their workspace. The floor is covered with overlapping Persian rugs, and everyone is in uniform. The image lists the names, and the key figures of Operation Fortitude are all there.

It meant I got very curious about the woman, who is labelled Junior Commander Lady Jane Pleydall-Bouvier. When I went looking for more information about her, I discovered she was the daughter of the Earl of Radnor, from a very long aristocratic line indeed. She was in her early 20s at this point, one of three ATS women mentioned associated with the project at different stages. Her name comes up twice in a thousand-page history of the project, which I think rather entirely unfair.

I'm not saying Junior Commander Roberts is her, but she's certainly the inspiration. The book's Junior Commander Roberts is however also very young for that rank, with the same sort of bearing. Roberts, of course, does come from a family with some magic. She has enough to make the Pact and be aware of magical society, but not enough to have it trained (or she may have chosen other options, as her family seems to). It did make her the best go-between of the two parts of the project.

Chapter 12: The main house on the property that became Camp 020 is **Latchmere House**, built in the Victorian era and turned over to the British government during the Great War. Very early in the Second World War, it was requisitioned for dealing with spies (and housing them after questioning), since the location was reasonably convenient to London, but remote enough to allow separation and reduce the risks of escape.

The house itself is still standing, though there's now a modern property development around it. During this period, an addition was built on the back, as isolation housing for prisoners, with camp huts and other spaces throughout a significant area. The memoirs I read suggested that the main house was kept very quiet, but that some rooms were used by officers and other staff for quiet conversations, such as the one Claudio is invited to.

Chapter 13: Shapeshifting has a number of possible mechanisms in Albion (as Cammie explains). The one she and Ibis both use is learned, with techniques for bringing clothing and carried items along with you if you learn that part. (You can read more about Ibis's experiences with shifting, including the trouble with Orion's great-uncle, in *Magician's Hoard* and *Chasing Legends.)*

When Cammie shows up in earlier books, she is inquisitive and sharp witted. When I started thinking about what she was like as an adult, I knew she shifted into some sort of mammal with teeth and a hunting instinct. **Stoats** have a number of fascinating aspects. First, there's the winter coat (when they're known as ermine and highly valued for their fur) versus the summer brown coat.

Second, they have a specific hunting technique when going after prey like rabbits (who can be ten times their size and weight). They will bounce around energetically, getting closer and closer to the rabbit. The rabbit watches, fascinated and entranced. Suddenly, surprise stoat, who has over a few minutes moved close enough to pounce. There are videos on YouTube (though many do involve actual hunting behaviour, some do not, and those are often labelled).

I was looking at videos of 1944 dancing, and what would have been common in the intersection of American and British troops, when I suddenly stared at some of the fantastic moves of **swing dance** in the period. The flips, leaps, and other movements made me immediately think of the stoat videos I'd been watching. Of course Cammie is also a swing dancer. She's made for it.

Chapter 17: I mentioned **Camp Griffiss** earlier, but it was in fact one of the main camps for the planning and some of the training for D-Day, in a wide range of huts in Bushy Park. Very little of the original camp remains, but there's some information online with maps and other details. There were about 8,000 men living at the camp by April 1944.

Cammie's friend mentions '**going northwest**', which is a very general reference (there's a lot of possible northwest from Richmond), but that includes Bletchley Hall, where a lot of the most cutting edge cryptography and signals work was going on, including breaking the Enigma code. Cammie, as she mentions, is in fact a trained cryptographer. **Giles**, her apprentice master, has his romance in *Wards of the Roses* and also appears in *Country Manners* (also in the *Winter's Charms* collection).

Chapter 24: I did quite a lot of digging into the historical forms of the puzzle that's often called **Knights and Knaves**. If you've seen the movie *Labyrinth*, you've seen one well-known version of it, about who is telling the truth and who is lying. I couldn't quite date this version back far enough, but I'm taking a slight liberty and saying the magical community uses it.

Chapter 34: The various fae creatures that Hypatia is thinking about - like the **ech-goblins** - are drawn from common folklore in the various places. The names are rather suggestively similar, though.

Chapter 35: Paperfolding became extremely common in the 1850s, both as an art or craft form, and to teach small children better manual dexterity. This was the time of the growing kindergarten movement, and the idea of learning through play and experience of the world. **Bell-flowers** or campanula are one of many different flowers I found folding instructions for. There are a number of varieties for the language of flower meanings, but bellflowers generally have to do with gratitude, constancy, support, and romance. The different colours can also mean different things, with magenta being romantic love.

Chapter 36: *Punch Magazine* was the venerable British humour magazine that ran for many years. Like a number of similar publications, it had topical cartoons with often clever captions.

Chapter 37: Given the presence of a stoat, I couldn't quite resist a reference to (probably) **Leonardo da Vinci**'s famous painting of Lady with an Ermine. The pose is charming, and of course it's one that Cammie would want to make use of. I suspect that paintings with similar subjects might have been more common in Albion.

Chapter 38: At this point, I have a running joke that whenever I look up the historical weather (and can get the information, which of course varies by year and location), it's doing what I want it to do. In this case, there was a significant heatwave in the London area at the end of May 1944, followed by storms and flooding.

Thank you again for reading! If you'd like to know more about when new books are coming out and all sorts of other fun details, my newsletter is the place to be. I do have some extensive extras planned for *Illusion of a Boar*, and you can get them via the newsletter as soon as they're available. I do plan to come back to these four down the road, with a romance for Claudio around 1950. There's also a bit more about Orion's arc in *Three Graces*, out in December 2023.

ALSO BY CELIA LAKE

Four Walls and a Heart

Land Mysteries

Best Foot Forward

Nocturnal Quarry

Old As The Hills

Upon A Summer's Day

Illusion of a Boar

Three Graces

Other stories

Complementary

Winter's Charms

Forged in Combat

Learn more about the world of Albion and future books at my website, celialake.com. Additional information linking characters, places, and timelines is available at bit.ly/celia-lake-wiki

Sign up for my newsletter to be the first to hear about future books and learn about fascinating bits of research. Happy reading!